Wicked Tongue

Darren Bane was born in Bristol, England, in 1969. He spent more than 12 years working as a journalist before 'going straight' and becoming a police force press officer for another 12 years. These roles furnished him with a valuable and inspiring insight into major crimes from the perspective of the police investigation teams and the media. He has self-published a number of books in different genres, which have sold all over the world. *Wicked Tongue* is his first crime thriller.

Wicked Tongue

Darren Bane

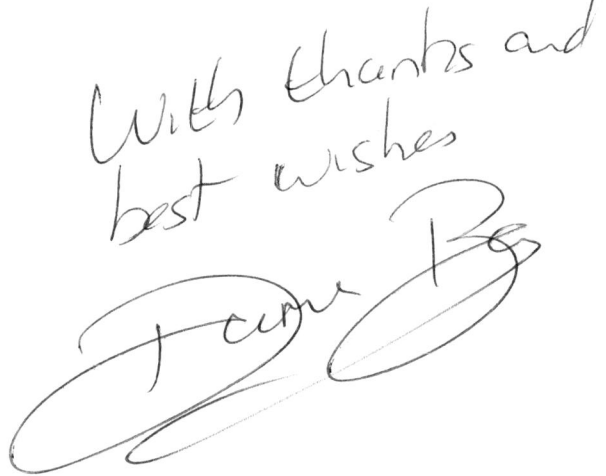

db books

2021

Copyright © 2021 Darren Bane

The right of Darren Bane to be identified as
the author of this work has been asserted by him
in accordance with the Copyright, Design and Patents Act 1988.

All rights reserved. No part of this publication may be reproduced, stored in or introduced into a retrieval system or transmitted, in any form or by any means (electronic, mechanical, photocopying, recording or otherwise) without the prior written permission of the publisher. Any person who does any unauthorised act in relation to this publication may be liable to criminal and civil claims for damages.

First published in 2021 by db books through the self-publishing platform Lulu
www.lulu.com

ISBN: 978-1-291-48066-5

db08

db books
www.darrenbane.co.uk

This is a work of fiction.
The names, characters and incidents portrayed in it are the work of the author's imagination. Any resemblance to persons, living or dead, events or locations is entirely coincidental.

"My son, keep your tongue still, and keep your friend.
A wicked tongue is worse than any fiend.

My son, full oftentimes, for too much speech,
has many a man been killed, as clerics teach."

Geoffrey Chaucer
The Canterbury Tales: The Manciple's Tale. 1395.

"Something wicked this way comes."

William Shakespeare
Macbeth. 1606.

Then

One

Daddy died today. And I'm sad, so sad.

I found him in his workshop at the bottom of the garden. That's where he always went when Mummy yelled at him.

Mummy shouted at him a lot.

Today she shouted at me, too. She told me to fetch my "good for nothing excuse for a father" and tell him that she was going to give his dinner to the dog if he didn't go back to the house.

The dog eats a lot of Daddy's dinners.

I walked across the lawn to the old wooden workshop at the far end of the garden, where Daddy used to sit at his desk, reading magazines or carefully making little plastic models out of kits; he had a large collection of little fighter planes and bombers from the Second World War.

I smiled as I got closer, because I could hear Daddy's music playing. Daddy liked listening to music in his workshop. Sometimes, I would hear him singing his head off, and he always seemed so happy. Other times, he would try to get me to sing along and this makes me laugh because Daddy's music is old, and silly. But he likes it, and it makes him happy. I like seeing Daddy happy.

When I got to the workshop, I thought Daddy had fallen asleep at first. He had done this many times before.

He was slumped in his favourite big black chair. One of his arms was stretched across the wooden desk. His head was resting on it.

I spoke to him, but he didn't answer.

I reached out and touched his shoulder. I wanted to get his attention, but I didn't want to frighten him. But he did not respond to my gentle touch.

I didn't really want to wake him up. I imagined that he was dreaming of being in some other place where nobody shouted at him, and he was happy. But I knew that if I didn't fetch him, Mummy would shout even louder at both of us.

I lightly shook his shoulder a bit harder. His head slipped from his arm and rolled onto the table with a gentle thud.

That's when I realised that his eyes were open.

Usually, when Daddy looked at me, his mouth would smile and his eyes would smile, too. Don't ask me how, but they did. There was a glow, a sparkle, in his eyes.

Daddy always smiled when I went to see him in his workshop. He always looked so pleased to see me. His eyes always shone, and that made me smile inside, too.

But on this day, his eyes looked very different. They were not shining. They looked glazed, slightly dull, and strangely empty. There was no light in his eyes. There was no life in his eyes. It was as though everything had been switched off.

I felt my heart start to pound, and tears start to well behind my own eyes. I knew something was very, very, wrong.

Maybe, I thought, he was not just *dreaming* of some other place where no one was shouting at him. Perhaps he was there. I hoped so.

I always thought people were supposed to look peaceful when they died. But Daddy didn't look peaceful.

He looked sad. So very, very, sad.

I looked at his desk. I saw a glass bottle with a small amount of golden brown liquid in it, and no cap on top. Next to the bottle was a small, chunky, glass which also contained a little of the same liquid. It smelled strong and reminded me a little of some kind of medicine.

Next to the glass was a white plastic round bottle which I knew was supposed to be filled with pills.

I thought pills were supposed to make people feel better, not kill them. I thought pills were meant to take people's pain away.

Rest in peace, they say. But Daddy looked troubled. Troubled, tormented, pained and just so very, very, sad.

I know Mummy and Daddy used to shout at each other a lot. Well, Mummy used to shout, Daddy just seemed to sit there and listen. If he tried to say anything, she would shout even louder. And then, when he didn't want to listen to her shouting any more, he would quietly slip out of the house and walk to his workshop.

I stared at his face, hoping he would suddenly wink at me; hoping that his lips would suddenly form that familiar warm smile that made me glow from the inside out, hoping that he had been toying with me, teasing me, playing a practical joke.

But this was no joke. Usually, when I found him in his workshop with a bottle nearby, he had a very rosy glow to his cheeks, almost as if he had been playing with Mummy's make-up.

But there was no warm, rosy glow this time. His face was a ghastly pale, blue-grey colour.

I wanted to hear his voice, so badly. I wanted to see his smile. I wanted to take him by the hand and walk back to the house with him together. But when I reached out and touched his hand, I recoiled in shock at how cold and firm it was. It didn't feel real.

Daddy was gone. He was really gone. And he was never, ever, going to come back.

I didn't know what to do. I felt so completely and utterly lost. I had a horrible sickly feeling in the deepest pit of my stomach. I slumped to the floor and rested my head against his leg.

I heard Mummy's voice. She had opened the back door of the house. She shouted across the garden. She called my name, she called Daddy's name. She said something about us both being as bad as one another. And she said something about the dog having *my* dinner, too.

I lifted my hand and wrapped it around Daddy's leg as tight as I could. We sat in a deathly silence as a tragic torrent of more tears than I thought any one person could ever store up inside them started to flow from my eyes.

Two

Mummy cried today. And I'm mad, so mad.

I've cried so much since Daddy died, I don't think I've got any more tears left. I'm mad because my tears were for Daddy, but Mummy's tears seemed to for herself.

When the policemen came to the house, Mummy told them she did not know how she was going to cope without Daddy's money.

How would she pay the bills? How would she feed me?

We had to go to a special room, like a court, where they talked about Daddy, and how I had found him, and what made him die.

A man said Daddy had written three notes; one to Mummy, one to his own Mummy, my Nanna, and one to me. I did not know Daddy had written to me. When I found out, I asked Mummy if I could see the note but she said it would upset me too much.

It upset me more that she would not let me see the note. It was *my* note, not hers. She had one of her own. Why wouldn't she let me see what Daddy had written to *me*?

She sent me to bed and told me to never ask about the note again. It was not important. What *was* important was that Daddy had gone and had left us to face life without him. She said he had been very selfish. She called him a coward. But I think he was very brave.

I went to bed. I wished I could speak to Daddy.

I heard Mummy and Nanna arguing.

With Daddy gone, it seems like Mummy needed someone else to shout at. I thought it would be me. Maybe it will be, soon. But for now, it's Nanna.

I crept to the top of the stairs so that I could hear them better.

I heard Nanna tell Mummy that she had no right to keep the note from me. Nanna said I had a right to see it.

Mummy shouted at Nanna and said Daddy had caused her nothing but trouble and upset all our lives and now, even when he was dead, he was still causing trouble.

Nanna was crying. But Mummy wasn't crying. She was shouting. Shouting at Nanna, and blaming Daddy for everything.

Nanna came to my room to say goodnight before she went home. And that's when she showed me the note Daddy had written to me.

Mummy didn't know that Nanna had taken it, and she showed it to me.

Daddy told me he loved me very much, and that he was so very sorry that he left me. He said Mummy had a wicked tongue. That was the words she used; *wicked tongue*. And he said he could not cope with her shouting at him anymore.

Daddy told me that he was frightened that, one day, Mummy might shout at him just a bit too much, and that he might lose his temper, and then he didn't know what would happen. He did not want to take the risk, so he decided he would rather die.

He asked me to do my best to look after Mummy, and he said that if Mummy ever used her wicked tongue against me, I should speak to Nanna.

And then Daddy asked me to forgive him for leaving me.

I do forgive you, Daddy, I do.

But I'll *never* forgive Mummy for making you so sad that you felt that the only way to be happy was to die. No, I'll never forgive Mummy for that.

Never, ever, *ever*.

Three

Mummy died today. And I'm glad, so very, *very* glad.

There were no tears today.

There was peace and quiet.

I sat at the bottom of the stairs, next to her crumpled body. I stared at her for what felt like forever, but she didn't move. I was still not sure if she was just knocked out, of if she was dead.

It didn't matter.

All that mattered was that her wicked tongue was quiet. I had made sure of that.

I stared at the blood pouring from her mouth onto the carpet.

I smiled because I knew that if she saw that stain, she would be so angry that she would have shouted louder than ever. But if she does wake up, and if she does see that blood stain, well, good luck with shouting about it.

I think I would enjoy watching her try.

I think it would be funny.

But the truth is, I know she's never going to wake up.

Her eyes were closed, and I couldn't see her breathing. But maybe people don't breathe much if they have been knocked out.

One of her legs was twisted in a very strange way. I can't bend *my* legs like that. I tried, and it really hurt.

I don't really know what happened; really, I don't.

Mummy had been shouting at me, I remember *that*.

She had been shouting at me a lot since that special court hearing. She would tell me that I was good for nothing and was just as useless as my father. She even said, more than once, that she wished Daddy had taken me with him.

What a horrible thing to say. I was very upset and cried a lot.

Nanna telephoned and she could hear that I was upset, so she came to visit, and Mummy started shouting at Nanna again. Nanna asked Mummy to stop shouting at me, and Mummy told Nanna to leave us alone. Mummy said if Nanna had raised Daddy properly, he would not have been so useless and she would not have had to shout at him as often as she did.

Nanna told Mummy she had made Daddy's life a misery. But this didn't make Mummy sad; if made her shout even louder. She said some horrible things to Nanna.

I told Mummy, "Daddy was right, you do have a wicked tongue."

When I said this, Mummy knew I had read the note Daddy had written to me. And she looked angrier than ever.

She ordered me to go to my room while she shouted at Nanna.

She told Nanna she should never come to our house again, she was no longer welcome. Nanna started crying and said she was sorry, but Mummy wasn't listening.

She grabbed my wrist and held it so tight that it hurt, as she pulled me up the stairs. She shouted at me to go to my room and shouted some more because I had not gone upstairs the first time she asked.

She dragged me by the hand. I didn't want to go because Nanna was crying and I didn't want her to cry.

I wanted to cuddle her and make her feel better.

But Mummy dragged me to the top of the stairs.

Nanna told her not to be so rough with me, but Mummy said Nanna should not tell her how to raise her son, because Nanna had not raised her own son very well.

Mummy let go of me when we got to the top of the stairs, turned and shouted - no, she screamed - at Nanna. She told her to never ever come back. She told her that she would never, ever, ever be allowed to see me again.

"You don't mean that," said Nanna.

"Oh, I do!" shouted Mummy. "Get out now, and NEVER. COME. BACK!!!"

"You really do have such a *wicked* tongue," sobbed Nanna.

I remember there was so much noise. I couldn't shut it out. Mummy was shrieking at Nanna; Nanna cried like her heart had just been ripped to pieces. And then I heard another voice, too, a voice even angrier than Mummy's.

It took me a while to realise that it was *my* voice.

And I don't really know what happened after that, honestly.

It's all a blur.

I can remember Mummy turned to me, looking very surprised because of how loud I was shouting.

Then…then…nothing but tiny flickers of something happening, but it's not clear. It's like - like - the only way I can think of describing it is that it was like I had seen red.

The next thing I *can* remember clearly is me sitting next to Mummy's body at the bottom of the stairs. Blood was pouring from her mouth.

I felt Nanna's hand softly touch my shoulder.

"Oh, my poor boy," she said, "what did she make you do?"

"Mummy won't be shouting at anybody, ever again," I said.

Nanna pulled me away from Mummy and gave me a huge hug. I turned my head to look at Mummy one more time.

One last time.

"Don't look back," said Nanna. "*Never* look back. It's over,"

"Yes," I said. "It's over."

And it was.

For a while…

Now

Four

Amanda's gagged today, and I'm glad, so glad. I haven't felt this glad since…well, it doesn't matter. What *does* matter is that she can't use that wicked tongue of hers.

It's too late to save her poor, pathetic, husband, of course.

But better late than never.

She has no idea what I intend to do, but I can see the pleading in her eyes; 'please, please, don't do this, whatever *this* is'.

As I look down on her, I wonder what frightens her most?

Does she think I'm after her money? This black widow's wealth is evident, from the lavish fittings in this large house to the expensive car on the drive. And it's definitely displayed in her clothing and how she smells. One bottle of that perfume probably costs as much as many people earn in an entire day.

Does she think I want her body? Are those terrified eyes waiting for me to rip open that designer-label satin blouse, rip off her presumably expensive underwear, and have my wicked way with her?

I run my eyes over her, slowly, deliberately. I see a fresh wave of fear overwhelm; she knows that I *am* now checking her out in *that* way.

I nod and allow myself a shallow smile of approval. She has just the right amount of curves in all the right places. Women many years younger than Amanda would love to have a body like hers.

Does she fear being physically violated in the most personal way, while being powerless to prevent it? No wonder she looks so scared. Or maybe, just maybe, she's actually just a little bit turned on.

I am. My whole body is tingling and buzzing with an almost adolescent intensity. It's quite unexpected. It's quite intoxicating.

Robbery or rape? It doesn't matter what she thinks.

She'd be wrong on both counts.

I achieved my main aim the moment I forced a crumpled-up handkerchief into her mouth and tied a scarf around the back of her head to hold it in place. I silenced her wicked tongue.

As I look down on her, I'm practically drooling as I imagine myself ripping that remorseless flap of foul flesh right out of her mouth.

Where did *that* come from? That isn't me! I don't talk or think like that. That's not the real me. But it *is* a part of me. A part of me I haven't heard from in a long, long, time. I suddenly feel detached, as if I'm having a surreal, out-of-body, experience, watching someone else tie up and gag this woman.

Amanda tries to speak, but the gag is too tight. Her mouth must feel raw and dry. All she can manage are pitiful whimpers, high-pitched, muffled moans, and anxious glances from those petrified, pleading eyes, which release sad tears down her face, smearing her make-up.

Her noises make the red mist rise again. I remember why I'm here.

Perhaps she thought I intended to kill her for some reason, maybe suffocate her. That's what her eyes told me when I forced the gag into her mouth. She sniffs hard, trying to take in as much air as possible, relieved that she can still breathe through her nose.

As she inhales, she involuntarily snorts and I can't help but giggle.

"That's right," I spit. "Snort like the filthy fucking pig you are."

She shudders, as the venom in my voice sends a new wave of chills shooting down her spine.

I have shaken Amanda to her very core, I can see that.

But now, there's a new look in her eyes, one that says, 'what could I *possibly* have done to warrant such spiteful hatred?'

I step towards her and she cowers. I lean over her, deliberately far too close for her comfort, and check the ropes that are pinning her arms behind her, securing her firmly to the wooden chair in the dining room at the back of the house.

The red marks on her wrists tell me she's been twisting and turning her hands, trying to release them, but the bonds are too tight. I made sure of that. She isn't going anywhere.

Well, except straight to Hell, of course.

I step back again, and she visibly relaxes just a little, presumably relieved that the imminent physical assault she had been fearing has not begun. Her buttons remain fastened, her clothing is intact.

I tower above her, satisfied that she is firmly bound and gagged.

My heart is thumping. It's almost a sexual thrill, but one far better than any physical act. Perhaps this is the kind of prolonged ecstatic sensation that those who practice Tantra get to experience and enjoy.

Amanda's eyes dart around the room desperately, but no white knight will be riding to rescue this damsel in distress. Why would there be? No one knows she's in danger.

If anyone had been passing when I knocked on her front door a short while ago, they wouldn't have seen anything suspicious.

Amanda was surprised to see me standing on her doorstep and didn't want to speak to me at all, but ushered me inside, for fear of any short exchange being overheard by her nosy neighbours.

"There's been enough curtain-twitching among those gluttonous gossips recently," she muttered, as she beckoned me in.

She led me to the kitchen at the back of the house and gestured for me to wait in the adjoining dining room while she made tea. While she had no intention of talking to me in any depth, she hadn't forgotten her manners.

I heard her fill the kettle with water and the distinctive clinking of expensive china cups being removed from a cupboard.

I closed the partially-glazed door which divided the dining room from the conservatory, causing the room to darken. The private garden had walls. There would be no witnesses.

I took a thin pair of latex gloves from the pocket of my trousers and pulled them on, before moving one of the wooden chairs from under the rectangular table which dominated the room. I turned the chair so that the seat faced the door to the kitchen.

I slipped off my small back-pack and pulled out some rope, a large handkerchief and a scarf, all of which I placed on top of the table.

Amanda stepped into the room and her eyes flicked from me to the re-arranged chair. She met my gaze again with a mixture of bewilderment and disapproval.

She then noticed the items on the table.

She was about to speak, presumably to unleash that wicked tongue of hers, and demand to know what was going on, but I didn't give her the chance.

I took two quick steps towards her and, in a swift, sudden, movement, raised my arm across my body and swung it back as hard as I could, my knuckles crunching into her cheekbone.

She was dazed and disorientated. I grabbed her by the wrist, spun her around and forced her down into the chair.

As she struggled to regain her senses, I jumped onto her lap, preventing her breathless body from taking in any air. I pinned her down, roughly forced her hands behind her and bound them with the rope. I felt a powerful, intoxicating, surge of adrenaline coarse through my veins, as if it had been injected into me with a high-pressure syringe.

I then shoved the crumpled handkerchief into her mouth. It pressed down on her tongue, so she couldn't scream or call out. I grabbed the scarf and knotted it tightly around the back of her head, holding the gag firmly in place. It was so tight that I could see the scarf cutting into the skin at the edges of her mouth.

I climbed off her lap and loomed over her, admiring my handiwork. That's when she inhaled and made her snorting noise.

I checked her bonds and then towered above her, hitting her with a look of complete and utter contempt as her eyes darted around the room, looking desperately for some sign of hope.

I stroll confidently out of the room and climb the stairs, leaving her to wallow in her fear and contemplate her fate, alone and in silence.

I wander into the master bedroom and find a large jewellery box standing prominently on the sideboard, the lid of which is partially open. I can see that it is full of chains and gems. If I *was* a robber, I'd have just thought all my Christmases have come at once.

I open the wardrobe doors. There are enough designer coats, dresses and shoes here to supply a high-end boutique.

But there's no menswear, not a single suit, shirt, tie - not even a stray sock. There's nothing here to suggest that Amanda once shared her life, let alone this room, with someone else.

There are no photographs anywhere, no sentimental snapshots of a once-happy husband and wife. It's as if she has tried to erase her late husband from her memory; it's as if he had never existed.

I allow myself a small smile.

Amanda is probably thinking I am ransacking this room, emptying her jewellery box into a bag.

Maybe she is relaxing, reassuring herself that this is, after all, 'just' a burglary. Maybe I had expected the house to be empty. Perhaps she is comforting herself with the thoughts that, soon, this will be over, her dignity will be intact, and all she will have lost are just a few trinkets.

I hope that's what she's thinking, because the only thing she'll have got right is that, soon, it *will* all be over.

I close the wardrobe door and pause, staring at a full-length mirror.

The figure staring back at me looks so different to the way I feel. I raise my arms, tilt my head, turn my body one way and then the other, and my reflection mirrors the movements perfectly.

My reflection.

But it doesn't look like me. Does it? Really?

It certainly doesn't *feel* like me.

That face shows no sign of the constant rage I feel, this insatiable hunger, a fiery compulsion to act; I've *got* to do this, I've got no choice. It's not my fault. It's my mother's fault.

I *want* to do this.

I don't know where this feeling comes from, or where it has been hiding, but right now, it feels good. Real good.

After what I feel is a suitably uncomfortable period of time for Amanda, I return to the dining room.

Her expectant eyes look at me, hoping I will issue some veiled threat to 'keep quiet or else' as I prepare to flee with her valuables.

I watch as her hopeful expression turns to crestfallen despair, when she sees my hands are empty. No swag bag, no pockets bulging with diamonds and pearls.

I raise my hands to confirm they are empty, and her eyes widen as she sees my gloves; clearly, she had not noticed them before.

She tries to scream, but can't dislodge the gag, and all I hear is a muted, hoarse, moan. She squirms and struggles in her seat, presumably fearing once again that I might be planning to rape her, after all.

I reach into an inner pocket of my coat, with an almost theatrical motion, and pull out a folded newspaper page.

This is not what she had been expecting.

"I read about your husband," I say, keeping my voice as dull and monotone as possible, not allowing any trace of emotion to be evident, which isn't easy, because inside my intense excitement is building up so much, I feel like I could burst at any time.

But no, I am determined to be the volcano; dark, foreboding, stony-faced, calm, menacing and quiet on the surface, with nothing to outwardly betray the molten maelstrom brewing beneath.

I unfold the newspaper slowly and show her the headline.

She turns her head away. She doesn't want to see it, she doesn't *need* to see it. The words are etched in her memory.

"Look at it," I say, softly.

She shakes her head. She knows exactly what it says.

"Look at it!" I hiss, with such pure, undiluted, hatred that she involuntarily turns her head back to meet my accusing glare.

I turn the newspaper around, so that the report is now facing me. "It says your husband left a suicide note," I say, "but it *doesn't* say what he wrote."

The raw fear in her eyes has subsided.

My reference to the newspaper report seems to have allayed any lingering fears that this might be a crime of passion. She knows now that this, whatever this is, has some connection to the recent death of her husband.

There's a new look in her eyes. It's not fear any more, it's…it's anger! She's actually angry at me now! And that feels like a red rag to a bull.

A euphoric wave washes over me from somewhere so very deep down inside. It rises up and flows through every fibre of my being. It is so intoxicating. I *like* this feeling.

I lean in close, so very, very close, to her, so close that she can feel my hot breath on her neck.

Her body tenses, and for a fleeting moment, I suddenly do have an incredibly strong urge to touch her. Maybe I *should* rip open that blouse or shove my hand up her skirt.

"I've *seen* the note," I whisper, my lips lightly brushing her ear lobe.

She shudders.

"I've read it. Every. Single. Tragic. Word."

I pull away, stand upright again and loom menacingly over her.

There's a mixture of confusion and denial on her face.

How could I have read the note? It was private, it was addressed to her. She has seen it, a police officer has seen it, and the Coroner has read it. But that's it. She finds some steely resolve. I'm lying, I have to be. That's what she's thinking. I can't have seen the note.

"He blamed you," I hiss. "You drove him to it. He couldn't live with you anymore. You and your wicked, *wicked*, tongue."

I pour every ounce of contempt into those last three words and I watch with tremendous satisfaction as what little colour she has left in her face suddenly fades.

Any anger and accompanying new-found strength she had been trying to muster suddenly slips away and dissolves.

The renewed look of fear in her eyes tells me that she understands; somehow, impossibly, I *had* read the note. It's the only way I could know those specific words written by her late husband.

"Yes, Amanda," I say, "you've got a wicked, *wicked*, tongue."

I reach into one of the deep outer pockets of my coat and pull out a pair of shiny surgical scissors, with long, thin, razor-sharp blades, expertly crafted for clean, precise, incisions.

Her eyes widen so much I wonder if they are going to slip effortlessly out of their sockets.

I can't resist a smile as I spot some liquid trickling down her toned calf, creating a small stain on the spotlessly-clean carpet.

I watch her struggle again, trying to summon every tiny ounce of strength she has left, but it doesn't take long for her to accept that her efforts are futile. I smile again when I see her shoulders slump.

She is exhausted.

She is drained.

She is deflated.

She is defeated, resigned to her fate.

I suddenly sit heavily on her lap again, forcing her to choke a little because air wants to escape from her mouth but can't.

I playfully tease and taunt her, waving the scissors back and forth in front of her face.

I slip my fingers into the holes so that I can open the blades and move my hand behind her. She winces, as if she is expecting to feel the blades sink into the back of her neck at any moment.

But no, that would be far too easy; far too quick. As tempting as it is to plunge the scissors into her neck, she needs to suffer, she needs to hurt, she needs to learn the true meaning of fear.

The scissors snip effortlessly through the scarf, which falls to the floor, releasing its grip on the handkerchief in her mouth.

Amanda starts to cough and splutter and is able to spit the handkerchief onto the floor, together with some bloodied saliva.

She gasps for breath, gratefully taking in huge gulps.

She looks at me intently, her expression suggesting she is torn; does she try to scream, or should she thank me for removing the gag and showing her some mercy? Perhaps I should release her hands next?

I smile. Oh, dear Amanda, your fate was sealed the moment you invited me into your lovely home.

"Wh-what do you want?" she says, hoarsely.

I lower my head and touch her nose with my own as I stare intently into her weary eyes.

"Shut up!" I sneer, sadistically. I may have removed the gag, but the very last thing I want to hear is her voice. That cruel voice, speaking with that wicked tongue. "That's what I want. I. Want. You. To. SHUT. UP!"

"Please," she begs. "I'll give you anything. I'll *do* anything. Please."

"Please…," I mimic. Then I suddenly shriek, "SHUT UP! *That's* what I want you to do!" as I raise the scissors in my hands again.

It's time to silence her forever.

Five: Kat

Hannah nearly knocks me off my feet when I step into the open-plan newsroom. She's so excited, I wonder if she won the lottery at the weekend, or if her boyfriend proposed to her.

"Something's going on," she gushes. "Tony was sent out as soon as he got here and Patrick's been on the phone non-stop."

Tony was the Herald's one and only staff photographer.

I glance across the large rectangular room. Glazed partitions divide the far corner from the rest and through the glass I see Patrick, the Herald's editor, sitting behind his desk, phone clasped to his ear.

"What is it?" I ask, as I pull away from Hannah and walk across to my desk.

Hannah shrugs her shoulders. "Dunno. But it must be pretty big. Maybe it's a murder or something."

I feel a shiver run down my spine, but it's a feeling of excited anticipation rather than fear or sorrow. A murder! Yes!

I quickly admonish myself. What am I turning into? How can I be *thrilled* at the prospect that someone may have been killed?

"Murder?" says Ross Barker, another member of the Herald's small editorial team. "We should be so lucky."

I gaze at the editor's office. Patrick is still on the phone.

I watch him intently as I shake off my coat and drape it over the back of my chair, my curiosity well and truly piqued.

He looks up and catches my eye; I quickly look away, my cheeks burning, feeling like an embarrassed little girl who has just been caught staring at someone she has a secret crush on but who is far too shy to say anything or do anything about it. Not that I have a crush on my boss. Of course I don't. But it was that kind of awkward feeling.

I slowly lift my head. Patrick's still looking at me, but he's also waving one of his hands, beckoning me over.

I exchange a quick glance with Hannah, who shrugs her shoulders again in that vacant, ditzy way of hers, and cross the room. I'm about to knock on the door but Patrick makes a dismissive gesture as if to say, 'don't bother', and invites me inside.

"Got it," he says to whoever he is talking to, as he points to the empty chair on my side of his desk. "Yes, I appreciate that, thanks. Please keep me posted, no matter what time. Cheers."

He replaces the receiver. "Kate," he says, as I sit in the chair, "how are you? Good weekend?"

I smile. Patrick keeps forgetting I prefer to be called Kat; I think it sounds better. But I'm not inclined to correct him. I don't want to appear rude and fall foul of the boss so early in my career.

"It was OK," I say. I shift a little awkwardly in my seat, aware that Hannah and Ross are almost certainly watching us like hawks.

"Good," he says. "We've got a big story breaking."

"Hannah mentioned it," I say. "But she didn't say what is was."

"That's because we don't know," he smiles. "Not for sure. I had a tip-off yesterday about lots of police activity in Mountview Rise."

I know Mountview Rise; it's a long, winding, cul-de-sac on the Hillside estate overlooking the town, with thick woodland on the steep slope behind it, which is popular with dog-walkers, joggers, courting teenagers and drug users. Some of the most expensive homes in town are on Hillside, and Mountview Rise houses the best of the best.

"I've sent Tony there, but it's cordoned off. Police aren't telling him anything, and with the way that road twists and turns, he can't see anything, either," Patrick says.

"So, what do you think it is?" I ask. I can feel my heart pounding in my chest. This could be it! A *proper* story, the kind of story that made me want to become a journalist in the first place.

"It could be a murder, assault or a rape, maybe a robbery which ended up with someone being injured. If you're a robber, Hillside has to be on the top of your hit list. My source said she saw what she thought might be a body bag on a stretcher being put into an ambulance, but couldn't be sure if the person was dead or unconscious or just injured, if it was a person. All I know for sure is that it must be pretty serious. I was just talking to the police press office. There's a media conference at Town Hall at ten thirty. I want you there, Kate."

"Me?" I feel a sudden rush of blood to my face. I know my cheeks have turned crimson, thanks to a combination of nerves, excitement and pride.

"Well, you've told me a couple of times you'd like to be our lead 'crime reporter'…"

"Yes! I do!" I say, probably with a bit too much enthusiasm.

"Good," he says, warmly. "Everyone's staying tight-lipped so we're not going to know anything more until the press conference. I suggest you hand over anything you *were* planning to do to Hannah."

"What about Ross?"

"Oh, he's too busy turning himself into our off-diary investigative reporter, apparently," he says, with a smile which suggests he may be indulging or humouring Ross a little.

I step out of his office and return to my desk in a daze.

"Everything OK?" asks Hannah.

"Huh?"

"Are you alright?"

"Sure," I grin. "Yes. I'm going to a press conference."

I hurriedly make my excuses and dash down the corridor, hoping to reach the ladies' room before I hyperventilate. I make it. Just.

I lean on the nearest sink, stare at my reflection in the mirror on the tiled wall before me, and allow myself a small, nervous, smile.

"Well, Kat, this *is* it, the proverbial big one."

I take a couple of deep breaths.

I turn on the tap, collect some cold water in my hands and splash it onto my face to cool the burning and to hopefully encourage my skin to turn a paler shade of scarlet.

"This is what it's all about," I tell myself. "Flower shows, charity cheque presentations and council stories are staple weekly newspaper fare, but this is the front-page lead and *that's* where I want to be."

I've been working at the Herald for nearly six months. In terms of 'hard news', I've covered some court cases, an inquest and recently spent several weeks at a high-profile planning enquiry.

But none of those generated this kind of buzz, the anticipation of knowing that something *very* newsworthy has happened.

I'm surprised that Patrick himself, or Mervyn, the chief reporter, aren't going to cover it. But then, they've probably 'been there and done that' numerous times in their careers; perhaps, for them, the buzz is simply not as intoxicating anymore. The novelty has worn off.

I can't imagine *ever* growing tired of this kind of feeling.

The best way for young reporters like me, Hannah and Ross to learn is by *doing* the job. That's where smaller local papers like the Herald come into their own; they let young newshounds off the leash and take their first steps into this crazy career, under the guidance of experienced, maybe slightly jaded, journalists who are counting down the days to retirement, who are happy to mentor to the next generation.

I'm so glad Patrick chose me, it's a huge vote of confidence. I expect Hannah's glad, too. I'm not sure hard news will ever really be her thing and it sounds like the egotistically ambitious Ross already has his sights fixed on some off-diary stuff.

"I hope it *is* a murder," a voice deep down inside me says and I immediately chastise myself again. No! A murder means someone's life has been prematurely ended by someone else. Brutally. How can someone intentionally take the life of another? How could I *hope* for that? I shake my head. I'm in danger of enjoying this too much!

But then, look at the alternatives. I definitely don't want it to be a rape, I think I would find that too uncomfortable.

I study my reflection again. My cheeks are slowly returning to their normal colour. I'll be able to go back to the newsroom shortly without looking flustered, and then head out to the press conference.

My cheeks redden all over again as another thought occurs to me. I wonder if Dan will be at the press conference.

I shake my head. Actually, I hope he *isn't* there, because this is my first really big story. I've no idea what it is, but I *do* know it's big, I can feel it, and that means I need to focus fully and be at my very best. I don't need to be distracted by Dan.

A memory flickers into my mind before I can stop it.

We're walking to our cars after another long day at the planning enquiry. I'm moaning about feeling tired and bored; ironically, moaning because I want the proverbial *big*, 'juicy', story to come my way.

Not that multi-million pound plans to extend the local airport aren't big news; neighbours are furious, not to mention climate campaigners and environmentalists. But it's not *exciting* enough.

It warranted a mention on the front page, with several full pages of copy inside. But it wasn't 'sexy' enough to make the front-page lead.

Dan casually draped an arm around my shoulder and gave me a gentle squeeze, as if to console or comfort me. He did this a few days ago, almost as if he was 'testing the water', and on that occasion, he quickly removed his arm.

But this time, as soon as I felt his arm around me and his hand on my shoulder, I took it in my own, so that he couldn't pull his arm away.

I think I surprised myself more than I surprised him. But this - whatever *this* is - had been building up over the past few months, ever since we first met, if I'm honest.

It was easy to deny it over the months, as I never quite knew when I might bump into him again.

But the planning enquiry saw us spend more than eight hours a day, every day for almost three weeks, sitting next to each other, having lunch together, getting to know each other.

When we got to the car park, I released his hand but he didn't move away. Instead, he moved closer and, against my better judgement, I let him kiss me. No, I did more than that. I kissed him back.

I shake my head. See? Dan *is* a distraction.

It's been a couple of weeks since the enquiry finished, and our paths have only crossed once since, the Friday before last. And I'm *definitely* not going to stand here and let *that* flash back into my mind.

I've thought about little else since, except for the odd moment when something work-related has occupied my mind, but now it looks as if I've got something to *really* distract me from day-dreaming about a couple of kisses that should never have happened.

The biggest story of my career is a heartbeat away. I can feel it.

I give my reflection a stern, assertive, stare.

"This is it, Kat Russell. Don't mess it up. Carpé diem and all that. Come on, girl, you've *got* this."

Six: Dan

The police usually host press conferences at their HQ just outside the city, not some twenty miles away in this sleepy little seaside town.

It means there's a good chance this story will be too parochial for me to spend any time on.

I work for a regional news agency, finding local stories which we sell to national newspapers and magazines, because it's simply not viable for them to have staff of their own in every town and city.

Agencies like mine often cover court cases or stories like the recent airport planning enquiry, when it makes financial sense for London-based media to use an agency rather than have one of their own staff away for several weeks, with all the associated accommodation, food and inevitably large bar bills, too.

I'm hoping this press conference will be about something which will be of enough interest to the nationals to warrant keeping me on it, but not newsworthy enough for them to send a staffer down.

And if does interest them, I'll get to spend some long overdue time back in my hometown. I can stay with parents and catch up properly with friends.

I'm hoping Patrick will be covering it for the Herald; he still tends to cover the bigger stories himself. Plus if he *is* here, it will confirm it's something decent as he'll undoubtedly have been tipped off by someone, as he's very well connected. But I'd love to just catch up with him. I started my career at the Herald and picked up plenty of tricks of the trade from its experienced editor, who I have a lot of respect for.

The press conference is taking place in one of Town Hall's old meeting rooms. Four rows of five chairs have been placed in front of a rectangular table which is next to a side door. Behind the table is a roll-up, free-standing banner bearing the police crest.

Three radio journalists are already here, one from the BBC, one from a regional independent outfit and the other from the town's own community radio station, judging by the branding on her microphone.

There are no TV cameras here. The police haven't gone out of their way to publicise the press conference, so it hasn't found its way onto the radar of local TV yet, who would need to know a lot more before deciding to devote any of their precious time and diminishing resources on it. I only found out about it because I know someone who works in the police press office; he told me about it almost in passing, and then seemed to try to backtrack a bit, as if he'd said too much.

The main door to the room opens and Kat anxiously peers in.

Any initial disappointment I may have had at not being reunited with Patrick soon fades. I'm glad Kat's here. Patrick knows the best way to encourage a young journalist's talent is to throw them in at the deep end to see if they sink or swim. That's what he did with me, and just over two years ago, my career took off, the agency snapped me up, my salary doubled, and I will probably never have to write another 'golden wedding anniversary' story ever again.

Now it seems Patrick considers Kat to be his next rising star.

But it's not her journalistic qualities that have caught *my* eye.

We spent a lot of time together at the airport planning enquiry, chatting and flirting. I took a chance by putting a friendly arm around her shoulder briefly, and didn't get a slap in the face. So a few days later, I chanced it again, which led to a *very* enjoyable kiss.

She then started playing hard to get, until just over a week ago, when we met at the official opening of a new restaurant at the local college, for student chefs to test their growing culinary skills on the public, who get to dine out for a fraction of the usual cost.

Kat hasn't replied to any of my texts since then, which has been disappointing, but I knew our paths would cross again sooner or later.

As she enters the room, I can't tell if she's pleased to see me or not, but she does, at least, make her way straight over to the chair next to mine; I guess I'm a friendly face in what could otherwise be quite an intimidating environment if you're not used to it.

She looks pretty hot. Tailored, sharp-creased trousers, which I know will be clinging tightly to her perfectly pert backside. I wish I was standing behind her right now, so I could fully admire the view. She's also wearing a figure-hugging white blouse which is just thin enough to afford me a teasing outline of her bra, and a dark blue jacket, which matches her trousers.

As usual, her jet-black hair is pulled back tightly into a ponytail which reaches halfway down her back. I've only seen her let her hair down once (in more ways than one!), at the college restaurant launch, and I'd love to pick up where we left off *that* night.

"Hi," she says, a slight quiver in her voice, "what's the scoop?"

I stare at her mouth and remember how sweet it felt to kiss her, and just how much I'd like to kiss her again.

"Sorry?" I say.

She blushes; it's cute. She *knows* what I was thinking, I'm sure.

"You must have some idea what's going on, otherwise you wouldn't be here."

"Maybe I had an ulterior motive," I say, as I hit her with what I hope is a suggestive smile, but before we can say any more, the side door opens and two plain-clothed police officers emerge and sit behind the table while Paul Brooks, my police press office contact, stands to one side and nervously asks us to switch our phones to silent.

Detective Chief Inspector Simon Fisher is one of the force's most experienced officers. Paul introduces him and explains, "DCI Fisher is the senior investigating officer in this case. Acting Detective Inspector Alexandra Nicholas is deputy SIO."

Alex is an ambitious officer who has risen rapidly through the ranks thanks to a graduate fast-track scheme.

I asked her out about 18 months ago, and we had a couple of dates. It didn't go anywhere, but didn't end badly, so I'm pleased to see her. It might be useful to have a 'friendly face' on the inside.

"DCI Fisher is going to make a statement," says Paul. "There will then be a short period for questions, but there will be no one-to-one interviews."

DCI Fisher stands and clears his throat. He's tall, wiry, clean-cut, in his late forties and has a calm, naturally reassuring, manner.

"Good morning, thank you for coming," he says, scanning the room and making direct eye contact with each of us in turn. I catch Alex's eye and her mouth twitches by way of acknowledgement.

"It's my solemn duty to inform you that we have launched a murder investigation," DCI Fisher says, and I hear Kat let out a little gasp. I smile as I remember the adrenaline kick I felt when I was in her position. You never forget your first time.

"Police were alerted early yesterday afternoon after the body of a woman was found at her home in Mountview Rise. Paramedics attended, but sadly, the woman was pronounced dead at the scene. Our sincere condolences go to her family at this terribly tragic time."

DCI Fisher pauses and pours himself a glass of water.

He continues, "A postmortem examination is taking place right now, so I'm not currently in a position to be able to confirm the cause of death. However, the circumstances in which the woman was found make it clear that she *was* murdered. We will know a lot more when we get the results of the PM. We know that the victim was seen in her front garden by a neighbour at around four o'clock on Saturday afternoon. We want to hear from anyone who may have seen anyone acting suspiciously in the Hillside area between four o'clock on Saturday and two-thirty yesterday afternoon. Was there a stranger in the street? Was there a car lurking in a suspicious manner? Did anybody see or hear anything unusual?"

I glance at Kat, who is scribbling furiously in her notepad; her shorthand is incredibly neat whereas mine has become sloppy over the years. I smile as I imagine us writing secret little notes to each other in shorthand. I wonder if we'd be able to translate each other's outlines.

DCI Fisher continues, "We've closed Mountview Rise to allow specially-trained forensic officers and dogs to thoroughly search the area. Uniformed officers are conducting door-to-door enquiries, which are likely to take some time."

I can't remember the last time this town had a murderer in its midst. I think I'm *definitely* going to be sticking around for a while, and if Patrick lets Kat lead on this for the Herald, she and I are likely to see a lot more of each other over the next few weeks. She can play as hard to get as she wants; her kisses told me she's interested, and now I've got the chance to break down her resistance, like I did after we spent prolonged time together at the planning enquiry.

"In the meantime," DCI Fisher says, his authoritative voice shaking me from my thoughts, "if anyone has any information, no matter how irrelevant they think it might be, please contact us. Is a member of your family acting differently? Oddly? Out of character? Did someone come home on Saturday evening or Sunday morning with blood on their clothes?"

Kat gasps again and my ears prick up. Bloodstained clothes? That suggests our victim suffered a violent demise.

"We owe it to the family of the victim to find whoever was responsible for her death as soon as possible. In the meantime, we are putting on extra patrols in the Hillside area, to reassure local residents. Again, I would urge anyone who has any information about this crime to come forward, either by calling the police non-emergency number, 101, or anonymously through Crimestoppers."

He nods at Paul, an indication that he has said all he wants to.

The confident, head-strong BBC radio journalist already has her hand up and clearly isn't interested in waiting to find out if there is to be any protocol for the short question-and-answer session.

"Who found her?" she asks, radiating the kind of sense of self-importance some broadcast journalists seem to have in spades.

"The victim was found by her son," he says. "He doesn't live at the address. He found her early yesterday afternoon."

The other reporters have their hands up, but the BBC girl seems determined to monopolise what little time has been set aside for questions. "What about motive? Was anything stolen? Did she disturb a burglar? What is it about the circumstances of her death that make you sure it was murder if the postmortem hasn't been done yet?"

DCI Fisher raises his voice. "We're in the very early stages of this investigation," he says, pacing his words deliberately in order to maintain his calm façade. "We're keeping an open mind about motive. As I've *already* said, while the postmortem has not been concluded, there is enough evidence to satisfy me that this *is* a murder. And no, I am not prepared to divulge any further details at this time."

"Were there any surveillance cameras in the area?" The other reporters glare at the BBC journalist, because she is hogging the limelight, exuding an arrogance which says 'I'm the BBC, so you simply *have* to listen to me and answer my questions.'

But there's one obvious question that she has *not* asked, presumably because she thought the answer won't be released until the postmortem is complete.

DCI Fisher raises his eyebrows impatiently. "Searching for CCTV footage is part of our enquiries. If anyone has any footage that may be of use to us, they should get in touch. The main reason for speaking to you this morning is to appeal for anyone with any information about this case to come forward and tell us anything they know."

"Are you looking for a weapon?"

The detective's body language suggests she's getting under his skin now. Mind you, I think she's having that effect on all of us judging by the frustrated looks being exchanged by the other radio reporters. Some broadcast journalists think they're *so* superior.

DCI Fisher sighs heavily. "We're still examining the scene for *any* evidence," and while he hasn't directly answered the question, the way he clamps his mouth shut says he has no intention of elaborating.

Paul steps forward, although he looks like a rabbit in headlights. This press conference is about to end.

I quickly stand, raise my hand, and say, just loud and assertive enough to drown out Miss BBC, but not so loud as to appear as obnoxious, "Excuse me, DCI Fisher. Daniel Barton, Southern News Service. If the murder was reported by the victim's son, presumably you know who the victim is. Can you tell us, please?"

I smile inwardly, as I see Miss BBC curse herself for failing to ask such an obvious question, one which will enable us all to go off and carry out some investigations of our own, no matter how much, or how little, the police tell us

The look on DCI Fisher's face suggests he had been hoping we'd all get so preoccupied with thinking about the cause of death, and the possible motive, that we'd forget to ask about the identity of the victim.

But I *had* asked, and because I'd asked respectfully, he was not really able to refuse to answer. And, since he has already told us that the son found the victim, her identity is known.

"Thank you, Daniel," he says, glaring at Miss BBC as if he was telling her *'that's* the professional way to ask a question'. She, in turn, throws me a disapproving scowl.

"The deceased *has* been identified. She was Mrs Amanda Shepton, a 54-year-old who has lived on the Hillside estate for many years."

I hear another gasp from Kat. Something stirs at the back of my mind. Amanda Shepton; I *know* that name but can't quite place her.

Miss BBC is about to ask yet another question, but DCI Fisher is already on his feet, throwing a dark look at Paul who looks like a nervous wreck and who hasn't been much use at all. "That's all we're able to say at this stage."

"But DCI Fisher…," Miss BBC begins.

"That is *all*," he says, sternly. "As soon as we are able to release any further information, we will. In the meantime, I'd just like to reiterate that if anybody has any information whatsoever that can help tell us who killed Mrs Shepton, and why, then we urge them to please come forward. Thank you."

He turns, nods at Alex, and they leave through the side door.

Miss BBC gets up and practically pounces on poor Paul, to bombard him with more questions, no doubt. Perhaps I'll give him a call later, as a bit of a welfare check. And, of course, to see if I might be able to find out if he knows anything more. I'm likely to have more chance of getting something out of him than I am from Alex.

The two other radio journalists are busy; one has pulled out her mobile and is talking presumably to her office, and the other is rewinding and playing back her recordings.

I'm going to have to phone my office, too, to submit the first report and get it to the nationals for tomorrow's editions. Then the fun really begins, as we get to turn detective and try to find out all the things that the police wouldn't, or couldn't, tell us.

I turn to look at Kat.

All the colour has drained out of her face and, as clichéd as it sounds, she looks like she has seen a ghost.

She's staring ahead of her, blankly, and I hear her whisper three, barely audible, words. "The black widow."

Seven: Alex

Simon didn't say much as he strode out of Town Hall and marched to the police station, which was a five-minute walk away, or two-and-a-half if you walked like he did.

The press conference took place at Town Hall because the police station simply doesn't have a room suitable for anything remotely formal or 'public'; it's in serious need of some investment.

The civilian at the front desk buzzed the internal door open and we took the lift to the incident room on the third floor.

"Tam," barked Simon, as he led me into his office.

Detective Sergeant Tam Fawcett is a burly, no-nonsense Scot and a third-generation 'old-school' detective who followed in the footsteps of his father and grandfather in joining the police straight from school.

Tam was convinced he'd be appointed Deputy SIO when we were both called in yesterday. After all, as he delights in reminding me at every opportunity, he would have earned the promotion, his credentials coming from the street rather than, as he says with such obvious distaste, the classroom.

From the second Simon named *me* deputy, Tam started giving me the evil eye. It feels as if he now has me under close surveillance, ready to pounce on the slightest indication of indecision. And woe betide me if I make a mistake or choose a different course of action to the one he would take, or, Heaven-forbid, get something wrong.

He's like a vulture, circling overhead, waiting to swoop.

Tam closes the door to Simon's office behind us.

"How'd the press conference go, guv?" he asks.

"You know the media," Simon sighs, "whatever you tell them, it's never enough to satisfy their insatiable hunger. That BBC woman was really pissing me off. At least Daniel showed some decorum."

"Daniel?" says Tam, who turns to me with a raised eyebrow. "You mean Danny Barton, the former Herald man?"

Simon nods.

Tam gives me a smug, knowing, look, a veiled warning that he has just acquired a little piece of ammunition he may be able to use against me, should the appropriate opportunity present itself. Unfortunately, he saw me out with Dan once, and would undoubtedly take great delight in trying to undermine me by accusing me of sleeping with the enemy, or some other kind of jealous, juvenile, jibe.

"I'd have preferred to wait before speaking to the press, at least until we had the PM results," Simon says, frustration written all over his face. "But that amount of police activity on Hillside was never going to go unnoticed. Someone tipped off the Herald, their editor rang the press office last night, so our hand was forced. Better for us to feed the sharks than have them scavenging for themselves."

"It's not like we had too much to actually tell them," I offer.

"That makes it all the worse, lassie," says Tam, who is unable to disguise the contempt in his voice. "All we've done now is dangle a little bit of bait for them, and without much more to go on, they'll be off now foraging for any little morsels they can get their sleazy little hands on."

"We had to tell them the victim's name," says Simon.

"Well," says Tam, "I guess the feeding frenzy will have already started."

Simon nods. "That's why we've got to move fast. We're lucky that Amanda was well-known in town. The media know we won't be saying anything else until we've got the PM results, so the hacks will just be busying themselves compiling tribute pieces and getting shocked responses from friends to the news of her death, so that should buy us a little bit of time."

"So, what's the plan, guv?" asks Tam.

"I'm going to the mortuary. I want the PM results yesterday. Tam, I want you to sift through the statements uniform have taken from neighbours; see if it throws up anything useful. Find out if there was any CCTV. Alex, speak to the scenes of crime team; find out if their examination of the house threw up anything."

"Especially Amanda Shepton's tongue," says Tam, and I wince.

"Tam!" snaps Simon.

The Scot shrugs his shoulders, raises his eyebrows, and mouths an innocent "what?" The truth is that, as much as I'm no fan of his abrupt manner, it was almost inevitable that it would be Tam who would address the elephant in the room.

I shiver, as if this was one aspect of the case that I was hoping would go away, one element of this grisly affair that, perhaps, I had dreamed up in my over-active imagination as I tossed and turned in short, restless, deeply-disturbed, sleep last night.

Restless, because we had a murder on our patch.

Deeply disturbed because of Amanda Shepton's tongue.

I can't shake the image of her.

When I arrived at her house yesterday afternoon, Amanda was tied to a chair in the dining room. We couldn't risk contaminating any potential forensic evidence, so we left her in that undignified, degraded, manner while the Scenes of Crime Officers and medical experts did their work.

I'm not particularly squeamish; you can't afford to be if you're going to get anywhere in this line of work. I've seen dead bodies before; a few too many for my liking, if truth be told.

But there were two things about Amanda Shepton's body that made me feel particularly uncomfortable, beyond the fact that she had died bound and gagged in her own home.

The first was the absence of any obvious cause of death; that was unnerving. No little round bullet wound to the head or heart. No sign that she had been stabbed. If she had been strangled, there would have been bruising or ligature marks. There was *nothing* obvious.

But the second, far more disturbing, element was the amount of blood around her mouth. Had she been hit or beaten, there would have been bruising, cuts and marks all over her, not just around her mouth.

The examining doctor then announced, "Some, if not all, of her tongue is missing."

He was reluctant to theorise further, advising us to wait for the full postmortem, but we needed something, so we pushed him.

Based on his preliminary examination of the body and the scene, he said the most likely scenario was that Amanda Shepton had bitten through her own tongue, and either swallowed it or spat it onto the floor, which prompted an uncomfortable search.

I can't comprehend just how terrified she must have been, to have bitten through her own tongue!

"I'll be back as soon as I've got the full PM results," says Simon. "Once we know how she died, we'll have a better idea of what we're dealing with."

He leaves the room without another word.

I'm sure Tam is gearing up for another snide remark, but my phone chirps. "Excuse me," I say gratefully and brush past him, through the incident room and out into the corridor.

It's a text message from Dan, asking if I want to 'grab a coffee'.

How naïve does he think I am? He doesn't want coffee, he wants information. If he thinks I'm naïve enough to feel compelled to have an off-the-record chat for 'old time's sake', then he's sadly mistaken.

I never thought there was any real relationship potential with Dan. I only agreed to go out with him because a lot of guys, other than police officers, seem intimated when they find out what I do.

Dan knew, but asked me out anyway. And he has got a cute smile and nice green eyes. But the truth is, I like my men tall, dark and rugged. What's Dan? Five-eight? A slight paunch, probably the result of too many liquid lunches, an occupational hazard for journalists; at least, it used to be among the 'old school', and I had enough 'old school' to contend with at work without bringing it into my personal life, too.

Dan is a little more ragged than rugged, I'm afraid. Besides, judging by the way he kept glancing at that pretty young reporter next to him, I think he's found a new muse. She was petite and far more feminine than I am; I've always been a bit of a tomboy and I think Dan desires a much more 'girlie' girl.

He's nice enough, and seems to have a fairly decent moral compass considering his chosen profession. But he isn't nice enough to convince me to commit career suicide by having informal conversations with the media, certainly not at this stage of the enquiry.

I delete the text, walk over to my desk, and call the Scenes of Crime office.

Eight: Kat

I feel like I'm in a surreal trance, a dazed state of denial, detached from reality, unable to accept what I've just heard.

I'd expected, perhaps even hoped, though I feel ashamed to admit it, that the press conference would reveal there had been a murder.

But I wasn't prepared for finding out that the victim was someone I had come to know, respect and like.

I spoke to Amanda Shepton last week, at the inquest into the suicide of her husband. We've spoken many times since I joined the Herald, and while we weren't likely to socialise and become best friends, we were definitely developing a positive rapport.

She was relieved and genuinely grateful when I promised not to report some of the things that had been said during the hearing.

I've never experienced the loss of a family member or dear friend.

Amanda's death is the first time I've had to face the death of someone I've felt any kind of connection with. That was upsetting enough. The fact Amanda had been murdered only made it worse.

I think about her son, Mark, who found her body, and what he must be going through, having lost both parents in such a short space of time.

I could almost feel sorry for him, if it hadn't been for the way he spoke to me.

But then, maybe he isn't grieving for his mother. He wanted her to be dead, didn't he? He said so. Right to her face, right in front of the Coroner, right in front of me. When I think of the look in his eyes, and the spite and hatred in his voice, it suddenly occurs to me that perhaps he didn't discover her body; perhaps *he* killed her. After all, it had been Mark who had called his mother the 'black widow'.

I feel my eyes start to moisten as I think about Amanda. She's dead. *Dead!*

"Kat? Kat? Are you OK?"

I shake my head. I can hear a voice. It's real and yet it isn't.

"Kat!"

Dan is looking at me intently. "Are you OK? You look very pale."

I can't speak. Oh, for goodness sake, girl! Toughen up!

"Come on, let's get you out of here. I think you need some fresh air," Dan says, as he takes my arm and helps me to my feet.

The radio reporters have all pounced on poor Paul, the police press officer, trying to persuade him to record an interview with them, so no one notices us, as Dan guides me out of the room.

We reach the main reception area of Town Hall and Dan leads me to a bench against a wall, alongside a water dispenser. He takes a small paper cup from a pile and fills it with cold water.

"Sit here, drink this and don't go anywhere," he says.

I look at him as if he has spoken to me in a different language.

"Did you get that?" he says. "Wait here, I'll be back in a minute."

I slowly sip from the cup as he walks across the reception area to the far corner, which is much quieter. He pulls out his phone and notepad, makes several calls, and then comes back to me.

"Feeling better?"

I nod. But a wave of panic suddenly explodes out of nowhere. "Shit! It'll be all over the radio and I haven't even called the office yet."

Dan smiles. "It's OK, don't panic."

"Don't tell me it doesn't matter because the Herald is only a weekly paper," I snap defensively. "We've got a website! People will expect the local paper to be reporting on this."

How will I explain myself to Patrick? He gave me a huge vote of confidence by choosing me to cover this press conference and how do I repay him?

"It's all taken care of," says Dan, putting a comforting hand on my shoulder. "I called Patrick, and I've given him the story. It's not like we're competing for the hot exclusive yet, is it? We were all given the same info at the press conference. I didn't tell Patrick anything different to what you would have told him."

I don't know what to say! Dan has suddenly transformed from a distraction which I hadn't decided was welcome or not into my knight in shining armour.

"I told him we were in one of those stuffy old rooms in Town Hall where the air doesn't circulate. He knew exactly what I meant. I told him you felt a bit unwell, so I'd file your copy for you."

"*My* copy?"

Dan gives me a sheepish grin. "Yeah. I told him you'd written it but gave it to me to phone in, because you needed to get some air."

"Thanks," was all I was able to mumble. I felt so relieved, I could cry. I felt so grateful, I could kiss….no, no, not *that* grateful.

"I told him you'll be back later to write up the full story."

"Later?"

Dan's grin grows just a little wider.

"Yeah, I, er, I told him I was taking you for a coffee first."

Since he has just saved my career, never mind the fact that I still feel a bit shaky, I'm hardly in a position to refuse.

"I'm sorry I snapped," I say, as we walk slowly across town. "You know, about the whole weekly-paper thing."

"It's alright," he smiles, and I feel a bit of colour rush back to my cheeks. Oh, Dan, if we weren't competitors, I think I could definitely fall for you. *Could* fall? I hear my inner voice tease.

I smile because I know I'm about to be reminded of a kiss. Not the one in the car park after the planning enquiry, but the other one, from just over a week ago. No, Stop. There's no point torturing myself.

We walk to an independent coffee shop in High Street. Dan orders a couple of cappuccino's while I find a table near the back.

I'd always thought journalism was a competitive, dog-eat-dog industry, everyone trying to out-do each other to get the scoop.

Dan could easily have filed his copy and left me to face the embarrassment of being responsible for the Herald, the local paper, being the last media to report the biggest story in this town for years.

As I watch him order the drinks, my mind meanders back to the first time we met; better to go there than to return to our last kiss. I feel myself begin to blush at the mere thought of it.

It was the second day of my second week at the Herald. The new Town Mayor had just taken up position and had organised a 'welcome drinks reception', which the Herald had an invitation for.

Since I was the newest member of the team, Patrick thought this would be a perfect networking opportunity, a chance for me to get to know some of the key people in town, members of the council plus prominent businessmen and charity representatives, and, of course, to give them a chance to get to know me.

Ultimately, being a successful journalist is all about the contacts and relationships you make.

I felt like a frightened little girl in a big wide world, a timid fish out of water. Most of the people there were a lot older than me and all seemed very familiar with each other, which I found quite intimidating.

I stood awkwardly in a quiet corner, cradling a glass of wine in both hands, because I was shaking so much I couldn't risk holding it in one hand.

When someone who was not unattractive, and who looked closer to my age than just about everybody else in the room, smiled at me and walked towards me, I instantly relaxed; I was no longer little miss no mates, a shrinking violet cowering in the corner. I didn't go weak at the knees at the sight of him, although he was quite cute. I think it was his unassuming, rather than arrogant, confidence which appealed to me.

"You must be from the Herald," he said.

Was it that obvious? Was I wearing a hat with an ID card shoved into the brim with the word 'Press' emblazoned across it?

"I'm Dan; I used to work there. I'm with Southern News now," he said. "You might actually be sitting in my old seat in the office!"

That was probably the first of many times that I blushed in his presence. I wasn't really used to someone flirting with me in the 'real world'. I'd had two boyfriends while I was at university, and a few dates, but nothing remotely significant since.

Then again, it was only my second week in the job. My second week of being a 'grown-up' adult in the real world.

It occurred to me that my stereotypical images of what working life would be like were being shattered. Surely Dan shouldn't be talking to me? If he covered this patch as well, then we were competitors, bitter rivals, even. We should be glaring at each other over our notepads, determined to out-do each other and get the scoop before the other.

It was clear, from all the nods and greetings from various people as they passed by, that Dan was known to many of the guests, so I felt so grateful when he said, "As much as I'd really enjoy spending the whole evening making small talk with you, we're here to mingle with this fair town's finest. And since you clearly don't have the foggiest idea who's who, I'll make some introductions."

And so it was that someone who should be my fierce foe guided me around the room, introducing me as the Herald's latest star recruit.

More than one crusty councillor smiled and said something along the lines of me following in Dan's footsteps, or that I had a tough act to follow, while others suggest he was a fine example of the best of my profession, and I could do a lot worse than learn from him or, come to that, from Patrick, as his absence from the room was noted by many of the people I was introduced to.

After about an hour, Dan excused himself in order to obey the call of nature, but I no longer felt like the 'odd one out' and I didn't have to stand by myself for very long.

Dan had paved the way, and a couple of different people he had introduced me to earlier came up to me and said hello for a second time, including the Mayoress, who was very sweet.

"Have you lost your chaperone?" she said.

I looked around, as it suddenly occurred to me that Dan had been gone for a little longer than I had expected. I spotted him across the room, deep in conversation with a couple of older men in suits.

"Apparently," I smiled.

"Never mind him, let me introduce you to some of the people who *really* make the town tick," she said, with a warm smile. "Come and meet the girls."

Before every introduction, Dan had leaned close and whispered the name and gave me a brief biography of my soon-to-be new contact.

I tried to ignore the tingle that ran through me each time I felt his breath on my ear.

Then as the Mayoress took me on a whirlwind tour around the room, I was being introduced to many of the same names, just a different gender.

After a while, the Mayoress asked, "Have you met Amanda yet? Oh, you must meet Amanda."

And that's when I first spoke to Amanda Shepton.

"She married into money," the Mayoress said, "got herself a wealthy sugar-daddy so she's never needed to work, lucky thing. But she *has* thrown herself into supporting numerous charities and other organisations in the town. She's Chair of the Women's Circle, a trustee of the local hospice, and has connections with the museum and theatre."

Amanda wore her wealth well. She oozed opulence and evidently enjoyed being a renowned socialite among the great and good of the community.

When she greeted me, she was polite and gracious enough, although I couldn't help but think she lacked the natural warmth that I felt from the Mayoress. Amanda's painted smile seemed a little forced.

Still, what did I know? She was obviously very popular, as many within the room seemed to gravitate towards her.

I should not, I told myself, be so quick to judge others. After all, when Dan had walked me around the room earlier, a few of the elected councillors had simply assumed I was his 'plus one' and raised their eyebrows when they were told that I, too, was a journalist. Surely this skinny little waif-like woman was too frail to be a hardened hack? I could see it in their eyes.

Perhaps I wasn't being fair in so readily judging Amanda by first impressions. Indeed, as the weeks went on, she and I spoke many times and I had started to warm to her, although I remained convinced that beneath all the airs and graces, smiles and air-kisses, something stronger, even a little formidable, was lurking.

She seemed to have warmed to me, too, especially after I wrote a few pieces promoting and praising some of her fund-raising activities.

I came away from that evening with a clutch-bag full of business cards and feeling a lot more confident about my ability to fit in and to be able to do the job I was being employed to do.

And I was in no doubt that I owed a lot of that new-found confidence to Dan.

"Feeling better?" he says, pulling me back into the present from my little wander down memory lane.

I nod. "Thanks," I say, and then sigh. "I feel so stupid."

"No need," he smiles. "I was a nervous wreck when I covered my first murder. You really shouldn't worry about it."

I smile, reassured, and thank him again for phoning an initial report in to Patrick.

"No problem. It was nice talking to him again. You'll learn a lot from 'uncle' Patrick. That's what we called him. He knows everyone who's anyone in town, and he'll make sure the Herald gets the inside story on this case, you'll see. I might be able to break the latest updates as they happens, but it'll be you who gets the real *inside* story."

Dan's starting to tease me. Or is he flirting? I know he wants to take things further with me, with us, I can see it in his eyes. But like I told him after our last kiss, 'we' can't happen, because if anyone found out, there would surely be concerns about a conflict of interest.

That's why, despite my 'little lapse' at the college restaurant opening, I've been resisting him. That's why I haven't replied to any of his texts. 'Little lapse?' says my conscience. 'Who are you kidding?' I shake my head, I've been trying not to think of Dan in that way ever since that night, when I very nearly lost all my self control, but then he comes to my rescue today and makes things just a little more difficult for me.

"I'll be the one chasing all the scoops that Patrick pushes your way," he says, and he winks and has the cheek to run his eyes over me.

"Well, he's *my* source now, not yours," I say.

And then Dan's smile fades, his face clouds over and he becomes all serious for a moment. His eyes are suddenly no longer as soft. I'm no longer with Dan the potential suitor, I'm with Dan the journalist, and he catches me completely off guard when he asks, "So, why did you refer to Amanda as the black widow?"

Nine: Dan

For a split second, I worry that I've gone too far.

Time has been flying by in the coffee shop, and I'm suddenly conscious that I'm going to be expected to come up with an update soon, if I'm to be allowed to stick around on this story.

And with Kat covering it for the Herald, I definitely *do* want to stick around.

She looks horrified, and I'm nervous that she's going to have another funny turn when I pop the 'black widow' question.

"You heard that?" she says, sheepishly.

"Yes," I nod.

She looks at me and I fully appreciate those mesmerising eyes, like pastel blue sapphires. They say that the eyes are the windows to the soul; what I see right now is a soul in torment.

Kat was already feeling insecure, after her funny turn at the press conference. Now I had hit her with the 'black widow' question. And there's something in the way she looks at me when I ask her that tells me that my inner journalist was definitely going to want to find out more. It was just a case of whether or not Kat will tell me.

Maybe, if she had not turned all pale at that press conference, there would be no question; she *wouldn't* answer my question. She might even go so far as to suggest I read all about it in this week's Herald.

It's probably what I'd have done, if I was in her shoes.

I see a lot of myself in her (and that's not a metaphor, although, come to think of it…stop it, Dan, focus); that determination to succeed, that driving desire to prove she's got what it takes. And, of course, to have that little something extra up her sleeve, that little exclusive extra which would put her ahead of the press pack.

"I knew her," Kat begins, slowly, as if carefully considering each sentence. "I'd spoken to Amanda quite a few times and I was getting to know her, so when the DCI said she was the victim, it was a real shock."

I nod sympathetically, but my inner journalist is aching for her to get to the good bit, because my instincts tell me there *is* a good bit.

"I first met her the same night we met, at the Mayor's drinks."

I nod again, in what I hope looks like an attentive way. Yes, fine. And?

"You must remember her. She does – she did – loads of charity work all over the town."

"Her name's familiar, but I didn't do many charity stories, I tended to focus on the front-page stuff. And I've met a million and one people since I left the Herald. Her name certainly rings a bell. But that doesn't explain why you called her the black widow."

This is it. I've called her out. Come on, Kat. I've helped you out today. Don't hold out on me now. Give me something back.

"It's something her son called her, at the inquest."

"Inquest?"

"Amanda's husband died, and the inquest took place last Monday; a week ago today, in fact. The report was in last Friday's Herald."

My inner journalist is now alert and extremely attentive.

Kat smiles. I think she likes the fact that she knows something I don't; that she has the upper hand on me.

"I was the only reporter there," she says. "I guess it didn't look interesting enough on paper to catch the attention of anything other than local media. It's not as if there were any suspicious circumstances."

"How did he die?"

"He took his own life," she says. "Hooked a hose to the exhaust pipe of his car, lowered a window just far enough to feed the hose through, sat in the car, played his favourite music, and slipped away as the engine fumes filled his lungs."

"OK. I hadn't heard about that. It's pretty sad, though."

"Their son, Mark, was at the inquest and was not at all happy."

"I'm not surprised, after losing his father like that."

Kat slaps me playfully on my arm. "No, listen. All the way through the hearing, it struck me as a bit odd. Here's this guy, Sam Shepton, he's 62, joint head of a very successful accounting business. He's got a decent home, has had a long marriage to a glamorous younger wife, and yet the coroner said Mr Shepton had written a note to say he was chronically depressed."

"Was it a case of all work and no play?" I ask. "Maybe the pressure of work was too much? Maybe Amanda wanted more attention. Maybe he had an underlying health condition, and decided to take his own life before things deteriorated."

"Maybe," Kat says, but there's a slight twinkle in her eyes as she straightens her back and leans towards me, as if she is worried about being overheard. "The thing is, the coroner mentioned the note, but he didn't read it out. All he said was he was satisfied that Mr Shepton intended to take his own life. That's when Mark jumped to his feet and started yelling at his mother, accusing her of making Sam's life a misery and driving him to kill himself. And it was Mark, Amanda's own son, who called her the black widow."

"Wow."

Kat nods. "He really went for it, saying people had no idea what she was really like. He called her a wicked witch, a black widow and a whole load of other horrible names. He only stopped when the coroner threatened to jail him for contempt."

"Was any of this reported?" I ask.

"I was the only journalist at the inquest. I told Patrick what had happened, and…"

"…he took the moral high ground," I nod. I can just imagine it.

Patrick was a solid local newspaper editor, who believed in good, honest, local reporting. He wasn't afraid to criticise, he wasn't afraid to challenge those in authority when he felt he had due cause, and hold them to account. But he would have decided that publishing Mark's emotional attack on his mother would have constituted an unnecessary intrusion into the grief of a family in mourning. There were clearly some underlying issues between Mark and his mother, but Patrick would not have wanted the Herald to be accused of adding insult to injury for the sake of a sensationalist headline.

Patrick didn't do sensationalist.

Besides, if I know him, he would have been straight on the phone to the coroner's officer to find out what was in that suicide note.

The coroner's officer would have told him, because they've known each other for years, and Patrick would have decided that whatever Mr Shepton's reasons for killing himself were, that level of detail did not need to be featured on the pages of a responsible publication like the Herald, which was proud of its high standards.

The black widow line would, however, be the stuff stories are made of for the tabloids my agency serviced.

I share these thoughts with Kat - well, except for the last bit, about the tabloids. She nods, and tells me that her report of the inquest only made about six paragraphs in Friday's paper. Patrick told her suicides were extremely sad, and while the Shepton's were well-known enough to warrant the inquest being reported, the circumstances of his death would only make for extremely depressing reading. The Herald was about informing people, not prompting them to wallow in misery.

I make a mental note; I know the coroner's officer, from my time at the Herald. Perhaps I should renew that acquaintance, see if I can persuade him to tell me what was in the suicide note. He can be quite a prickly character, but if I don't ask, I won't get.

Something else occurs to me.

"Do you think Mark was just lashing out because he needed someone, *any*one, to blame for his father's death, and his mother was an easy target? Or do you think it runs deeper than that?"

Kat doesn't hesitate to reply. "Oh, definitely deeper. The way he spoke to her, it was as if he absolutely hated her. He said…." she pauses, and suddenly I get the impression she is worried that she has said too much - or that she is about to.

"Go on," I prompt, gently. "What did he say?"

"Well, at one point, he…he…"

I see the first glisten of a tear forming in the corner of her eye, and she feels it, because she lowers her head and wipes it. She takes a deep breath, composes herself, and continues.

"At one point, he turned to his mother and said to her 'it should be you who is dead, not him. I wish it was you. I hate you. You're a black widow and I wish to God *you* were dead, and not Dad."

"Wow," I hear myself say again.

Kat is on the brink of crying but is holding herself back. She clamps her mouth shut and glances towards the ceiling, as if trying to pull back the tears which are threatening to stream from her eyes.

"And then…then he turned to me, and said if I dared to print anything he just said, I would wish that *I* was dead, too."

Her voice breaks as she finishes the sentence. I want to put an arm around her and console her, but it's probably not the right time. My mind is racing. "What did you do? That must have been frightening."

"The police sergeant who gave evidence stepped in and told Mark to calm down."

"Your hero," I say.

"Well," she says, affording me a wry smile. "He *was* quite cute."

She's flirting with me! Maybe even trying to make me jealous. That's a good sign. But right now, I'm actually too preoccupied to think about anything other than this murder.

"Sam Shepton kills himself," I say. "Mark blames Amanda, and less than a week after he publicly says he wishes she was dead, he - *apparently* - finds her dead in her home."

Kat stops sniffling and looks at me intently, her eyes burning brightly, the natural journalistic fire inside her reignited and overpowering any other emotions she is feeling.

"Do - do you think Mark killed his own *mother?*"

"Why not?" I say, matter-of-factly. "Sounds like he made it pretty clear he blames her for his father's death."

I let out a little cry of frustration. "Stupid, stupid, stupid…" I say. "*That's* what I should've asked at the press conference."

Kat looks confused.

The police hadn't told us much, but there's one question they probably *would* have been able to address: how do they think the killer got into the house? Did he break an upstairs window? Did he pick the lock on the front door?

"I should've asked if there was any signs of forced entry, and I bet the answer would have been no," I say.

"Which means the killer didn't *break* in," Kat adds. "Amanda either let him in, because she knew him, or he had his own keys."

"Bingo," I say. "Gold star for Sherlock Russell over there. Move over, DCI Fisher, Barton and Russell here…"

Kat interrupts me with a wry smile. "Russell and Barton," she says.

"OK, Russell and Barton here have solved the crime. It's a classic revenge killing. She drives her husband to kill himself, so their distraught son kills her. I bet if we did a bit of digging, we'll discover Mark was a daddy's boy. There's nothing like keeping it in the family."

I pause. "You know, Kat, you and I make a great te…"

I can't finish the word because when I look at her, she has turned a ghostly shade of white all over again.

"He…he said if I quoted him, I would wish *I* was dead, too. I'm not sure that I want to do any digging."

I can understand why she's anxious. It's not unusual for reporters to be verbally attacked, sometimes physically assaulted, by people because they don't want to see their names in print, either because they think it's too private, and none of our business.

Or because they've got something to hide.

But Kat said her report was only six paragraphs long, so there wouldn't have been room to quote Mark, even if she'd wanted to.

Of course! The coroner's officer would have told Patrick about everything that had happened at the inquest, including Mark's outburst and his threat to Kat, even if she hadn't told her editor herself.

Patrick wasn't just taking the moral high ground by not giving the story much coverage in Friday's paper, I'm sure he thought he was being 'responsible' and protecting Kat.

I shudder. I hate the thought of Kat being in danger.

But I'm also feeling excited. The black widow line, the possibility that a grieving son may have murdered his own mother in retaliation for the suicide of his father, is something that will definitely keep the tabloids interested.

I walk Kat back to her office and resist the urge to pop in and say hello to Patrick; I don't have time. I've got an updated story to file, and a lot of work to do. My nose for news is twitching like a hay fever sufferer at a flower show.

I'd really like to know what was in that suicide note.

Ten: Alex

"Amanda Shepton died of fright," Simon says, as he scans the pathologist's report he has brought back from the mortuary.

"Is that actually a thing?" I ask.

I hear Tam tut. Of course it's 'a thing'; that's what he's thinking. After all, Simon isn't one for telling jokes in an incident room.

"What we're about to discuss doesn't leave this room," says Simon, sternly, "otherwise, we won't just have self-important divas from the local BBC to deal with, we'll have sleazy crime reporters from every wretched red-top and trashy tabloid in our faces. Clear?"

"Crystal, guv," says Tam, through slightly gritted teeth.

"Clear, boss," I say.

He thumbs through the papers in the folder and then starts reading to us. "A sufficient shock to the system can trigger an involuntary surge of adrenaline, which stuns the heart so severely that it stops beating," Simon says, reading from the report. "They call it broken heart syndrome in the US. Around ninety percent of reported cases involve older women. Not that 54 is particularly old."

Simon turns the page he is holding over. "The release of adrenaline is a response controlled by the automatic nervous system. There will be a rapid heart rate, dilated pupils and increased blood flow to the muscles. The release of adrenaline triggers calcium channels in the heart to open. Calcium rushes into the heart cells, which causes the heart muscle to contract. As the calcium pours in, the heart muscles can't relax. It says here that if someone is scared enough and has a large quantity of adrenaline reaching their heart, they can develop an arrhythmia called ventricular fibrillation, an uncoordinated contraction of the heart that makes it quiver and not beat regularly. It leads to a drop in blood pressure, and without blood for the brain, you lose consciousness. A terrifying event can trigger this cardiomyopathy."

He drops the folder onto his desk. "All of which basically amounts to the fact that Amanda Shepton was scared to death. Literally.

"Jesus," I say, involuntarily.

"Bit late for prayer," sneers Tam. "She's with JC now, anyway. Well, unless she went 'downstairs', of course."

"Enough, Tam!" Simon snaps. "There's no room for your gallows humour in my incident room."

"Sorry, guv," says Tam, who lowers his head but glances at me and fires a few daggers, more out of embarrassment than anger.

Given the absence of a visible cause of death, I had prepared myself for pretty much any conclusion from the PM. What I had not considered was that Amanda Shepton may have died from fear.

I shudder. What could possibly drive someone to torture, taunt and hurt another human being so much that their heart gives out in sheer fright? What kind of monster are we dealing with who can actually scare someone to death?"

I am definitely not going to be meeting Dan for that coffee.

"Tam, anything from the door-to-door?"

"Nothing we didn't already know, guv. Woman two doors down saw Amanda in her front garden at four on Saturday afternoon. After that, no sighting until her son found her Sunday."

"CCTV?"

Tam shakes his head. "A few of the houses have some of those video doorbell contraptions, but they cover their own doorsteps and not much more. And, naturally, the Shepton house does not have one of those doorbells."

"Alex? Anything from SOCO?"

"It looks like the killer explored the house," I say. "A partial footprint was found in the master bedroom. Mrs Shepton had enough jewels in there to fund a small country, and it's not exactly hidden away. Her jewellery box was on top of the sideboard, in plain sight, but hadn't been touched, so I think we can rule out robbery as a motive."

"The pathologist says there was no evidence that Amanda had been sexually assaulted," says Simon.

"So what the hell was the motive?" asks Tam.

"Whatever it was," I say, "I think she knew her killer."

Tam raises his eyebrows at me, unable to hide his surprise.

I could have shared this with him as soon as I had finished my call to SOCO earlier, but I chose not to. It sounds a bit childish, now I come to think about it, but I wanted to be able to tell Simon something potentially significant that Tam did not know, as if, in some silly, playground-politics kind of way, I was getting one up on him.

"Why do you say that, Alex?" asks Simon.

"No forced entry," I say. "Whoever killed Amanda Shepton, he did not break into her home to do it. She must have let him in."

"Or," says Tam, trying to steal my moment, "he had a set of keys."

"You're thinking of Mark Shepton?" says Simon.

Tam shrugs his shoulders. "Maybe."

"You think someone could hate his own mother so much that he could frighten her to death?" I say. I love my parents and couldn't, for one second, think of ever harming a hair on my mother's head, let alone anything else.

"We are going to need to talk to him," says Simon. "He knows we'll need a statement, but I wanted to wait until we had the PM results, and also given him a bit of time to come to terms with what has happened."

"Unless he already knows," smirks Tam. Jeez, the guy just can't help himself.

"W-what about her tongue?" I hear myself ask. I'm not at all sure I want to know the answer, but I don't want to prolong any verbal sparring with Tam.

Simon pauses for what seems like an eternity, and there's a very uncomfortable silence between the three of us. Then, he takes a very deep breath, and says, "It's the opinion of the pathologist that Mrs Shepton did *not* bite through her own tongue, as had been initially suggested by the examining doctor at the scene. The full postmortem examination has led the pathologist to conclude that her tongue was forcibly removed by her killer. And this act was a sufficient enough shock and trauma to trigger the release of adrenaline which led to her death."

I wince as I feel an involuntary acid reflux. I can't even begin to comprehend what she must have experienced in the last moments of her life, let alone consider how depraved someone must be in order to forcibly remove someone else's tongue.

"Fuck!" says Tam. He looks genuinely agitated, and for once, I see no trace of his usual cocksure, bullish bravado and there's something in the way he looks at me that tells me he wants to say more. But only if he is prompted.

So I take the bait. "What are you thinking, Tam?"

"You remember what the doctor said? That she bit through her own tongue and either swallowed it or spat it out?"

I nod.

"She *didn't* swallow it. The killer *took* it," says Tam. "We searched and didn't find it on the floor. The logical conclusion is that the killer snatched a souvenir from the scene. To the victor, the spoils, and all that."

Simon doesn't react. He simply stares impassively at Tam.

"Tell me, lassie," Tam continues, what kind of killer do you think collects trophies from his victims, eh?"

I'm inclined to say some kind of mentally-disturbed psychopath, but the increasingly smug look on Tam's face tells me that all his alpha male arrogance is returning, and that he wants to be the one to reveal the answer.

"Go on," I say.

He pauses, for maximum dramatic effect, and I regard him closely. He has a kind of permanently scowling, scrunched-up face, as if he has been punched head-on multiple times.

"A serial killer," Tam says, softly. "I don't know if our man has killed before, or if this is his first, but one thing I'll put every penny I have on is that he *will* kill again."

"No," says Simon. "This is personal, very personal. I think this is a one off…"

Tam interrupts him, and I feel my jaw drop a little at the sheer arrogance of the man. "Come on, guv, you're in denial."

"I'm *what*?"

"You're in denial, because you know that if there's the slightest suspicion that we've got a serial killer at large, we're going to have one terrified town on our hands, with everyone wondering who's going to be next."

There's a twinkle in Tam's eye. It's almost as if he *wants* this to be a serial killer. Isn't it sickening enough that a woman has been killed in such a cruel, callous way? Does he really want there to be more victims? More tongues taken as…as trophies?

I almost gag as the thought passes through my mind.

"If the press finds out her tongue was taken out by her killer," I whisper.

"There'll be a media circus," says Tam. "We'll hit the headlines in every national paper and TV news channel in the country. Fancy yourself on News at Ten, Nicholas? We'll make a man of you yet."

I *really* want to pummel the pug-faced prick. But there's something I want more; I want to find Amanda Shepton's killer and rid the streets of someone so sick that he tormented a woman until she died from fright.

I take a tiny crumb of comfort in convincing myself that Amanda probably, hopefully, passed out before her tongue was torn out.

"Perhaps he hangs the tongues on his wall, like a hunter hands the heads of the animals he has shot. Or maybe he wears them around his neck, like a macabre necklace or a badge of honour."

"Tam!" barks Simon. "The killer didn't take her tongue as a trophy, OK? I know exactly where Amanda Shepton's tongue is."

Tam and I both glare at Simon. He's holding out on us! We need to know what he knows if we're to have any chance of leading this investigation and catching this brutal bastard.

"Samples have been sent to a forensic lab, to confirm beyond all doubt…," says Simon.

"Confirm what?" asks Tam, unable to hide the look of bewildered disappointment from his face, as if his sick desire for us to be facing a serial killer was being dragged away from him.

Simon swallows hard, looks up towards, perhaps through, the ceiling, and then fixes Tam with a chilling, steely stare. "Amanda's tongue is in her stomach."

"But you said…." the Scotsman started.

"She *didn't* bite through it and swallow it," says Simon sternly, not letting Tam interrupt.

Tam glances at me, as if he is expecting me to suddenly reveal something to him. Then he turns back to Simon, who takes a very deep breath, and says, "The killer took Amanda's tongue out of her mouth, chopped it into small pieces, and then fed them to her."

My cheeks puff out as they fill with bile, and I lift a hand to my mouth to prevent myself from throwing up. Biting her own tongue and swallowing it sounded horrific enough; having it ripped out of your mouth, cut up, and then forced back *into* your mouth takes this to a whole new level of depravity.

"That's why I'm convinced this is not the work of a serial killer, Tam," says Simon. "We're looking for someone who had one hell of a grudge against Amanda Shepton. This was a very personal murder. I've asked the forensic lab to see if they can give us any indication as to whether some sort of instrument was used to remove the tongue or…or whether he ripped it out by hand. Nothing obvious has been found at the scene, so if the killer did use a knife of some sort, then he must have taken it with him."

For once, even Tam looks lost for words, and there's a very uneasy silence in the room.

Simon glances at us both grimly, as if he thinks we haven't fully taken in what he has told us. He pauses, then says, "The pathologist found every single bite-size piece of Amanda's dismembered tongue inside her stomach."

Eleven: Kat

I've been sitting in Patrick's office ever since Dan walked me back to the Herald building.

I'm still finding it hard to believe that not only is Amanda Shepton dead, but that she was murdered. I just can't get my head around it.

There's no doubt that Dan definitely did me a huge favour when he phoned Patrick from the press conference. It seems the radio reporters were so busy scrabbling around trying to find someone from the police to provide just a few seconds of audio for the story that they had missed their eleven o'clock news broadcasts.

The story wasn't big enough to warrant interrupting the regular programming with a 'breaking news' flash, so the radio stations wouldn't mention the murder until their next news at noon.

That meant, despite my fears of having let the side down, that the Herald was among the first to break the story after all, as Patrick had quickly posted the information Dan gave him onto the paper's website.

Before the rise of the digital era, big stories like this would always be very difficult for weekly papers. The dailies and broadcast media would always be able to release up-to-date developments on any story often on the same day, if not quicker, whereas it could be days before local papers would be able to publish their first reports.

Of course, the flip-side is that weekly papers, in theory, knew their communities a lot better than the bigger media, so while the likes of the Herald would always be playing catch up in terms of the latest updates, we should have the relevant contacts and local expertise to be able to get a more in-depth, meaningful, inside story.

Things are different now, of course. We've got our own website and social media channels, so we can update stories on a twenty-four-seven basis, just like the 'big boys'.

But we've still got the edge on them because we do still have that local expertise and knowledge, too.

That's where we can really come into our own.

"Are you alright?" says Patrick, shaking me from my thoughts.

I nod. "I still can't believe it."

"When I heard there was something going on in Mountview Rise, I wanted you to cover it because I knew you had a good relationship with Amanda, and that she's the kind of person who keeps her finger on the pulse. I thought you'd cover the press conference and, when we knew what was going on, you'd visit Amanda to see what she knew."

I'm suddenly experiencing mixed feelings, and am also feeling a little stupid. I'd flattered myself, thinking Patrick chose me to attend the press conference because of my journalistic merits. But no, it was because I'd fostered a relationship which we might be able to use in order to help the Herald get an exclusive, and scoop the other media. It makes perfect sense, of course. Any Editor, like any senior manager, needs to know how to make the best use of their available resources. I really do need to toughen up a bit when it comes to the profession. For a moment, I allowed myself to bask in the glory of being Patrick's 'favourite', the 'teachers pet', the chosen one. But, of course, his decision to send me to the press conference was purely practical, and my growing little ego had been brought back down to earth.

"If I'd had any idea that Amanda was the victim in all this, I'd have never sent you," says Patrick. "I'm sorry, Kat."

I smile inwardly. And there was the kindly, avuncular, editor coming through again, being more than the 'practical' journalist.

"If you'd rather Mervyn covers this, I'd understand," Patrick says. "If you feel that you're too close to it…if you can't detach yourself, if a story becomes too personal, it can cloud your judgement."

"Please," I say, "don't take me off this story. It's *because* I'm close to it that makes me want to cover it even more. If I end up playing just a tiny part in bringing Amanda's killer to justice…"

Patrick nods again, and smiles warmly. "I understand," he says. "But if, at any point, it *does* become too much, you must tell me."

"I will." I almost gush the words out, because I'm relieved. I couldn't bear sitting in the newsroom watching and listening to someone other than me working on this story. That would be soul-destroying. This is my story. *My* story.

"The police will probably release a statement later today, once they've got the PM results, assuming that the PM yields something conclusive. If not conclusive, they'll have sent samples to forensic labs for toxicological tests and the results of those can take weeks."

"The police may not know the cause of death, but the DCI said he was satisfied that it was murder, so there's clearly something they know that makes them think that," I say.

Patrick smiles, almost as if I've just passed a little test, to show how my journalistic mind is thinking. Then he seems to make his mind up for certain. "Right. I'm going to get Mervyn and Hannah to do the big tribute piece for this week's paper; they'll speak to Amanda's friends and reps from all the organisations she worked for. I want you to focus on the criminal investigation."

I'm suddenly starting to feel like teacher's pet again and I know that I'm consciously having to hide the pride from showing on my face.

"W-what about Ross?" I ask.

"Oh, he's got some 'big scoop' of his own breaking, apparently, so I'm quite happy for him to focus on that, and also satisfy his little ego by filling the rest of the paper while you all work on the murder story."

I can imagine Ross seeking some plaudits for helping to 'keep it all together' while we're all otherwise engaged, although I am curious as to what his own 'breaking story' is.

"We need to turn detective ourselves, to some degree," says Patrick. "We need to support the police investigation, of course. We also need to reassure the local community. But, as you say, we can also play our part in catching the killer."

I feel a tingle run through me again, a thrill. This *is* what it's all about.

"You'll probably have to put some extra hours in," says Patrick. "If the police release an update at nine at night, we need to be on top of it, for the website."

Again, I feel that burst of pride. "Got it, sir," I hear myself say.

"Get onto the police press office, make sure they've got your contact details. Give them your mobile number. I'll see if I can get in touch with the SIO directly. You never know."

"W-what about Mark?" I say.

"Mark?"

"The inquest. He - he said he wished she was dead. Dan and I were talking, and we both think Mark might have done it. Should we tell the police?"

Patrick's face becomes stern. "We've got to be careful," he says. "Especially after the way Mark behaved at the inquest. But we do need to deal in hard facts, the truth, not any rumour, speculation or hearsay. Think about what he said, calling his mother a black widow. Knowing what we know now, that might be relevant, it might not, but that's not for us to decide. I'm sure the police will be aware of everything that was said at the inquest. We can support the police investigation, but we are not judge and jury."

"OK."

"And no matter what any other media reports, however tabloid-like their reports might become, we play it straight, support the police and treat this in the right way."

"Of course," I say.

I'm half-expecting him to warn me against talking to Dan anymore. I think I would, if I was in his position.

"Dan's a decent journalist," says Patrick, almost as if he can read my mind.

"He seems to be," I say, appearing as nonchalant as possible.

Patrick's smile widens, and I can feel my cheeks start to redden.

"I think he likes you," he says, and I don't know how to respond. I don't want to think about it, really. I certainly don't want Dan to be a factor in this, a reason for Patrick to let someone else cover this story. I don't want Patrick to think I will share whatever I know about this story with Dan. Maybe I shouldn't have told Patrick about the conversation Dan and I had shared about Mark.

"I - I don't know about that," I say, but I know I sound a little flustered, and not at all convincing.

"He certainly didn't have to do what he did, phoning some copy in here," says Patrick. "He's a good man. Well, of course he is, he's been trained by the best." Patrick winks, and I feel myself start to relax.

"I - I guess so," I say.

"There *is* a line between business and pleasure," says Patrick. "As long as you know where that line is, and I'm sure you do, then good luck to the two of you."

Bloody hell! It's as if he knows that there's something between Dan and I. Or that there could be.

Then again, Patrick isn't stupid, is he? And he's right, Dan had no reason at all to send the story over to the Herald. But he did. And I think Patrick respects that, as do I. But there is, I think, a gentle warning here. I *can't* get too close to Dan, no matter how much I might want to

"So," says Patrick, "let's crack on. I don't want to read about any black widows, unless it's something that the police give us. What I want you to do is put together a list of questions that we can justifiably put to the police. Do they have any suspects? What did the PM reveal? What do they think the motive was? Any signs of a break-in? There's a whole pile of questions we can put together, so get to it."

I return to my desk, my head buzzing, but my overall feeling being one of relief. Ultimately, Patrick could have taken me off of this story, but he hasn't. It's mine.

Before I start work on my list of questions, I pull out my phone and send a quick text to Dan. *Thanks for today. I owe you one.*

I didn't expect such a prompt response, but my phone vibrates before I've even had chance to put it back into my pocket.

I can't help but smile when I read Dan's reply. *I look forward to collecting.*

Twelve: Dan

After escorting Kat to the Herald's office, it only takes me a few minutes to walk to my car.

I send another text message to Alex; I sent one from Town Hall just after the press conference, and another while Kat and I were in the coffee shop.

I don't think I seriously expect to get a reply, but you know what they say, nothing ventured, nothing gained, and all that. And they also say it's not what you know, but who you know.

There are no hard feelings between Alex and I, so she may speak to me. Likewise, I need to get hold of Paul, too. I'm confident I'll be able to get something more out of him, although he may just have been totally frightened off after being pounced on by that trio of radio reporters at the press conference.

I sit in my car and think about everything Kat told me; Sam Shepton's suicide. Mark Shepton describing his mother as a black widow, and then threatening Kat herself! Now, Amanda Shepton is dead. And police are, so far, being very tight-lipped. No PM results, but DCI Fisher being 'satisfied' she was murdered. A suggestion of violence, but no further detail.

A short drive across town takes me to the mortuary and offices of the Coroner, which are in a detached building on the grounds of the town's general hospital. I know I don't have any chance of speaking to the coroner, or the pathologist, but I'm hoping I can grab a few words with the Coroner's Officer.

A young administrator sits behind the desk of the small reception area.

"Is the Coroner's Officer in?" I ask, politely.

"Is he expecting you?"

"Er, no. Just tell him it's Dan Barton, an old friend."

She picks up a phone and a short while later a door behind her opens and Warren James saunters out from his inner sanctum. It's over two years since I've seen him, and he hasn't changed one bit. I think he's even wearing the same suit!

He has a craggy, weathered, face and walks with a slightly ghoulish gait. I had always thought that there was something slightly sinister about Warren, something a little creepy, although if you spent all your time dealing with death, perhaps anyone would become somewhat sombre.

I am going to have my work cut out for me here, I know that. Warren is no fan of the media. He made no secret of the fact that he felt we had no place at an inquest; there was no justifiable reason, in his view, for a perfect stranger to sit in a room with grieving family members at a time of extremely personal distress for them.

He tolerated the attendance of journalists only because the law allowed them to be there.

I've seen him at inquests, when some journalists approached family members at the end of the hearing, for their reaction to the verdict. Warren would wade in and basically push the journalists out of the building, like a nightclub doorman ejecting an unruly drunk from the premises.

Patrick had nurtured an uneasy alliance with Warren. Patrick had promised that no reporter from the Herald would ever approach a grieving family directly; they would go through Warren first. After all, some families did find some comfort in speaking, through the media, publicly about their loss, and paying tribute to their loved one.

Warren appreciated Patrick's offer of using him as the 'middle-man'. In Warren's eyes, it was far more respectful.

Patrick also argued that journalists sometimes approached the family not to ask awkward or potentially upsetting questions but just to check some basic facts, such as the correct spelling of an unusual surname. After all, Patrick had said, a newspaper report of the inquest could be upsetting enough; it could be even more distressing to emotional family members if names were spelled incorrectly.

Journalists have a legal protection, a 'privilege', if they report accurately, and contemporaneously, anything said during an inquest, even if, in other circumstances, it could be considered slanderous.

Patrick promised Warren that any Herald journalist would always report responsibly, sensitively; his recent decision to omit the reference to Mark calling Amanda a 'black widow' was testament to that.

As a result, Warren was always just a little more accommodating - it would go too far to suggest welcoming - towards Herald journalists, while being barely tolerant to anyone else.

This was the first time I've seen Warren since I left the Herald. I was hoping he would remember me and would remember that I had followed the 'informal rules' agreed between himself and Patrick, and that I had always been respectful.

His eyes bore into me as we face each other in the small reception area. I feel quite uncomfortable.

He nods towards the door he just came out of and I follow him into his little room.

"Thanks for seeing me," I say. "It's been a while. How are you?"

His eyes narrow and his mouth twitches. "I'm quite sure that my welfare is the least of your concerns," he says, his gravelly voice containing no hint of warmth. "I'm afraid the post mortem on Amanda Shepton only finished a short time ago, so you'll need to speak to the police. There's nothing I can tell you about it, I'm afraid."

I feel an involuntary chill dance down my spine.

"I know that," I say. "I'm not here about Amanda Shepton. I'm here about Sam Shepton."

Warren involuntarily raises an eyebrow. He'd clearly been anticipating hearing from the media in the wake of Amanda's death. But he had not, apparently, expected a question about Sam Shepton.

"Tragic," he says, solemnly. "As is any situation where someone feels compelled to take their own life."

"I agree," I say. And then, because I know from experience that there's no beating around the bush with Warren, I decide to come completely clean and be totally honest with him.

"What I'd really like is to know why Sam Shepton took his own life," I say, being careful to use Warren's own language, rather than 'suicide' or 'killed himself'. I know Warren would appreciate the gesture, and the respect it indicated.

Before he can answer, I add, "But I don't expect for one minute that you'll tell me. But what I would really appreciate is if you would be able to confirm something that happened during the inquest itself since this would, technically, be in the public domain."

"Go on," he says.

"And…well, if you're not willing to tell me, perhaps you could give me the name of the police officer who gave evidence at the inquest."

My mind briefly recalls my conversation with Kat. Do I really need the name of the officer because of this case, or am I sub-consciously trying to check out the 'competition' when it comes to Kat?

"Anything said during the course of an inquest is, indeed, technically, in the public domain. But you weren't there to hear it."

"But you *were*," I check myself. I don't want to appear remotely argumentative, as that will get me absolutely nowhere. "I know that Kat, er, Kate, from the Herald, was there. I spoke to her earlier."

Warren stares at me impassively. The old phrase about getting blood out of a stone springs to mind.

"There was a girl from the Herald there," Warren says. "She heard everything that was said. And I had cause to call her editor when the paper came out last Friday, because her report of the inquest was… appropriate, written with sensitivity and respect."

"Did Mark call his mother a black widow? Did he also threaten Kate, if she published the black widow line?"

Warren stares at me, through me, for a few seconds.

"Kate was very shaken up," I say. "And you *know* the Herald, there's no way that Patrick would use the black widow line."

"But *you* would?" he says, disapprovingly.

I shrug my shoulders. "Maybe, if it was in the public domain. But between me and you, I've only heard this from Kate. And I don't want to drop her in it, especially after Mark threatened her. In my view, whether he is grieving or not, he had no right to threaten her when she was just doing her job."

Warren twitches, and I know I've struck a nerve. Warren wants, and expects, certain standards of behaviour at inquests from everyone who attends, from police officers and journalists to grieving relatives.

Warren presses a few buttons on the computer keypad on his desk.

"Mark Shepton's behaviour at the inquest was inappropriate," he says.

"Are you saying that he *did* call his mother a black widow?"

"The officer who spoke on behalf of the police at the inquest was Sergeant Tom Davey," Warren says, evading my last question.

I involuntarily clench my fist but just manage to prevent myself from pumping it with a triumphant 'yes'. I knew Tom quite well from my Herald days. In fact, I'm pretty sure I've still got his mobile number. And I'm pretty sure he isn't too much of a threat to my intentions towards Kat.

I know that Warren has told me everything he is likely to, so I thank him for his time.

"It was nice to see you again," I say, as I offer him my hand, which he doesn't take.

"I'm sure," he says.

I walk to my car and pull out my phone, scanning the contacts lists. Yes, there he is, Tom Davey. I just hope he hasn't changed his number. Tom was involved a campaign to crackdown on car crime a few years back, which I gave plenty of coverage to.

He remembers me when I call him, and I immediately pull the legal ace out of my sleeve. "I'm not wanting you to tell me anything that could put you in an awkward situation," I say, "I just need to confirm a couple of things that were said in open court, at the Sam Shepton inquest, that's all." I then add, purely because I know flattery is always a winner, "as you know, anything that is said in open court is in the public domain. I've been told by one person who was there about something, and I just wanted to corroborate it from a respected source."

My little charm offensive worked; Tom clearly remembered Mark's outburst at the inquest, and in particular the phrase 'black widow'. He also recalled how Mark turned on Kat, too. "Is she your replacement at the Herald?" he says. "She's definitely better looking."

I let the comment pass, thank Tom, promise to buy him a pint the next time we meet, and hang up.

I call Paul next, to find out if there's any news of the PM results.

Paul is quite comfortable dealing with fluffy, pro-active PR stories about positive police initiatives, but, as he showed at the press conference, I'm not at all sure he's cut out for the serious crime stuff.

He stutters and stammers when I get through to him, as if he is terrified of being quoted, and being caught saying something he shouldn't, but promises to call as soon as the PM results come through.

I drive to my parents' house and tell them I need to crash in my old room for at least a few days, which Mum is delighted about.

I let her mother me for half an hour, then retreat to my room to write my next story. This is panning out quite nicely for me; there will be enough interest in the story for my agency to keep me on it, for sure.

I'm quite convinced that at least a few of the tabloids will find a few paragraphs for the 'black widow' line.

I'm equally convinced this investigation won't take very long, as the more I think about it the more likely it seems that Mark killed Amanda, and I'm sure this has not escaped the attention of the police.

I phone an updated story over to my office, with the hope that the next story should contain the results of the PM.

All in all, it's been a pretty good day.

I feel bold. I text Alex again. *Are you looking at Mark Shepton for the murder of his mother?"*

Since she hasn't responded to any of my other messages, there's no way she'll reply to this one. But you never know.

My phone chirps and I pick it up. I'm not disappointed to discover that it's not a message from Alex, because it's a very welcome message from Kat. *Thanks for today. I owe you one.*

I lie back on my bed and close my eyes. I'm back at the new college restaurant, just over a week ago, with Kat, her long hair released from its usual ponytail, cascading in dark waves over her shoulders and down her back. She had squeezed into a figure-hugging little black dress and heels.

We had an enjoyable meal, and there was some flirting, some reminiscing over our conversations when we spent so much time together at the planning enquiry, and then talk turned to our kiss.

We walked slowly to the nearby council-owned car park, where we've both left our cars.

On the premise that I needed to re-tie a shoelace, I stooped down and let her walk a few steps ahead. She had a short jacket over her shoulders, but I got to fully appreciate how sexy she looked from behind in that slinky little dress.

Our cars were next to each other, which was no accident on my part. When we reached them, there was one of those funny little 'will we, won't we kiss' moments between us.

We did kiss, but as we were in quite a public place, she ensured it was quite short.

Somehow I persuaded her to jump into the passenger seat of my car, which is larger than hers, and we kissed again. This time, it was much deeper, much more passionate.

I pulled her across to me and allowed my hands to run over her stomach and brush lightly over her breasts and then behind her, up to her neck.

I found the zip at the back of her dress and gave it a slight tug.

"No," she said, breaking the kiss. "No, Dan. Stop, please. We shouldn't. We mustn't. We can't. Whether I want to or not, this won't work, not with us working for different papers. We can't."

"We can," I said.

But her mind was made up and I certainly didn't want to drive her away from me.

"No, it's not right. We can't."

But the look in her eyes suggested she wanted to. She really wanted to. And that made me want her even more.

I text her my reply. *I look forward to collecting.*

Thirteen: Alex

The testosterone in the small interview room is almost palpable as Mark Shepton and Tam size each other up, like two over-excited stags who are about to start rutting.

Mark turns to me and gives me an intensely chilling look which sends shivers down my spine.

The small table between us will offer me no protection if he decides to attack, and I have no doubt Tam would feel no inclination to rescue me.

Simon had intended to give Mark a few days before asking him to come in and make a formal statement about his mother's death.

But our hand has been forced by today's national newspapers.

The words 'black widow' were plastered prominently across the front of many of the Tuesday morning tabloids and, irrespective of our own thoughts on the matter, the media were blatantly and unashamedly suggesting that Mark must surely be the prime suspect.

None of the stories had a proper byline - the name of the writer. The articles were all attributed to 'Staff Reporter' or 'Echo Reporter'.

I'd learned a few things during the few evenings out Dan and I had shared - it was inevitable we'd end up talking 'shop' - one of which that a 'staff reporter' byline typically meant, ironically, that the article was not written by someone on that particular publication's payroll, but by an agency reporter.

Someone like Daniel Barton.

Warren James had called Tam yesterday afternoon to say that Dan had paid him a visit, and had asked about Sam Shepton's inquest. A few hours later, the national papers are all carrying the black widow story; you don't need to be a rookie detective on their first day on the job to put two and two together and put Daniel Barton's name on these stories.

Simon felt we had no option but to bring Mark in for questioning, and gave me the dubious delight of being question-master.

While Mark keeps staring at me like that, I'm in no hurry to begin, so I flick through some of the documents before me.

Simon remains adamant that this was a very personal killing, and it seems the pathologist agrees, much to Tam's chagrin; he'd still much prefer us to be looking for a serial killer.

No robbery, no sexual assault and, more significantly, no forced entry. Mark may not live with his mother anymore, but the first officer who went to the house after Mark called the police had already established that he had his own set of keys.

It's the whole business of her tongue that still turns my stomach. We'll only be able to begin to try to understand that when we have a better idea of what the motive was.

And while I'm no fan of 'trial by media', I have to admit that, at this early stage in proceedings, Mark is as good a suspect as anyone else.

As soon as we read this morning's papers, Tam called Warren and confirmed what had been reported; Mark had, indeed, called his mother a black widow, had said he wished she was dead, and had even made a threat against the girl from the Herald if she reported any of it.

So while we have no clear motive, we can safely say there was no love lost between Mark and his mother.

Then, of course, there is the fact that Mark raised the alarm. That makes it textbook amateur hour when it comes to establishing an alibi. I'll put a month's wages on him saying something like, "If I'd killed my own mother, do you think I'd be stupid enough to call the police myself from the murder scene? No, I'd have run a bloody mile away!"

We may be speaking to Mark a bit sooner than planned, but I can't help but think if we manage to get a confession out of him, then we can have this case wrapped up in no time.

Mark has already declined any legal representation.

Why would he need a bloody lawyer? He hasn't been arrested, and he is, in his words, "obviously completely innocent?"

I slip the papers back inside the folder and begin the procedural formalities, acutely aware that Tam is watching me, almost with the same intensity as Mark.

"Mark, you didn't like your mother very much, did you?"

"No shit, Sherlock," he says. "Did you work that out all by yourself, or did your little office boy here give you a hand?"

I very nearly allow a little smile to show, as I can imagine the angry look on Tam's face. I can't bring myself to look at him, I think I'd enjoy it too much.

Mark starts smirking.

"You think this is funny?" I ask.

He tuts. "Not really," he says. "But I do think *you're* a fucking joke. You and everyone else in this pig pen."

"You haven't answered the question," says Tam.

"Eh?"

"*Acting* Inspector Nicholas asked you about your relationship with your mother, who has been murdered," says Tam. He emphasised the word 'acting' in a way that suggested he found it distasteful.

"Don't you know?" mocks Mark. "Haven't you seen the papers? Or can't you read?"

My eyes dart down to Tam's hand resting on his thigh. He has clenched his fist and his knuckles are white.

"Maybe you don't *need* to read the papers, since someone must have given that stuff to the media," says Mark.

"Answer. The. Question," Tam spits, through gritted teeth.

Mark smiles at him sarcastically, then turns to me, mimics Tam's voice, and says, "No, *acting* Inspector, I didn't like my mother very much. I fucking hated her. I still do. Satisfied?"

I stare at him. He's twenty eight and is a typical alpha male; he is stocky, solid, strong. He's a prop forward in the first team of the town's rugby club, and his whole demeanour suggests that he fancies himself as something of a 'tough guy'; he's certainly quite intimidating. But while he had initially made me feel a little uncomfortable, his attitude has grated with me; he isn't acting like a grieving son, he is acting like someone who is on the defensive. Someone with something to hide.

And for me, that's like a red rag to a bull.

"Did you hate her enough to tie her to a chair, rip out her tongue, chop it into pieces and feed it to her?" I say.

I hear an intake of breath from Tam.

"What the fuck?" says Mark, the smirk wiped clean from his face.

We would normally be a little more diplomatic in revealing the results of the postmortem examination to the next of kin.

"I've got the pathologist's report here," I say. "Ever heard of cardiomyopathy, Mark?"

"Eh?" he grunts.

"Your mother was scared to death, Mark. Scared. To. Death. And yes, that is a thing. Her tongue was ripped out, and the shock of that frightened her so much that it killed her. So, tell me, Mister Shepton, do you still think this is funny?"

He looks shocked.

Just when I had really started to believe that this would be a quick case to solve, because Mark was our man, I find myself unsure. Either he is an extremely good actor, or he was genuinely shocked by what I'd just told him. It wasn't the reaction of someone who knew what I was going to say; who knew, because he was there.

Then again, my sudden abrupt tactics had drawn a gasp from Tam, too, so maybe Mark had been simply caught off guard by my approach.

He takes a few moments to consider what I'd told him, and then seems to regain his composure.

"For the record," Mark sighs, "I did *not* kill my mother. Did I hate her? Yes. Did I say that I wished she was dead? Yes. Am I sorry that she has been murdered? Not particularly. Am I the one who did it? Don't be so fucking stupid. Why on earth would I kill my mother, phone you lot and then wait at the scene of the crime for you to arrive, with her blood on my hands?"

"So," says Tam, smugly, and I throw him a look. I'm supposed to be leading this interview. "You admit her blood is on your hands?"

"Not like that, you fucking clown. I found her, didn't I? Was your magnifying glass not strong enough to see the blood pouring from her mouth? Of course I had her blood on my hands. I'd rushed over to see if she was still alive, for fuck sake."

"Mark Shepton," I say, before Tam can ask anything more. I then choose to mock Mark in the same way he had mimicked Tam earlier. "*For the record,* did you murder your mother, Amanda Shepton?"

"No, I fucking didn't," he says. "If I'd have killed her, I wouldn't have reported it as soon as I'd finished. I'd have left her stinking carcass there to rot."

"Where were you on Saturday night," I say.

"What?"

"Where were you, Saturday night? It's a simple enough question. Or do I need to get someone in to help you with the long words?"

"Bitch," he says.

"The pathologist believes your mother was killed on Saturday, some time between eight and eleven. Where were *you* on Saturday night, Mark?"

"I was out."

"Out?"

"Yeah, out. O. U. T, out."

"Where?" I ask.

"Mountview Rise, by any chance?" Tam suggests.

"Fuck you!" says Mark. "I was out, OK? I go out most Saturday nights after a game. I play rugby for the Warriors. I was in town on Saturday night. A few pubs, then I went clubbing."

"Who was with you?" I ask. "Who can we check with?"

"I can't remember."

"Convenient," sneers Tam.

"I can't fucking remember, because I was pissed out of my head, OK? I was absolutely shit-faced. I can't remember which pubs I went to, or who was there. But I was in town."

"Are you sure?" Tam says.

"What?"

"Well, if you can't remember where you were, isn't it possible that you actually did go to Mountview Rise, ripped your mother's tongue out and frightened her to death, because for some reason you blame her for your father's suicide?"

"You fucking c..." Mark stands up and pushes the table towards us with such force that I am nearly thrown from my chair. Tam leaps from his chair and squares up to Mark. Two alpha-male meatheads, ready and willing to exchange punches.

"Sit DOWN, both of you," I yell, so loudly that they're both taken aback. I have surprised myself. But I really don't know what else to do. I certainly wouldn't have been able to break them apart if they had started fighting.

Mark and Tam stare each other down for a few more seconds. I shoot Tam a glowering stare. "Sit DOWN, Detective Sergeant," I say.

Tam reluctantly obliges and, since his opponent has given way first, Mark visibly relaxes just a little, and sits.

"I didn't kill her," he says.

"Then help me find out who did, and why," I say. "Do you know anyone who hated your mother enough to want to kill her?"

Mark's sardonic smile returns. "Yeah," he says. "I do. Me."

I sigh. I want to bang both their heads together.

"Why, Mark? Why did you hate her so much?"

He shakes his head. He doesn't want to tell me.

"I hated her," he says. "*Hated* her. But I didn't kill her."

"Then help me. Tell me where you were on Saturday night. We can check it out and eliminate you from the enquiry."

"I told you, I was in town."

"Where, Mark? There are plenty of pubs and clubs in town. And you can't tell me you went into town on your own. If someone can corroborate your story, it's in your interests to tell me who they were."

"I don't know, because I was pissed! How many more times."

"Then I have to ask you, Mark, if you were so blind drunk that you can't tell me where you went or who you were with, isn't it possible that you *did* make your way to your mother's house? Isn't it possible that you were so upset by the inquest that you went out the next weekend, got very, very, drunk, and then…"

"I DIDN'T KILL MY MOTHER!" he yells. "I wish to fucking God I had done. I'd like the shake the hand of the man who did. But it WASN'T ME!!!!!"

"Let's take a break," I say.

Fourteen: Kat

I've got a million and one feelings and emotions running through me right now; I don't know whether to laugh ironically or cry. I don't know whether to run a mile and crawl under a stone somewhere or go and find Daniel Barton and smack him in the face.

I don't know whether I should be feeling anger or fear.

When Mark Shepton turned on me at the inquest, there was such fury in his eyes, I had no doubt that he meant what he said.

He knows I was the only reporter at the inquest. If he thinks it was me who gave that story to all the papers, he'll come after me, I'm sure.

I pick one of the tabloids up from Patrick's desk. The paper shakes in my hands as I read it again. The nationals have, to all intents and purposes, accused Mark of killing his mother. His motive was revenge for the suicide of his father, who was chronically depressed. Every paper says Mark called his mother a black widow, and that he shouted out at the inquest that he wished she was dead.

I was the only reporter there.

The only person I told the whole story to was Dan.

Patrick then tells me he knew about it. It turns out that he and the Coroner's officer talk to each other quite frequently and openly. I hadn't told him about Mark myself because, knowing Patrick, he'd not let me cover anything other than a flower show for months.

No, these newspaper reports *must* have come from Dan.

I can't believe I kissed him. I can't believe I kissed him good and proper in his car. And I can't believe I considered doing a lot *more* than kiss him. The thought of that makes me feel sick now. Yesterday, he was my noble, gallant, knight in shining armour. He was my hero.

Today, he has gone from hero to zero. He wasn't being a kind, considerate, friend. He wasn't acting out of compassion for me. He was simply sweet-talking me to find out what I knew and I fell for it, like the naïve, gullible, little girl that I am.

Or was. But no more. Never again.

My phone buzzes. It's a text message from Dan. *Morning. I hope you're feeling better today. Maybe we can meet up later. What do you say?*

The text makes me even more furious. He's got some nerve! Does he really think I'd want to talk to him, knowing that anything I say may be taken down and appear in print in tomorrow's papers?

That thought immediately tells me how I should reply to him.

No Comment.

Dan replies instantly. *?????*

I wonder whether I should reply again and, if I do, what should I say, but before I can make my mind up, Patrick comes back into his office, carrying a couple of coffees. I quickly pocket my phone. But not quickly enough.

"Dan?" asks Patrick.

I nod.

"Don't be too hard on him," says Patrick. I can't quite believe what I'm hearing! Is my editor defending someone who has betrayed my trust in such a cruel way?

Not for the first time, it's as if Patrick can read my mind.

"It's a different world, writing for the tabloids," he says. "And don't forget, Dan did file some copy on your behalf yesterday. He had no reason to. No obligation to. He did it because he's a decent bloke."

"He can rot in Hell as far as I'm concerned," I say.

"You're taking it too personally," he says. "Remember what I told you yesterday. If things become too personal, it can cloud your mind."

"My mind has never been clearer," I say.

Patrick nods.

"Dan hasn't stabbed you in the back quite as badly as you think he has," he says. "I spoke to Warren James earlier. Dan went to see him yesterday, and was asking about what was said at the inquest, and who the police officer was. It was Sergeant Davey, and Dan knows him quite well."

"So?"

"So, Dan may not have been aware of the black widow line if you hadn't mentioned it to him, *but* what he gave to the nationals wasn't based only on what you told him. He's got it from other sources, too."

I think the look on my face tells Patrick that his words are falling on deaf ears. Everything is still just a little too raw at the moment.

"Anyway," he says, "never mind all that, because there's been a development. I've just got word that police are interviewing Mark Shepton this morning."

I can't help but smile. Patrick, not Dan, is the kind of journalist I want to be. Some people might say he's unambitious, spending all his career on a small weekly paper in a small insignificant town. But look at him, a big fish in a small pond, with contacts everywhere. People who trust him, who talk to him, who tip him off.

Dan was right when he told me at the press conference yesterday that Patrick would ensure the Herald would get the inside story on this case. I might have lost all my belief in Dan Barton, but I *do* believe he was right when he told me that.

"The press office hasn't said anything," I say.

"They probably won't for a while. They're waiting to see how it all pans out. Imagine; if he suddenly cracks and confesses, then the case is closed, all nice and neat. If he gives them an alibi, they'll need to check it out, and might need our help with that."

"I can't believe you've got tipped off like that, it…it's brilliant," I say.

"It's all about making contacts," says Patrick. "Just like you were doing with Amanda. Being a good journalist is not so much about what you know, it's about who you know. And it's about treating people right, so that they trust you."

"NOT like Danny Barton, then," I say.

"Danny is a decent man, Kat, trust me. If it's any consolation, if I was in his position, I'd have probably done the same as he did. Now, get onto the police press office, ask them if they can confirm, on the record, if anyone has been brought in for questioning. We'll need to start putting together some background on Mark, just in case."

I return to my desk. I didn't want to hear Patrick say he would have done the same as Dan. But deep down, I know it's true. And I know that, if I want to get anywhere in this job, I'd be expected to do the same, too.

My phone rings. It's Dan. Against my better judgement, I take the call. "What?" I say.

"Kat! I've been trying to get hold of you. Are you OK?"

"I'm fine. Not that you care."

"What?"

"Come on, Dan. You took advantage of me."

"What?"

"You took advantage of me!"

"Well, I'd like to, but…"

"In your dreams, Dan. You betrayed me, and I don't really have anything else to say to you right now."

"Betrayed you? Kat, I haven't got a clue what you're talking about."

"Really?"

"Really. What's going on?"

"Pick up a paper, Dan. Read all about it," I snap, and hang up. I am no longer going to be distracted by Danny Barton. I'm no longer going to need a knight in shining armour. I am going to stand on my own two feet, and I'm going to give one hundred percent of my attention to covering the murder of Amanda Shepton.

I'm glad the police have got him. I was worried that he would come after me as soon as he saw the papers. He scared me at the inquest.

I'm sure he's capable of killing. I'm absolutely positive that he hated Amanda.

What I don't know is why.

And I'm more determined than ever to be the first to find out.

Fifteen: Dan

I was stunned when I spoke to Kat on the phone. I had no doubt that, despite her demure appearance, there was probably quite a strong character lurking not so far below the surface, but I had no idea just how feisty she could be.

Having taken her advice and 'read all about it', I can see why she's angry with me.

The tabloids really went to town with the 'black widow' line and Kat has understandably assumed I simply ran with everything she said.

She didn't give me a chance to explain that I had confirmed what she had told me with someone else. And it goes without saying, or at least, I'd like to think it does, that if I was really pushed to reveal my sources, then I'd say it came from Sergeant Davey.

But there isn't an issue, not really.

Hopefully, when Kat takes some time to think about it, she'll see that there's no real betrayal here. Granted, I was not at the inquest, and yes, I admit I wouldn't have known about the black widow line if Kat hadn't told me.

But it wasn't something that had been said to her privately, in confidence. It was something that had been said at an inquest. It was, legally, in the public domain. And I had confirmed with one other person directly and, I like to think, with Warren indirectly (because while he didn't confirm it as such, if I had been way off track, I've no doubt he would've had no hesitation in correcting me.)

I had not divulged something that had been secret, or known only to Kat.

And it's not as if it was something she was saving for herself, to run in the Herald on Friday. Patrick wouldn't run the black widow line from an inquest, it would be disrespectful. He would only run it if it came out in a court case.

Of course, with hindsight, if I'd have known the tabloids would go that crazy about it, I'd never have given them the line.

But it was done now, it was out there. It was published and, it appeared, I was to be damned.

Although it goes against my better judgement, I think, deep down, that I've already decided if I get any decent tip-offs or new lines about this case, I'm going to share it with Kat. Call it a goodwill gesture.

I've left messages with a few old contacts of mine; I've reached out to find out if anyone has any idea about who would want to kill Amanda Shepton.

While Sergeant Davey confirmed what had been said at the inquest in the 'public domain', I hadn't been able to persuade him to give me any insight into the content of Sam Shepton's suicide note. Perhaps that would shed some light on just why Mark hated his mother so much. I wonder if he would tell Kat, if she asked him.

What I know for sure is that I have absolutely no chance of getting anything else out of Warren James. He'll probably never talk to me again after he reads today's papers.

The police have been a little cagey about the PM results. A short statement was issued late yesterday afternoon to say that the results of further forensic tests were needed before the police would be able to confirm the precise cause of death.

This usually suggests that drugs, or perhaps some sort of poison, are involved, as it means forensic tests are being carried out on blood samples, stomach contents and, perhaps, DNA evidence recovered from the scene.

I phoned Paul after the statement was released, and he insisted there was nothing to add to the statement. He sounded as if he was living on his nerves, terrified of saying the wrong thing. I'd only have to hint that I was seeking something off the record, and I think he'd have had a seizure.

I seem to have burned enough bridges on this case already; I don't need to do any more damage.

I considered trying to call Alex but again, I didn't want to make things worse. I might need to call on her in the future.

I finally accepted that it was time to do something I had hoped I could avoid doing; door-knocking. Visiting Mountview Rise, talking to the neighbours, trying to find any little nugget of new information that might help things along, and, more importantly, help me make amends with Kat.

There are worse ways to spend a sunny morning than to wander up and down Mountview Rise, to get a teasing glimpse of how the other half lives.

It's quiet now, peaceful, quite idyllic. Only a single strand of blue and white police tape hanging loosely across the entrance of the Shepton's house is the only indication that anything untoward has happened.

Most of the people I speak to all say the same thing; they're deeply shocked to hear that Amanda was murdered, some of them are afraid that the killer might target them next, although police have apparently tried to reassure them, without going into any detail, that they are treating this is an isolated incident, although officers have advised people to ensure their home security is up-to-date, and said that they should remain vigilant.

They haven't been quite that forthcoming with the media yet.

If the police truly do think this is a one-off, it suggests they might have some idea of who did it. It also suggests that they think it might have been personal, rather than a burglar who was caught in the act, and lost control of his senses, or something like that.

That means I need to get to *know* Amanda Shepton; the people living in her street aren't likely to be able to help. I need to get to her friends, those 'ladies who lunch', those confidantes and people who truly know her.

Sometimes, I think I'd quite like to work for the police, being truly on the inside of an investigation. Maybe I should go for a job at the police press office, which would be the next best thing.

I'm sure Paul knows a lot more than he's letting on. Maybe he knows what Sam Shepton wrote in his suicide note. I'm certain he must know more about the circumstances in which Amanda Shepton was found. We've still not been given a definitive cause of death yet, which has got my nose for news twitching.

I call Paul, using his mobile rather than the main office number.

"There's no updates at the moment," he says. "All I can say is that it's the early stages of the enquiry, we're following up a number of leads, and we're still appealing for anyone who has any information to come forward."

"Yeah, thanks," I say. "I've got the corporate lines. I need a bit more than that, mate."

"I'd have thought you'd had enough for at least one day," he says.

"What do you mean by that?"

"I'm assuming the reports in today's tabloids came from you."

"Yeah, well, you know the media. Insatiable thirst and all that."

"The investigating team is staying very tight-lipped. Only the most senior officers know the full story so far, and they're playing their cards very close to their chests."

"You mean Simon and Alex? Any chance of you arranging for me to have a chat with them?"

"In a word, no."

"I need something, Paul, come on, mate. How many officers are on the investigation team? Was there any sign of a break-in? Any update on the cause of death? There must be something you can give me that won't upset the applecart."

"I can't," he says. "It's being kept very tight."

"I guess I'll have to run the old 'police are refusing to comment' line, then, won't I? It won't make you guys look very good, and does nothing to reassure the community, but if the police won't speak…"

"Come on, Dan, you know that's not going to be very helpful."

"Then give me something so that I can be helpful," I say.

There's an uncomfortable symbiotic relationship between the police and the media; it's a real love-hate thing. Most of the police, especially the higher up the ranks you go, seem to have an in-built, deep-running, distrust of the media.

But they know that the media is often the most effective way to get their key messages out to a wide audience, whether it be an appeal for witnesses, a crime prevention message, or call to action.

We police by consent in this country, and that relies heavily on public confidence in policing. Nothing undermines that confidence more than a report which says police declined to comment, as this can be interpreted as 'we're not interested' or 'we don't care'.

At the same time, journalists need the police. We want them to talk to us. We want them to trust us to treat the information we are supplied with responsibly, because if we don't, they'll find a reporter who will, and if other reporters get an update that I can't get, well, why would an editor pay my wages if I'm never first to break the news.

I don't like 'bullying' Paul by threatening him with the 'no comment' line, but I know it works. I know that the Chief Constable often takes his communications team to task when he reads 'police declined to comment' in any media report.

"Hang on," says Paul. "I'm just going to step into the corridor."

I can hear him moving, and then he speaks to me again, his voice a low, harsh, whisper. "Look, you didn't get this from me, OK. There's no sign of any break-in. Shit. Look, that has to be off the record, Dan. And that's all I can say. Honestly."

"Alright Paul. Thanks, mate."

I don't want to push too hard, otherwise he'll never take a call from me again. It's not much, but it does give me something to go on. No break-in. So either the killer is an expert lock-picker or, as is quite common with murder cases, the victim and the killer knew each other.

That would make Mark a *very* decent suspect.

I might be able to convince Kat, in time, that she wasn't the only source of the story I gave to the tabloids, but if Mark assumes it was down to her, will he make good on his threat?

I have an extremely uncomfortable feeling that I may have put Kat in danger. If something happens to her because of a sodding story I've written, I'll never forgive myself.

My phone rings.

"Are you the reporter who has been knocking on doors in Mountview Rise this morning?" says a voice. "You gave your business card to one of my friends who lives there."

"So?"

"I'm Stuart Shepton. Sam Shepton was my brother. I've got some information for you."

Sixteen: Alex

I hadn't called for a break just because I felt Mark Shepton and Tam needed some time to cool down. In all honesty, I think I'd have quite enjoyed watching the pair of them knock the living daylights out of each other.

But no, I called a time-out because I want to strike while the iron is hot, and get the ball rolling on either confirming or, hopefully, completely discrediting Mark's flimsy alibi.

"Tam, I want you to track down the other members of Mark's rugby team. Find out if they *were* out on Saturday night, and if Mark was with them. Get someone to speak to the council's CCTV control room, and all the main pubs and clubs. If Mark *was* out on the town, then at least one of those cameras must have caught him. But don't hold your breath; I'm not really expecting you to find any."

"You think he did it, then?" asks Tam.

"And you don't?" I counter.

Tam shrugs his shoulders. "I don't think Mark's a serial killer."

"Nor do I," I say. "But I *am* starting to believe he killed his mother. We know he hates her, even if we don't know why. We've also proved he's got a fiery temper, and it doesn't seem to take too much effort to press his buttons."

"I think he's all mouth and no trousers. Sure, he'll happily throw his fists around on the rugby pitch, but tying his mother to a chair and cutting her tongue out? Nah. I don't think so."

"All the more reason to investigate his alibi then, eh? If we prove he was in town, then he probably isn't our man. Can you check it out?"

"Sure. What are you going to do?"

"I'm going to go back and talk to Mark."

"Eh? Without me?"

"Yes, Detective *Sergeant*," I say, relishing the opportunity to pull rank and remind him of the hierarchy. "Somehow, I think you and Mark will only antagonise each other, and that won't get us anywhere."

Tam sulks off with his tail between his legs and I head back to the interview room, for round two with Mark Shepton.

I grab a couple of coffees from the vending machine and return to the lion's den.

"Captain Caveman not with you, then?" says Mark. "Did you send him back to rub two sticks together or something?"

"Actually, he's going to be pulling out all the stops to check out your alibi for Saturday night," I say calmly. I pause and then add, "One way or the other."

I put a coffee on the desk in front of him. "I'm not sure how you take it, so it's just black, I'm afraid," I say.

He smiles. "What's this, the good cop, bad cop routine? The grunt couldn't intimidate me into some kind of confession, so you're trying the sweet and soft approach?"

"Something like that," I say. "I just think it would be far more productive to try and talk like two human beings, rather than have two meat-heads wanting to kick the proverbial out of each other."

He smirks briefly, then looks away, and takes a sip from his coffee. "Thanks," he mumbles.

"Put yourself in my shoes," I say. "Just take a step back and look at this from my point of view."

He looks up and I can see that the animosity has gone from his face; he's curious.

I continue. "Amanda Shepton, a well-respected member of the community. Her husband tragically takes his own life. At his inquest you make it very clear that you blame Amanda for your father's death. Less than a week later, she is found dead. You apparently find her body and call the police. You can't seem to remember where you were on Saturday night, or who you were with. You do tell us you were very drunk. And I think you'll agree that we've seen today that you seem to have, er, anger management issues, shall we say. The evidence strongly suggests that Amanda knew her killer. No forced entry. So, she either invited her killer in or…or he let himself in with his own set of keys. When you look at all this, surely you can understand why the finger of suspicion might be pointing at you right now."

Mark sniffs hard. "Yeah, I s'pose," he says.

"Where were you on Saturday night, Mark?"

"I told you. I can't remember."

"Can't? Or don't want to?"

His body language suggests he is starting to become agitated again, which I don't want. It feels as if I might be starting to get through to him, I don't want him to revert to his natural neanderthal state now.

"Why did you hate your mother so much, Mark?"

"Why do you fucking think?" he says. "Dad would still be alive if it wasn't for her."

"Did you love your father?"

"What?" He looks genuinely offended and hurt. "Of course I did. I loved him. I miss him."

"So," I say, lowering my voice, because I'm about to take a big risk, and I need to tread carefully. "You love your father. You hate your mother. It seems that you had more reason to kill your mother than anyone else."

"I. Didn't. Kill. Her," he says, his voice trembling a little, as if he is struggling to contain his emotion. Not anger, this time, but sadness. "But I wanted to. Fuck knows, I wanted to."

"But if you didn't, who did? Who, out there, could possibly want to kill you mother more than you?"

He shrugs his shoulders. "Dunno."

"Really? Is that the best you can do?"

He's still playing a very defensive game, which does suggest a guilty conscience. Or could it be he is protecting someone else? Or maybe there's something else. Something else that he simply doesn't want us to know. But we *need* to know. Tam still seems sure this has all the hallmarks of a serial killer. Simon is sure this is personal.

All the evidence we've got so far, such that it is, tells me this is personal, which makes Mark the prime suspect. Unless he can point me in another direction, which he doesn't seem to be in any hurry to do. Maybe it's because he can't.

"Mark, if you hated your mother so much, why did you go to her house on Sunday, when you say you found her body? Surely you weren't making a social call? Surely, if you hated her so much, you wouldn't have wanted to see her at all after the inquest."

"I'd have been quite happy never to see that evil bitch ever again," he says, the bitterness and anger clearly evident again.

"So, why were you there?"

"For my sister," he mumbles, so low I can barely hear him.

"Your sister?"

"Yeah. Sarah and my parents used to have a video call every Sunday lunchtime, so Mum and Dad could talk to and see Gemma, their grand-daughter. Sarah called me because she wasn't getting a reply from Mum. It had been less than a week since the inquest, so Sarah was worried about Mum and asked me if I'd go and check up on her."

"I see," I say, as I make a note of this. "Of course, I'll need to talk to Sarah, to confirm this."

"Knock yourself out," he says.

"Where does she live?"

"Canada."

"Canada?"

"Yeah, Canada. She wanted to get as far away from our fucking mother as she could, so she went three-and-a-half thousand miles away. Dad was devastated, heart-broken that his little girl had been driven to escape all the way to other side of the bloody world."

"Tell me about your parent's marriage, Mark. How did your mother make your father's life a misery? Why didn't he divorce her, if he was so unhappy?"

"It's all about keeping up appearances, isn't it?" says Mark. "She fitted the perfect stereotype of the kind of wife a man of his standing should have, and she loved the lifestyle that a man of his wealth could provide. It's as simple as that."

"Are you saying the marriage was a sham?"

"Pretty much," Mark sighs.

"Your dad was an accountant I believe, is that right?"

"Yeah. A family firm. My grandfather founded the business, made a huge success of it and, when he retired, his two sons took over."

"Two sons?"

"Yeah. My dad, and my Uncle Stu. They worked hard at it, too. Long, long, hours, but they reaped the rewards. They made good money, and that made them attractive propositions for gold-digging little bitches like my mother, who fluttered her eyelashes at him and bagged herself a rich sugar daddy."

"What was the age difference between them?"

"Ten years. It worked. To start with, it worked. It suited them both. Dad had a trophy wife who had enough airs and graces about her to look the part alongside him at the occasional swanky business do, and she got to enjoy all the trappings of being a kept woman. I don't think she loved him at all, certainly not for the last few years. They were always fighting. But she loved his money. That's probably the only reason she didn't leave him. She made his life a bloody misery, but he was a proud man. She looked the part, and was willing to act the part when required. He didn't want there to be any wagging tongues if they got divorced. He was old-fashioned like that; he believed marriage was for life. It was all about reputation for Dad, and he always felt that a failed marriage would bring shame upon the family."

I can feel the resentment oozing from every pore on Mark's body.

"It should've been me," he says, softly.

"What should?"

"It should've been me who killed her," he says, and this time he can't hide the tremble in his voice. "It should've been me. I wanted to kill her, I really did. It should've been me. I couldn't even do that for my dad."

"Then if you didn't," I say, "who else would? Who else knew about the unhappy marriage? Your sister?"

He shakes his head. "Nah. Sarah couldn't hurt a fly. But…but Uncle Stu could. He hated Mum almost as much as I did."

Seventeen: Kat

I was both surprised and pleased when the Mayoress agreed to meet me for coffee to talk about Amanda.

It's Wednesday morning, and we're sitting at the same small table, hidden away at the back of the quaint, cosy, coffee house, that Dan I shared earlier this week.

Elizabeth Page was the one who first introduced me to Amanda, at that drinks reception to celebrate her taking up office. That, of course, was also the first time I met Dan.

But I'm not here this morning to talk about, or think about, Dan, or, as Elizabeth had described him, my 'chaperone'.

No, I'm here to talk about Amanda.

I had called Elizabeth and told her that, as she might expect, the Herald was planning to run a full tribute to Amanda this Friday, honouring her work with various charities around the town. I'd already collected a number of glowing testimonials from several people, who all expressed their shock at what had happened.

But Elizabeth said she would rather speak face-to-face than on the phone. The coffee shop was just around the corner from the Herald's office, so I was happy to oblige.

Elizabeth looks tired. There's heavy make-up around her eyes and I'm sure she has been crying recently; a lot.

She greets me with the same warm smile that she had when she whisked me around that room introducing me to the great and good of the town, only the smile seems less natural today, more forced.

"Amanda liked you," Elizabeth says. "She spoke about you several times. She was very grateful for all the coverage you gave her for the various charities she was involved in."

"I didn't know her that well," I say, "but I always enjoyed our chats. She seemed very nice."

"I guess that's why I wanted to speak to you, face-to-face," she says, a little enigmatically.

"I'm happy to include any quotes from the Mayoress in the tribute piece," I say.

"What sort of things have other people said?" she asks, and I get the impression she is expecting me to say something unpleasant. It's almost as if she is waiting for me to say that people have been dishing the dirt on the deceased, if there is any dirt to be dished. But the truth is, as I explain to Elizabeth, everyone has had nothing but praise for Amanda, for her commitment to the various causes she got behind and for being an inspirational driving-force behind many successful fund-raising campaigns.

Elizabeth looks relieved.

"It's all been glowing tributes and, of course, shock and sorrow at what happened to her. It doesn't seem as if anyone has a bad word to say about her," I say, "which makes her death even more tragic."

"Have you spoken to her family?"

I shift awkwardly in my seat, unsure exactly how to respond. I think about it for a moment. "I, er, well, I don't think Mark is interested in speaking to any journalists at the moment." I don't think it's my place to tell her that I know about Mark being interviewed yesterday. If she raises it, then I can say that I know. But I don't want to become the source of any other gossip. I've already been bitten by that particular bug once this week, I have no desire to repeat the experience.

"When someone reaches a certain level in society," Elizabeth begins, "there are certain expectations. Expectations that you feel a certain, er, duty and responsibility to try to meet."

"I'm not sure I follow you," I say.

"Oh dear," she replies. She looks flustered, uncomfortable. "I was just hoping that people were not speaking ill of the dead, that's all."

"I've heard nothing but good things," I say.

"I'm so pleased," she says. "It's just that, well, there can be a big difference between someone's public profile, and their private life and I just didn't want, well, I just didn't think it would be right if anyone took an opportunity to smear Amanda's good name."

I suddenly feel a little defensive. "I'm writing a tribute piece," I say, "not a character assassination."

"I know, I know," she says. "That's why I wanted to speak to you, and nobody else. It was so upsetting, what those newspapers said yesterday. All those horrible, horrible, headlines. I guess I was just hoping that the Herald wasn't going to print that kind of filth."

"We're not, I can assure you of that," I say, and Elizabeth visibly relaxes.

"It's just so unfair, isn't it?" she says. "Horrible things are said about someone when they've got no opportunity to defend themselves."

"That's the way the tabloids work, unfortunately. But we're not the tabloids. We're only interested in the truth."

We each take sips from our coffee and sit in silence for a few minutes. The thing is, Elizabeth has dangled a carrot in front of me that I simply can't ignore.

"I - I was at Sam Shepton's inquest," I say. "The coroner didn't go into any detail, but did say that Mr Shepton had left a note, which basically said he was very depressed. And then, well, just like the papers reported yesterday, Mark lashed out, and blamed his mother for his father's death."

Elizabeth nods, and I can see the unmistakable glisten of tears forming in her eyes.

"Mark," she whispers.

I glance around, as if I'm half-expecting to see Mark step out of the shadows and stomp towards us.

"He - he threatened me," I say softly. "At the inquest. He had a go at his mum, just like the reports. And then he turned on me. He told me if I printed anything he said that I would wish that I was dead."

Elizabeth puts one of her hands on top of mine. "Oh, you poor thing," she says. "You must have been terrified."

I know I probably shouldn't say too much more, but I like Elizabeth. I've liked her from that first night we met her. And I suddenly feel like I need someone who is close enough to this case to understand, but not so close that it is complicated. In other words, not Patrick, because he's my boss and I need him to have confidence in me, and certainly not Dan.

I feel my lip quiver as I tell Elizabeth that I've been frightened of Mark coming after me, after the national newspapers came out yesterday; I've been terrified that Mark may make good on his threat and, until this moment, I don't think I've been willing to admit just how scared I've been.

"He scares me, too," says Elizabeth. "I've known Amanda, the whole Shepton family, for a very long time. Mark and his mother were always at loggerheads."

"Do….do you think he could be capable of killing her, though? Taking the life of his own mother?" I ask.

Elizabeth shakes her head sadly. "I loved Amanda," she says. "I have huge respect for all the time she dedicated to worthy causes. She didn't have to; she could easily have led a life of leisure. But she gave a lot of time to doing a lot of good. And I respected her for that. And I also loved her as a friend."

"I can see that," I say.

"But, that doesn't mean that I agree with everything she said and did. That doesn't mean I agree with the way she always conducted herself. Remember what I said earlier; there can be a big difference between someone's public persona, and the person they are privately."

"What are you saying?"

"Mark loved his father and he loved his sister. He blamed Amanda for taking both of them from him."

"But surely even that wouldn't be enough to make him want to kill her? If anything, you'd have thought Sam Shepton's death would have brought the family closer together."

"Oh Kate," says Elizabeth. "Amanda messed with her son so much. Everyone has their limits, and Amanda definitely pushed Mark beyond his. Do I think he was capable of killing his mother? Am I surprised at the suggestion?"

I shift forward on my seat, because I desperately want to hear Elizabeth answer her own questions.

"After what she did to him, to be honest, the only thing that surprises me is that he didn't kill her sooner."

Eighteen: Dan

The offices of the accountancy business that Stuart Shepton ran in partnership with his brother, Sam, are located in a converted Regency-style house in a picturesque crescent just off the town centre.

As I stand before the white-painted stucco façade, I can't help but wonder why, if Stuart has some information relevant to the murder of his sister-in-law, he wants to tell me, rather than the police.

But I guess there's only one way to find out.

My dad always used to encourage me to consider accountancy as a career. I'd ask him why on earth would I want to spend all my days number crunching, and he'd reply, "Have you ever seen a poor accountant?"

As I step into Stuart Shepton's office, I can finally appreciate what my father meant, and for a brief moment I regret not taking his advice.

The room is tastefully furnished, and you can almost smell the pound-signs in every piece of furniture.

Stuart himself cuts a diminutive, unassuming figure who greets me with a limp handshake.

But I think his suit is probably worth more than my entire wardrobe. "Thanks for coming, Mr Barton," he says.

"It's Dan, please," I reply. I look at the empty chair on the opposite side of Stuart's large, ornate, desk, and I almost feel unworthy to sit in it.

He sits behind the desk.

"I, er, I'd like to offer you my sincere condolences," I say.

"If you mean, with regards to the death of my brother, then I thank you," he says. "If you are referring to the more recent death of…of *that* woman, then all I can say is good riddance to bad rubbish."

I have a feeling that this is as close to swearing as Stuart Shepton ever gets.

I pull out my pen and notepad, and flip to an empty page. "So, Mr Shepton, what did you want to tell me?"

"The police interviewed Mark yesterday," he says.

I'm intrigued. Mark couldn't have been arrested, because otherwise the police would surely have said so. When someone is arrested, proceedings become active under the Contempt of Court Act, and this can - or should - curtail what can and cannot be reported. In essence, when proceedings are active, the media shouldn't publish or broadcast anything which could potentially jeopardise a court case, for example anything which might influence the opinion of a potential jury member.

However, unless police make the media aware that proceedings are active, then they are none-the wiser. I'll certainly need to confirm this with the press office. If anything, the fact that Mark has been questioned at all provides a new line, a suitable follow-up to yesterday's headlines which named him as the prime suspect.

Stuart confirms that Mark was not formally arrested, which is a relief because it means there's nothing to prevent me from reporting that he was questioned. Readers can make their own minds up about what this implies.

"Do you think Mark killed Amanda?" I ask.

"God knows he had every reason to," Stuart replies, without hesitation, although I suspect it means the answer is 'no'.

"But?" I prompt.

"No," he says. "No, I don't think Mark killed his mother."

"Do you have any idea who did?"

It takes Stuart a few moments, but then he nods, and I begin to feel a little surge of adrenaline race through me.

"Mr Shepton, may I ask, if you have information about a potential suspect, why are you telling me, and not the police?"

"Because the police have a one-track mind, and seem hell-bent on pinning Amanda's murder onto Mark. It would be a quick, convenient and therefore relatively inexpensive, result."

Spoken like a true accountant, I think to myself.

"Are you worried that the police won't believe you?"

"Why should they? I'll be accused of clutching at straws by making wild accusations because I'm desperate to protect my nephew."

He pauses, as if he was about to say something else but then had second thoughts. And then he returns to plan A. "I'm also giving you a chance to redeem yourself, as a representative of all the media."

"What do you mean?"

"Yesterday's papers," he says. "Totally out of order. Mark has been accused, tried and convicted by the media before the police even went near him. The media seemed quick enough to name Mark as public enemy number one, it seems only right that the media should have a chance to redeem themselves and put the record straight."

I swallow hard. I have no intention of letting Stuart discover that I'm responsible for those headlines yesterday. He clearly has a need to let off some steam, and I am conveniently in the firing line. It's probably just as well he doesn't know that I supplied that story.

"I don't trust the police and for that matter, don't particularly trust the media, either. I just happen to consider you and your lot to be the lesser of the two evils. Er, no personal offence intended."

"None taken," I say, though not with any true conviction. "But, if I may, I will say that while the coverage in the papers was, I admit, somewhat sensationalist…"

"That's putting it mildly."

"…I would say that the facts, as reported, are exactly that. They're true. I've spoken personally to a police officer who attended the inquest and Mark did call his mother a…"

"I know," Stuart interrupts me abruptly. "I was there, young man."

I feel about three inches tall. Stuart loved his brother. Of course he would have been at the inquest. Hmm. I wonder…

"May I ask, have you seen the note that your brother wrote, which was referred to by the Coroner?"

"Yes," Stuart says.

"You'll know that the Coroner referred to it, but didn't read it out, like they sometimes do. It may help me to better understand the story if I knew what Sam wrote."

"All it will help you do is write some more sleazy headlines," he says, and I see he is a little angry, which had not been my intention, "and cause even more hurt to Sam's family, to Mark and to Sarah."

"Sarah?"

"Mark's sister. My niece. She lives in Canada with her husband and daughter. She came over for Sam's funeral, but had to return home before the inquest."

"I see."

"Mark would never have gone to his mother's house had it not been for Sarah. Mark wanted nothing to do with his mother. But Sarah was worried, because she hadn't been able to reach her, and it was so soon after the inquest…well, I don't know what Sarah thought, but she was worried."

"So she called Mark and asked him to check on his mother, which is when he found her dead?" I surmise.

He nods. "Actually, she called me first," he says. "She knew that Mark blamed Amanda for Sam's death. But the truth is, so do I. And to my shame, I told Sarah I had no intention of checking on Amanda. I didn't care if she was sitting inside her house, rotting. Sarah then called Mark, and he went and found his mother."

"W-what exactly did he find?" I ask, seizing an opportunity.

"Her, of course," he replies. He sounds a little frustrated, or impatient. I'm pretty sure he has no idea how the whole police-press relationship works during a situation like this. Does he assume that the police tell us everything? Does he think the police tell us nothing?

"That's why I have no interest in talking to the police," he adds. "Mark swallows his pride to go to check on his mother, which is the last place on earth he wants to go to, and the last person on earth he wants to see, but he goes because his sister asked him to. Then he finds his dead mum, tied to a chair in her dining room, and as if all that isn't bad enough, is then accused by you lot of being the killer."

Tied to a chair! No wonder DCI Fisher felt 'satisfied' that this was a murder enquiry long before the PM results came through.

"Mark found the body. It's no secret that he hates his mother. It's no stretch for the police to assume that he didn't actually find her as such, but was there all along. To a degree, I can understand why he's such an obvious suspect."

"To a degree?"

"Yes. Mark had every reason to kill his mother. She'd certainly gone out of her way to provoke him and give him cause. But let me ask you this; if Mark killed his mother, why Saturday? Why not as soon as he found Sam's body in his fume-filled car? Why not after the funeral? Why not immediately after the inquest? Why wait until Saturday?"

"I don't know," I say. "Grief and emotions work in mysterious ways. Perhaps he went to check on his mum, like his sister asked, and they got into a fight, and he just lost it."

"The only reason he went to 'check on his mum', as you say, is because Sarah asked him to. Sarah asked him to because she had not been able to get hold of Amanda for their weekly video call. And Amanda wouldn't have missed that call by choice. The only reason Sarah couldn't get hold of Amanda is because Amanda was already dead."

I rapidly scribble down some notes.

"You say Mark had every reason to kill Amanda; it's clear that he blamed her for Sam taking his own life. Was there, well, any other reason why he might kill her?"

"Plenty," says Stuart. "They had a huge falling out a while back. They hadn't spoken for months, which personally, I think is the final straw that broke the camel's back and drove Sam over the edge. He doted on his family; he couldn't bear all the internal turmoil."

"What did Mark and his mother fall out about?"

"It's private. And it's irrelevant."

"Irrelevant?"

"Of course it is, because Mark did *not* kill his mother, no matter how many reasons he had for doing so."

"You seem very sure of that, Mr Shepton, which leads me to the big question, then, doesn't it. If Mark didn't kill his mother, then who did?"

Stuart Shepton gazes at me with an uneasy look, which reminds me of his description of me as the 'lesser of the two evils', and then he leans forwards and says, "I think it was probably her last lover. The toyboy she jilted and refused to take back."

Nineteen: Alex

I always try to finish work on time on a Wednesday, as I like to catch up with a couple of girlfriends for a mid-week drink, and a chance to put the world to rights.

I was just wrapping things up and thinking about daring to reach for my coat when Tam and I were summoned to Simon Fisher's office for a 'where are we so far' chat.

Tam has been giving me a wide berth so far today; I think he's sulking about me doing the second half of Mark's interview without him. It also means I haven't got a clue how far he has got with the tasks I asked him to look at.

I've spent most of today reviewing statements from people living in Mountview Rise. I also did a bit of research on the Shepton accountancy firm. I've tried to get hold of Stuart Shepton, but every time I call, I am told he is in a meeting and can't be disturbed.

I've left my number twice, but he doesn't seem to be in any rush to call me back. It feels like the Shepton family, or what's left of it, really isn't in too much of a hurry to help find out who killed Amanda, and why.

Maybe it's because they already know.

I did manage to track down a number for Mark's sister, Sarah Matthews, in Canada. I called her at lunchtime, bearing in mind that Canada is about five hours behind us, so it would have been just before eight in the morning local time.

Sarah told me she was making arrangements to come back to the UK to attend Amanda's funeral, which will take place at some point over the next few weeks.

She also confirmed what Mark told me; that she had tried to call her mother, as per their usual Sunday routine. When her mother didn't reply, Sarah was concerned. She thought maybe her mother may have chosen to get drunk, as she dwelled on the aftermath of the inquest, so she called Stuart, to ask if he would check up on Amanda.

Stuart refused - yet another sign of the Shepton family's apparent contempt for the matriarch - so Sarah called Mark.

So that part of his alibi checked out, at least.

"Sarah," I said, "may I ask, why did you move to Canada?"

"Well, if you must know, it's because my husband is Canadian. We met at university in the UK. We chose to live in Canada because, to be honest, I prefer the lifestyle. The open fires in the campsites in the summer; the guarantee of a white Christmas and the skiing in winter. I just fell in love with the place."

"Oh," I said, unable to disguise my disappointment.

"Does it really matter? Is it relevant to anything?"

"Not really. It's just that, well, we spoke to Mark yesterday. We needed to take a formal statement from him, since he was the one who found your mother's body and alerted the authorities. And during that conversation, he suggested that the reason you went to Canada was because you wanted to get as far away from your mother as possible."

"Did he?" she said.

"Yes. Sarah, is that true?"

"Look, it wasn't a particularly happy household in Mountview Rise. Mark and Mum, in particular, were often falling out, but all families have their problems, don't they? And those things are private. Or they should be. No family should be made to air their dirty washing in public. The main reason I came to Canada was for love; the love of my husband and my love for the way of life over here."

"Fair enough. I just need to ask you one more thing Sarah. And I'm sorry, but I do need to ask."

"Go on."

"Do you think Mark is capable of killing your mother?"

There is quite a long pause, and for a moment, I think the phone had gone dead.

"Sarah?"

"I don't know," she breathed. "I just don't know."

So, while she had corroborated Mark's account of asking him to check on their mother, her account of why she chose to live in Canada was not consistent with Mark's version of events.

Simon strides into his office to find myself and Tam waiting for him in stony silence. "Afternoon," he says. "I'm sorry I wasn't around yesterday, I had a long-standing commitment that I simply couldn't change and had to attend a senior officers' seminar for most of today, but I've got every confidence in you two."

"Cheers, guv," mumbles Tam.

"I guess the first thing I need to know is, do we have a problem with the press? I was a bit surprised with some of the coverage I saw yesterday."

"Not as surprised as we were," I say.

"Do we know the source of those stories?"

"Barton, guv," says Tam, before I have chance to reply. "I spoke to Warren James, and he told me Barton had been to see him and was asking about the Sam Shepton inquest. Barton was also asking about the contents of Sam's suicide note."

I feel my cheeks start to burn. I knew that Tam and Warren had discussed Dan visiting the Coroner's officer, and that Tam had been asked to call Warren back after we had seen the papers, to check that what had been reported, while distasteful to us, was factually correct. But this was the first I'd heard about Dan making enquiries about the suicide note.

"Nothing about the note was reported," says Simon, "so I'm assuming Warren gave short shrift to Dan, as he usually does to the media."

"I'm sure Alex could have a word with Barton, if you want her to, guv. I believe they know each other, privately."

Simon glances at me suspiciously, and I scowl at Tam. Here he goes again, playing stupid games.

"Bottom line is this," says Simon. "The whole black widow thing, and Mark's outburst, happened at the inquest, so I'm not entirely surprised that it's got out. What I don't want to get out is anything concerning Amanda's tongue. Is there any reason to suspect that the press have got wind of this?"

"None, boss," I say, beating Tam by a fraction of a second.

"Let's hope it stays that way, shall we?" Simon says.

"Mum's the word, guv," says Tam.

"Alex, how did the interview with Mark go?"

I tell Simon about the interview, and Tam winces when I say it got a little 'lively' at one point.

"Does Mark have an alibi?"

"We've been checking it out," I say. "He says he was in town, but was too drunk to remember where he was, or who he was with. I asked DS Fawcett to see if there's any CCTV from the pubs and clubs on Saturday night."

"Tam?"

"We've spoken to all four of the main clubs and most of the pubs. The head barman at Langley's can remember a group of rugby players being in, but doesn't know their names. We're still collecting and reviewing the CCTV footage; it's going to take some time."

"What about Mark's team-mates?"

"We haven't interviewed them all yet," says Tam. "Those we have spoken to have been as vague as Mark himself has been. Yes, they were in town, yes, they're pretty sure Mark was with them, because it's an all for one, one for all kind of team, they say. But when pressed, none of them could swear Mark was there, on the basis that they were all far too pissed to remember anything clearly. They can't even tell me, for sure, which bars they went to, which doesn't help. Bloody piss-heads."

Simon listens attentively.

"Alex, based on everything we know so far, what's your gut feeling? Did Mark Shepton kill his mother?"

"I think so, boss."

"Why?"

"His alibi can't be corroborated; he can't say for certain that he didn't get so drunk that he didn't go to his mother's house and kill her. There was also a discrepancy in what he said about his sister. He said she moved to Canada because she hated Amanda as well. But I've spoken to the sister…"

"Good work," says Simon. "And?"

"Her husband is Canadian. They chose to move there for the lifestyle."

"I don't blame them," says Simon. "Lovely place."

"We know Mark had very strong negative feelings towards his mother, but he won't elaborate. He blames Amanda for the suicide of Sam Shepton, but I think there's a lot more to it. The hatred Mark has for Amanda runs very deep. I still think he's holding out on us."

"Which, in itself, is cause for suspicion," says Simon.

"He does protest that he's innocent, and even suggested his uncle, Sam's business partner, also had an intense dislike for Amanda. But other than being to blame for Sam's suicide, there's nothing much more than that."

"Have you seen Sam's suicide note?" Simon says.

Tam and I exchange glances.

"No, I haven't," I say.

"Sorry, guv, no," says Tam, and I'm glad about that.

"I *have*," says Simon. "Not many have seen it. Mark has, and I assume Sarah has seen it. I believe Sam's brother has seen it, as has the Coroner, Warren James, and Sergeant Davey, who was the senior officer at the scene. He recovered the note, read it, and passed it on to the Coroner's officer."

"OK," I say, but I must admit I don't know where this is going.

"Sam loved his family. And in his note, he wrote about his tremendous sadness at what he considered to be the break-up of his family; his brother no longer visited as often as he used to, Sarah had moved to Canada and, as the final straw, Mark moved out. He blamed Amanda for all of that. And he said there was increasing distance between them. And he said he felt he could simply no longer live with what he described as Amanda's wicked tongue. It's a phrase he repeats several times in the letter. He says Amanda's wicked tongue drove a wedge between him and his brother; he says her wicked tongue drove Sarah to emigrate, and her wicked tongue forced Mark to leave home."

"Wicked tongue," I whisper.

Simon nods. "This was a very personal crime. All the evidence strongly suggests that the killer went to that house with the sole intent of murdering Amanda Shepton. It was brutal, it was very personal. And I can't help but think that the fact that the killer ripped out her tongue and fed it to her was because the murderer felt that Amanda had a wicked tongue. How better to silence it than to tear it out and cut it into pieces?"

"Guv," Tam starts. "Look, I know it all points to Mark at the moment. But I'm just not sure. I don't think he's got it in him."

"You still think it's a serial killer, Tam?"

"Aye, guv, I do."

"Need I remind you that this killer didn't take Amanda's tongue as a trophy. It's inside her stomach. He fed it to her. That screams out to me that this was extremely personal. And from everything we've got so far, no one seemed to want Amanda Shepton dead more than Mark."

"I agree, boss. Mark has got a fiery temper. I think he did get very drunk on Saturday night, probably started thinking about his father, his mind drifting back to the inquest. I think he got blind drunk, went to confront his mother, not necessarily with the intention of killing her, but that she may well have argued with him and he saw red, lost it, and killed her in a drunken rage."

"I'm with you for most of that," says Simon. "But I don't buy the drunken rage bit. The scene was too tidy."

"Too tidy, and aside from a pretty useless partial footprint, no significant evidence found at the scene. I think our killer was very careful, I think he was forensically aware. That's not the way of an over-emotional, grieving son who see's red in a drunken rage."

I grit my teeth. I think Tam simply wants to disagree with anything that I say. I've got no doubt that if I suggested I believed this was the work of a serial killer, Tam would be championing the one-off theory.

"Tam, let's just say, for a moment, I'm willing to consider the serial killer theory. What's the motive?"

Tam shrugs his shoulders. "Maybe we've got someone who has a thing for rich widows. Maybe it's someone who had their heart broken by an older woman. I don't know. Maybe we'll have a better idea when he strikes again."

"*If* he strikes again," I counter.

"When," says Tam. "Assuming he hasn't done so already."

Simon thinks about this for a moment.

"OK, we take a two-pronged approach. We need to cover all bases. Tam, go through the files, check with other forces. Look for any murders with a similar MO from the past, oh I don't know, five, ten years, for starters? See if you can find anything which might link any other death to that of Amanda Shepton. If this man has struck before, I want to know about it."

"Yes, guv," says Tam, who flashes me a smug 'I told you it was a serial killer' kind of look.

"Alex. Everything we've got so far points towards Mark. But we've got nothing yet that would come anywhere close to getting a conviction. So I want you to focus on building a case against Mark. Either corroborate his alibi, or destroy it. Try to find out exactly where he was on Saturday night, and who he was with. Get the team to chase up the CCTV footage again and review it. Sooner rather than later, I either want to clear him, or nail him to the wall."

"Got it, boss," I say.

"I'm going to think about that suicide note a bit more," says Simon. "I can't shake the feeling that there's a link between the repeated use of the phrase 'wicked tongue' in Sam Shepton's suicide note, and his wife being murdered by having her tongue torn out just a few weeks after his death. I will try to find out if anyone else has had access to that note. I'm going to speak to Warren James and Sergeant Davey. I don't need to remind you that the contents of that note remain completely confidential and is not for the public domain. Is that clear?"

"Yes, guv."

"Yes, boss."

"Oh, and talking of the public domain, I suggest we prepare for another press conference on Friday. You know the sort of thing, preparing for the one-week anniversary of her death, that kind of thing. Bottom line; whether this is a serial killer or not, we don't want any more newspaper headlines like we saw yesterday. So let's crack this case, and crack it quickly."

Twenty: Kat

"After what she did to him, to be honest, the only thing that surprises me is that he didn't kill her sooner."

Elizabeth's words continue to echo around my mind, as they have done ever since we said our goodbyes in the coffee shop earlier.

I'd asked her to tell me exactly what she meant by that, but she clammed up. She wanted to pay a tribute to her friend, she didn't want to bad-mouth her. In fact, she said she feared she had said too much already, but I promised her the tribute in the paper would only include the positive comments she gave me.

Still, it's got me thinking.

Mark blamed Amanda for his father's suicide; that's a fact. And in many people's eyes, that would probably be motive enough to prompt Mark to want to take out his grief and anger on his mother.

But ultimately, it was what Amanda did to Sam that prompted him to take his own life. I've always been of the opinion that Elizabeth is someone who says exactly what she means; and when she said "after what she did to him", she was referring to Mark. My interpretation of what she said was that it was a clear implication that Amanda had, in some way, directly wronged her son, beyond driving his father to kill himself.

And perhaps cumulatively, whatever this wrong was, add it to the death of his beloved father, and suddenly there is enough, perhaps, to drive any man over the edge, to lose his temper completely and take matters into his own hands.

I finish the tribute piece; it could take a full two pages, as there were plenty of people who were willing to pay tribute to Amanda, and I know Tony has been asked to go through the Herald's photo archives and dig out some of the many pictures the paper has published of her over the years.

I've also drafted my first front-page lead, too, with the few firm facts we know so far about the actual murder.

Most of the stories for Friday's edition will be signed off today, but the front-page lead will be held until the last possible moment tomorrow, in case there are any updates or new statements from the police.

I'm trying to figure out how I can find out more about Mark and his relationship with his mother.

Is it my job to find out? Surely, this is something the police would be doing. They've probably covered it all when they questioned him yesterday. I've spoken to the press office a couple of times, but all I could get out of them was that, at this time, nobody has been arrested in connection with the murder of Amanda Shepton.

I don't know if it is my job to find out more, but I just have an aching feeling deep down inside that I *want* to find out more, I need to find out more.

But how?

Patrick calls me into his office; he has read my tribute piece, and loves it. He was particularly pleased that I'd been able to include some comments from the current Mayoress. Well, her title is officially Mayor. I guess it's just force of habit that I've referred to her as Mayoress. I like to think I'm a bit of a feminist, (but not a militant activist) but even so, some old habits die hard.

"Any update from the police?" he asks.

I shake my head. "They've still not clarified the cause of death," I say, which is another aspect of this matter that has got me very curious. Of course, this is my first murder story, so perhaps this is normal. But it strikes me that, having examined the body at the scene, and now having had a full postmortem, I'd have thought the cause of someone being murdered must have been quite obvious.

At the press conference, the DCI had said he was 'satisfied' that this was murder, and that was even before the PM had taken place. Let's think about that logically; what would the alternatives to murder be? An accident in the home. She spilled something on the kitchen floor, slipped, and cracked her head on the hard surface.

Another option could be that, with all the emotional upheaval of losing her husband, and her son's outburst at the inquest, perhaps the stress simply became too much for her, and her body responded by having a heart attack. That, of course, would mean death by natural causes.

Another option would be that a grief-stricken widow, again in the wake of the conclusion of the inquest, the last formal proceeding, the last 'farewell', if you like, deciding that she didn't want to live without her husband, and taking her own life.

But DCI Fisher said he was satisfied that Amanda was murdered, even without knowing the actual cause of death. That means he's sure that her death was deliberate, not accidental. It means he is sure that her death was not self-inflicted. Why would he be so sure, before the PM results?

A voice in my head provides the answer. 'He's sure because the circumstances in which she was found means she would have been incapable of inflicting any injuries upon herself' and the most obvious thing that springs to mind is that she must have been tied up.

I share my thoughts with Patrick.

"It's a possibility, for sure," he says. "Usually, once a PM is done, police more often than not are a little more forthcoming about the cause of death. Maybe you should try the press office again, see if you can get anything out of them."

I turn to leave his office, but hesitate.

"What about Mark?" I ask, and I tell him what Elizabeth had said earlier.

Patrick thinks about this carefully.

"As you say, it's no secret that he hated Amanda, and no secret that he has a temper. But if police had any firm evidence, I'm sure he would have been arrested by now. Of course, that's not to say he isn't a prime suspect, just that they don't yet have grounds for arrest."

"I want to do some digging," I say. "See if I can find anyone who knows Mark who might be willing to talk."

"I'm not sure what there is to be gained by that," says Patrick. "We wouldn't be able to print anything like that. At least, not yet."

I seize my opportunity. "I agree. But if he does get charged, then at some point, won't we want to do some kind of in-depth background piece? Anything I am able to find out now could be saved for publication when it is appropriate."

He smiles. "You've got the natural curiosity and drive of a *real* journalist. And you never know, you wouldn't be the first reporter to beat the police to solving a murder case."

I feel my cheeks redden and I know I'm beaming with pride.

I'm about to leave the room to plan just how I am going to turn detective, when he stops me. "Kat; Tony is meant to be going to the rugby club tonight, to take a pre-season team photo. We always print a photo of the new squad at the start of a season. Since it's highly likely that Mark will be keeping a low profile, why don't you go with him? On the basis that you're seeking some quotes about how they feel about the forthcoming campaign. And if an appropriate opportunity arises, but only if it feels right, perhaps you can discreetly ask a few questions about Mark, too."

I feel a thrill shoot through me. Yes! This is definitely the kind of thing I had hoped I would find myself doing as a journalist.

Patrick smiles again; you don't need to be an expert in body language and reading people's expressions to see that I am into this. But then his smile fades. "Kat. I don't want you to do anything silly, OK? I don't want to put yourself in a vulnerable situation if you do decide to do some digging on Mark, OK? I've only suggested the rugby club because Tony will be with you, and he can certainly handle himself."

"Understood," I say, and leave the office to let Tony know that I'll be coming with him to the rugby club.

Ross is switching off his PC, his day's work done.

"Well, look at you," he says, "the cat who got the cream! It must be exciting to know you've got your first front page lead coming up."

"It's great," I say.

"Well, don't get too used to it," he says. "I'm snapping at your heels. I'm working on something that will put me on page one as soon as I get it finished."

"Sounds exciting, what is it?" I say.

He taps his nose enigmatically. "Watch this space."

There's no point going home now, so I take the opportunity to catch up on emails and a few other bits of admin that have built up while I've been caught up with working on the tribute piece to Amanda.

For a fleeting moment, I think about Dan. And about what Patrick said. Maybe I was a bit harsh on him; after all, Dan did help me out on Monday, big time. Why do that, if you're only intending to stick the knife in? I don't know.

Thankfully, I don't have time to be distracted by this any longer. Tony is waving his car keys at me. "Come on then, scoop, he says.

I grab my coat.

"Tony," Patrick calls from his little cubbyhole. "Look after her."

"Will do," says Tony. "Come on, Kat."

I can think of worse things for a girl to do that watch a squad of strapping rugby players be put through their paces.

The rugby club is a ten minute drive across town.

The Warriors are a lower-league side, so there's no elaborate stadium or anything like that. There's the main pitch itself, which has one small shed-like stand, with three rows of benches, which looks out over the half-way line but which is about a third the length of the pitch as a whole.

There's another grass area which is used to warming up and training, a car park and a modest two-storey clubhouse, with changing rooms, showers and equipment stores on the ground floor, and a bar and kitchen above, with a terrace which overlooks the pitch.

The players are in a group, gently jogging around the edge of the pitch, when Tony and I pull up.

Tony is well-known to all the staff at the club, as he pops in to take some pictures for the Herald at every home game, and has already been there several times over the past few weeks, capturing the pre-season friendlies.

Tonight is the last training session before the league campaign begins, and is traditionally the time when the team photo is taken.

There are three coaches on the sideline, and they greet Tony warmly. One of them makes no secret of eyeing me up, and I suddenly feel very self conscious. I hope I'm not blushing too much.

"They've only done a gentle warm-up," one of the coaches tells Tony. "We didn't want them to get the new kit all dirty before you've had a chance to catch their ugly mugs on camera."

Tony introduces me as a journalist, and I can immediately see the suspicion that clouds over their faces. "She just wants a few quotes about your expectations for the season," Tony explains. "Since she's new to the paper, she thought she'd do it face to face rather than on the phone."

They seem to buy this, thankfully, and visibly relax. They clearly know and trust Tony. It just goes to prove Patrick's point again; it's not so much what you know, but who you know, that's going to get you anywhere in this business.

One of the coaches blows harshly on a whistle and calls the squad over. "Right you rabble, let's get in between the posts at that end, and see if we can achieve the impossible and make yourselves look respectable."

A few of them grin at me and, for the first time in my life, I have a true appreciation, if that's the right word, of the phrase "undressing with the eyes", because a few of them are definitely looking at me in a way which is both flattering and intimidating.

"Who's this?" says one, "a new cheerleader?"

"She's a journalist," says one of the coaches, and there are some raised eyebrows in response. I presume they thought I was 'with' Tony.

"I'll give you a quote, sweetheart," says one, "but we'd have to have an in-depth interview."

"Pay no notice to them," says the coach. "It's just typical dressing room banter."

"Boys will be boys," I say, with a smile that I know almost certainly looks forced. Tony and I follow them across the pitch, where they gather under the 'H'-shaped posts.

As we walk, I decide it best to keep up pretences, so I pull out my notepad and ask the head coach, Dave, how preparations have been going for the season, and what his expectations are.

"Of course," he says, "I don't need to tell you, I'm sure, that the lads have been somewhat distracted this week, because of the murder."

I raise my eyes upwards and say a silent 'thank you'. I had come here with Tony, but with no real game plan, and not a clue how I might possibly raise the subject, but now Dave has just offered it to me on a plate.

"It must have been a big shock," I say. My eyes scan the squad as they organise themselves into a couple of rows for the photo, just to confirm that Mark is not among them. "How have they all taken it? How, er, how is Mark?"

"There's no 'i' in 'team', and that goes double for this lot," Dave says, proudly. "They're a close-knit bunch, and they've been rallying round, offering Mark as much support as they can."

"That's good to hear," I say. "Mark is very much one of the lads, then, so to speak? A typical rugby player."

"Typical? He's one of the best we've got, love. Rock solid, he is. You wouldn't want to get on his bad side, that's for sure."

I wince. I'm pretty sure Dave didn't intend this to sound like a threat, it's just a figure of speech. But it did halt me in my tracks momentarily.

"So you've had contact with him this week, then?"

"He's never been out of contact," says Dave. "The lads were all out on the town last Saturday, celebrating a decent win in the last pre-season friendly."

"Was Mark with them? After all, that's only a few days after the inquest..."

Dave's face darkens a little. "I wasn't out on Saturday myself, but I'd be very surprised if Mark wasn't out with them on Saturday. Of course, we haven't seen too much of him since..."

His words trail off, and I nod. "Of course. Anyway, you say this whole tragic business hasn't affected the team too much?"

"It was a shock, of course. But these are grunt and groan rugby players, sweetheart. These are *real* men, they take most things in their stride."

I wince at the 'sweetheart' bit, but remind myself that I really am in full alpha-male territory here. I turn to make sure I know exactly where Tony is.

The players are all lined up in two rows. Those in the front row are squatting down, those behind them have their arms folded.

"All present and correct?" asks Dave.

"Not yet, coach. One missing. Always late on parade."

One of the other coaches turns towards me, but shouts to someone who is behind me, beyond me. "Come on Shepton, we haven't got all night."

My heart skips a beat.

"Jeez," the coach says. "That man will be late for his own fu…" and he stops himself, for fear of incurring Mark's infamous wrath.

Mark Shepton jogs past me, glances at Dave and says, "Sorry I'm late, been kinda busy," and takes his place in the back row.

"Fantastic," says Tony, who stands in front of them with his camera raised. "All look towards me; let's smile for this one. We'll do the intimidating 'face down the opposition' photo after."

This gets a few laughs from pretty much all the players.

Except Mark.

He has just spotted me, standing a good few paces behind Tony and the coaching staff.

"What the fuck is she doing here?" he says, and he breaks ranks. He takes two steps towards me. "I'm talking to you, you cold-hearted bitch! What the fuck are you here for? Trying to dish some more dirt? Trying to get a few more choice phrases you can sell to the papers for tomorrow's headlines!"

I don't know what to say, and I don't know what to do. I'm rooted to the spot, unable to move, and my legs are turning to jelly.

Marks face is reddening and he takes another two steps towards me.

"You're fucking scum!" he seethes. "And you're not welcome here."

"Mark!" says Dave. "Mark, come on man, you're out of order."

"*I'm* out of order?" he turns on Dave and for a moment, I think he is going to flatten his coach. "This little bitch might look all sweetness and light, but she's fucking scum. It's her that put all that shit in the papers this week."

Dave glares at me, as if he's asking if this is true.

I shake my head vigorously and try to fight back the tears that are threatening to flow. I can just about manage to say, "I didn't…"

"Leave her alone!" says Tony. "She's just doing her job."

His heart was in the right place, but unfortunately it was the wrong thing to say. It was like a red rag to a bull.

Mark turns towards Tony, strides up to him and stands so close that their noses are practically touching. A few of the other players tell Mark to calm down, to go back to them, but he isn't listening.

"Some fucking job! She's a fucking leech, just looking to make headlines out of other people's misery."

Tony stands his ground and glares back at Mark, who then turns to me again.

"You! You keep your fucking nose out of my business. If you print another word about me or my family, I swear to God I'll…"

"You'll what?" says Tony. "Attack a young girl for doing her job? Some bloody man you are."

Mark swings a club-like fist and knocks Tony right into the air.

He steps forward and looks as if he is about to deliver a kick to the ribs but is suddenly swamped by several other players, who are wrapping their arms around him, pulling them away.

"Fucking scum!" yells Mark. "I'll kill you! I'll fucking kill you!"

Two of the coaches are helping Tony to his feet. Blood is pouring from his nose.

Dave looks at me and says, "Are you OK?"

I nod, and he says, "I think you'd better go."

There's at least six other players gripping Mark tightly and, to be truthful, struggling to hold onto him, as his fury seems to keep building.

Two of the coaches escort Tony and I back to his car, while Mark continues to scream and swear at us.

I can't stop shaking as I get into the car. I don't think I've ever been so scared.

But at the same time, I'm more determined than ever to find out what I can, prove that Mark killed his mum, and see that gets locked up like the wild animal he clearly is.

Twenty One: Dan

I'm not entirely sure what I was expecting from my meeting with Stuart Shepton, but it certainly wasn't what he told me.

On reflection, hearing that Amanda had been tied up is not that much of a surprise. Sure, I was a little shocked when he first said it, but when I think about it, it's kind of obvious.

Even now, police haven't confirmed the precise cause of death, yet they haven't opted for the traditional 'we're keeping an open mind' line; DCI Fisher has made it clear he is satisfied that it's murder. And he's no mug. He's one of the most experienced, and respected, officers on the force.

He wouldn't publicly say he thinks it's murder unless he truly believes it; and since he announced this before the PM results, then it all becomes clear; the circumstances in which Amanda was found satisfied him that it was murder. She was found tied up. People can poison themselves, people can hang themselves; people can shoot themselves, even stab themselves. But you don't hear of people tying themselves up.

Of course, the police press office are never going to confirm this in a month of Sundays. I may try to get an off-the-record steer from Alex. But to be honest, that can wait; the fact is, Amanda was murdered.

What's of far more interest to me right now is the 'jilted toyboy lover'. This scenario throws up a whole pile of new questions. That's assuming, of course, that it's true. But then, why would Stuart Shepton lie to me?

My cynical sub-consciousness says it could be that Stuart Shepton has come up with this to divert attention away from himself. From what he told me, he disliked Amanda intently himself. And even if he didn't, it's blatantly apparent that he is in fairly close contact with Mark, so perhaps some of Mark's rather strong opinions about his mother have rubbed off on his uncle. Maybe Stuart and Mark are in it together.

But I don't think so.

What I do think is that Stuart doesn't trust the police at all; he doesn't trust the media much more. But he definitely doesn't believe that Mark killed his mother.

Of course, there is this falling out between Mark and Amanda that Stuart mentioned. Some might think Mark had enough of a reason to kill his mother because he blamed her for Sam's suicide. But if there was some big falling out as well, it sounds like this could provide Mark with yet more motivation.

Yet Stuart was quite insistent that Mark did not kill Amanda. This seems to be more than a case of family loyalty to me; I think Stuart truly believes it.

And so, the toyboy.

This has become my focus. It's a totally new line. And, now that I come to think of it, given Stuart's distrust of the police, then it's a line that I bet the investigation team don't know about. Suddenly I have a bargaining chip with Alex; I could offer an exchange of information.

But first I'll need to confirm the toyboy line. I need to find him.

I've left a message for an old contact of mine at the local authority communications team, and I'm waiting for a call back.

The toyboy. Did Sam Shepton know that his wife was sleeping around? Is this what pushed him over the line, the final nail in his coffin, so to speak?

As I understand it, the Shepton's were fiercely proud of their social status. If Amanda's indiscretions became the talk of the town, it would do untold damage to their reputation, and their standing in the community.

Did Mark know? This could help explain his blatant animosity towards his mother. Of course, it could also add more strength to the argument of what Mark's motive might be for killing his own mother.

The thing that has got me particularly intrigued is the way Stuart Shepton worded what he said. Like DCI Fisher, I think Stuart chooses the words he uses with great consideration.

"The toyboy she jilted and refused to take back."

When did she jilt him? Before Sam killed himself, or after?

Presumably this toyboy knew that Sam Shepton was dead.

Did he expect the black widow to continue, or resume, their relationship? Was he expecting to be the main man, rather than the other man? Did Amanda shock him by turning her back on him?

That would make this a crime of passion.

Many people have been killed for less.

Stuart Shepton was a convincing talker. I find myself having serious doubts about Mark Shepton and am much more inclined to think that Mr Secret Lover Boy may be our killer. A bruised heart, a spurned lover; if he can't have Amanda, then no one else would.

My mobile rings. The caller ID reads 'Vicki FitzGerald', my contact at the local council. We worked together at the Herald, but while I chose to progress along the journalism career path, she took the other common 'poacher turned gamekeeper' approach.

She left the Herald about six months before I did for a job on the local council. It paid a lot more, and the hours were a little more regular, which suited her as she loved the social side of life.

"Hey stranger," she says. "Long time no speak."

"Vicki, hi, how are you? Thanks for calling back."

"I'm fine, mate. But something tells me this isn't a social call."

"No, it isn't," I say. "But it should be. Or at least, I should've made a social call a long time ago. We'll have to catch up at some point."

"Yeah, that'd be good. So, you know I always love a good gossip; did things ever pan out with you and that copper you were seeing?"

"No, it didn't," I smile, "although, now that you come to mention it, I'm about to renew our acquaintanceship. She's deputy SIO on the Amanda Shepton murder."

"Of course," says Vicki. "I should've guessed you'd be working on that. Was that your handiwork in the nationals yesterday? The black widow thing?"

"Er, yeah, it was."

"Sweet."

"What about you? Has someone swept you off your feet yet?"

"I've got a handsome hunk that I'm pretty loved up with," she says, and I can hear the smile on her face. "But come on, enough of the small talk, what do you want?"

"I need you to do me a favour," I say.

"I figured that much."

"I need you to check the electoral roll for me, strictly off the record, of course."

"Naturally," she says. Technically, of course, I have no right whatsoever to ask her to do something like this. It's one of the old tricks Patrick taught me. Another former Herald hack had gone to the local authority, and Patrick did exactly the same thing with him.

Vicki and I had always got on well so when she went to the local authority, I knew I'd always have a useful contact on the 'inside'. And she knew that I'd always do my best to put a positive spin on anything she was particularly keen to promote on behalf of the local council, in return.

"I'm trying to find someone, and it's a fairly unusual surname, so I'm hoping there won't be too many of them in town."

"Go on."

I review the notes in my pad from my conversation with Stuart Shepton. "It's Eliasson; one 'l', double 's'."

"Give me half an hour or so."

She calls back in just over twenty minutes and tells me that there are four households with that name registered. I asked her if she had a list of all the people living in each of the houses.

"What do you think this is? Amateur hour?" she says, and then runs through the names.

The second name of the third household is Pieter Eliasson.

"Bingo," I say. "Give me the address again, please?"

I note it down.

"So, what's this got to do with the Shepton murder?"

"I honestly don't know," I say. "It might be nothing. But then again..."

"Keep me posted, scoop."

"Thanks Vicki. Look, I'm in town for a few days, staying at my parent's place. We'll have to have that overdue catch up."

"If your lead, that I've had absolutely nothing to do with, of course, works out, then you're paying," she says.

"Done."

The Wellington estate was a middle-class area on the outer edge of town, mostly decent-size semi-detached houses, with just a few terraces scattered between them.

Wellington Way was one of the main roads that dissected the estate; it was a long, quite wide, thoroughfare. Pieter Eliasson lived at number 280. I found a parking space nearby.

Stuart was reluctant to tell me too much about Pieter; I wonder if he is afraid that, if this proves to be a significant lead, he'll find himself having to speak to the police.

What he did tell me was that Amanda spent quite a few hours each week working in the offices of a large local charity, a hospice, where she would co-ordinate fund-raising activities.

Sam and Stuart's accountancy provided their services to the hospice free of charge, as a goodwill gesture. And Stuart said he became aware of there being a chemistry between Amanda and Pieter, who also worked for the hospice, running its social media channels.

He didn't know if Pieter started working there after his relationship with Amanda started - perhaps he joined the hospice as a way of spending more time with her - or if it was just a coincidence. He didn't know if this was where they met, or if they met somewhere else.

What he did know was that there was definite chemistry between them.

Stuart wasn't prepared to tell me how he knew, for sure, about the affair, or that Pieter had been 'jilted' and that Amanda had refused to take him back. He was quite uncomfortable talking about such personal issues, he said he felt that it was a betrayal of sorts. Yet at the same time, with the police seemingly so intent on pinning the murder on Mark, Stuart felt obliged to tell someone just enough to enable them to do some detective work of their own. And that someone was me.

I'd say the woman who opened the door had to be in her mid-seventies. Perhaps, I thought, Pieter still lives with his parents.

"Hello," I say, and I flashed my 'Press' card at her. "Is Pieter in?"

"Pieter?" she says. "Why would you want to speak to my grandson?"

"I believe Pieter worked at the local hospice, with Amanda Shepton. I, er, I don't know if you've heard about what happened…"

"Yes, yes," she says, "terrible business, terrible. That poor woman."

"Indeed. Well, I'm doing an extended obituary on her, because of all the good charity work she did, and I'm trying to track down and speak to as many people as I can find who worked with her, to give them chance to pay their own tribute to her. Someone suggested that Pieter knew her quite well, so, er, here I am."

"Oh, that's nice," she said. "Please wait here, young man."

She closes the door. Through the frosted glass panel, I see her stand at the bottom of the stairs, and I hear her call Pieter's name.

The door opens slowly and Pieter regards me apprehensively. I know Stuart had described him as a toyboy, but I'm taken aback by just how young he looks.

"Nan said you want to speak about Mrs Shepton," he says.

"That's right," I say, and I show him my Press card. "I'm doing an obit, and because she did so much work for so many local charities, I'm trying to speak to anyone I can find who worked with her, to give them a chance to pay tribute."

"Tribute?"

"Yeah, you know. Say something nice about her."

"I've got nothing nice to say," he says.

"Oh, really? That's a surprise," I say, lying through my teeth of course, while thinking that this might be easier than I thought. "You worked with her at the hospice, didn't you?"

"Yes."

"That's what I thought. Well, perhaps I've been misinformed, but I was under the impression you and Amanda worked together a few times."

"We did."

"But you didn't get on? I haven't found anyone who's had a bad word to say about her."

"We got on fine."

"It must have been a terrible shock to hear she had been killed."

"I suppose."

"Suppose?"

"Yes. It was a shock."

"Well, lots of people who knew her are paying tribute to her in my article. It would be nice to get one of her co-workers from the hospice to talk about her."

"There's plenty of others. Speak to someone else. I don't want to talk to you. I think you should go. I don't want my name on anything to do with Amanda," he says, and he starts to shut the door.

"Is that because you were sleeping with her?"

He freezes. I can't see his face, because it is obscured by the door, but I can see one of his hands on the doorframe, and it's trembling.

"What?" he whispers.

"You heard," I say. "But if you don't want to say anything, that's up to you. I think it will sound pretty weird if I have to write that someone who was so close to her didn't want to contribute to her obituary. Saying that her lover said 'no comment' does seem a bit odd."

The door opens again. He's in pieces. It seems he is torn, not sure whether he wants to start crying or shrieking, or to start kicking the shit out of me. He looks quite skinny, so I'm not too worried if he does choose to start throwing any punches.

"You can't print that, you can't say anything like that."

"Well, I need to say something," I say. "My editor is expecting me to produce a full piece, from all the people who knew her well and shared time with her. And who better than someone who loved her."

"Loved her?" he says, raising his voice. "Loved her? I fucking hated her. She - she broke my fucking heart, that cold, cruel, witch. I can't say anything nice because I've got nothing nice to say, I fucking hate her."

"I guess that definitely counts as a 'no comment' then," I say, as I turn away.

"Isn't an obituary meant to be for people who are sad that someone's dead? Well, I'm not sad. I'm not sad at all. I'm glad she's dead, OK. Is that what you want me to say? I'm fucking glad she's dead. She got what she deserved. There. You can quote me on that!"

Twenty Two: Alex

Wicked tongue. I can't get those words out of my head. Sam Shepton repeatedly spoke of his wife's 'wicked tongue' in his suicide note.

And when she's murdered, her tongue becomes a focus for her killer. There simply *has* to be a link. All I can think about is who has seen the note.

I felt a pang of embarrassment when Simon had asked if I'd read it. It simply hadn't occurred to me, and a moment of relieved delight when Tam said he hadn't read it either. This would have been just the kind of morsel the vulture was waiting to swoop on.

There's no way I could go out with the girls tonight now. No, I needed to stay in the office and think things through.

Naturally, they were disappointed when I offered my excuses. I like to think the disappointment was fuelled because they enjoy my company but I suspect they were far more interested in seeing what gossip I might share about the murder, which is, of course, the talk of the town. Thankfully, they know me better than that.

I sit at my desk and write out a list of names, starting with Mark Shepton. Then Stuart Shepton, who appears to have no intention of returning my calls. The coroner. Possibly the pathologist? I put a question mark there. Warren James. Sergeant Tom Davey.

These are the people we know have seen the suicide note.

For a moment, I think about adding my name, Tam and Simon to the list. But we've only just become aware of the contents. If there is a link between what Sam wrote and the murder of his wife, then that 'link' has to have happened between the time the note was found, and Amanda's death. Which rules out Tam and I, for sure.

I don't know how long Simon has been aware of the contents.

I laugh. I think I'm over-tired. Am I actually seriously even thinking that the boss might be a suspect? That's crazy.

I look up and gasp. Warren James is standing in the doorway of the incident room, staring at me intently. "Shit!" I exclaim.

The outer edges of his narrow mouth turn up just a fraction.

"I'm sorry," he says. "I didn't mean to startle you."

My heart rate slowly returns to normal. He offers what I guess he thinks is a reassuring smile but if anything, it makes me shudder again. There's something about him that gives me the creeps. Maybe it's the way he lurches when he walks, almost zombie-like.

Maybe it's the way he lurks in doorways, like an ominous ghostly presence. Maybe he spends too much time in the world of the dead.

"That's OK, I just didn't hear you."

"You looked engrossed in your work, so I was trying not to disturb you. I'm looking for DS Fawcett."

"And you've found him," booms that familiar Scottish brogue. I'm assuming Tam has been in the men's room or standing outside having a cigarette or something.

Warren steps out of the doorway to let Tam in. He crosses the room and grabs his coat. He glances at me. "We're off for a drink," he says, and with a dismissive wave of the hand, he and Warren disappear.

I walk to the door and watch them stomp down the corridor. I can't help but think of them as two old relics left behind from a bygone age, and that thought makes me smile.

Suddenly, Tam turns and his eyes meet mine. Shit. I didn't want him to see me. "Don't work too late," he says, and then has the gall to wink at me!

Warren turns, to see who Tam is talking to. The pair of them then exchange glances, Tam says something that I can't hear, and he and Warren both start laughing like a couple of conspiratorial schoolboys in the playground.

Warren James. He's on my list. He knows what the suicide note said. Is he capable of tearing someone's tongue out? There's certainly something sinister about him, so I wouldn't put it past him.

Of course, it's highly likely that someone on that short list of people who we know have seen the note have not kept the contents to themselves. Did Stuart Shepton tell his wife? His children? Did Mark share the contents with his cousins? His sister?

Did Sergeant Davey talk about it?

What about Warren? Has he discussed it with anyone?

Has he discussed it with Tam?

Now, there's a thought! For a moment, I have a sense of perverse satisfaction run through me. Yes, Warren tells Tam and, for some reason, there's something about those words that turns Tam into a killer!

I shake my head as I return to my desk.

Maybe I should take a break; this case is definitely starting to get to me.

I spend some time reviewing the statement we took from Mark.

It's really nagging at me, him protesting his innocence, yet us finding nothing to support his alibi.

I've no idea how long I've been at my desk; I may even have dozed off, but I'm suddenly startled by the shrill ringing of the phone on my desk. The tone tells me it's an internal call.

"DS...sorry, Acting DI Nicholas," I say. I still haven't quite got used to the sound of my temporary promotion. Perhaps *very* temporary, if I don't make any meaningful progress on this case.

"I'm glad it's you ma'am," says a voice, and I shudder. I really can't get used to being called that. It makes me feel so old or, at least, old-fashioned. But then, I guess I'd rather be called ma'am than sir. "It's Sergeant Davey, I've got the short straw and I've just started the night shift on the community beat team."

Another shudder. First Warren, now Sergeant Davey, another name on my list. This case is making me paranoid. Or, if not paranoid, then certainly a little jumpy.

"How can I help, Sergeant?" I say.

"I just thought you'd like to know, ma'am, I've sent someone round to the office of the Herald. We took a call from the editor; their photographer was assaulted a short while ago."

"I'm not sure why that would interest me," I say, a little impatiently. Aside from this being an occupational hazard for any press photographer, I'm sure - not that I would put the Herald in the same league as the more intrusive paparazzi, this is a community policing matter, not one for me. Unless, I suddenly shudder, unless the assault is so serious that the photographer is fighting for his life. If there's the possibility that this could become a murder, then of course we need to know.

"How serious is it?" I say.

"The snapper's gone to the hospital, suspected broken nose."

"I see. So, why have you called…"

"He says he was attacked by Mark Shepton. I thought you'd want to know."

He doesn't have much more information. An officer has been sent to the Herald's office, and they haven't yet taken a statement from the photographer; they're going to wait until he's had his hospital treatment first.

I pull my contacts book out of my drawer. The Herald switchboard won't be staffed at the moment, but I'm sure we've got a number for the editorial office here somewhere, just in case we needed to get hold of them 'out of hours'.

I find it and call the number.

It rings for a quite a while before it's answered. "Newsdesk?"

"Patrick Harding please."

"Who's calling?"

"Acting DI Alex Nicholas, from the…"

"Patrick speaking," says the voice.

"I'm calling in relation to an allegation of assault against Mark Shepton."

"One of your constable's is here at the moment, talking to one of my reporters, who witnessed the assault," he says.

"That's good," I say. "My colleagues will do it. I just wanted to talk to you myself because I'm on the team which is investigating the murder of Amanda Shepton."

"I guessed as much," he says. "How can I help?"

He tells me what he knows, including the fact that the photographer was with Kate Russell, who was verbally threatened by Mark at Sam Shepton's inquest. I'm assuming that Kate is the reporter I saw sitting next to Dan at the press conference. Patrick confirms that she is leading on the murder story for the Herald.

"In all the circumstances, we didn't make a formal complaint about the threat Mark made to Kat at the inquest; she was shaken but not hurt, and it's understandable that Mark would be emotional, irrational, so we let it go. But I'm not prepared to let this go; Mark has broken Tony's nose, and it took half a dozen rugby players to restrain him."

"I'm sorry to hear that," I say. "Although I am wondering what your thinking was, sending your people to the rugby club having had a member of your team already threatened by Mark. Which you *should* have reported."

"We really didn't think Mark would be there, in all the circumstances. I thought he'd be keeping a low profile, after you lot interviewed him yesterday."

"I'm sorry, what?"

"I know he was interviewed yesterday. Don't worry, I'm not planning to run that in the paper, unless you want to confirm it."

"How did you know we interviewed Mark?" I say, and immediately curse myself. I'm just extremely grateful that Tam wasn't here to witness exactly the kind of basic error he has been waiting for. I've just inadvertently confirmed that we've had Mark in.

"Well, I know for sure now," says Patrick. "Look, we're not on opposing sides, here, detective. I've no intention of adding any more stress to your life as I'm sure you're under plenty of pressure."

"Thank you, I say. Yes, we've spoken to Mark. He hasn't been arrested. We needed to take a statement from him because he was the person who found his mother's body, and alerted the authorities."

"The DCI said that at the press conference, so presumably there's nothing wrong with us saying that Mark has given a formal statement."

"I suppose not," I say. "I'd still like to know what you were hoping to gain by sending someone to the rugby club, even if you thought Mark wasn't going to be there. Were you expecting one of his team-mates to give you some gossip? To rat on Mark and implicate him?"

"If they had done, believe me, we'd have been in touch," says Patrick. "They were there predominantly to take the annual pre-season team photo and get a few quotes about their hopes for the new league campaign."

"Really?"

"Yes," says Patrick, his tone friendly but firm. "I appreciate that the Amanda Shepton murder is occupying your attention twenty-four-seven right now, but the Herald isn't a one-page paper. The world hasn't come to a stop just because of a murder in town; while Amanda Shepton will make Friday's front page, we've still got all our other pages to fill."

"Of course," I say.

"I should also say that we will be reporting that our photographer has been assaulted, although we'll be limited in what we can say if he is arrested. That's if Tony agrees, of course."

"He hasn't been arrested yet," I say. "We need a full statement from your photographer, first."

"Don't rush," he says, his tone becoming friendlier again. "At least, don't arrest him until after we've gone to press."

I can't help but smile. "I'm sure that can be arranged," I say. "I don't suppose, in return, you can tell me how you found out about us speaking to Mark?"

"It wouldn't be right for me to reveal my sources," he says.

"Of course not, I understand."

"While I've got you on the phone, can I ask if there is any significant update to the investigation at the moment? We do go to press tomorrow lunchtime? I should tell you that, despite the reports in the national papers yesterday, we're not running anything along the lines of 'black widow', or Mark verbally attacking Amanda at the inquest. We want to report this responsibly."

"I appreciate that," I say, and I can't help but warm to him. Like most police officers, I'm generally cautious and distrusting of the media, but Patrick seems very sincere. I always thought Dan had a decent moral compass for a journalist. I can see now where he got it from.

"There's really nothing else I can tell you at the moment," I say. "We may hold a press conference on Friday, but I don't suppose that will be of any use to you, as the Herald will be out by then."

"We've still got a website," he says.

"Of course. As soon as we are able to say anything more, we will make sure the Herald knows about it."

"Thanks," he says. "Oh, and don't forget to let me know if you do arrest Mark over the assault on Tony. Or for anything else…"

"I will," I say, and hang up.

My first thought is that I have no doubt whatsoever that Mark Shepton has a volatile, fierce, temper. If someone even starts to press the right buttons, he loses control quickly, easily and extremely.

Tam is still not convinced that Mark killed Amanda. He still prefers the serial killer theory.

I'm more certain than I've ever been that Mark killed his mother. But not just because he blamed her for Sam Shepton's suicide. I want to know - I need to know - what buttons Amanda pressed to make her son see red.

I'd also like to know who is feeding the Herald with information. Surely Tam wouldn't be so determined to make my life uncomfortable that he would speak to the media? I wouldn't be entirely surprised. But would he, really?

My phone buzzes. There's a text message from Dan. *Can we meet ASAP? Quick drink. Just the one. Need to talk.* I suddenly feel an almost overwhelming craving for alcohol. I glance at my watch. The girls are probably on their third round by now. But I can't join them. They'll bombard me with a million and one questions that I won't be able to answer. It will be like being in a press conference, but with the audience having no concept of what I may, or may not, be able to say.

At least Dan will be more realistic.

But no, I shouldn't meet him. I can't meet him.

I text him back. *Hi. Sorry, rather busy. Another time, perhaps.*

I thought he would reply with a simple 'OK'. But instead, he sends me another text which says *Exchange of info?*

Nice try! He's still sniffing around for some inside info; I guess after he provided the tabloids with the 'black widow' line, he's under pressure to feed the sharks with their next juicy tidbit. Maybe, since he left the Herald, his moral compass has shifted a bit.

I text him back. *More than my job's worth. Sorry.*

I put my phone on my desk; Dan's a bright boy, he'll have got the message now, loud and clear, I'm sure.

My phone buzzes again. *Please. You might not want to talk TO me, but you WILL want to hear what I've got to say.*

He's persistent, I'll give him that.

I wonder if he's got the same sources as the Herald? I wouldn't be surprised, since he used to work there. I wonder if he wants me to confirm that Mark Shepton has been interviewed.

His emphasis on me not talking to him but that I would want to listen has intrigued me. I'm tempted.

My phone buzzes again. *Pretty please.*

Twenty Three: Kat

"Are you going to arrest him?" I ask.

"Not my place to say, Miss," the young police officer replies. "We need to take a full statement from Tony; and we'll need him to make a formal complaint. But, er, between you and me, it seems pretty straight forward and I wouldn't be surprised if we did pull him in soon."

I nod. The officer thanks me for my help, and Patrick offers to escort him out. The front door will be closed at this time of night, so the only way in and out is through the secure staff entrance.

Patrick returns to the newsroom.

"Are you OK, Kat?"

I nod.

"I'm sorry," he says, and when I see the expression on his face, I can see that he truly means it. "I should never have let you go to the rugby club. I put you in danger."

"None of us thought Mark would be there, remember?"

"All the same, we didn't know for sure, did we? I put you in danger. The tabloids might pay danger money, but the Herald doesn't."

"It's not your fault," I say. "I wanted to go."

"I know. You've got a fire inside you, a true journalistic heart. But all the same, Mark is clearly a very dangerous and unstable man."

"He's a fucking animal!" I say. It just comes out, instinctively. I lower my head, bashfully. "Sorry, sir."

"Don't be," he says. "After what you've been through, you must be quite frightened?"

"Frightened? I'm bloody furious!" I think I surprise my editor as much as I surprise myself.

"I'd understand if you wanted to take a step back from all this. Mervyn and I can take it on…"

"No!" I interrupt.

"No one will think any less of you, if you decide it's too much. But I won't force you to walk away. The choice is yours. If you would rather someone else take this on, then fine. If you do want to stay with it, despite being threatened twice now, then I can understand that, too. I could make that decision; part of me thinks I should. But I'm not going to. The choice is yours, Kat."

"No!" I say. "It's my story. Please."

He nods. "OK. But we do need to tread carefully."

"I know. But don't take me off this story, please. I want to nail that son-of-a-bitch."

He smiles. "Then you can start by amending the front-page lead."

I look at him, unsure of what he means.

"While you were speaking to the police constable, I had a phone call from Acting DCI Nicholas. She confirmed the tip off I'd had that they questioned Mark yesterday. He wasn't arrested, so we can't say that. But we can report that he has been, how does the old cliché go, helping police with their enquiries? If we word the piece right, I'm sure people who pick up Friday's Herald will be able to read between the lines."

Yes! Never mind Patrick's clichés, what about the pen being mightier than the sword? I'm no competition for Mark's brute strength, but I can use the power of words to bring that caveman down.

"Have you told Dan?" Patrick asks.

"Sorry?"

"Does Dan know what happened tonight?"

"Why should he?" I say, and I know I sound a little more defensive than I intended to.

"Oh, I don't know. I just thought that you and he were, well…"

"We're not!" I say. "I haven't really spoken to him much."

"You're not still blaming him for Tuesday's tabloids, are you?"

"I don't know," I say.

"He's a good man," Patrick says. "And he likes you, I know he does. I think you'd make quite the couple."

I smile, so that he knows I'm not taking it the wrong way, when I reply, "I didn't realise matchmaking was part of your managerial duties."

He returns the smile as he turns and walks back to his office.

I realise just how clever he is.

Less than half an hour ago, I was a trembling bag of nerves, let alone a ticking time-bomb waiting to explode.

Right now, I'm feeling quite calm and relaxed, and I'm ready to do what I do best; fight Mark the best way I know how to.

He doesn't hesitate to let his fists fly, but words are my weapons.

I'll find a way to write the front page lead in such a way that, wherever he goes, people will be pointing their fingers at him; whether he is arrested or not, anyone who buys the Herald this week will be able to read between the lines, and will all know that the foul-tempered bully that is Mark Shepton is also a murderer.

Twenty Four: Dan

I know Alex was reluctant to meet me, so I chose a backstreet bar which isn't particularly popular and which has lots of high-sided booths.

It's about as discreet a public meeting place as there could be.

I find a cubby hole at the back of the bar and review my notes while I wait for her arrive.

I spot her and get up to go and meet her and buy her a drink.

She looks good, and for a moment, I think it's a shame that things didn't 'happen' between us; close-cropped, mousey-blonde hair, almost shaven at the back, slightly longer on top. She's wearing trousers, naturally. I don't think I ever saw her in a skirt. I certainly couldn't imagine her slipping into a sexy little black dress, like the one Kat wore…steady, I tell myself. This is business, not pleasure.

We carry our drinks to the table.

"Thanks for coming," I say. "It's nice to see you."

"You, too," she says. She takes a greedy gulp from her glass, which suggests she badly needed that drink.

"Everything OK?" I ask.

"Oh, you know," she says. "Bit of a 'thing' going on at work. It's been quite busy."

"Really?" I tease.

"But then, you know that, don't you? You must have hit just about every front page in the country yesterday."

I lower my head. "Yeah," I say, "I was a bit surprised about that. I didn't expect the nationals to go as mad with it as they did."

"Well, that's the media for you. Totally unpredictable."

I raise a glass to her.

"You weren't at the inquest," she says, "I know that much. So how did you get the black widow line? I can't imagine you spoke to Mark. If you'd approached him, you'd almost certainly have the bruises to prove it. And I can't imagine Warren James would've said too much either; he's notoriously nervous about speaking to journalists."

"You're right," I say. "His mouth was like a clam which had been superglued. He didn't say much at all. Just the name of the officer who gave evidence at the inquest. Who I've known for years."

She nods, and her expression tells me that this is one mini-mystery solved. I'm hoping she'll see this disclosure as a goodwill gesture on my part, a sign that I'm willing to give just as much as receive.

"I can't stay long," she says, "it's been a long day."

"I'm sure. Look, I'm not really expecting you to be able to give me anything, but if I tell you a few things that I've learned, you could at least let me know if I'm on the very wrong track. Then I'll need to decide what I use or not."

She's about to interrupt me and say that she's not in a position to give me anything, but I raise a hand to stop her. "Then I'll tell you something which you'll definitely want to know."

She doesn't answer. She just gives me a 'hit me with what you've got' kind of look.

"I've spoken to Stuart Shepton," I begin, and her expression changes to one of looking fairly impressed.

"Well done you. That's more than we've been able to do," she says, and I can tell she's a little annoyed.

"It's the power of the press," I say, "or something like that."

"And what did the elusive Mr Shepton have to say?"

I glance at my notepad.

"He told me he isn't inclined to speak to the police, because he thinks that all you're interested in is proving that Mark killed his mother."

"All *I'm* interested in," says Alex, "is finding *whoever* killed Amanda Shepton, why they did it, and bringing him, her or them to justice."

"But by the sound of it, Mark is the prime suspect," I venture.

"I can't discuss that, you know I can't."

"But you have spoken to him, haven't you?"

"Yes."

I stop myself for a moment. That was a bit easier than I thought. Thanks Alex, at least I have *something*.

"Is that on the record?" I ask, hesitantly.

Alex nods. "It seems to be this week's worst-kept secret. But make sure you get it right. Mark Shepton was *not* arrested. He was brought in because he was the one who found Amanda's body, and he was the one who called the police and ambulance. So, yes, we have interviewed him."

"Gotcha," I say. "But is he a suspect, too? He did call his mother a black widow, that he hated her and wished she was dead. I know that, if I was in your shoes, I'd have been taking a good, hard, look at him."

"Mark Shepton has been helping us with our enquiries," she says, formally enough to tell me that this is the last time she is going to answer this particular question, "predominantly on the basis that he found her body and reported her death. Naturally, as part of those enquiries, we have examined all the relevant circumstances."

I scribble some notes and I can see now that she is feeling a little anxious. I didn't get chance to get to know her too well, but I do know her well enough to know that her career, and particularly her new promotion, mean the world to her, and she will not want to compromise that. I've got nothing to gain by stitching her up. I just hope she believes that.

If she doesn't know, hopefully she soon will.

"There's something else Stuart told me," I say, and she now looks nervous. It stands to reason that she knows a lot more about this case than I do. But I wonder just how much more? What does she know that she is so obviously worried about me finding out?

"Go on," she says.

"Stuart said that Amanda Shepton was tied up when she was found."

I'd love to play cards with Alex, I suddenly decide. Because if that's the best she can do for a poker face, then I'd be quids in.

"It adds up," I continue. "At least, it does to me. It explains why, even before the PM had taken place, your boss said he was satisfied that her death was murder. Normally you'd all be keeping an open mind until the PM results were confirmed. I don't suppose you're prepared to confirm that she was tied up, are you?"

"No, I'm not," Alex says.

I don't particularly like the idea of the next question, but it is kind of obvious, and it is one that I need to ask. "Can you flat-out deny it?" I ask.

I know full-well that the police have a policy of not lying to the media. They may not always be completely forthcoming with the 'truth, the whole truth, and nothing but the truth', but the general policy is that they do not lie; it would destroy any credibility and public confidence, which they rely on.

She takes her time to think about this, weighing up all the pro's and cons. If she goes 'no comment', will I run the story anyway, and then the police will look stupid, because the public may think, 'don't they know? How can they *not* know? It's a simple yes or no.'

If she lies, and it later transpires, through a court case, for example, that she has lied, then her reputation - and career - is in ruins.

If she tells me the truth, well, it depends what she says. If she says the truth is Amanda Shepton was not tied up, then that means Stuart Shepton lied to me. And I can't, for one miniscule nanosecond, figure out why on earth he would possibly want to lie about something like that. If the truth is that Amanda was tied up, well, I've had it confirmed from a reliable police source, and I can run it.

I'm pretty sure that this is exactly the kind of thing that's running through Alex's head right now.

Finally, she fixes me with a piercing stare and I have a momentary idea of what it might feel like to be on the receiving end of an Alex Nicholas interrogation.

Then she says softly, "No, I can't."

"Sorry," I say, "I'm not clear. Can't what? Comment…?"

"I can't….," she pauses. One last internal thought process and deliberation; after all, once it's said, it's said. "I can't flat-out deny it."

"Obviously, Mark knows," I say, "and Sam knows. I presume the sister knows. So if I did go ahead and publish this, there's no outstanding family member who could be distraught because they are learning about it through the media rather than from the police. And since you've already openly declared it a murder enquiry, this fact merely reinforces why you've done that."

She squirms in her seat a little. "It's not like printing this would compromise an active line of investigation, is it? I'm not speculating on the cause of death, or trying to establish if a weapon was used and if so what type? Merely that she was tied up."

"I can't flat-out deny it," she mumbles.

I feel sorry for her. I know she is going to relay this conversation to her boss some time soon, and it's going to be very uncomfortable for her. But I've got something to help with that.

"Thanks Alex," I say, raising my glass.

She gives me a resigned smile.

I put my glass down loudly, look her directly in the eye, and say, "Does the name Pieter Eliasson mean anything to you?"

She shakes her head. "Should it?"

"It will," I say, and, although I hate to admit it, I'm quite enjoying this little moment, this rare 'I am ahead of you for once' situation, this 'I know something you don't know' position that I'm in, thanks to Stuart Shepton.

"Presumably we're getting to the bit that you said I will want to hear," she says, hopefully.

I nod. "Sam Shepton told me about him, and earlier this evening, I door-stepped him at his home on the Wellington estate."

"Who is he?"

"Well, right now, he's a nobody," I say, doing my best to prolong my little moment.

Alex takes the bait. "OK then, who *was* he?"

"Well, until very recently, he was Amanda Shepton's toyboy. Her lover. And if you think Mark has a chip on his shoulder when it comes to his mother, that chip is the size of a one-man rowing boat compared to the Titanic-size chip Pieter has."

Alex pulls out her own, police-issue, notepad and begins to write, as I tell her everything Pieter told me during the hour or so I shared with him earlier. A very bizarre, uncomfortable hour, in which I witnessed a flood of tears and the wailing of a love-struck broken heart, to a fury and rage which, quite frankly, scared me a little. I even saw some pictures of the two of them together.

"Why are you telling me this?" Alex asks, when I finish. "Why are you giving this to me, rather than talking to the tabloids?"

"Because it's the right thing to do," I say. "Because I'm pretty sure that Pieter Eliasson killed Amanda Shepton. It's a classic crime of passion; she broke his heart. He couldn't have her, so the only comfort he could take was to ensure that no one else could have her, either."

"We're going to need to look into this," she says. "I, well, it would be the 'right thing' if you don't print anything about this just yet. Give us time to see how credible a suspect he really is."

I nod. "Fair enough; just make sure that, if it does pan out, I get some kind of exclusive."

"If this turns into anything substantial, you'll have earned it," she says.

I'm pleased. It's a classic, mutually-satisfactory 'you scratch my back, I'll scratch yours' scenario.

Alex takes another deep drink.

"So," she says. "How are things going with your little reporter friend?"

"Eh?"

"Oh, you can't fool me. I saw those gooey eyes you were making at her during the press conference."

"You mean Kat?" I say, somewhat thrown.

Alex nods. "How is she? Not too shaken up, I hope."

"Shaken? Why should she be? Alex? What are you talking about?"

"Oh," she says, "the two of you looked pretty cosy at the press conference, I assumed you'd have known."

"Known what?" My heart is starting to race, and Alex is looking at me with the same expression I was looking at her with a short while ago, that 'I know something you don't know' look.

"Well," she says, "since we're in the mood for sharing, and since you clearly care about her, because it's written all over your face, you should probably know that she was threatened by Mark Shepton tonight."

"What? When? Where?"

"The rugby club. I don't think she expected Mark to be there."

"The stupid cow," is all I can say. "Is she alright? Did he hurt her?"

"She's fine," Alex says. "Just shaken. But it apparently took six men to hold Mark back."

"Bloody hell!" I say. I'm already on my feet, pulling on my coat. Kat will either be at home or, knowing her, as it's a Wednesday night, she'll still be at the Herald's office. "Did he touch her? Did he…?"

"Her? No. The Herald's photographer wasn't quite so lucky, though. He's currently at the general, being treated for a broken nose."

"Shit!!!"

Momentarily, the journalist in me rises to the fore again. "Has Mark been arrested?"

"Not yet," says Alex. "We need to take a statement from the photographer first. Uniform are dealing with it."

"I, uh, I've got to go," I say.

"I know," she says, as she stands and pulls on her coat.

I fumble for my phone. I'm going to call Patrick, I think, rather than Kat. She hasn't exactly been responsive to me since the papers came out yesterday, so I think it would be a better move for me to use Patrick as a peacekeeper.

Alex and I step out of our booth, and I'm very distracted, still trying to grab my phone from my pocket, so I don't realise that someone has left the adjoining booth until I bump into him, with such force that my phone clatters to the floor.

I retrieve it, rise, and turn towards the man, ready to apologise.

"Mr Barton," he says impassively. "Imagine, finding a journalist staggering around inside a pub."

Warren James flashes me one of his trademark sinister smiles and steps aside, revealing a shorter, stocky man standing behind him with, if anything, an even more sinister sneer etched on his face.

"Well, well," says the man, "if the devil could cast his net."

"Sergeant Fawcett," says Alex, formally polite, but I can sense the uncomfortable tension between them.

"*Acting* Inspector Nicholas," says the man. "Well, now, if these walls had ears, what secrets would they tell?"

Twenty Five: Alex

I curse my wretched luck. I know Dan chose what he thought was a pretty safe place for us to meet.

I should have known that it was just the sort of dark and dingy backstreet dump that the likes of Tam and Warren James would feel right at home in.

"Not leaving on my account, I hope?" says Tam.

"Not at all," I say, attempting but, I fear, sadly failing, to appear composed. "I'm about to call the boss."

"Aye," nods Tam. "Probably a good idea. Walls do have ears you know. Probably best he hears directly from you first. You know how quickly rumours can run around this tiny little town of ours. Well, don't let me keep you. See you tomorrow."

With that, Tam strides out of the bar, with Warren lurching behind him.

"Who was that?" asks Dan.

"Tam Fawcett. A thorn in my bloody side. A DS. He's got a bee in his bonnet because I got the deputy SIO gig over him."

"I got the impression he isn't your number one fan," I say.

"That's not like you," I say, "understating things. Usually you hacks are blowing things out of all proportion, but that has to be the understatement of the year. I've got to go. I need to get to the boss before Tam does."

Dan nods. "Yeah. I need to call Kat."

We go our separate ways.

I pull out my phone and call Simon. "Are you still at the nick, boss?"

"I was about to leave," he says. "Why?"

"Hold fire, I'll be there in ten minutes. I've got a new lead," I say. If Simon knows that I've been spotted 'fraternising' with the enemy, he doesn't let on in anyway.

"I'll put the kettle on," he says.

The incident room is dark when I get there. The only illumination is the faint glow of artificial light radiating from Simon's office.

"I thought you were long gone for the night," he says.

"No rest for the wicked," I reply.

"I don't have you pegged as the wicked type," he says. Oh please! What I definitely do not want right now is to have the boss start flirting with me. Or am I being over-sensitive? Over-anxious? I've got the jitters, that's for sure.

"So, what's going on?" he asks.

"Boy, where to start," I say.

"That good, eh?"

I smile. "OK, the easy part. Uniform are looking into an allegation of assault; the Herald sent a reporter and photographer to the rugby club tonight, apparently to talk about preparations for the new season."

"And?"

"And Mark Shepton lost his temper and broke the photographer's nose."

Simon raises an eyebrow.

"The photographer is in hospital and hasn't made a statement yet, but I suspect Mark will be arrested for that. There were plenty of witnesses."

"I see. I guess we'll just have to keep an eye on that. Are *we* any closer to being able to arrest him?"

I shake my head. "No. We're still looking into his alibi but at the moment we can't corroborate it, or disprove it. I can't believe there's no CCTV."

"Maybe we should widen the search. Maybe they didn't go to any of the bigger bars. We're going to need to ask at *all* the bars in and around the town centre."

"I'll get onto it tomorrow," I say. "Boss, I met Dan Barton for a drink tonight. You know, the journalist."

Simon turns from his computer screen, telling me that I now have his full, divided attention. He smiles, "Correct me if I'm wrong, but it wouldn't be the first time, would it? And while I don't need to remind you of the potential issues of talking to a journalist, how you choose to spend your personal time, and who you choose to spend it with, is not really any of business. Although, of course, if I *did* have any say in the matter, I'd much prefer you not to be socialising with a journalist."

"It wasn't personal, it was professional," I say. "But, er, as it happened, we were seen by DS Fawcett and Warren James."

Simon nods. "Ah, so you thought you'd confess your sins and beat Tam to the punch, eh? Look, I know you two don't get on, but I'm not particularly interested in whatever beef you two have with each other."

"I want to be honest with you," I say, "and knowing Tam, he will try to make a big deal of it, make it into something it's not."

"Well, Alex, I appreciate your honesty. Even if your motive is a little misplaced; you're only telling me now because you don't want Tam to beat you to it. But I really don't have time to waste on the internal squabbles between two members of my team."

"It's not that," I say. "It was truly a professional meeting. Dan told me he has spoken to Stuart Shepton, which is more than we've managed to do. Seems he is a deep-rooted distrust of the police."

I then tell Simon that Dan knows that we interviewed Mark Shepton yesterday, as, indeed, does the Herald. I also told him Dan knew about Amanda being tied up and that, when push came to shove, I wasn't in the position to deny it.

"I was in an impossible situation, boss," I say.

"Sounds like you handled it as best you could. Dan's right, this would've come out sooner rather than later. In some ways, it's a relief. I won't have to face any more 'why are you so sure it's murder' questions."

He suddenly looks panicked. "D-did Dan say anything about the tongue? Either the line in the suicide note or, or…"

I shake my head, and Simon's relief is also obvious.

I'm relieved, too. I feared Simon might give me a bollocking for meeting Dan and confirming that Amanda had been tied up. But the boss is renowned for being fair, and I honestly don't think I could've played things any other way with Dan.

"So, enough of the small talk. What's this new lead you mentioned on the phone?"

"Pieter Eliasson," I say. "Amanda's former toyboy, who appears to have been very unhappy that she didn't want to continue their relationship after Sam Shepton died."

"Bloody hell!" says Simon. "Is it credible?"

"My money's still on Mark, to be honest," I say. "But I don't think we can afford *not* to check this out. It seems he's been bottling up his emotions and when Dan pressed him, the floodgates opened. He's an emotional mess."

"It certainly paints a very different picture of Amanda Shepton. Did her husband know about her affair? Was Pieter her only toyboy? Or were there others? Was *this* what pushed Sam Shepton over the edge?"

"I'm thinking that this is what pushed *Mark* over the edge," I say. "I think he knew, and this was just one step too far."

Simon considers this. "It's possible. We're going to need to ask him, I guess. But we should probably speak to Pieter first."

"I've got an address," I say.

"The boy Barton really did come good," Simon says. "Are you sure his interest in meeting you was purely personal?"

"Positive, boss. He's completely smitten with the reporter from the Herald that he was sat next to at the press conference."

"Ah," says Simon, who switches off his computer.

"Are we done, boss?"

"Not yet," he says. "Come on, I think we should pay Pieter a visit."

"Really? Now?"

"Let's strike while the iron is hot, shall we?"

"Don't we need a warrant?"

"From what you've said, he was more than happy to have Dan's shoulder to cry on. Somehow, I don't think we're going to need a warrant. I'll radio the community team on our way out, we may need some back-up, depending on how it goes."

I follow Simon into the elevator. We leave the building through the back door which leads to the small staff car park.

I wonder if, perhaps, it's a bit too late to go knocking on doors. It's nearly ten-thirty, after all.

But Simon is very determined. I can tell that he's been hoping we'll get a decent break in this case sooner or later. While I'm not anywhere near as convinced as Dan that this Pieter chap is Amanda's killer, if Dan is right and this Pieter guy was sleeping with Amanda, then Mark's grudge against his mother suddenly seems a whole lot bigger.

We pull up outside the house. There's a dim light on behind the curtains across the biggest window at the front, which I assume is the lounge. There is a brighter light on in one of the upper floor windows.

Simon marches purposefully along the path to the front door. I have to practically skip a few steps behind him in order to keep up.

He thumps the door with an authoritative knock.

For a while, we wonder if anyone is going to answer. Simon is about to rap on the door when we see a crack of light in the hall as an inner door from the lounge opens and a stooped figure slowly shuffles towards the front door.

There's the sound of hands fumbling with a security chain, and then the front door opens.

"Yes? Yes? Who's calling here at this time of night?"

Simon and I exchange glances. Dan had told us that Pieter lives with his grandmother.

"Sorry to trouble you so late, ma'am," says Simon. "I'm Detective Chief Inspector Fisher. This is Acting Detective Inspector Nicholas. We need to have a word with Pieter, if we can."

"Not without any ID, you don't," she snaps.

"Quite right, too," says Simon, a wry smile on his face. He pulls out his ID card.

"Oh! Oh my goodness. Hang on, please. Hang on."

She shuffles across the floor to the bottom of the stairs. "Pieter? Pieter! PIETER! Come down, please. There are a couple of police officers here who want to speak to you."

There's another voice. "What's that, Gran?"

"Come here, Pieter. There are two police officers here."

She tuts, and then returns to the front door. "Goodness me, where are my manners," she says. She fumbles with the security chain, releases it, and opens the door. "Please, please, come in."

We step into the hall.

She looks a little flustered. "Oh, where on earth is that boy? Pieter! PIETER!!!"

"May I go upstairs?" Simon asks.

"What? Oh well, I suppose so. If the mountain won't come to Muhammad, then Muhammad must go to the mountain."

"Thank you ma'am," says Simon, who pauses. "Er, which room is he in?"

"Do a one-eighty at the top of the stairs, and it's the door right in front of you. Bedroom at the front, right above our heads."

Simon strides up the stairs in twos.

"May I get you a cup of tea?" the old lady asks.

I hear heavy footsteps walking across the floor above.

"Alex! Call for support. He's done a runner!"

The elderly woman looks confused. I pull out my mobile, press one of my quick-dial buttons and get through to the Headquarters control room.

"Why don't you go and sit in the lounge?" I suggest to the woman, who nods. I make sure she's settled and then I go upstairs. I find Simon in a bedroom at the back of the house. The window is wide open.

Simon has a torch in his hand and is shining it out of the window.

"He's jumped out of the window. It looks like he put his foot through the conservatory roof," he says. "I'd say that suggests something of a guilty conscience, wouldn't you?"

The sound of sirens fills the air. "I'm going to take a look out back," says Simon. "Since we're here, why don't you take look around his room at the front?"

I nod.

There are three main rooms upstairs, plus a bathroom and toilet, which are next to each other at the top of the stairs. Simon is in the back bedroom. The master bedroom is at the front and next to it, above the hallway, is the smallest of the three rooms.

It turns out that Pieter's bedroom is the room Simon is in. The box room is a study or home office. It's dominated by a desk with a large computer screen on it.

The computer is still on, and there's a half empty cup of tea next to the keyboard. The liquid is still warm. Peter definitely left in a hurry.

I move the mouse to wake the screen up.

The website for the Herald is now in front of me. Simon was reading Kat Russell's first report into the murder of Amanda Shepton.

I look at the wall opposite the computer desk. There's a floor-to-ceiling shelf unit, laden with books, boxes, DVD cases and, propped up against them on every shelf, photographs. I recognise Amanda straight away. I assume that the other person in the photo is Pieter.

He looks young; I'd say mid-twenties at the most.

Most of the pictures of them were taken indoors; sitting together on a sofa or at what looks like a patio table. All the photos show just the two of them. There are no pictures of them that appear to be taken in a public place, or at least, where there are other people around.

In some of the photos, they have their arms around each other.

I note that a picture on the third shelf is a duplicate of one lower down, so I take it and slip it into the inner pocket of my coat.

I'm momentarily distracted by the flicker of blue flashing lights from the street outside, and the sound of multiple voices. I hear one voice ask if there are any dogs available. Someone orders someone else to enquire about the helicopter.

I turn back towards the computer desk. There's a small unit under one side of it, which contains three drawers. They're lockable, but the key is still in the lock. Pieter definitely left this room in a hurry.

The top drawer doesn't have much in it. Some pens, a couple of USB drives, a stapler, some sticky tape, nothing of any interest.

I open the second, slightly larger, drawer.

There's only one thing in this drawer, a large book.

I open it and start flicking through the pages. I then turn to the back and start flipping through it in reverse, my heart-rate increasing with every page I open.

Pieter kept a diary. And I've just found it.

Twenty Six: Kat

"Don't you have a home to go to?" says Patrick.

This is definitely the latest I have ever been in the office. But then, the evening was somewhat disrupted earlier, so I've stayed on to help Patrick with some last-minute copy-writing and proof-reading.

I've amended my report on Amanda's murder for the front page, but it won't get signed off until the very last minute tomorrow, in case something else develops.

We're a weekly paper and yes, we've got a website and our own social media channels, so we can update stories around the clock.

But, like many local weekly papers, the bulk of our readership is in the older age bracket, and some of them don't use social media or the internet for news, they rely on their weekly paper, and that's why I want to make sure that whatever appears on the streets on Friday morning is the most up-to-date account of what has happened this week.

"I could ask you the same thing," I say.

"Oh, Mrs Harding accepted many years ago that there are three in our marriage; her, me and the Herald," he says.

"Any children?" I ask.

"Just the Herald," he says. "That's my baby."

Patrick briefly popped out earlier and returned with two bags of chips from a takeaway just down the road, which didn't touch the sides.

He also took a phone call from Tony, who was now at home. Tony said he had every intention of making a full statement to the police about the assault on him, but had no particular desire to see it featured in this week's paper.

I'm just wrapping up when he takes another call in his office.

He stands up and sheepishly approaches me.

"That was Dan Barton," he says.

"Oh?" I say, trying to look disinterested.

"He's at the back door. He heard about what happened at the rugby club and is asking after you. Should I let him in?"

I shrug my shoulders. "You're the boss."

He smiles and leaves the room.

I'm tired. I'm really not sure I want to have a showdown with Dan right now. Yet, I kinda *do* want to see him, too.

Patrick appears at the door, with Dan lurking sheepishly behind him. "Look what the cat dragged in," says Patrick.

"Hey, Kat," Dan says.

"Dan."

"I heard about what happened? Are you OK?"

I nod. "If it's a welfare call you're making, I'll give you Tony's address. He's the one with the broken nose."

"I'm sorry to hear that, but to be honest, I'm not particularly concerned about Tony."

I should be angry at him. I want to be angry at him. But I'm not. It's good to see him.

Patrick looks at us with a knowing look in his eye. "If you two don't get out of here pretty sharpish, I'll give you some work to do, Dan."

"Actually," he says, "I may have a little bit of work for *you* to do."

He then turns to me. "Kat, look, about Tuesday, the tabloids."

I cross my arms.

"I had no idea they'd go to town with the story. I really didn't. But all the same, it wasn't from you. Tom Davey told me everything. I got it all from him. I've known Tom for years. OK, I guess I'd probably never have heard about it in the first place if you hadn't mentioned it. But I swear, if I couldn't get it confirmed from a different source, I'd never have filed that copy. I'm sorry."

"It's done," I say. "But, for the record, apology accepted."

"Have you gone to press yet? I presume not."

I glance at Patrick who gives a slight shrug of his shoulders, as if to say, 'let's see where this goes'.

"Most of the paper's done," I say. "But we're not signing off the front page lead until tomorrow."

"Just to show there are no hard feelings, I want to share something with you," he says. There's a pleading in his eyes. Part of me doesn't want to forgive him for what happened, but part of me can't help myself. And here he is, not only checking on my welfare, but apparently willing to make amends. "I'm not going to give this to anyone until tomorrow night. That means that whatever I give to the tabloids for their next story will hit the streets at the same time as the Herald."

"OK," I nod. "What've you got, and what do you want in return?"

He visibly relaxes. "I'll settle for us being friends again, that OK?"

"Done. So come on, don't keep me in suspense," I say.

"I spoke to Stuart Shepton, Mark's uncle. He seems to think the police are fixated on Mark as the murderer."

"I can't possibly imagine why," I say.

"No, but listen. He told me Mark was interviewed by the police yesterday; not arrested, but he was questioned for a few hours."

"I know," I say, and I do my best to hit Dan with an expression that says I'm not particularly impressed. I glance at Patrick.

Dan smiles. "Yeah, of course you'd know that."

Patrick feigns innocence and retreats to his room.

"Did you know that Amanda Shepton was tied up? That's how she was found. That's why the police could be certain it was murder, even before they got the PM results?"

"No, I didn't know," I say, turning away briefly because I don't want Dan to know that he has now well and truly got my attention.

"Police confirmed it. Of course, you don't have to take my word for it. Check with them."

I close my eyes, and try to picture the scene. Poor Amanda! Tied up and killed in her own home.

"There's more," says Dan.

"Well, I should hope so," I say. "That's only about one extra sentence you've given me so far."

He hesitates, as if trying to make his mind up whether to tell me or not. After all, we're rivals. Or *are* we? I suspect the Herald has a very different audience demographic to most of the tabloids.

"To be honest, I doubt Patrick will run anything on it," says Dan. "But at least if I let you have it, you'll know I'm being upfront and not hiding anything from you."

"Go on," I say. I can feel a rising buzz of excitement.

"Stuart Shepton told me Amanda had a young lover. I tracked him down earlier and the guy broke down. He's in pieces."

"Wow," I say. "I can't believe it! Amanda was unfaithful? I - I don't know what to say. Wow."

"I've told the police," Dan says. "I felt I had to, really. So they know. If you make some sort of enquiry tomorrow, in terms of new leads or possible suspects, they might confirm it. And again, you'll get it in time for Friday's paper."

My mind is reeling, as Dan gives me the name and address of Amanda's apparent toyboy, and about how he was broken-hearted that she wouldn't continue their affair after her husband died.

What did the Mayoress tell me? "There can be a big difference between someone's public profile, and their private life." No shit!

"Anyway, look, I've got to go. It's been a long day and all that. And besides, I've given you all my new lines, so I'm going to have to try and come up with something else tomorrow."

I'm a little sad that he's leaving, but I'm also pleased. I was worried we might have an awkward moment of exiting the office together, at which point I'm sure he'd offer to walk me to my car, and we've been *there* before. I may have forgiven him for the whole 'black widow' thing, but I haven't forgiven him quite that much. Yet.

"Oh," I say. "OK."

"I think the police might be having another press conference on Friday," he says. "If I don't see you beforehand, see you there?"

"Sure."

He shouts out to Patrick. "Nice to see you, Pat. I'm outta here."

"You know the way," says Patrick.

Dan walks towards the door and turns. "Kat, one more thing."

"Yes?" I say, half-expecting an invitation for a drink or something.

"Promise me you'll keep away from Mark Shepton. He may not be a killer, but you're not exactly top of his Christmas card list."

"I'll try, but I can't make *any* promises," I say. "I'll go where the story takes me. The lover is an interesting new line, but my money's still on Mark being the killer. And I'm going to bloody well prove it."

Dan smiles and leaves the office.

"Told you," says Patrick, who startles me as I hadn't heard him come out of his office.

"Told me what?"

"He likes you. And I can see you like him. Do I need to start saving for a new hat?"

"Not yet, sir," I say, as my cheeks start to burn.

"Come on. I think our work here is done. I may not be a young suitor, but as I'm the only candidate left, let me walk you to your car."

"Sure," I say. The car park isn't too far from the back door of the office, but now that I come to think of it, I don't particularly want to make that short walk by myself.

As we head down the stairs, my phone rings. I recognise the number; Sergeant Davey. We'd exchanged numbers after he stepped in to protect me from Mark at the inquest. Patrick and Dan are always telling me that a good journalist is about making contacts. Tom and I swapped numbers and I told him I'd be very grateful if he could tip me off about anything that might be of interest. His expression suggested his definition of 'grateful' might be a world away from mine; but if it got me a tip-off or two, that was all part of this game, wasn't it?

Of course, the most likely scenario was he had heard about my most recent run-in with Mark, and might be making a welfare call.

"Sergeant Davey, hi," I say.

"Hi Kate," he says.

"It's Kat," I say politely.

"Sorry," he says, a little flustered. "Kat. I'm calling because you asked me to tip you off about anything interesting, particularly if it was close to the time the Herald goes to print."

My heart starts beating faster. Not a welfare call, a tip-off! And at this time of night, it is likely to be something quite interesting.

"I remember," I say, "what have you got?"

"I've just been asked to pull together as many officers as I can for a search for someone we wanted to talk to tonight, but who did a runner. Actually, he jumped out of a bedroom window."

"OK," I say. "What did you want to speak to him about?"

"It hasn't been confirmed," he says, "but the call came from Acting DI Nicholas, on behalf of DCI Fisher, so it's a fair assumption that it's in connection with the Amanda Shepton case. We've got some dogs coming down, and also the police helicopter. I presume this is the kind of thing you want to be tipped off about?"

"Bloody hell, yes," I say. "Where is it?"

"Wellington Way," he says, and I almost drop my phone.

That's where Dan told me the toyboy lives!

Twenty Seven: Dan

It's been a long day, but definitely a case of 'never a dull moment'.

My boss will be furious if he finds out I gave the toyboy line to the Herald, but in all honesty, it was a means to an end.

I don't think for one minute it's the kind of story the Herald will run, at least, not yet. But if it turns out that Pieter *is* the killer, then at least they've got enough information now to be forewarned and to put together a background case which can be used if he comes to court.

I'm sure they can use the line about Amanda being tied up. It might be a little 'sensationalist' for the Herald, but it *does* provide some clarity over the whole 'we know it's murder but we aren't explaining why' confusion; and all the family already know.

While the job of weekly papers like the Herald is not to provide shock stories for the sake of it, it does pride itself on informing its readers about newsworthy items, and there's no doubt that this murder is the talk of the town.

My parents haven't stopped talking about it since I returned to sleeping in my old room for the foreseeable, and just about everywhere you go, there are people gossiping and speculating.

But more significantly, me telling Kat everything I learned from Stuart Shepton has seen me get back into her good books, hopefully.

I send Patrick a text, thanking him for letting me visit Kat tonight, and he replies almost immediately. *Just make sure you don't upset my staff*, complete with a smiley face emoji.

It's not *me* upsetting Kat that he needs to worry about, it's Mark. The truth is, after those tabloid headlines, I was worried that Mark might assume she was responsible for it and I made my mind up earlier today - when I became convinced that it wasn't Mark who killed Amanda, it was Pieter - that I would contact Mark and confess that I supplied the story to the tabloids.

But after hearing about what Mark did to Tony, I'm keeping my mouth shut and making sure I steer well clear of Mark myself.

I only hope that Kat has the common sense to do the same. Whether he's a killer or not, he's definitely a loose cannon with an extremely short fuse, and a firm fist.

I get home and fire up my laptop to type out my next story. I will be good to my word. I'm not going to file it tonight, I don't want any of the papers to use it tomorrow. I want to ensure the next national update hits the streets the same day as the Herald.

I think about Alex, too. Not in the same way as I think about Kat, of course. But I feel sorry for her; I know she has worked hard for her promotion but as well as ensuring she proves herself worthy of that, she has to contend with morons like this Tam bloke.

What an arrogant ass.

However, seeing Tam tonight has given me another moral dilemma; not so much because of who he is, as who he seems to keep close company with.

Tam and Warren James looked as if they were as 'thick as thieves'; I used the phrase deliberately.

I don't want to upset Alex; I know our exchange of information tonight is further than I would ever have expected her to go. I can't imagine, for one moment, that I'd be able to push her any further.

But the fact that Tam seems to think she got promoted ahead of him means he has an axe to grind with her, and I confess that my inner journalist is currently screaming at me to take advantage of that.

I consider myself a fairly good judge of character; it's a useful trait in my business. I believed Stuart Shepton's tip about Pieter as something genuine, rather than an attempt to divert me from Mark, and after chatting to Pieter, that proved true.

While I've only met Tam briefly, his whole manner, added to what Alex told me, suggests that he wouldn't hesitate to stick the knife into her back if the chance arose; I think he would be more than willing to bend the rules if it meant there was the possibility of undermining her.

So I wonder; if Tam *is* as thick as thieves with Warren, how hard would it be for me to persuade Tam to find out, if he doesn't know already, what Sam Shepton wrote in his suicide note. I have a hunch that Sam didn't necessarily pull any punches in his parting shot.

Of course, now that I know about Pieter, the real cash cow will be if Sam Shepton's suicide note mentions his wife's infidelity. That could be good enough to not only get me back into the nationals, but could get me back onto the front pages.

I'd be curious to speak to Pieter again, although if my judgement of character is anywhere near as good as I think it is, I'd put money on Alex not going home after we left the pub but going straight back to base and telling her boss.

So perhaps the update will be 'Shepton killer arrested after journalist tells police about her toyboy lover,' or something like that.

My big concern is Alex; if I find out from Tam what is in the suicide note, will it compromise her in any way? I hope not. Besides, while I know journalists are traditionally proud of protecting their sources, I don't think I'd need to be pressured too much into dropping Tam's name into the conversation, if it came down to it.

Come to think of it, rather than piss Alex off, I could end up doing her a favour, and getting that moron kicked off the case for leaking information to the media!

My conscience likes that train of thought much better than the idea of dropping Alex in any kind of trouble. My only issue then becomes Warren. Tam would undoubtedly argue that Alex is the media's mole, and that Tam saw Alex with me in the pub, something that would be backed up by Warren.

I've got a lot to think about, to weigh up. But the over-riding feeling I have is an increasingly strong desire to find out what Sam Shepton wrote and, more importantly, did he know about Pieter?

Ah yes, young Pieter. What a turn up for the books that was.

When I hit him with the "Is that because you were sleeping with her?" line, he didn't only freeze, he looked like the proverbial rabbit in the headlights.

Then he exploded, and said, "I'm fucking glad she's dead. She got what she deserved. There. You can quote me on that!"

At that point, I had expected the door to be slammed in my face.

I had actually started walking down the path, but he called me back, which surprised me.

"Don't," he said.

"Don't what?"

"Don't quote me on that."

I could see tears already welling in his eyes.

"I don't want police to think I killed her," he said, softly.

"Did you?" I heard myself say.

The rabbit-in-the-headlights look reappeared. "Do you think I would tell you if I had? Stupid, I might be, but not *that* stupid."

"Off the record then," I said; I had a hunch that this kid was pretty naïve, as well as emotional, which also means not thinking clearly.

"OK, off the record. I did love her. I loved her like crazy. And I thought she loved me to. There's a fine line between love and hate, mister."

"Sounds like you want to talk about it."

He looked at me as if I was mad for a moment. What I saw was a confused, hurt and very frightened young man. I also saw a man who was desperate to talk to someone.

"Part of being a good journalist is being a good listener," I said.

"Off the record?"

"Yeah, off the record."

So he invited me in.

"Pieter, are you alright?" asked his Nan

"Yes, I'm fine Nan. I'm just talking to this journalist for a while. It - it's about the charity."

"Oh, that's nice dear," his nan said. She came out of the lounge, announced that it was past her bedtime anyway, and let us use the front room.

"Does she know?"

"She knows I was seeing someone. And she knows I got hurt. But she doesn't know the details."

We went into the lounge and Pieter opened his heart. He had to pause a few times, because he would sob intermittently. He told me he was twenty-four and had lived with his nan since his parents divorced messily a few years ago, with neither of them apparently wanting any parental responsibilities attached to their new-found freedom.

Two years ago, Pieter went to a nightclub, got separated from his friends, who all paired off one by one as the night wore on, and got picked up by Amanda.

That woman is full of surprises. Prowling around nightclubs at her age? Given her social standing and apparent pride?

According to Pieter, they fell in love, or so he thought, and she told him that her marriage was a sham; she even had her own bedroom.

Pieter confessed to not having had a huge amount of experience with women, but he's pretty sure that most of the 'girls' his friends were preoccupied with were just that; little girls, compared to Amanda, who was, apparently, 'all woman'.

It didn't take long for Pieter to declare his love for Amanda, and to suggest they move in together, or if that wouldn't work for her, then they could elope.

She said she'd think about it. He kept asking, she kept thinking.

When he found out that she spent quite a few hours each week at the offices of the local hospice, he quit his college course and got a job there, just to ensure he could spend more time with her.

All the while, she said her home life was miserable. She barely saw her husband, because he worked all the time, and she was forever arguing with her son.

"Do you know what about?"

"Anything and everything, by the sound of it."

Finally, he said, Amanda confessed she would never leave her husband.

"It was the money," said Pieter. "I couldn't compete with that. She loved the lavish lifestyle her rich husband provided. I live with my Nan."

At this point, Pieter pulled out his wallet and showed me three photos of him with Amanda, which he obviously carried with him everywhere. He started crying then, as he recalled how Amanda then admitted that she did love him, at which point he delivered an ultimatum.

He demanded that she choose between her husband and him.

"She chose the money," he said.

So they split up. He was heartbroken; he lost his job, started drinking heavily, stopped going out, and was inconsolable.

He would frequently loiter round Mountview Rise. That's how he learned about Sam Shepton's death; he saw the funeral cortege.

Pieter contacted Amanda again; he offered his condolences, and he offered himself, assuming that, now she was free from her marriage, but still entitled to the money, that there was now no reason for them not to pick up where they had left off. They could finally be together, officially. No more sneaking around, no more hiding. They could declare their love and become a couple.

But she just laughed at him.

And that destroyed him.

"It was bad enough that she wouldn't take me back," he said. "But she actually laughed at me. Called me a pathetic little love-struck boy. And from that moment on, my love turned to hate."

"I don't blame you," I said.

"I'm not sorry that she's dead," he said. "It's a bit of a comfort, actually."

"A comfort?"

"Yes. It's like, I can't have her anymore, but nobody else can, either. That would have been the hardest thing to take; if I'd have gone out somewhere and seen her with another man. I don't think I could have handled that."

"You really loved her, eh?"

"Yes. And then it turned to hate."

"I hated her more than I thought it was ever possible for one person to hate another," he said.

"Did you hate her enough to kill her?" I asked. Bold, I know. But I'm not really sure this puny little kid would have it in him.

"Off the record?" he said.

I nodded. Then a completely different look came over his face. He suddenly looked much older, much colder, and very sinister, as he said, "If I told you that, I'd have to kill you."

Twenty Eight: Alex

I glance at my phone; it's very nearly midnight. I can't believe I'm still in the office.

Simon stayed at Pieter's house; he wanted to co-ordinate the search from the scene, and also speak in more depth to Pieter's nan, who was clearly quite distressed, and said she had no idea why her grandson ran or what was wrong with him.

She allowed me to bring Pieter's diary with me after I explained it may help us to better understand what was going through his mind.

I've got a police radio on my desk so I can monitor the search. We've got some dogs out and the helicopter, with its thermal imaging camera. I'm not expecting Pieter to be at large for long.

I thumb through the pages of his diary, and it certainly makes me see Amanda Shepton differently; I believe the commonly-used term these days is 'cougar', although she is the last person in this town I would have expected that label to be attributed to.

Pieter describes their first meeting in a nightclub. It was only after she took him home that she told him she was married, but that her husband neglected her needs, and, as happened so often, was away working, leaving her with the prospect of spending the night alone in their king-size bed.

Pieter describes subsequent liaisons in explicit detail. He notes in an account of one of their early liaisons that Amanda had a birthmark in an intimate place, and he his able to describe this in the kind of graphic detail which could only come from seeing it with his own eyes.

Had Amanda ever been in a position where she denied sleeping with Pieter, this level of detail from him is likely to have been sufficient proof to the contrary.

Every Thursday evening was 'ladies night' for Amanda; she and a number of her well-to-do friends would meet, for drinks and gossip, each taking their turn to host the evening while the husband of the house would dutifully oblige by making himself scarce.

It would seem that, within her circle of friends, Amanda was not alone in using this time for drinks, gossip, and a lot more besides, with all of them agreeing to keep other others' secrets, and most of them picking up virile young men from clubs.

I pause. This paints a very different picture of Amanda Shepton than the wealthy wife and dedicated charity worker.

It doesn't take long for Pieter to start describing strong emotional feelings to Amanda. He talks about going to work at the hospice, and the two of them occasionally enjoying illicit encounters in her office there.

I flick through quite a period of time in which Pieter is very happy being given a comprehensive sexual education from his experienced lover.

But then the tone starts to change. He confesses his love for her. She returns the sentiment. He says he doesn't care what people will think and say, he wants to be with her, and begs her to leave her husband, but she refuses.

She tells Pieter that her marriage may lack love in the physical sense, she respects her husband, and does not want to hurt him. And she admits that, if she left her husband for Pieter's bed, she would lose access to the lavish lifestyle that she enjoys. And she was not prepared to do that for Pieter, or anyone.

He speaks of his frustration, distress and, increasingly, anger.

There is no suggestion that Sam Shepton knew about his wife's indiscretion.

But there *is* mention of Mark.

It would appear that, on one occasion when it was Amanda's turn to play the genial host, Mark, who had moved out of the house a few weeks before, made an unexpected visit. While he didn't actually catch Pieter and Amanda in a compromising position, Mark put two and two together, threatened Pieter, and said some "awful things to his mother".

Interesting. So Sam may have been oblivious, but Mark was aware that his mother was cheating on his father, adding, I feel, to Mark's motivation for killing his mother.

And then Sam Shepton died.

And Pieter is delighted. He sees this as the way being paved for his love for Amanda to be 'official'. Amanda is now widowed *and* wealthy; they will no longer have to sneak around, snatching clandestine kisses and snatched moments of passion.

Pieter writes about how he wants to sing from the highest mountain about their love. But Amanda continues to deny him.

And there is definite anger. "She has ruined my life, so I am going to ruin hers", he writes. "I'll show her what a 'silly little boy' I am" and "If I can't have her, I'll make damned sure no one else can have her either. I'll make damned sure she is damned. She has broken my heart into a million pieces, she has destroyed me. And I'm going to make her suffer for it. I'm going to make her suffer so bad. I don't just want to ruin her reputation, I want to hurt her, really, *really*, hurt her."

Then comes his last entry, written just last Thursday evening.

He followed Amanda to the venue for that weekly social and hammered on the door. He was shown inside and, in his words, "humiliated" by her in front of all her friends. He felt embarrassed and shamed. He was then ordered to leave, and as he pulled the lounge door closed behind him, he heard the ladies start to laugh. And somehow, he knew they were laughing at him.

As he described it, "Amanda had thrust her dagger deep into my back. But as I hear her gossiping about me with her friends, and laughing, she was twisting the blade. I'll make her sorry she made fun of me. Somehow, I'll make them all sorry. The sound of their cruel wagging tongues will give me nightmares for the rest of my life. I swear, somehow, I'll make that heartless witch sorry if it's the last thing I do."

Less than forty eight hours later, Amanda was killed.

I close the diary.

My gut feeling tells me that Mark is still a more likely murderer than Pieter, but I can't ignore the reference to 'cruel wagging tongues', and the manner in which Amanda was killed.

Tam was convinced that the nature of her death suggested a serial killer. While Amanda was clearly Pieter's primary tormentor, is it possible he may also target the other members of her social circle?

I make a note to follow this up in the morning.

We may have to ask Mark for the names of some of the people in that social circle. That's a conversation to look forward to. But then, it could be in his best interests, if it reduces our interest in him.

I don't know. For some people, just writing their thoughts down in a diary, however emotive or extreme they might, is sufficient therapy, expressing their angst can be a relief; a problem shared is a problem halved and all that, even if you're sharing the problem in writing, to yourself, rather than with anyone else.

Does Pieter really have what it takes to kill Amanda?

My radio crackles. It's Simon. They still haven't found Pieter.

Simon thinks the youngster may have taken shelter at a friend's house. The helicopter is picking up plenty of thermal traces of people inside their homes, but no one apparently 'on the run' or hiding in some undergrowth in and around the estate.

Simon tells me he wants to keep the search going for a while and see if Pieter can be flushed out.

He also tells me that Kat Russell from the Herald has turned up on the scene, having been tipped off about police activity in the area.

"What has she been told?" I ask.

"An interesting question," Simon says. "We haven't told her very much at all, but someone has."

"What do you mean?"

"We told her we were engaged in the search for a person of interest but that, with it being a live operation, we were unable to provide any further information, and we suggested she make contact with the press office first thing in the morning."

"Fair enough," I say. "We'll have to brief the press office. The Herald goes to press tomorrow, so she will be in touch quite early."

"I'm sure she will. There were plenty of police cars in the area, but she was specifically interested in Pieter Eliasson's home. She asked an officer near the house if he could confirm that the search was connected to the Amanda Shepton murder enquiry, and then asked if we could confirm that this was the home of someone suspected of being Amanda's lover, so she's getting her information from someone."

I was shocked.

"Tell me," says Simon. "Your 'friend', Danny Barton. You said he was quite smitten with Miss Russell. Do you think he is smitten enough to be sharing information with her?"

"Either that, or she has spoken to Stuart Shepton as well," I say.

"It seems Stuart is happy to talk to anyone except us," says Simon. "And that's something we're going to need to rectify. We may need to make a personal visit. We do need to keep a tight lid on this."

"OK, boss." There was something in the tone of his voice that made me feel a little uncomfortable. Was he suggesting that he thought I might have told Kat? I hope not.

Still, it does pose an interesting question. If Dan *didn't* tell her, do we have a leak? Because that's the last thing we need.

If he is worried about me getting too 'close' to any journalists, I hope he will pause for a moment and remember that if I had not met Dan, we wouldn't know anything at all about Pieter Eliasson.

"I'll probably be late in tomorrow," Simon says, shaking me from my thoughts. "It depends how long this search takes. If so, can you add something else to you 'to do' list. I want you to chase up the national forensic lab, see if they've been able to look at Amanda's tongue."

I involuntarily shudder at the mere mention of it.

"Are you waiting for anything in particular?"

Yes," he says. "I need to know if they've found any evidence that suggests how her tongue was removed; did the killer rip it out or did he use something else to remove it."

"Something else?"

"Yes," he says. "Pieter's nan let me have a good look around his room. After you found the diary, you didn't check the final drawer, but I did."

"Oh? What did you find?"

"An extremely sharp knife."

Twenty Nine: Kat

Ever since I developed an interest in journalism, when I was very young, I've dreamed of yelling the legend, "Hold the front page!"

Now that the opportunity has presented itself, it's more of a nightmare than a dream.

I came to work early, to update my copy for the front-page lead. In addition to reporting that Mark had been questioned and Amanda tied up, I wanted to add something about last night's activity.

I didn't think Patrick would use the line about Amanda possibly having a lover but I was prepared to fight for the inclusion of a line that police were searching the Wellington estate for a 'person of interest'. I don't like using police jargon, but on this occasion it would imply that this was a direct quote from the police, a more reliable source than gossip between neighbours or a rumour from social media.

I actually wanted to add "a police source confirmed the search was connected with the murder of Amanda Shepton" since it isn't speculation, it's a fact, but I don't want to cause any problems for Sergeant Davey. A good journalist protects their sources.

Patrick also arrived some time before nine, keen to review my copy as soon as I wrote it.

All was going well until Alex Nicholas called just after nine.

"Is that Kat?" she said.

"Yes." It crossed my mind that, having never actually spoken to her directly before, she called me 'Kat'. Did this mean Dan had spoken to her about me? I wonder what he said.

"I know the Herald goes to press today and I wanted to ensure you had the latest information. Half-an-hour ago, we arrested the man we were looking for on the Wellington estate last night, on suspicion of assaulting a police officer and causing criminal damage."

"Criminal damage?"

"Yes, he allegedly smashed the window of a police car. He was quite agitated and determined not to come quietly."

She paused, and then said, "He's also been arrested on suspicion of the murder of Amanda Shepton."

"Wow!" I said. "Thanks for letting me know, I appreciate it."

Actually, that wasn't true; it meant I had to completely re-write my story, as proceedings are 'active', so we're very limited in what we can report for fear of being accused of prejudicing any potential trial.

"May I ask," she said, "how you found out about the search last night? You arrived so quickly. Do you live nearby?"

"We had a tip-off about police activity which might be linked to Amanda's murder."

"I see," she says. "Can you tell me *who* tipped you off? It could be someone we may be interested in talking to."

"No," I lied, "It was an anonymous tip-off, saying there was lots of police activity, and she thought it must be to do with the murder."

"I see. Well, I won't keep you. You'll need to update your story."

I hung up, rose from my chair, turned towards Patrick's office and yelled, "Hold the front page!"

I tell Patrick everything Alex told me.

"We have to play this straight," he says. "We'll still run the two-page tribute to Amanda, but we need to re-write the murder report. We can't mention she was tied up or name Pieter, unless he's charged, and can't suggest he may have been Amanda's lover."

"I know," I sigh heavily. I know what's coming next.

"We'll still run it on the front," he says, "but it'll be a side column. We can't really say enough to make it fill the space of the lead."

"Have you got anything to replace it with?" I ask.

"I'm not sure," he says, pensively. "I'll worry about that, you worry about a new version of your story, concise and factual."

"On it," I say.

"And Kat, well done."

"Sorry?"

"You got the tip-off last night, you've got some nice photos of the police in Wellington Way. If it turns out that Pieter *is* the killer, we've got some nice stuff we can use when the time is right, that no one else has got. Well done. Contact building is what it's all about."

My disappointment at losing the front-page lead has been compensated for a little by a growing sense of pride. I think back to the little pep-talk I gave myself on Monday morning and smile as I start typing a new story. Yes, I *have* got this.

Ross saunters in, around ten minutes late as usual, and is immediately summoned into Patrick's office. Seconds later, he's at his desk, collecting a pile of papers, and then returns to Patrick.

He emerges nearly forty minutes later and punches the air triumphantly. "Yessss!" he says, "front-page lead *and* an 'exclusive' tag on my byline."

"Congratulations," I say.

"Thanks, Kat," he beams. "Sorry you lost the lead," he added, in a voice that carries not the slightest hint of genuine sincerity.

"I didn't *lose* it," I say, a little more bitterly than I'd intended. "It's an occupational hazard of ongoing police investigations."

"There's always next week," Ross teases.

"So, what's the big scoop then, Ross?" I say, thinking that if he's going to gloat all day, the most diplomatic thing I can do is show a little interest. He was flying so high on his success, there was no way I was going to win any tit-for-tat verbal exchange right now.

He tells me that he enrolled in an evening class at the local college a few weeks ago, but this was just a 'front'; he was collecting supporting evidence for a story that had to be absolutely watertight before Patrick would even consider using it.

This 'undercover work' as he puts it - I smile at his dramatisation of events - started while I was covering the airport planning enquiry for days on end. The former Deputy Head of the college's Apprenticeships and Business Partnership department, Phillipa Player, visited the Herald to say she'd been forced out of her job, after more than ten years, by Lisa Davidson, who became head of the department five months ago and who has made Phillipa's life a misery from day one.

Phillipa said she could only conclude Lisa felt threatened by her experience and knowledge, and rather than take advantage of her expertise, seemed determined not to build any kind of professional relationship with someone who should have been her right hand.

Instead, she started undermining Phillipa at every opportunity.

Lisa's daughter, Laura, was soon appointed to the team, despite performing poorly during the initial stage of the recruitment process. Phillipa said she would not have put Lisa through to the final interview, with the most senior college staff, but was strong advised by HR that, given who she was, she ought to put Laura through to the next stage.

Phillipa was ordered to line-manage Laura. There were soon issues with the quality of her work and her attitude towards other college staff, resulting in Phillipa receiving repeated complaints, which policy said she should raise with Laura at their regular one-to-one meetings.

Whenever Phillipa did this, Laura ran straight to Lisa like a spoiled, petulant, child. Lisa then accused Phillipa of being unduly harsh and not managing Laura properly.

Finally, Lisa announced a departmental restructure, apparently necessary to achieve budgetary savings, and Phillipa's post was deleted.

She complained to the Board of Governors, accusing Lisa of misconduct and being a bully, but her claims were dismissed

Phillipa told Ross she believed her experience was just the tip of the iceberg, and if someone from the Herald looked into it, they would find a culture of intimidation, bullying and inappropriate practices at the college, emotive words that were like a red rag to a bull.

After compiling his story, Ross did the responsible journalistic thing of seeking a response from the college.

Journalists are trained to ensure that, whenever they cover a story in which one party makes allegations against another, they should be backed up with evidence, rather than being based on one party's word against the other, and that the party the allegations were being made against should be given right of reply, to balance the article.

The college not only refuted the allegations but made counter claims of Phillipa not performing her duties to acceptable standards.

But she had kept, and shared with Ross, her performance reviews from the past decade, which consistently praised her work.

Ross said the principal had telephoned Patrick, saying he presumed the Herald didn't intend to stoop to such gutter-press standards as to touch such a scurrilous story as this, particularly if it wanted to continue to benefit from the college's considerable advertising spend with the paper.

Ross said Patrick didn't take kindly to the principal's patronising tone and veiled threat, presumably intended to intimidate the editor.

Ross tells me that, during his evening classes, he ingratiated himself with some other staff, and gleaned enough information, albeit anecdotally, to support Phillipa's claims.

Phillipa also said she was forced to sign a Non-Disclosure Agreement when she was made redundant, upon pain of having to re-pay any severance money, or, as she described it, 'silence' money.

But she hadn't only lost her job, she lost her relationship after becoming very depressed, and then lost her house, as she couldn't find a new job which paid anything like her college salary.

Phillipa told Ross that, NDA or not, she had nothing left to lose, so turned to the Herald. While her situation isn't likely to change, she felt exposing wrongs at the college may prevent other people from suffering as she had.

My own journalistic instincts tell me this story *should* be told. A key role of a local newspaper is to not only inform its readers, but sometimes to represent them and, where appropriate, to challenge those in authority on their behalf.

Ross says Patrick even took some legal advice this morning before deciding that his story could be used as the replacement page one lead.

Ross smiles. "Patrick said, and I quote, 'if that egotistical principal thinks I'm going to be intimidated by the threat of removing advertising, he's got another thought coming. The threat suggests even more strongly that college *does* have something to hide."

I have to give Ross credit; it sounds like he has done a very thorough job. And the story definitely *should* be printed.

I tell Patrick I have filed the new version of the murder story. It's a lot shorter, but factual, and 'safe'.

"Keep checking with the police press office every half hour or so," he says. "If they were to charge him before two o'clock, we'll just about be able to squeeze that line into the paper. If not, we'll need to update the website in any event."

He looks a little flustered and I ask if he is OK.

"It's been a while since we've had to change things so close to deadline. I need to lose a few stories on page four to accommodate the full story Ross supplied. We're going to be going right down to the wire with this one."

I turn to leave him to it but he calls me back and asks if I feel alright, following my run-in with Mark last night. I tell him I'm fine.

"You had a late one yesterday, so if you want to finish early today, you can. Just brief Mervyn, he can keep an eye on things for you."

"You've had a long week, too," I say. "Are you leaving early?"

"I'm going one better," he says, with a wry smile "I'm taking tomorrow off. I think the college principal will be on the war-path once he sees tomorrow's front page."

"You're not going into hiding, are you?" I tease.

He laughs. "I plan to spend a few hours playing golf, the perfect place to relax after a long week. And it just so happens that some very senior police officers can quite frequently be found at the club some Fridays. I may find out how strong a suspect they think Pieter is. If the college principal does come calling, Mervyn can deal with him. Merv has an incredible way with people; I swear the United Nations should employ him as a peacekeeper; the world would be a much better place if Merv was allowed to flex his diplomatic muscles. He could charm anyone into submission. Well, except Mark Shepton. That one has a foul temper, so please steer clear of him, Kat."

Pieter's arrest will remove suspicion from Mark over Amanda's murder, but *I'm* not convinced. My story still says Mark was questioned; after all, it's an indisputable fact. Of course, I haven't said 'on suspicion of murder', but I haven't said why he was questioned. I've left it vague. How readers choose to interpret the facts is up to them.

Ross is going after one bully with his story; Mark may not be a killer, but he's a bully, too. After what he did to Tony last night, and the way he threatened me, while the police may think they've got their man for the murder, I'm not ready to let Mark off the hook just yet.

Thirty: Dan

"This morning, we arrested a twenty-four-year-old man in connection with the murder of Amanda Shepton. We're going to question him later today. We have a warrant and are conducting a thorough search of his home on the Wellington estate," says Alex.

She then tells me that they had quite a few officers, a couple of dogs and the force helicopter out late last night after the suspect ran away when they tried to speak to him.

I was right, then; Alex went straight back to work last night after I told her about my visit to Pieter.

She apologises for not telling me sooner, and says she told Kat first, because she knew the Herald goes to press today.

"Dan, how much did you tell Kat about the guy in Wellington Way?" she asks.

"Pretty much the same as I told you," I say. "Why?"

"Nothing really. It's just that she turned up at the scene last night quite quickly."

"Last night?"

"Yes, she was there quite soon after we were."

"Damn!" I say. "Look, I just told her pretty much what I told you."

"So you weren't Kats anonymous tipster, then?"

"Alex! If I'd have known there was manhunt going on last night. I'd have been there myself."

"Well, someone has tipped her off. And it's made Simon jumpy."

"I promise you, it wasn't me, Alex."

I think - I hope - she believes me because she then teases me. "It sounds like the girl from the Herald has scooped you."

"I guess so," I say. I'm annoyed that I didn't know about the activity last night. Alex could have told me. Come to that, Kat could have told me. If it wasn't for me, neither of them would know about Pieter at all, yet it seems I'm the last to know about the latest developments.

As for Kat's 'anonymous source', I suspect it's Tom Davey. He co-manages the community beat team, so if he was on duty last night, he'd have been called on to help provide resources for the search.

Ultimately, it doesn't really matter who her source is right now; it doesn't matter much right now that neither Alex nor Kat felt obliged to return a favour and give me some information.

What does matter is that there has now been an arrest, and for that I am grateful.

Just before Alex called me, my boss called and said at least two of the nationals were seriously considering sending their own reporters to town, to follow up on the 'black widow' line and see what other dirt they can uncover.

The fact that an arrest has been made is likely to dissuade them from wasting their own time and resources on something if it looks like the case is already closed, so they'll leave it to me.

"What's your gut feeling?" I ask Alex. "Do you think Pieter's the killer?"

Alex laughs. "Do you honestly expect me to answer that?"

"A little guidance wouldn't go amiss," I say.

"Nice try," she says. "I'm going to be interviewing him shortly, so we'll see what he says. That's assuming he is fit to be interviewed."

"Fit?" I say. "Why do you say that? What happened? Did you guys have to zap him with a Taser or two?"

"No, nothing like that," she says. "He was as high as a kite when we caught up with him this morning. I think he assumed we'd given up the search, so he came out of whatever hidey hole he'd been in and returned to his nan's house just before eight-thirty and we were waiting. He was either extremely drunk, or high; I suspect the latter."

"Interesting," I say.

"And that is very most *definitely* off the record," she says. "I can't believe I just told you that."

"Don't worry," I say, "I can't do much about it while he's under arrest. But I might pop out to the Wellington Estate though. I'll need to put together a background piece on Pieter, in case he does turn out to be our man."

"Who?" Alex teases. "I haven't confirmed the name of any individual, and nor would I at this stage."

"I know you won't talk out of place to the media, but it seems that *someone* is."

"And it definitely wasn't you?"

"It wasn't me. It couldn't have been. I didn't know about the manhunt, did I? Nobody told me." I think the tone of my voice suggested that I feel Alex could have told me, because she then promises to keep me informed of any developments with Pieter.

"Good luck with the interview," I say. "Is there going to be any end-of-week press conference tomorrow, to give us all an update?"

"That very much depends on how the interview goes," she says. "I *will* keep you posted."

"Thanks," I say, and I'm just about to hang up when something else occurs to me. "Oh, one more thing. Mark. Are you going to charge him with assaulting Tony, the Herald's photographer?"

"Not sure yet. Tony hasn't decided if he wants to make a formal complaint. Maybe he's worried Mark and some of his meathead mates might come after him if he does. I'll let you know as soon as I do. We could do with charging that one with something, that's for sure. He's a bloody menace."

"Can I quote you on that?" I laugh.

"Sod off," she says, although I can hear the smirk in her voice.

I phone some copy into my boss and, not surprisingly, he tells me I'm going to need to do some digging and find out as much as I can about Pieter.

I text Kat, to ask how she is after being confronted by Mark again. Her reply is quite curt. *Frustrated.*

Why?

Because I'm getting a bit sick and tired of people pussyfooting around me like I'm some delicate fragile flower. I'm not a little girl.

Sorry I asked.

There was a pause before her next text to me. *Sorry, too. I'm just getting a bit fed up with everyone asking how I am and telling me to be careful. Patrick, Mervyn, Hannah, now you. I am fine.*

Guess you don't want a drink later then to celebrate your front page lead?
I don't have the lead. The arrest put paid to that.

I know when to pick my battles, and this is one that I feel that, the longer I stay in it, the worse the outcome will be for me. I think the most diplomatic move for me is to quit while I'm, well, not ahead, but not yet out of the game. Run away to have a go another day.

While I wait to see if Alex makes good on her promise to keep me posted, I know that the best thing I can do now is head out to the Wellington estate, knock on a few doors and see what I can find out about Pieter.

Thirty One: Alex

Things are moving fast, which is exhilarating and also a relief.

There's nothing worse than a long, drawn-out murder enquiry, where every lead takes you to a dead end.

While I'm a little disappointed that Mark Shepton appears to no longer be our prime suspect, the fact that we've got a strong alternative so quickly is encouraging.

Simon sent the knife he found at Pieter's house to forensics for a full analysis; hopefully some DNA to link Pieter to Amanda.

Another thought occurs to me. Pieter mentioned in his diary that Mark had threatened him. Was it possible that Mark killed Amanda and is trying to set up Pieter? Or is that me clutching at straws because, deep down, I'd love to be able to charge Mark with something.

Simon's gone back to the Wellington estate to oversee the search and talk a little more to Pieter's poor grandmother.

Tam has asked to track down Amanda's friends who belong to the social circle mentioned in Pieter's diary. That book has been useful, but there's always the chance it just contains the wishful fantasies of a deluded young man with one hell of a crush on Amanda rather than a factual account of events. It'd be a huge coincidence if he simply had a fixation on our murder victim, but stranger things have happened. That's why Tam's been tasked with finding those friends, to see if they can confirm that Pieter and Amanda were lovers.

I guess we could talk to Mark about it, too, since Pieter mentioned being threatened by him. Maybe I'll leave *that* to Tam, too. I'm sure he and Mark would enjoy the prospect of going another round with each other.

We've still got a few detectives collecting and studying CCTV from Saturday night, too, although it seems now to be more a case of confirming that Mark is not a suspect than confirming he is.

The particularly good news for me is that Tam's task of finding Amanda's friends means he won't be interviewing Pieter with me.

I'm waiting to be allowed to talk to Pieter. There's no doubt he's under the influence of something, and I'm pretty sure it isn't alcohol. We need him to sober up, or come down, before we can talk to him.

He told us he doesn't have a lawyer. But given the seriousness of the charges he could face, the duty solicitor has been asked to advise him, and is with him now.

The lawyer looks young and is probably used to dealing with burglaries, car crime and cannabis cases. The startled look on his face suggested this is the first time he's been asked to advise a murder suspect, which means he's unlikely to prove too much of an obstacle.

"Told you Mark wasn't our man," says Tam, as he brushes past me on his way out to track down Amanda's friends.

"We don't know anything yet," I counter.

"Bullshit," says Tam. "We've got him. We've already got enough evidence to send him down, and he's a bloody nervous wreck. Getting him to confess under interrogation should be easy, even for you."

"It's going to be a damn-sight easier without you trying to pick a fight with the suspect," I say.

"Just don't fuck it up, Alex. Get the confession," he sneers.

"Don't you have somewhere to go, Detective *Sergeant*?" It's not really my style, but if there's one way to end a verbal spar with Tam that he can't argue with, it's to pull rank. And I'd feel uncomfortable using such tactics with anyone else. But not Tam.

He snaps his heels together and performs an extremely over-exaggerated salute. "Yes, ma'am!" he says, and stomps away.

I phone Kat and then Dan, to tell them about the arrest.

I knew the Herald went to press today, so wanted to make sure they had the update early; I know it will mean a re-write of the story, and it's always nice to try and keep the local newspaper on-side. If this investigation becomes prolonged, and the public start to turn against the police, accusing us of incompetence for not solving the crime quickly enough, we may need at least one media outlet with us.

I wanted to tell Dan, too, because the truth is we may not have become aware of Pieter for some time, if at all, if he hadn't told us. So I wanted him to hear the update from me, rather than the press office.

My next call is to the press office, to tell them to issue a formal statement about the arrest.

I check in with the team working on the CCTV. Nothing yet.

An email arrives for Simon, copied to me, from the forensic lab in Chepstow. They fast-tracked their analysis of Amanda's tongue.

In answer to Simon's questions, there are two key conclusions. The forensic team is satisfied that every piece of Amanda's tongue is accounted for. Her killer chopped it up and fed every single piece of it back to her. I shudder.

Secondly, having analysed the pieces of her tongue, the experts have concluded it wasn't ripped out by hand. It was cut out, most likely with a very sharp knife, something like a modelling knife, or a very sharp pair of scissors with narrow blades, such as surgical scissors.

I'm not sure if the knife that Simon found fits the bill. But we should know soon enough.

My phone rings. It's Simon.

"Uncanny timing, boss," I say.

"Since you've answered your phone, I'm guessing you haven't started interviewing Pieter yet."

"No, not yet."

"Good. We found a loose floorboard under his bed. There's a large stash of what looks like cocaine, together with the usual drug-related paraphernalia. It's a *very* large stash."

"I knew he was on something."

"It means that, whatever happens, we'll be able to charge him with something; possession of Class A drugs, assault on a police officer, criminal damage. Plenty. Given that you've not been able to start the interview yet, I'm going to ensure we get the application in early to detain him beyond 24 hours."

I agree, and then tell Simon about the email from the forensic lab.

"The knife we found wasn't a modelling knife," he says. "But there's a few cutting tools with the drugs under his bed. We'll get them all analysed. Keep me posted. I need to speak to Granny again."

Finally, I get word that I'm able to interview Pieter. I call across the incident room and ask DC Jackson to join me.

I'm grateful that I get to share this interview with a decent detective rather than Tam.

I pick up some paperwork, Pieter's diary, and lead DC Jackson into the interview room.

Pieter looks shell-shocked. He's jittery, anxious, nervous.

The duty solicitor doesn't look any more composed.

Pieter's cuffed hands are clasped together; they look red and sweaty and his eyes look as if he's been crying.

I go through the formalities and then fix Pieter with a stare which he can only return for a couple of seconds before turning away.

I wonder if he's capable of killing someone. Sure, anyone under the influence can find the mental strength to do almost anything. But could he physically do it? He's not exactly the alpha male type. Whereas Mark is stocky and strong-looking and, frankly, something of a grunting neanderthal, Pieter is skinny and, if anything, a little effeminate.

I shuffle through the papers, making sure Pieter sees his diary. He squirms uncomfortably. I'm no body language expert, but I'd say he's acting like a guilty man. Maybe, though I hate to admit it, Tam is right and it could be quite easy to get a confession.

"Let's cut to the chase," I say, firmly. "For the record, Pieter Eliasson, did you kill Amanda Shepton?"

His eyes widen, his mouth opens and closes a few times, and he wrings his hands together, before finally gasping, "No! No, I didn't."

"Who knows what a man can do when he's high, Pieter, eh?"

His eyes open even wider. The lawyer looks as if he's thinking about intervening, but I throw him a look which tells him to sit still and keep quiet. Thankfully, he obliges.

Pieter's response suggests he's less afraid of being accused of murder – perhaps he believes this is just too far-fetched, or is he truly convinced that he's innocent – and more worried about being charged in connection with the cocaine, because my suggestion that he may have been high tells him I know about his stash of drugs.

Thinking back to what Simon told me, I'm assuming the quantity of drugs he found was larger than anyone would need for personal use, which means we could charge Pieter for possession *and* supply.

I pick up the diary and place it in the middle of the table.

"An enlightening read," I say.

He squirms uncomfortably again.

"You can make this easier on yourself," I say, "by co-operating with us. We've got your diary. We've got your knife, which is being forensically examined, we've got your cocaine, and we've got you bang to rights for assaulting a police officer, resisting arrest and criminal damage. So why not save us all a lot of time and earn just a little bit of leniency when it comes to sentencing by confessing to your crimes."

He nods vigorously, which surprises me and the duty lawyer.

Tears start streaming from Pieter's eyes.

I need a few moments to compose myself. "Are you, are you saying…"

"I'm s-saying I admit having the coke and the knife. And yeah, I sell the coke. I don't really remember assaulting the police officer and damaging the police car, but if you say I did it, then I must have."

He pauses and swallows hard.

"Go on," I say, while I involuntarily clench one of my fists. Come on, Pieter, come on, just say it! Because right here, right now, I'm absolutely willing to accept that you *did* kill Amanda. "Pieter?"

He lifts his head and stares at me. He looks completely broken.

"I, I didn't kill her," he whispers. He glances at the diary. "Those words…I can see why you might think I did it."

He starts to sob openly. Proper, deep, sobs.

"She broke my heart, and I hated her for that," he blurts out, in between sobs. "But I could never hate her enough to kill her."

"What about thinking that if you couldn't have her, no one could?"

"I was angry," he says. "I was hurt. But I didn't hate her. Not really. I loved her."

He's quite convincing, I'll give him that.

"I think we should take a break," the duty solicitor says, so quietly the first time that I ask him to repeat himself.

I nod and announce, for the purpose of the recording, that the interview is being suspended. "I'll get someone to bring you a drink," I say, nod at DC Jackson and we leave the room.

"What do you think?" I ask, as we return to the incident room.

"He's terrified," DC Jackson replies. "He looks guilty as sin."

"I'll be happier if we get some DNA on the knife," I say.

"You don't think he did it?"

"I'm not sure. If he was high, he may be capable of anything. I'm just having a hard job picturing him being strong enough to force Amanda into a chair, tie her up, and…" I pause, stopping myself just in time. I'm not sure if DC Jackson knows about Amanda's tongue, and I don't want to be the one to tell him.

That's the bit I'm having most doubts over.

Pieter has motive; he probably *was* high, which can cloud your judgement, and, perhaps, give you a strength you may not usually have. But is that quivering wreck of a man, no, not a man, a boy, a frightened little boy. Is this frightened little boy capable of cutting out Amanda's tongue, chopping it into pieces and feeding it to her? I don't know.

Amanda had one bruise on her cheek. We think she was hit hard enough to disorientate her, enabling the killer to tie her up. I just can't picture Pieter being strong enough or aggressive enough to do that.

"Inspector Nicholas?" The voice shakes me from my thoughts. I turn and find myself face to face with DC Foreman.

"I've been going through some of the CCTV from the clubs and bars from Saturday night," he says. The excited look on his face tells me that he has found something.

"And?"

"We've got footage of nine of the rugby players in The Crow's Nest just after seven-thirty. Mark Shepton is there."

"Are you sure?"

"Positive. CCTV isn't always the best quality, but there's a few seconds of him standing at the bar, front and centre. No mistake, it's definitely him."

"Shit!" I say, and apologise immediately.

"But," DC Foreman continues, "we've got some further footage, from Benny's, at ten-forty. It's darker there, and there are fewer cameras. But we've got a couple of clips. There are eight members of the rugby team identifiable."

"And Mark?" I say, hopefully.

He shakes his head. "No. It's probably not enough to *prove* he wasn't there, but you'd have thought that, since the others can be seen clearly, he'd have been caught on camera at least once."

"Unless he was avoiding the cameras for some reason," I say.

"I don't think he was there. I, er, I've gone through the statements from the rugby players. They all pretty much say the same thing; they were too drunk to remember exactly where they went and when, but they're all adamant that they stayed together for the whole night, because they always do, they're a team."

My mind is beginning to race.

I know the cameras don't cover every corner of every bar. I know Mark not being caught on camera at Benny's doesn't prove he wasn't there, but when you see him front and centre at the Crow's Nest and then noticeably absent from Benny's, it does look suspicious.

I need to return to the interview room and continue my interrogation of Pieter.

But right now, I've only got one question running through my mind. If Mark Shepton wasn't in Benny's with the others, then his team-mates were lying for him, covering for him. Why?

Where the hell *was* Mark Shepton on Saturday night?

Thirty Two

According to the old saying, fortune favours the brave, and it definitely seems like Lady Luck is smiling down on me today.

So much so that I'm absolutely convinced that I've found my true calling; my purpose, what I was destined to.

It's what I have to do, what I need to do, what I must do.

It's what I *want* to do.

It's like something deep inside me, which has been dormant for so long, has finally been awakened. And now that it's awake, it doesn't want to go back to sleep, ever.

It's like this inner force, this power, this…this demon has been activated, like a sleeper agent in a spy film, who has been hypnotised or mentally conditioned and doesn't even know he's an agent, until the key word or phrase is used; the phrase that unlocks and releases the sleeping demon buried so very deep within.

I feel like I've been activated and switched on. And I don't know where the off switch is. I'm not sure if there *is* an off switch.

The town centre supermarket is open almost twenty-four-seven. The morning papers have been delivered but are still in their bundles on the floor, waiting to be placed on the shelves.

I pull a copy of the Herald from beneath the bundle's plastic ties.

The front page is an inspiring read. And a call to action.

I pick up a few supplies and head across town.

Alongside the main college building is a very narrow side road, poorly-lit and not covered by any of the town centre's CCTV cameras.

Some way down this road is an even narrower turning into a small private car park, which is used by the college's senior managers.

My luck is definitely holding out. I suspected - and it was truly nothing more than a hunch - that Lisa would arrive early today, probably to avoid as many other people as she can. I guess she hopes to scurry into her office and bury herself away, out of sight and, as much as possible, out of mind.

As I watch her pull into the car park, I'm pleased to see that Laura is not with her. I'm not sure I could deal with two of them.

Trees and thick bushes form the back wall of the car park, which has little room for vehicles to manoeuvre. The foliage is thick and hangs low; it's easy to hide in the dark shadows as Lisa's car moves forwards and backwards several times. It then slowly reverses towards me.

I reach into my supermarket bag and pull out a pair of surgical gloves, which I pull on. From an inner pocket of my long jacket, I pull out an eight-inch-long hatpin, which I carefully slip inside my left sleeve, with the razor-sharp point towards my hand and the ornamental head resting on the inside of my elbow.

I glance around anxiously, fearing another car may pull in. But my luck prevails. This is *definitely* meant to be.

As soon as the car stops, I emerge from the shadows, pull open the back door and climb into the seat behind Lisa. I let the hatpin slide into my palm, reach around the seat and press it against her neck.

The tiniest circle of red forms where the very tip of the pin pierces her skin.

"What the...?" she gasps.

"SHHH!" I hiss harshly. "If you so much as whisper, this pin goes all the way into your neck, and out the other side."

"Get out of my car!"

"LISA!" I say with such ferocity that she resists the urge to call out. "I'll get out of the car right now if you want me to. But if I do, then the next person I visit will be Laura. And I won't be as patient with her as I'm being with you. Nod if you understand."

She nods. I glance at her hands which are clutching the steering wheel. Her knuckles are white and her fingers are trembling.

"We need to talk," I say. "But not here. Drive. The woods on Hillside. If you try to draw attention to us in any way whatsoever, your life ends right here, right now. And then I go after Laura. Nod."

She does.

I hide behind the high headrest of her seat, but I keep the hatpin pressed against her neck as she slowly drives the short distance from the car park to the Hillside estate.

At the far end is a steep road which climbs to the crest of the hill, where a left turn takes you into the thick woodland which overlooks the town.

This road narrows the deeper you drive into the woods. The surface becomes noticeably more uneven the further you go, from a smooth, normal surface to a rough, stony track.

"There," I say, indicating a dark gap between two of the largest trees at the edge of the track. "Park front-end in between those two trees, kill the lights and turn off the engine."

I've no doubt that, not too many hours ago, there was probably another car parked in this exact spot, inside which two horny young lovebirds were able to make out because their parents wouldn't let them shut themselves away together in either of their homes.

Lisa's car has tinted privacy glass in the rear, which helps obscure the view of the interior to anyone looking in unless they are standing very close. If I get this right, anyone else in the woods this morning who see Lisa's car will assume they've stumbled upon a clandestine couple who are snatching some illicit pre-work pleasure.

I glance around; I can't see anyone nearby.

"Get out of the car," I say.

I open the rear door and get out of the car as she gets out of the front. I take her firmly by the wrist with my left hand and I wave the hatpin in front of her face as a warning of what will happen to her should she even *think* of trying to run.

"Get into the back," I say.

She hesitates but nervously obeys after I scowl at her.

I close the front door and climb into the back seat alongside her, pulling the door shut behind me.

My supermarket bag is in the foot-well.

They call it a 'bag for life'. I smile at the irony as I pull a length of rope from it.

"Turn away from me," I say, "and give me your hands."

"No!" she says, defiantly.

I thrust the hatpin towards her and rest it under her chin, applying enough pressure to encourage her to tilt her head up.

"Lisa, if you don't do exactly as I ask, when I ask it, then things are going to get much, *much*, worse for you. How? Because I'll knock you out-cold right now and when you wake up, Laura will be with us, and I'll make you watch as I rip off her clothes and violate her. Then I'll slit her wrists, and she'll slowly bleed out in front of you. You'll be helpless to do anything. All you'll be able to do is watch your precious daughter's life slowly drain away. But. Do as you're told, when you're told, and I promise, I *swear*, I won't ever so much as breathe in Laura's direction. If you understand, turn around and give me your hands."

She obeys and I tie her hands. She winces as I tighten the knots and the coarse fibres of the rope chafes against her wrists.

I twist her back round so she is faces the front of the car and shove her firmly back against the seat with such force that the back of her skull collides with the rear head restraint with a solid thud.

I reach into my bag again and pull out a copy of the Herald.

"Is - is *that* what this is all about?" she breathes.

"Isn't it enough?" I say.

"Did Phillipa send you?" she asks. "Did that wretched thorn in my side send you to frighten me? I'm sorry, but what's done is done, and she isn't getting her job back. Never."

"Well, now, it seems Phillipa was right, you really do have a vicious tongue, don't you?"

"I don't know what you hope to achieve, doing this," she says. "All you're going to do is get both of you into even more trouble."

I raise the hatpin right in front of her face.

"For the record, Phillipa doesn't have a clue who I am, or that I'm here. We don't know each other. But I *am* here on her behalf. What do I hope to achieve? Karma, Lisa. Karma. I'm going to make sure you never use that vicious tongue on anyone else. Ever! And, just in case you were in any doubt, let me make one thing absolutely crystal clear. The only person here in any kind of trouble is you."

I'm suddenly distracted by the sound of a dog barking outside.

There's a voice. "Buster! Buster, c'mere, boy. Not that way."

Lisa looks at me with a calculating look in her eyes. If she dares to call out, will I *really* stab her with the hatpin?

Footprints crunch on the twigs and leaves on the ground; presumably the dog owner is coming to retrieve his wayward pet.

My left hand clamps itself firmly over Lisa's mouth and I grip her nose between my thumb and forefinger.

I lean across her, lower my head close to hers and rest my chin on the gloved knuckles of my left hand, on top of her mouth.

The hatpin in my right hand is hidden beneath my body, but is now pressed against her breast, over the dark, desolate, empty space in her body, where decent people have a heart.

I move my head from side to side slightly. If curiosity does get the better of the dog owner, and he does decide to peer in through the window at close range, all he will see is what looks like a couple sharing a passionate kiss.

"Get away from the car, Buster. Come on; here."

The voice is very close.

Lisa makes a muffled sound and I release my grip on her nose, just enough to allow her to breathe. My body leans heavily against hers, pinning her down.

I lift my eyes, so that I can see the fear in hers. I can feel how tense she is. It's invigorating.

The footsteps fade away.

I pull away from Lisa and remove my hand from her mouth. She splutters and coughs as she gratefully inhales gasps of air.

I reach for the newspaper again and glance at the front page.

"This report does not paint a very flattering picture of you," I say softly, before injecting some venom into my voice. "But I know for a fact that this is only half the story."

She looks bewildered.

"I saw what Phillipa wrote to the governors, when she reached out, when she cried for help. When she spoke about how you took great delight in bad-mouthing and belittling her at every opportunity. You degraded her, you put her down, you insulted her, you humiliated her in front of her colleagues. How did she word it now? 'Lisa repeatedly abused and bullied me with her cruel, vicious, tongue, and that's just not right. It shouldn't be allowed to happen.' Yes, that's it."

I place the newspaper onto the seat next to her.

"But that corrupt, close-knit, college clique took your word over hers. Your cruel, wicked, words. Well, Lisa, I am karma. And I am going to make you eat your words."

Her eyes widen and it looks like she's about to scream so I clamp my hand tightly over her mouth again.

"You took everything from Phillipa. Everything. But I'm not as cruel as you are. I'm going to give you something that you didn't give her. I'm going to give you a choice."

I raise the hatpin in my right hand again, and I place it on the edge of her ear. "One firm push," I say. "That's all it will take. I don't know if it will be instant, or if it will take a while. But I'm quite sure it will hurt like hell."

She tries to say something, probably "no", "don't" or "please" but I can't make it out because my left hand is gagging her

"Not the ear?" I say.

She manages to shake her head.

I pull my right hand away from her ear, raise the hatpin in front of her face, and turn the sharp point towards her. I slowly move it closer to her face, and then up and to my left a little, so that it is perfectly lined up with her right eye.

"You know, the eyeball is full of liquid," I say. "If I push this into your eye, will it pop like a water balloon, or will it take a while to drain, as if it has a slow puncture? Will it slowly sag and slip out of its socket?"

Her eyes involuntarily open wide with fear.

"That's it," I say, and I push the hatpin so close to her eyeball that if she blinked, her eyelid wouldn't be able to close fully because it would hit the pin. How easy it would be to push it forward just a fraction!

"Not the eye, then?" I say.

I move the hatpin away from her eye and let it hover over her breast again. "I would just shove it into your heart, but I don't think you have one, so the pinhead will just be floating around in a hollow chamber."

Tears are starting to form in her eyes. She makes more muffled noises. The defiance she had been able to muster earlier has long gone.

I lift my left hand and force my fingers into her mouth before she has the chance to clamp her lips shut. I grab the end of her tongue and pull it out just a little.

"How about I use this pin to pierce that vicious tongue?" I say, as I tap the metal point a few times against the quivering flesh.

"I did say I'd give you a choice," I say. "That was the hard way, but there is an easier way."

There's a small fold-up table attached to the back of each of the front seats. I lean over and pull down the airplane-style table on the back of the front passenger seat. I reach into my bag and place a small water bottle on top of the table.

I then pull out some small bottles of pills and remove the lids.

She looks at me with pitiful, pleading, eyes.

"I don't want you to be disillusioned," I say. "You're not getting out of this alive. But I've got just about enough decency left in me that I'm giving you the choice to help dull the pain."

Tears now start to flow from her eyes.

"Please," she says. "I'm sorry. Please. I'm SORRY!"

"So am I," I say. "But as you said earlier, what's done is done."

I shove my gloved left hand roughly against her neck, grip her tightly by the throat, and force her head back against the high headrest.

"Please," she says, "Don't. I've got a daughter, I've..."

"Phillipa had a partner, a home, a job that she loved and was good at. But you and your vicious, wicked, tongue took it from her."

I'm gripping her neck so tightly that she is starting to struggle to catch her breath.

I lean forward, almost touching her nose with mine, and stare into her eyes as if I'm burrowing into the darkest depths of her soul.

I got lucky with Amanda. Her heart gave out when I started cutting her tongue, which was extremely satisfying. Luck has been on my side tonight, but I can't count on being *that* lucky again. Lisa is a hardened battle-axe of a woman, stronger than Amanda was.

I tighten my grip even further. My fingers and thumb snake up over her cheeks, squeezing them in hard and forcing her lips into an open pout.

I apply a little more pressure on her throat with the base of my hand, and she gags slightly. "Does that hurt, Lisa?" I say. "Does my hand against your throat hurt? Answer me, ANSWER ME!"

"Y-yes," she says, hoarsely.

"Are you in pain, Lisa?" I say, squeezing her cheeks even harder.

"Y-yes," she gasps.

"Well, it just so happens that I have some painkillers here. How apt. You're the pain. *I'm* the painkiller."

I push harder still against her throat, knowing that I'm starting to choke the life out of her.

I put down the hatpin, pick up a bottle of pills in my right hand and tip some of the small white tablets into her pouting mouth. I then pick up the water bottle.

Lisa tries to turn her head away from me and to close her mouth. But my grip on her throat is so tight, she can't move her head, and if it wasn't for my gloves, my fingernails would be digging deep into the flesh of her cheeks, as I'm squeezing so hard.

I tip some clear liquid into her mouth and just slightly release the grip on her throat. "Swallow," I say. "SWALLOW!"

She splutters and gags, as she realises that the bottle doesn't contain water, but vodka, which I'm guessing is burning her throat right now. When I left the supermarket, I emptied the water bottle into a drain and filled it up from a small bottle of vodka I had also bought.

I pick up the hatpin again and hold it in front of her eye.

"I swear to God, you evil bitch, if you don't swallow, I am going to push this into your eye, very, very, slooooooooooowly."

She swallows hard.

"There now," I say. "That wasn't so bad, was it?"

She looks at me as if she's thinking her ordeal might be over. That this is the worst of it. Oh Lisa. I'm only just getting started.

I put the hatpin down again, and force another pile of pills into her mouth, and more vodka, some of which trickles down the side of her mouth as she splutters, chokes and gags.

"Swallow! SWALLOW!"

I force her to tilt her head and squeeze her cheeks, in and out.

I've no idea how long it's going to take for this cocktail of painkillers and sleeping tablets, washed down with vodka, to make her feel drowsy and, quite frankly, I don't care.

She's already weakening, because my grasp of her throat is severely restricting her air flow.

What I do, *really*, care about is that her death is not quick. I want her to hurt, I want her to suffer, to feel such fear that she will welcome the darkness when it comes. She may even thank me for it.

The world will thank me, because after I'm done, there will be one less wicked tongue to cause such misery and pain. And that will make the world a better place, a happier place.

And that's good, right? That makes *this* right, doesn't it?

I pour more vodka down her throat.

Her eyes are just starting to glaze a little. She's finding it harder to focus on and follow the hatpin as I wave it back and forth in front of her face.

"I think you're ready," I say.

Her eyes look at me and I wonder what she's thinking.

Does she think I'm trying to make my mind up? Trying to decide whether I do pierce her eyeball with the hatpin, or do I shove it into her ear?

I smile and drop the hatpin into her lap.

She looks down, then meets my gaze again.

My right hand reaches into the inner pocket of my jacket, while my left maintains its vice-like grip on her throat, and I pull out my surgical scissors.

"You, and your vicious, wicked, tongue have caused so much pain and misery…"

"I'm sorry," she manages to say, though it's barely a whisper.

"Save it for Satan, when you meet him. He might forgive you, but I don't. It's time, Lisa," I say, as I lean close to her face again, and wave the scissors right in front of her eyes. "It's time for you to eat your wicked words."

Thirty Three: Kat

The police have secured permission to keep Pieter Eliasson in custody for a little longer.

I don't know whether that's a good sign or not.

I guess that, if he'd been able to give them a cast-iron alibi, he'd have been released already. So perhaps he is a strong suspect.

Then again, it could be that he's protesting his innocence, which means the pressure is on the police to collect as much evidence as possible, as quickly as possible, either to prompt a confession or build a case so strong that a conviction is inevitable.

I stare at the phone on my desk, almost willing it to ring.

I want to be distracted, occupied, so I don't have to indulge Ross in his triumphant gloating. Since he arrived this morning – he was in early today, for once, presumably keen to start his self-celebration as soon as possible - he's been proudly parading around the newsroom like a strutting peacock.

I avoided him for a little while when I first got in, by checking the police website and social media channels, and calling the press office, which is when I learned Pieter was still in custody.

I also found out police were still searching Pieter's house. I don't know whether that's a good thing or not. Does it mean they haven't found anything yet and are making sure they leave no stone unturned? Or does it mean they *have* found something, and they're just seeing if there is even more to find?

I know we're supposed to make all our enquiries through the press office, but I'm so tempted to call Alex Nicholas directly.

The press office said there are no plans yet for a media conference today; everything is hinging on how the interview goes with Pieter.

With my phone calls all made, and no significant developments to work on, I make myself a coffee and pick up a copy of The Herald.

Ross seizes his moment. "Read 'em and weep," he says. "Exclusive report by Ross Barker. Got a ring to it, don't you think?"

"Well done," I say.

"This week's Herald, *also* starring Kat Russell," he says.

Oh boy, it's going to be a long day.

Fridays are traditionally the most light-hearted day of the week. The new edition of the paper is out, the weekend is nearly here and our focus is on filling the later pages of next week's edition, which means writing the fluffy, timeless, 'filler' stories, from charity fund-raising events to previewing future events.

It's usually the one day of the week when we wander out for a pub lunch, too, although Patrick isn't here today to lead us, so I doubt we'll do that. Mervyn isn't much of a pub person.

He's not here at the moment. He was called upstairs by the advertising manager as soon as he got in. She had wanted to speak to Patrick but as he's off, she said Mervyn would 'have to do'.

The phone in the editor's office rings.

Whoever is calling is not taking the hint that Patrick would have answered by now if he was in. It rings for a while and, as soon as it stops, Mervyn's phone rings. Of course, I've got no way of knowing if it's the same caller, but I've just got a feeling…

Besides, if I don't take the call, I'm going to have to continue listening to Ross singing his own praises. I consider this to be a classic case of being saved by the bell.

I jab at a few buttons phone so that I can intercept the call.

"Herald newsroom," I say.

"I was starting to think you'd all taken the day off," a man says, curtly. The voice is familiar.

"No, we're here," I say.

"What about the editor?" he says. "Can I speak to Patrick?"

"I'm sorry. He's *not* here," I say.

"Ah. Up in the woods already is he? Probably explains why he isn't answering his mobile. There's a poor signal up there."

"The woods?" I say. "I don't think so. He's taken the day off and said he was going to play golf."

"Golf? Of course. Using mobile phones on the fairway is frowned upon by the great and good of the golf club" the man says.

"Is there anything I can help you with?" I ask.

"No, I don't think so. Mervyn not there?"

"He is in today, but he's in a meeting at the moment."

"I see. Well, I'll keep trying Patrick's mobile. I guess you can get Mervyn to give me a ring when he returns. He's got my number."

"And you are?" I ask, a little more abruptly than I usually speak on the phone, but then, I guess I'm just involuntarily speaking to this man it the same contemptuous way he is talking to me.

"James, Warren James."

I'm about to ask why he thought Patrick might be up in the woods but he hangs up before I get the chance.

My curiosity is piqued.

I'm tempted to ring the police press office to see if they're aware of anything going on in the woods, but they don't seem to feel inclined to go out of their way to be particularly forthcoming with information today.

I grab my mobile and walk into Patrick's office, shutting the door behind me, and call Sergeant Davey.

"Ah, my favourite local newshound," he says. "What can I do for you?"

"Well," I say, feeling a little apprehensive, but at the same time telling myself nothing ventured, nothing gained, "you could tell me what's going on in the woods."

"You *know* about that already?" he asks. "And I thought I was your favourite source."

"But you haven't told me anything," I reply. "Yet."

"Well, since you *asked*," he says, "and I don't like to lie, I can confirm that we are in the woods investigating reports of a body being found in a car. Looks like suicide."

"Oh?" I say. My hands start to shake. "What makes you say that?"

"From what I hear, there were several bottles of pills found in the car and an almost-empty bottle with a few drops of vodka in it."

I scribble some notes down on a piece of paper I find on Patrick's desk. "Do you know who it is?" I ask.

"Now you're pushing it," he says. "I'm too good to you."

"I know," I say. "I owe you."

"Promises, promises!" he says, and I shudder. I don't know how much older than me he is, but while his voice suggests an interest beyond professional on his part, my interest is absolutely professional, and *only* professional.

Still, if it takes a little flirting to loosen his tongue, where's the harm?

"Don't you have any idea who it is, yet?" I plead. "I could do with a break. You lot cost me my front-page lead by arresting Pieter Eliasson at the wrong time."

"Sorry about that," he says. "Hang on, why am *I* apologising? It was nothing to do with me."

"Well," I say, "I accept your apology on behalf of the force. But if you really want to make it up to me, you can tell me who you think the person in the woods is."

He pauses and for a moment I worry that I might have been a little too pushy. "Hang on," he says.

I hear some movement; I think he is walking. I hear a door close, and then a whisper. "You still there?"

"Hanging on your every word," I say.

"Well, you didn't get this from me, because ID hasn't been done yet. In fact, we've had trouble getting hold of the Coroner's officer, because he gone off gallivanting visiting relatives somewhere, but I hear it's Lisa Davidson, from the college. But that's strictly off the record. I suggest you get up there. And yes, you most definitely owe me now."

I make a mental note to buy him a posh box of doughnuts next time I go shopping.

My eyes involuntarily turn towards Ross. He looks so happy and proud of himself. I wonder how he would feel if it turns out that Lisa Davidson killed herself because of his front-page piece.

"I've got to go," I say, as I grab my count. "Tell Mervyn to call me when he gets back."

"What's going on?"

"Possibly next week's front-page lead," I say, with a slightly sarcastic smile, as I dash out of the room.

Thirty Four: Dan

Mum has a fry-up breakfast in one hand and a copy of the Herald in the other; I eagerly take both from her.

I feel sorry for Kat. Even though she didn't say as much, I know how thrilled she was at the prospect of a front-page-lead murder story.

Even with Pieter being arrested, I'd have thought Patrick and Kat would've been able to stretch enough detail out of the murder to keep it on the front.

Mind you, the story they *have* led with is quite the tale; not the kind of story Patrick would usually run, but there's a response from the college in it, so they've clearly done their homework and checked it out.

Talking of checking it out, there's no statement from the police to say that Pieter has been charged, so I need to find out what's going on.

I call Paul's mobile number. If I ring the press office landline, one of his colleagues may answer. I need Paul.

"Paul," I say cheerfully. "Still need to catch up for that drink at some point."

"Dan! Er, yeah, sure, mate. Good plan."

He sounds nervous. There's a quiver in his voice.

"Everything OK?" I ask.

"Yeah, of course. Y-you know how it is, never a dull moment behind the thin blue line."

"So, what's the scoop with Pieter? Has he been charged yet? Is he going to be charged or are you going to bail him?"

"I - I don't really know, I haven't been able to get hold of any of the senior members of the team this morning."

"Really? Are they still interviewing him then?"

"I - I guess so. They got permission to hold him longer."

"What about the search of Pieter's house? Was anything interesting found?"

"I - I…"

"That suggests it was."

"I can't…I'm not sure how much they want to say at the moment. It's all a bit manic."

"I see," I say. "Well, I've got Alex's mobile number, maybe I'll just call her, and cut out the middle man."

"That's not fair, Dan," he says. "Besides, if I can't get hold of her, you won't be able to either. If I could tell you anything, I would."

"I don't know," I say, "what's the point of having a friend on the inside if I know more than you do."

"What do you know?"

"I know you're questioning Pieter Eliasson in connection with the murder of Amanda Shepton. I know that Pieter was her lover."

"Her lover? H-h-how…?"

"It's my job to know. It's because I've got people who tell me things. Well, *some* people. But hey, what can you do, if you don't know anything, then you can't tell me. It must be frustrating for you, though, when a journalist knows more than you do."

"As it happens, I very much know something you don't know right now, otherwise you would have asked me about it already."

"Oh?"

"Yeah, oh."

"Well, you can't say that and not back it up. Am I just meant to believe you know something I don't, or are you going to prove it?"

"I was expecting your first question today to be 'what's happening in the woods on Hillside?'. I can only assume you don't know. But I do. Oh shit."

"What?"

"Not sure I should have told you that."

"Well, you can't unsay it, so you may as well tell me more. You know your secret will be safe with me. I can say someone who lives near the woods tipped me off."

He considers this, then says, "I'm not telling you this, but the reason I don't have an update about the Shepton murder is because the SIO, Alex and Tam have been called to the woods. There's a body in a car there."

Within five minutes, I'm in *my* car.

I reach the crest of the hill and turn to the woods, but I don't get very far. There are two police patrol cars blocking the road and, behind them, a taut line of police tape.

As I pull up on the side of the road, Kat gets out of the car in front of me. It seems she isn't wasting any time in building up some decent contacts; she's going to be a great journalist. Ha, who am I kidding? She *is* a great journalist.

I allow myself the pleasure of watching her walk away from her car for a few seconds. She's wearing another pair of nicely-fitted, sharply-creased, trousers, and she really does have a great arse.

She starts talking to a couple of police officers at the cordon and I get out of my car, before my mind starts wandering a little too far.

"What have I missed?" I say.

Kat turns and I'm disappointed to see a look of disappointment on her face. It's definitely an 'Oh, it's you' kind of look. I guess she was hoping she had this little scoop all to herself.

I introduce myself to the officers and ask what's going on.

"As I was just saying to the young lady here," one of them says, "a statement will be issued in due course." His colleague steps away, out of earshot, and I can see he is talking on his radio, presumably telling someone in authority that the news hounds - or wolves, if you will - are already gathering at the door.

I take a few steps away from the cordon and gesture to Kat for her to join me. "So, what's a nice girl like you doing in these woods at this time of a Friday morning?"

She blushes briefly. "Same as you, I guess," she says. "Although I didn't think a suicide would be of any interest to you."

"Suicide?" I say, and I can tell from the look on her face that she's now wondering what I know, as my instinctive response will have told her that I wasn't expecting her to say suicide.

I decide I've got no choice but to play it straight. "I just had a tip off that there was a body in car, that's all. I hadn't heard anything about a suicide. What makes you so sure it was suicide?"

Again, she hesitates. I give her a bit of a pleading look. Come on, Kat, I did tell you about Pieter, I say to myself.

She sighs. "I was told there were bottles of pills and a bottle of vodka found with the body," she says.

"Really?" I ask, and she nods. "Your source seems to have been a bit more vocal than mine; any idea who's in the car?"

She doesn't answer, but the look on her face tells me she knows. Or at least, that she has been given a name. Formal identification will not have happened yet.

"Did you see today's Herald?" she says. OK, I think to myself. Try and change the subject, play it cool.

I nod. "Sorry you didn't get your front-page lead."

"Did you read it?"

"Glanced through it," I say. "Not your usual Herald-type story, but it looks like your colleague did a thorough job."

Kat nods towards the cordon.

"What?" I say.

She nods again.

The penny drops.

"The woman from the college?" I whisper.

"That's what I've been told," says Kat.

"Shit!" I say. "Do you think she topped herself because of the Herald story?"

"That's why I'm here," she says. "I want to find out as much as I can. Ross doesn't know yet."

"What about Patrick?"

"He's off today, playing golf."

I smile involuntarily, as I remember how often Patrick would take a Friday off to spend it on the local golf course, although it wasn't all about the game. Quite a few councillors, businessmen and senior police officers often shared a round with him. The relaxed environment had been the source of much information to the Herald in the past.

"You didn't know it was suicide?" she says. "Honestly?"

"No," I say. "I thought it was connected to the Amanda Shepton murder."

She smiles. "What, we've got a serial killer in town? I doubt it. My money is still on Mark for killing his mother, and I'm going to prove it.

So, there's nothing for you to see here, this is a sad suicide. A bit like Sam Shepton. And you don't cover sad suicides, or so I thought."

I ponder on this. I don't know for sure who her source is, although thinking about, I could probably make a reasonable guess that a certain community sergeant probably wouldn't be too far off the mark.

One thing I do know is that Kat has certainly been told a lot more than I have. If it did turn out that Lisa Davidson killed herself because of the Herald's front page, Patrick will be devastated. The story was a bit sensationalist for the Herald as it was; if it transpires that it prompted Lisa to take her own life, well, I can't imagine how that might affect him.

But something about this doesn't add up. My instinct tells me that there is something not quite right.

"So, it seems a pretty clear case then," I venture. "Car in body, loads of pills, vodka? A sad, sudden, death rather than a suspicious death."

"Looks like it," says Kat. "Very sad. I'm just worried that the Herald will be blamed for it. That's why I'm here, to find out if anyone is suggesting it was our fault."

"I don't think anyone will be pointing any fingers at the Herald," I say. I've already decided that Kat has been quite forthcoming with what she has been told, which I take as a positive sign for future relations, so it's only fair that I share, too.

"Oh?" she says.

"I think there's a lot more to this than a straight forward suicide?"

"That's those national newspapers who pay your wages talking," she teases. "This seems quite straight-forward to me."

"OK," I say, and I fix her with an intent stare. "If this is 'just' a sad, sudden death, then why isn't it being handled by the community policing team?"

"I assumed it was," she says. "What do you know?"

"I know that the three most senior members of the Amanda Shepton murder investigation team are here."

Thirty Five: Alex

I'm doing everything I can to avoid making eye contact with Tam as we wait for Simon to join us in his office. And Tam knows it. I can feel the smugness radiating from him.

"I told you he'd strike again," he hisses; he just can't hold it in any longer. "There'll be more, too. I *said* this was a serial killer."

I bite my lip, a bit harder than I intended, and stare out of the window, willing Simon to come into his office before I see red.

It's been a few hours since Simon, myself and Tam were summoned to the woods. So much for the boss having the morning off, which is what he had planned to do.

I couldn't comprehend why we'd been called to what looked like a suicide, until examining doctor emerged from the back of Lisa's car, shook his head solemnly, and said, "Her tongue has been removed."

Tam smirked and I instinctively knew what he was thinking. "Amanda's killer didn't keep her tongue for a trophy," I said. "There's nothing to suggest anything different here."

Our radios crackled all at once. It was one of the officers at the cordon on the edge of the woods. There were two journalists there, asking for information about what was going on.

Simon threw me an accusing stare, which angered me. Did he think *I* tipped them off? And what, exactly, does he think I might have said to them? Until I got to the woods, I had no real idea of what we were dealing with myself.

"I wonder who they are," he said. "It won't be Patrick, because I saw him at the golf club this morning. So, it's probably Dan Barton and that young girl from the Herald."

He glanced at me again, but I threw the daggers from his eyes right back at him! He can't imply I may have spoken to the media if he's been on the golf course with the editor of the Herald! After all, which journalist was it who got the tip off about Amanda's murder? The editor of the Herald, I believe!

"Christ," said Tam. "The body has barely stopped breathing and the vultures are circling already."

Simon asked me to stop at the cordon on the way out and, if it does turn out to be Dan and Kat, to see if I can buy us some time, until we knew exactly what we are dealing with.

Simon's right to be wary; two murders in a week is going to end up attracting more than a little media attention, especially after those black widow headlines; the longer we can give ourselves before the full media circus rolls into town, the easier our task will be.

Simon allocated some other tasks to Tam and I and told us to drive back to the station. He wanted to stay in the woods for a while, and work with the scenes of crime officers.

Simon breezes into the room in a blur, shuts the door and throws himself into the chair behind his desk.

"Sorry, he says, a little breathlessly, "I took a bit longer than expected. I was getting something checked out."

"What have we got then, boss?" I ask.

"A bloody serial killer, lassie, that's what we've got," sneers Tam.

"Let's focus on what we know, rather than any speculation," says Simon, who throws a stern look at Tam. "One thing we know for absolute certain is that Pieter Eliasson did not kill Lisa Davidson. I'm not ready to totally eliminate him from the Shepton murder, but right now I'm assuming the same person killed both women."

Shit," I whisper involuntarily, as my peripheral vision catches Tam executing a small fist pump by his side, presumably out of Simon's sight.

"So, Alex, once we're done here, I need you to brief DC Foreman to charge Pieter with the drug offences, possession and supply, since he admitted as much in interview. Well done on that, by the way. And we can bail him for the murder."

I scribble some notes in my pad. "Righto, boss."

"The MO suggests it's the same killer," says Simon. "There's the tongues being removed; and it's not likely to be a copycat, because there's only a small number of people who know anything about the tongues being removed. It hasn't been in the public domain."

I feel a cold shiver run down my spine again. It really will be a full media circus if news gets out that we now have two dead women who have had their tongues removed.

"There's something else I need to tell you," says Simon. "Scenes of crime found a partial muddy footprint in the footwell at the back of Lisa's car. This is why I've been held up. I asked the lab to do a quick comparison of this footprint with the one we found in Amanda Shepton's bedroom. They're going to do a more detailed analysis, but it looks like they match. Add that to the missing tongues, and I think you'll agree it looks as if we are dealing with one perp."

Wow. That's the first word that pops into my head.

"I've asked for the PM to be fast-tracked, but if I had to put money on it, I'd say we're probably going to find Lisa's tongue in her stomach."

I stifle the instinctive urge to retch.

"We need to focus on working out why these women were targeted? Is there any connection between them?"

"The proverbial missing link," muses Tam.

"Did you talk to any Amanda's social group?" asks Simon. One of the tasks he gave to Tam back in the woods was to re-contact Amanda's friends, to ask if Lisa Davidson has ever been part of their little clique.

"I've only spoken to a couple of them, guv," says Tam. "They both denied knowing Lisa personally. One of the women knew *of* Lisa, because her son is at the college. But in terms of Lisa and Amanda knowing each other, I haven't found anything to confirm that yet."

"And what about CCTV?"

"There's one camera which covers the entrance area of the college," Tam reports. "But it only covers a tiny part of the road, and there's nothing on that. I called the college and found out Lisa has an allocated space in a private car park down a side road. Again, there's no CCTV of that area, either. The college is on the outer fringes of the area covered by the town centre camera network. We did find one piece of footage of Lisa's car. It was caught by the camera overlooking the car park at the far end of High Street. There's a glimpse of her car, which is driving away from the direction of the college."

"What time?"

"Just after seven-thirty, guv. There doesn't appear to be anyone in the passenger seat, although the images are not crystal clear."

"They never are, when it matters most," sighs Simon. "All this modern, digital technology we have these days, yet crucial CCTV images always seem to be so grainy."

"You said that footprint was found in the rear footwell, so it's possible our man was hiding in the back of the car," says Tam.

"Or she was going to meet him in the woods," I venture. "She could have been alone in the car."

"One thing bothering me, guv," says Tam. "If it is the same guy who killed Shepton, what's the deal with the vodka and pills?"

"I asked the doctor at the scene about that," Simon replies. "There will have to be full toxicological tests on the contents of Lisa's stomach, but the doctor said if those bottles had been full of pills, and she had been forced to swallow them, washed down with vodka, there would have been enough there to cause an overdose."

"There were no pills or vodka with Amanda, tho?"

"Maybe the guy got lucky the first time around?" says Simon, and I wince. Lucky? *Lucky?* Ask Amanda Shepton if she thinks her killer got lucky! "Maybe she died of fright as he cut her tongue out before he had chance to use his preferred method of murder. Perhaps he couldn't run the risk of getting lucky again; he couldn't bank on Lisa also dying of fright when he took her tongue, so the pills and vodka were the back-up plan, the fail-safe. One way or another, Lisa was going to die. Alex, how did you get on with the journalists at the cordon?"

"It *was* Dan and Kat," I say. "Kat said she had been told Lisa Davidson had killed herself in the car and was worried that it was because of the Herald's front page."

"What?" snapped Tam. "A hack with a conscience? Her career ain't going to go very far, then."

"What about Dan?"

"He said he thought it was connected with Amanda's murder because he knew that the three of us were there."

Simon's brow furrows. "Who the hell is tipping the media off?"

"No idea, guv," says Tam, who glances at me with an expression that says 'do you have any idea who you would like to try to blame, in order to divert suspicion away from yourself'?

"The thing is," I say, "is that I think I've bought us some time. I confirmed there was a body; I couldn't very well deny *that*, could I? I also told them that formal ID had not yet taken place, which is the truth. I said it wouldn't be helpful if we suddenly read a social media report naming Lisa before we had spoken to her family, and I think Kat and Dan respect that."

"Oh, they've *both* got a conscience?" scoffs Tam. "Can it be that you've managed to find *two* hacks with a heart? Or are they sharing one between them? Sorry, but I just don't think they can be trusted."

"We haven't got a choice," I say, raising my voice. "They've agreed not to print anything anywhere yet, until we brief them further."

"Brief them?" says Tam. "You promising little exclusives now, Nicholas?"

"I've bought us some time," I say firmly. I'm struggling to control my temper. He's really getting to me, but I don't want to give him the satisfaction of letting him know that. "We all know we'll have a mass of journalists down here as soon as it is suggested that we have two connected murders in one week. I've bought us some time. But there has to be a price."

"Fine," says Simon. "If we don't get any calls from any other media, then we'll sit on this for as long as we can, and when we do decide to release something, we'll give it to Kat and Dan first."

Tam throws daggers at me.

"Alex, how did you get on with Lisa's family?"

I sigh. In the woods earlier, Simon had given me the unenviable task of talking to Lisa's family. Had we been able to get hold of the Coroner's officer – it seems everyone wanted to have some time off today – I would have arranged for them come in and formally identify her body. That will have to wait just a little. But since Lisa had her college ID badge among her belongings and her driving licence, the bottom line is we know it's her. So my task was to tell her family.

I obtained a phone number from the college.

It turned out that Lisa's husband, Paul, has a high-flying job with a London-based finance firm, and works in the city four days a week, returning home for a three-day weekend.

Having established he was home, I arranged to visit, in the company of a specially-trained Family Contact Officer.

Laura, Lisa's daughter, was also at home.

"Lisa's husband and daughter are devastated, of course," I report.

"Husband?" Tam raises his eyebrows. "Our Lisa was not another black widow, then?"

I glare at him. How is it possible for an alleged human being to be so cold and insensitive? Then again, how is it possible that a man can have such an apparent hatred of women that he feels compelled to rip their tongues out?

"They said Lisa often left home quite early to go to work, but today she left a little earlier, because she knew there would be a lot of eyes on her because of the piece in the Herald."

"Any indication how Lisa felt about that article?" asks Simon.

I pull out my notebook, because I had written down what Laura told me when I asked that question. "By all accounts, Lisa was quite bullish about it," I say, as I scan my notes. "Here it is. According to Laura, Lisa said Phillipa was clearly an incompetent, bitter and twisted loser who won't get anywhere in life, and doesn't deserve to, and it really doesn't matter, because in a day or so, the front page of the Herald will be wrapping up someone's fish and chips before being tossed in the bin where it belongs."

"Och," says Tam, "she had a vicious tongue, that one."

I glance at him, and something momentarily occurs to me, but I don't have time to ponder on it, as Simon is talking to me.

"Anything else?"

"That's about it. The Family Contact Officer is waiting to hear from Warren James about arranging formal ID. I think Paul Davidson wants to read the riot act to the Herald's editor at some point. I did ask if they knew of anyone who would want to hurt Lisa, and they said no, except Phillipa Player, of course."

"What about any links with Amanda?"

"I didn't ask," I say. "I thought we should wait until we knew for sure that the two deaths were linked before I suggested it to the family."

Simon nods. "OK," he says. "I don't think, for one minute, she would have had anything to do with it, but we are going to need to speak to Phillipa, find out where she was this morning. And last Saturday night, for that matter. Alex, I'll leave that to you."

"OK, boss," I say.

"While we're covering all bases," Simon continues. "Tam, I want you to keep looking at CCTV, keep reaching out to Amanda's friends, and find someone from the team – someone who can handle themselves if the need arises – to speak to Mark Shepton, to find out where *he* was this morning.

"I can speak to Shepton," Tam offers.

"Somehow, I don't think he's likely to be very forthcoming if you try to talk to him. Diplomacy is not your strong suit," says Simon, and I can't help but smirk.

"There has to be someone, or some*thing*, that links these two women," says Simon, more a case of him thinking out loud than talking to us. Did Mark Shepton know Lisa? Did Phillipa know Amanda? Does Phillipa have a vengeful friend who wants to fight her battles for her? But how would Amanda fit into that?"

"We also need to decide when we speak to the media," I say, "and what we tell them. Undoubtedly, Lisa's family will be expecting to see us announce an investigation."

"I need to think about that," says Simon. "Leave it with for a bit. Now, let's crack on; you both know what I want you to do."

"Guv!" says Tam and marches out in quite a military fashion.

I walk away a little more wistfully because, as much of a pain in the proverbial as he is, something that Tam said earlier really struck a chord with me.

It might be that Tam has inadvertently just helped me find the missing link that connects the two victims.

Thirty Six: Kat

I glance at the clock on the wall; it's just gone four, and still no word from the police, which is frustrating.

Alex had spoken to Dan and myself at the cordon, and we agreed to say nothing until we heard again from her or one of her colleagues.

I've been monitoring all the police news channels, in case a statement is issued although I would like to think that Alex would be good to her word, and that I would hear something before any kind of announcement is issued more widely.

Of course, as Dan has told me on several occasions, there are sure to be a lot of things going on behind the scenes that we're never likely to know about, which can take time. Leads being followed up, alibi's being checked and so on.

Still, considering it is a Friday, I had hoped that some sort of contact would have been made before the weekend begins.

Ross has calmed down a little now. He's milked the admiration of Mervyn, Hannah and anyone else who has shown the slightest bit of interest.

When I came back from the woods, my colleagues asked me where I had been and why, considering how quickly I had dashed out. Ross even suggested he thought I had popped out to buy some celebratory champagne, for goodness sake!

I had to tell them the truth, which is that it could be something, could be nothing. And until I know which way it is, I'm better off not saying anything further at all.

Mervyn's phone rings, and as he's talking he glances at me with one eyebrow raised, in an expression which is a mixture of curiosity and surprise.

"Yes, yes, I'll come down," he says, puts his phone down, and slowly stands up, which seems to take considerable effort. "Popping down to reception," he says, as he shuffles past me.

He returns a few minutes later, with Alex Nicholas behind him.

I smile. All is forgiven, Alex, I think to myself. A personal visit is better than a phone call, any day. It somehow just seems more important.

Mervyn points towards Patrick's office. "You can use the editor's room," he tells Alex.

I'm about to get out of my seat to join her for my briefing when Mervyn speaks again, stopping me in my tracks. "Ross," he says, "someone to see you."

I glance at Alex with a puzzled look on my face. "Stick around," she mouths at me, before heading to Patrick's office.

I may have a puzzled look on *my* face but that's nothing compared to the expression that Ross is currently wearing; a combination of shock, apprehension and fear.

Hannah looks at me, her face asking if I know what's going on. I shrug my shoulders.

Ten minutes later, Ross returns to his desk. Without a word, he opens one of his drawers and pulls out a folder which I know contains all his notes and paperwork relating to his beloved front page lead.

He glances anxiously at me and then returns to the little room where Alex is waiting for him. His cheeks are red and there are beads of sweat on his brow.

"I - I need to go," says Mervyn. "I should stay, to support Ross, but I need to go…"

"Don't worry, Merv," I say. "I'll stick around. I could do with having a quick word with Alex, the, er, the police officer, anyway."

"Well, if you're sure," he says. I can see he feels a little embarrassed but I know Mervyn is a creature of habit; there's probably a social function or a hot dinner waiting for him, and it simply wouldn't be the done thing to be late for it. We may work a number of evenings during the week, covering council meetings and other events, but Friday evenings? Not unless there is something huge going on. "You can call me if you need anything. Or Patrick. He's probably home by now, I'd have thought."

"Don't worry, Merv," I say. "I'll hold the fort."

He shuffles out.

A short while later, Hannah also leaves. Her boyfriend is due to be taking her out tonight, and she needs a couple of hours to get ready for him. I can see she's torn; she tells me she assumes Ross is in some sort of trouble about today's front page. I think to myself, Hannah, you have no idea.

I'm alone in the large newsroom, with Alex and Ross still deep in discussion in Patrick's room.

Suddenly Ross lets out what I can only describe as some kind of squeal, and I watch him through the glass partition; he's on his feet and his quite animated. Alex is making hand gestures which suggests she is asking him to calm down.

What on earth is going on?

My mind drifts back to a conversation Dan and I had earlier today at the cordon in the woods, when I thought I was visiting the scene of a suicide. He reminded me that, if it was a straight-forward suicide, why was Alex, Simon and Tam at the scene? Surely they had more important things to do?

Dan also reminded me that we have never been given a precise cause of death for Amanda, either.

Then Alex came to see us, and essentially confirmed that the woman in the car was Lisa, and without blatantly saying it, strongly suggested that there might be foul play. More than that, she requested that Dan and I give the police some time before publishing anything, on the promise that we would be the first to hear anything, which is why I've been willing my phone to ring all afternoon.

And so, I'm now wondering, if Lisa's death is something other than a suicide, is Alex speaking to Ross because he might be a suspect, in the light of today's front-page story?

Ross is feverishly flicking through his folder, and then plucks out a piece of paper and offers it to Alex, triumphantly.

Alex snatches it from him in her right hand and studies it intently. Her left hand clenches into a fist, almost as if she is saying, 'result!'

She glances at me and our eyes meet. I turn away; it's not the first time I've been caught staring into that side room! I lift my head furtively and am relieved to see Alex has turned her attention to Ross again.

She picks up the phone on Patrick's desk and spends a few minutes talking.

Then she leaves the editor's office and walks across the newsroom to where I am sitting.

"Hey, Kat," she says.

"What's going on?" I ask. "Is Ross OK? Is he in trouble because of the front-page piece and because Lisa is now dead?"

Alex looks extremely awkward. And then she looks me straight in the eye with such a fierce gaze, it's as if she's trying to bore right down into my soul. "Kat, can I trust you?"

I'm thrown momentarily; it's not what I expected her to say. Not that I had any clue what she was going to say, but it certainly wasn't that. "Of course," I say. "Of course. You can trust me."

"I need to," she says. "All this pussy-footing around, it's crazy. We need each other, right? We need the Herald to print our appeals for information or, er, to sometimes not print something, if we ask. And you need us, to give credibility to whatever information you might have."

"That's about it," I say, still a little unsure of where this is going, although the look on Alex's face suggests that I'm about to find out.

"As you and Dan suspected," she begins, pausing as if fighting an internal battle, with the opposing voice shouting a final 'don't' in order to prevent her speaking to me. She closes her eyes, and her expression changes. Her face visibly relaxes, as if that internal battle has come to an end. "Here's the bottom line," she says, "and I must stress that you cannot publish any of this yet. Lisa was murdered. We think it's probably the same person who killed Amanda Shepton."

I probably look like a goldfish right now; I can feel my mouth opening and closing, but no words are coming out. "If you or Dan publish anything to suggest that, then we're going to have journalists from all the nationals swarming into town and that won't do any of us any good. I don't expect you'd welcome them any more than we would."

"Not really," I say. And I mean it. It's one thing for Dan and I to be covering this story, knowing that people are waiting for our reports.

But if the nationals start running it, who knows where it will go? They went crazy with the black widow headlines.

"I spoke to the SIO earlier; we are planning to issue a statement at some point over the weekend, saying a body was found in the woods, and that we're looking into the circumstances. I will make sure you and Dan get that statement a few hours before it goes out generally, OK?"

"Yes." I'm just about able to blurt the word out.

"The statement will give an update on Pieter's situation, and it will say he has been bailed in terms of the investigation into Amanda Shepton's death. The full PM for Lisa is taking place at the moment and we're expecting it to conclude that the cause of death was an overdose, a lethal cocktail of pills and alcohol."

"That's what I was told," I say. "But you said she was murdered."

"I know," says Alex. "Look, there are certain, er, common factors, which I simply cannot disclose at the moment, which strongly suggest Lisa was killed. And it's precisely because one of those factors has not been disclosed publicly at all which leads us to believe that the same person is responsible for both deaths."

I do my mute goldfish impression again.

"Simon has asked us to look into anything we can think of which might tell us if these two women were linked in any way, or which might suggest why these two women were targeted. That's why I came here tonight to speak to Ross. Having read his report, and the allegations against Lisa, I wanted to know if there was any further information he had which had not made it into print. And it turns out there was which, in my opinion, gives us a potential significant new lead. So, the reason I am telling you all this is to try to make you understand why we need time, and why we would be very grateful if you don't publish anything beyond the official statement. I'm sure that, when the time is right, we can find a way to reward you for your co-operation. I can speak to your editor, if you wish."

"He doesn't know about any of this," I say. "He's been off today."

"Ah yes," she smiles. "Playing golf, I believe. It seems you and I have an increasing number of things in common, Kat. We both know Dan…" She pauses and for split second, I think I see her blush.

She continues, "And both our bosses started this particular Friday at the local golf course."

I return her smile.

"I need to ask you something," she says, and suddenly the smile fades from her face. "I didn't know if Ross was going to be able to help me this afternoon. It was a long shot. But I ended up getting a lot more than I bargained for."

"What do you mean?"

"How well do you know him?"

"Well," I say, and suddenly I feel very awkward. "I've worked with him for about six months, so I guess I'm getting to know him."

"What time did he arrive at work this morning?"

I can't help but smile. "It's funny you should ask that," I say. "He's usually the last one in, quite often arriving after nine. But today…"

I pause, as it suddenly dawns on me where this might be going.

"Go on," she says, softly.

"Today, I came in a bit early because I wanted to check to see if there was any update about Pieter, and Ross was already here, and was quite hyper, which I assumed was because of his front-page lead."

"I see," she says.

"You're not suggesting…."

"I'm not suggesting anything," she says. "But you know I said we're trying to find some way to link the women. I had a hunch what the link might be, and Ross confirmed it. But I still didn't know how that piece of information could actually indicate who the killer might be; who is common to both women?"

"And?"

"The thing is, during our conversation, Ross became quite upset. I've left him in that room now, because I've called his parents to collect him. But he's going to have to come to the station to give a formal statement at some point."

"Why?"

"Because he has shown me some information from Lisa which was not included in his story, but which could have been a prompt for our killer. And also because he slept with Amanda Shepton."

Thirty Seven: Dan

It's been a whirlwind of a week, to put it mildly, and I can't think of a better way to wind down into the weekend than by sharing an unexpected late-afternoon/early evening drink with Kat.

I was pleasantly surprised to get a text from her and I know I responded far too quickly than I should have done. No 'treat 'em mean to keep 'em keen' tactics for me.

The fact that her text said she had some info to share meant, of course, that the primary motive for meeting was professional. But hey, it's Friday evening, so you never know. Perhaps there will be an opportunity to mix business with pleasure.

Within seconds, I get another text, this time from Alex, in which she apologises for not getting back to me yet and 'strongly suggests' I speak to Kat at the earliest opportunity.

Who am I to disobey an officer of the law?

So, for the second time in a week, I find myself lurking in the shadows at the far end of the King's Head. I've already discreetly surveyed the other clientele; there aren't many of us, so it didn't take long, and there are no familiar faces present; there's certainly no sign of Warren James or Tam Fawcett.

Kat walks in, makes eye contact with me straight away, and smiles. I'm delighted to see that she's still wearing those tight-fitting trousers, so I know she's come straight from the Herald office. Working late on a Friday, too. That's intriguing.

I buy her a drink and nod perhaps a little too enthusiastically when she suggests we find somewhere quiet to talk. I take a chance on lightly placing my hand on the small of her back as I guide her to a booth at the back of the bar.

"I'm assuming you've come straight from work," I say, "and the only possible reason for still being in the office of a weekly paper like the Herald at this time of a Friday night is because *something* is happening or has happened."

Kat glances around, displaying a mixture of anxiety and excitement, as if she is worried that someone might be spying on us, and she then tells me that Alex visited the office of the Herald this afternoon and spoke to Ross.

"Woah," I say, when she finishes talking. Because for five or ten minutes, it's been like sitting opposite one of those old-fashioned kids toys, where you pull a cord in its back, and it starts talking away at a rate of knots until the cord returns to its starting position.

And I was pretty much enthralled by every second of it!

Where do I start to process this? In what order? Do I want to talk about Alex telling Kat there were 'common factors' which strongly suggest Lisa was killed, even though the PM is likely to conclude she died from an overdose? Or should I start with this apparent link between the two victims which, somehow, Ross was able to confirm to Alex? No, I can't help myself. I know where I've got to begin.

"Ross slept with Amanda?" I say, with a small whistle. "It seems Mrs Shepton was quite the cougar. Didn't you tell me you thought he had the hots for you?"

"So?"

"I guess you just weren't old enough," I smile.

"I'm old enough," she retorts, defensively.

"Oh, I know," I say, and the smile instantly fades from her face.

"Don't," she says softly.

"But…"

"Please, we can't."

I like to think that I'm a fairly good judge of people, which means I know when to pick my fights. Something tells me that if I persist with the flirting right now, all I'm going to do is drive Kat further away, not pull her in closer, so I choose to change the subject.

"So, is Ross now the prime suspect?"

Kat shakes her head. "I don't think so. Alex said he's going to have to make a formal statement at the police station but I don't see him as a killer."

"Ah, but that's because he's a colleague. Take a step back and look at it from Alex's point of view. Ross has got links to both women. He slept with Amanda. Perhaps she used and abused him, like Pieter. So he killed retaliated by killing her. And that gave him a taste for it. Then perhaps he found himself sympathising with Phillipa a little too much and decided to take matters into his own hands and kill Lisa in retaliation for the way she treated Phillipa."

"I just can't picture Ross killing someone," Kat says.

"I can't picture me agreeing not to write about a murder, yet I'm doing it by the look of it. Mind you, my motives are purely selfish."

"Oh?"

"As it stands, one murder, with a strong suspect bailed, and a second death which looks like a suicide, with no obvious links, and that's of enough interest to the nationals to keep me here. If they think that the 'black widow killer' is still at large and has struck again, well, that's probably it for me."

"Well, we can't have that now, can we?" she says. I wonder if she has any idea just how much she is teasing me? Or is she oblivious to it.

"So, what now?" I say.

"Police will probably issue a statement over the weekend, once the PM is confirmed," Kat says. "And she said she'll give it to us first."

I nod. If Alex is so keen to buy some time that she will approach Kat like she did, then I've no reason to question whether or not she will honour her side of the bargain. We'll be the first to hear about any update.

"Any chance of you getting a look at the notes Ross made?" I venture. "See if you can work out what this link is that he confirmed to Alex."

Kat looks offended. "Spoken like a true tabloid hack!" she says. "No, I'm not going to go shuffling through his notes."

I shrug my shoulders. "Worth a try. Doesn't it bug you, though? The police want us to trust them, and buy some time, yet they are holding out on us a bit. Common factors around the circumstances of the deaths which they won't tell us. And a 'common link' between the two victims, which they also won't tell us."

"I guess what we don't know can't hurt us," says Kat.

Of course, deep down, I'm happy to agree to our deal with Alex.

Ultimately, it will keep the nationals at bay, stop them sending their own staff to town, and give me more chance to break Kat's defences down, so I should be grateful.

"So," I say, "where do Barton and Russell investigations go from here?"

"Russell and Barton," smiles Kat.

"Maybe I should do a bit more digging into Amanda's background. See if I can find any more jilted toyboys. I wonder if Lisa had a son? Perhaps Amanda had him, too. That might link the two women."

"You're definitely sounding more and more like a tabloid hack," Kat says. "You can look into Amanda if you want. I'm more interested in Mark."

"Mark?"

She nods. "Yep. I think I'm going to do a bit more sniffing around there. I'm sure he killed Amanda. Now I need to find something to link him to Lisa."

"Have you forgotten about what Mark did to Tony? Have you forgotten that he has threatened you? I think you need to steer well clear of Mark Shepton."

"I'll go wherever the story takes me," she snaps defensively. "Isn't that what a journalist does? Use their instinct, follow the leads, go wherever the story takes them? My instinct is still telling me that Mark is our killer."

"All the more reason to keep away from him," I say.

She sighs. "OK, I wasn't going to tell you this," she begins, and then looks a little embarrassed. Hmm, holding out on me, Miss Russell? Maybe I'm not the only one behaving like a tabloid hack.

"Before she left the office, Alex told me they had some CCTV from Saturday night. A bunch of guys from the rugby team, out on the town. Including Mark."

"OK," I nod. "Which kind of gives him an alibi and plenty of witnesses."

"Yeah, but there is more footage from later in the evening. And Mark isn't on it. It doesn't prove he wasn't still there, of course. It just seems odd that he's clearly seen earlier, but not later."

"I think you're clutching at straws because you want it to be Mark so badly," I say.

"He's an arrogant scumbag," she says, and I can't help but laugh. "What's so funny?"

"My usual reply, when someone says something like that, is 'he might be a scumbag, but he's very good to his mother', but somehow I don't think that's appropriate in this case."

She gives me a playful slap on my arm.

"Another drink?" I say.

She glances at her watch. "Shit, no," she says. "Sorry, I've got to go, I've lost track of how late it is."

"Time flies when you're having fun," I offer.

"I've got to go, I'm supposed to be meeting some friends."

"Well, I'm only going to let you go if you promise that it is some friends you are meeting," I say.

"What do you mean?"

"I mean, I hope you are meeting friends, and not going after Mark Shepton again. Please stay away from him, Kat. Promise me."

"Promise you?" I instantly know I've said the wrong thing. "Promise *you*? Why would I do that? It's up to me what I do, not you."

"I'm only thinking of…."

"Well don't! It seems to me you're thinking of…whatever…just a bit too much."

I raise my hands in a calming gesture. "Alright," I say, "no need to go overboard, I…"

"Overboard?" She's raising her voice. "I'm fed up with people tip-toeing around me like I'm some fragile little thing."

"I know you're not fragile," I say. "I just don't think you should mess around with Mark Shepton, that's all. I'm just looking out for you."

"Well, STOP looking out for me," she says. "And stop trying to tell me what to do. Who the hell do you think you are, you arrogant, presumptuous prat?" And with that Kat grabs her bag and marches out of the pub, leaving me, open-mouthed, in my seat.

Thirty Eight: Alex

"I think I've found a link," I say and I afford myself a small, smug, inner smile as I watch Tam's eyebrows rise involuntarily.

"Go on," says Simon, who turns away from his computer screen and stares at me in a way that makes it clear that I have captured his undivided attention.

"Both our women had their tongues severed," I say. I pause to take a breath, as I feel a sickening sensation in my stomach every time I think of Amanda, and now Lisa, having their tongues cut out of their mouths and into pieces. "And we know that Sam Shepton repeatedly spoke of his wife's 'wicked tongue' in his suicide note. Earlier, I went to the Herald to speak to the reporter who wrote the front-page story today. He has a lot of paperwork, and files, a lot of additional material which did not make it into print. Among his files was the formal letter of complaint Phillipa sent to the college board of governors."

"I presume there's a point coming at some point?" says Tam, and I glare at him.

"The point is that Phillipa made some extremely strong allegations of misconduct and bullying, and on several occasions she made reference to Lisa having a 'vicious, wicked tongue.' I think that could be our link. Both our victims are accused of having cruel tongues, and both are found dead with their tongues cut out and, er, fed to them."

"Jesus, Nicholas," says Tam. "Clutching at straws now, aren't we?"

"We can't rule it out, Tam," says Simon. "It's as good a theory as any other we've got to suggest why our killer targeted these two women."

"You're going soft, guv!" says Tam. "Don't tell me you're buying this shit?"

"You want to offer me an alternative theory?" says Simon.

"Mark Shepton," says Tam, which surprises both Simon and myself.

Tam regards me a little warily, and then nods ruefully.

"You might be clutching at straws with this tongue mumbo-jumbo," he says, "but I think you might have been right about Mark."

I'm almost lost for words. But only almost. "What makes you say that?"

"I went to see Mark today, as instructed," Tam glances at Simon. "I caught him at the gym that he owns, across town, not long after we left here this afternoon. I asked him if he had been to the woods this morning."

"And?" says Simon.

"And he clenched his fists, turned as red as a baboon's arse, and said, 'are you wankers following me everywhere now?' which I took as a yes."

He pauses, presumably for dramatic effect, and then explains that Mark told him he visits the woods early every morning and does a run. The uneven terrain on the hillside provides him with a decent workout.

"And yes," Tam concludes, "he was in the woods early this morning, too. Though naturally, he denies seeing anything suspicious. And I didn't really want to tell him too much."

Simon thinks about this for a moment, and then says, "If Mark *is* our man, then it won't do any harm if he thinks we've got him under surveillance. My only concern is, did he think this before you want to see him, Tam, or afterwards? Because if he already thought it, he would have been taking one hell of a risk killing Lisa if there was a chance he was being observed."

Shit, he's right! And I was just starting to think that the pendulum was swinging firmly back to that thuggish brute.

"Did we get any further with the CCTV?" asks Simon. "Have we got any trace of Mark in the town centre with his team-mates late on Saturday night?"

"Nothing of any note, boss."

"We need to keep at it," says Simon.

The sound of an email notification from his computer diverts his attention. I focus once again on staring straight ahead of me, at the window behind Simon's head, because I had no inclination to engage in any small talk with Tam.

"PM results are in," says Simon. "Cause of death for Lisa is 1A, overdose. The initial examination confirms that her tongue was chopped up and fed to her, but the pathologist can find no evidence that this contributed directly to her death. There will be toxicological tests to determine the levels of alcohol and blood in her system."

Tam and I both wince at mention of the tongue.

"It's the same guy, alright," says Tam.

"You mean, Mark?" I suggest.

"We've got some boxes to tick," says Simon, his tone suggesting he's in no mood to witness any more verbal sparring between myself and Tam. "Clearly, we can rule Pieter out of Lisa's murder. Alex, how did you get on with speaking to Phillipa today?"

"She's in Scotland, boss," I say. "Seems Ross was so excited about his story being promoted to the front page, he gave her a courtesy call. She was terrified that, ironically, Lisa would go on the warpath as soon as the paper came out, so she decided to go and visit her sister, who lives just outside Inverness."

"Och, lovely part of the world," says Tam.

Simon scribbles some notes in his pad. "OK. We'll need to speak to the press office tomorrow, get a statement issued about Lisa's death. I will speak to her husband tonight, and the Principal of the college. I've been with him most of the afternoon, so it makes sense for me to keep that contact going. Are our two friends from the media still behaving themselves?"

"So far," I say. "I don't think they want a media circus down here any more than we do."

"OK. Alex, you can brief them; tell them the PM results. We want to hear from anyone who was in the woods on Friday morning, say from between six-thirty and eight-thirty. You never know, if there were some early dog walkers or joggers, we may have some sightings of Mark, too. The press office can put the PM results out and say that there are going to be further toxicological tests. If we get asked if we are treating this suspiciously, we will say we're keeping an open mind, OK?"

I nod. Tam looks a little uncomfortable.

"Are we not going to be honest, guv, and say that it's a murder?"

"I'm not sure what good that will do," says Simon.

"But it's the truth. If word gets out that we've lied…"

"We're *not* lying," says Simon. "Well, not exactly. We're being truthful about the PM results, and further tests. Most people will think about the Herald front page, put two and two together, hear the words overdose, and assume it's suicide. That means we can keep any potential panic at bay just for a little while. The fact that we're still asking for information from anyone who may have seen Lisa could ultimately, of course, change our stance."

Tam is clearly unconvinced.

"Look," says Simon, "I know you'd love me to stand in front of the cameras tomorrow and announce that we're hunting a serial killer, but all we're going to do is bring the national spotlight onto the town. I'll speak to Lisa's family. If Mark turns out to be our man, although what his motive might be for killing Lisa is a complete mystery right now, he's hardly likely to strike again if he thinks we're watching him."

"I suppose," says Tam.

"And in the meantime, I want us to do some more work on this theory Alex came up with, about the tongue. I've been thinking about it and I'm going to consult a criminal psychologist, see if there is any merit in the idea that, somehow, the words of Phillipa Player and Sam Shepton have prompted someone to commit murder. I think I need an expert opinion on this one, some educated insight. In the meantime, we need to consider if there's anyone who had access to both the suicide note of Sam Shepton, and Phillipa Player's letter."

"There's one person who springs to mind," says Tam, who then immediately clamps his lips together, as if the words had escaped from his mouth without permission.

"Sorry?" says Simon.

"Nothing," replies Tam, sheepishly.

"If you know of someone who we should be speaking to, let's have it," says Simon.

"Well, we should speak to him, I guess," says Tam, with all the mannerisms of a man well and truly backed into a corner, "but only to see if he knows of anyone else who would have access to both those documents."

"And the 'him' in question is?" asks Simon, his impatience rising.

"Warren James," Tam mumbles.

"The coroner's officer?" says Simon. "Interesting. Obviously he would have had access to Sam Shepton's suicide note. But what makes you think he might also have seen the formal letter of complaint written by Phillipa Player?"

Tam's hand instinctively reaches for, and tries to loosen, the collar of his shirt. Not only does he look as if he has been backed into a corner, but has been forced flat up against the wall in that corner, with absolutely no way out.

"Sorry, guv, I don't know what I was thinking, I shouldn't have…"

"And right now, I don't know what you're thinking either, but we're not leaving here until you tell us. I know Warren had access to the suicide note. How would he have seen Phillipa's letter?"

Tam glances at me helplessly, then Simon. He then looks towards the ceiling. What's he hoping for, some divine inspiration? He'd be better off looking through the floor, surely. I know it's wrong, but I can't help but enjoy watching him squirm. His discomfort is, well, it's making me feel very good.

"Warren would have seen the letter from Phillipa, because he is a senior member of the committee that deals with such complaints. He's on the board of governors."

Thirty Nine: Kat

I'm not quite sure what prompted such a dramatic outburst in the pub earlier, and I feel terribly guilty about it.

I will apologise to Dan, of course, but not right now.

I think my little tantrum came out of my own self-defence mechanism, because he was starting to get under my skin again, starting to get too close, and I was starting to enjoy that feeling.

It's amazing that he feels so protective of me, that he worries about me putting myself in danger by going after Mark. It's very sweet. But, like I told him, I'm a journalist. I'll go where the story takes me.

I think I surprised myself as much as him. It's as if I saw red, as if I was rebelling against his desire to protect me by wanting to be even more reckless.

I wonder, for a fleeting moment, if this is what happened with the killer. Did *he* see red? Did something happen, or was something said, which made the red mist rise? Did *Mark* see red? Did someone light the fuse on that foul, explosive, temper of his? Did someone push him too far? Everyone's got their breaking point, haven't they?

I poured myself a large glass of wine as soon as I got home and there isn't much of it left, so I feel much calmer now.

I guess right now it makes sense if I put some space between Dan and myself. I'm determined to get to the bottom of this case, on my own merit as a journalist and not because anyone thinks I'm Dan's plus-one, or because I'm 'sleeping with the enemy', no matter how tempting that might be at times. I need to do this for this myself.

The phone rings.

It's Patrick. Mervyn had told him about the day's drama around Ross, and my editor had apparently spent the last hour talking to Ross' parents, while also trying to get hold of Simon, the SIO on the case.

I then bring him up to speed with pretty much everything I know about the Lisa Davidson case, and I also tell him about the 'deal' Dan and I have made with Alex.

Thankfully, Patrick approves, and agrees with the rest of us that there's nothing to be gained by having a media circus here, which will undoubtedly be focused on ramping up the 'black widow' lines, which means trying to dig up any dirt they possibly can on Lisa; as much as it appears as if she wasn't exactly the nicest person in the world, I'm sure her husband and daughter are missing her, and don't deserve to be surrounded by sensationalist hacks seeking salacious stories about her.

"What do you think it can be?" I ask.

"What?" says Patrick.

"Alex said there were 'common factors' about the deaths of the two women but won't say what they are. It looks like Lisa died from an overdose, but thinking about it, we've never yet had a formal cause of death for Amanda. Is the 'common factor' an overdose? We know Amanda was tied up, so it could be that whatever she OD'd on was forced into her mouth."

"Maybe I'll try to have a little chat with Warren," says Patrick, "see if I can get some kind of steer from him. He should know."

"Good luck with that," I say. "He's rude."

"Oh, he's not too bad when you get to know him," says Patrick. "He's just old-school, that's all. I'll try and get hold of him and see if I can get some kind of hint, although I think I'll tread very carefully, because he plays everything by the book, and if he tells the investigating team that I'm pushing, they might think we're going to go back on our agreement, and can't be trusted, and we don't want that. You seem to be doing a great job building a good rapport with Alex."

"Thanks," I say. A vote of approval from my boss is just the pick-me-up I need right now. "I wish I could say the same about Dan."

"Oh?" he says, and I instantly kick myself for letting that slip out.

"Don't tell me I've got to cancel my order for a new hat," he teases, and I feel myself blush. I tell him what happened in the pub.

"At the risk of incurring your wrath myself, I can see where Dan's coming from," says Patrick. "Mark is somewhat volatile, just ask Tony. And I don't need to remind you of what he might be capable of"

"Don't take *Dan's* side," I protest. "Aren't you meant to support your staff?"

"Of course I support you. I admire your drive. You're going to be a brilliant journalist. You're *already* a brilliant journalist, and that's why it's in my interests to do what I can ensure you remain in one piece. Just be careful, eh?"

Another man telling me to be careful, to take it easy. I wonder if he'd have said the same thing to Dan, if Dan was the journalist six months into his career, working on his biggest story so far.

"Look," he says, "take some time out this weekend. Go and do – well, whatever it is you do, have some fun, take a break. You've done some great work this week. I expect Ross will be off for a good few days, so we'll be short, so I'm going to need everyone fighting fit next week."

"But the police are going to issue a statement tomorrow."

The tone of his voice suggests that he knows he isn't going to win this argument. "Then write up the statement, publish it online, and then go and have some fun."

"OK," I say, and he *knows* I'm smiling.

I rent a flat on the edge of the town centre, which has become very popular with my younger sister, as it's the perfect place for us to stagger back to after a night on the town, although it's been a little while since we did that. Maybe it's time we did it again. Maybe that's just what I need right now.

I finish what's left of my wine and am about to go in search of more when my phone rings again. My instinct tells me it's Dan. Part of me wants to talk to him, part of me doesn't.

I pick up the handset. It's Alex!

I quickly shake my head, as if that's somehow going to shrug off the slight fog around my mind caused by the large glass of wine. I may not consider myself frail and fragile, but I will admit that I'm a bit of a lightweight when it comes to consuming alcohol.

"Hey," I say into the handset.

"Have I caught you at a good time?" she asks.

"Had a slightly bigger glass of wine than I expected," I confess.

"Sounds great! Wish I could."

"You still at work?"

"Afraid so. And I've got a few more things to do tonight before I finish, so if I was you, I'd top up that glass of yours, and have one for me, too."

Alex tells me the press office will be issuing a statement around midday tomorrow, which will give the initial PM results, but will emphasise that further tests are taking place.

She also tells me that Simon is making contact with Lisa's family, so that if I hold off until tomorrow morning to write the report, I'll be able to confirm Lisa's identity.

That, of course, does throw up another immediate question, but Alex is already ahead of me. "For the record, in case you were thinking of asking, because I'm sure other people will, there's no evidence to suggest Lisa's death has any connection to the Herald's front-page story today, although people will invariably draw their conclusions. I think it would also be fair to say, given my conversation with Ross, and the fact that I've had several messages from your editor, that the Herald is providing every possible assistance to us in our investigations."

"OK, thanks. So," I say, discovering that the wine has given me a little more bravado than I might otherwise have, "are you treating Lisa's death as murder or not?"

I'm sure I hear a little laugh from Alex before she answers. I think she knows I'm tipsy. "Officially, we're keeping an open mind. But as I said to you earlier, there are circumstances about this case which not only make us think Lisa was murdered, but that she was killed by the same person who killed Amanda. We just can't, well, really we just don't want this to be said publicly yet. We'll probably have to say more when we get the toxicology results."

"And presumably you can't tell me what these 'circumstances' are?" I ask, my new-found bravado suggesting nothing ventured, nothing gained.

"It's precisely because we didn't divulge these details that makes us sure we are dealing with two murders committed by the same man."

"And could that man be Mark?"

Alex pauses, and for a moment I wonder if the phone signal has cut out.

"OK, look," she says, "you've been true to your word, and haven't published anything about Lisa being murdered, and you could've done. I'm grateful for that, so let me tell you something about Mark."

I suddenly feel stone-cold sober, and a shiver of anticipation shoots up and down my spine.

"Mark is definitely a person of interest," she begins, her words slow and measured. "But you can't print that. Not yet. But we are able to place him in the vicinity of *both* murders within the right timeframe."

"Both?"

She reminds me that it was Mark who reported Amanda's death, and then tells me that Mark told Tam he was in the woods on Hillside this morning. In fact, he is in the woods almost every morning, apparently, as part of his regular fitness routine.

"So, what's his alibi?"

"For this morning? He doesn't have one. He admitted to being in the woods and denied seeing anything suspicious. As for Saturday night, he says he was out drinking in town."

"That should be easy enough to prove," I say.

"Not as easy as you might think. We've got CCTV of Mark in The Crow's Nest just after seven-thirty on Saturday night, with some other members of the rugby club. It looks like they then went on to Benny's. But we can't prove that Mark went with them. There's no CCTV. We've covered pretty much every bar in High Street and on the main strip along the seafront, everywhere between the Crow's Nest and Benny's."

"Which means...?"

"Which means that, right now, Mark's alibi for Saturday still can't be corroborated." She laughs again. "I can almost hear your nose for news twitching. Kat, don't get tempted to do too much digging around Mark, leave that to us, eh? He's dangerous, you know that."

I sigh. "They say it happens in threes. You're the third person to tell me this in the last couple of hours."

"Then hopefully you'll listen to one of us. Actually, I'm really going to have to go in a minute. I've got a house call to make..."

"A lead?"

"I don't know yet. But look, I haven't got time to call Dan and give him an update. I'm assuming he's one of the other people who have been warning you off Mark, so can you update him for me?"

"Er, well, I, uh…things are a little, er, *complicated* right now."

"Don't worry, I'll call him. But if you speak to him before I do, tell him I *am* going to call him. I've just got one thing I've got to do first."

"Thanks," I say. I feel as if I've let her down a little. But then it occurs to me that I was also her messenger earlier, too. "If he thinks you've only called me and not him for the second time running, he might think you're choosing sides," I say.

"You're right, I should be the one to call him. Oh, and Kat?"

"Yes?"

"Whatever's become 'complicated' between you two, try and sort it, eh? He likes you, and he's a good guy."

"I'll try," I say.

"You should. Let's catch up soon," she says, and hangs up.

The wine has definitely worn off now, and I pull out my laptop, typing up the notes from our conversation while it's all still fresh in my mind. I'm not sure I'll be able to read my tipsy shorthand quite so well if I left it a day or so. Besides, I can write something now for the Herald's website and social media channels tomorrow.

I reach the part of my notes that relate to Mark.

I felt a pang of exuberance when Alex told me they can place Mark at the scene of both deaths within the right timeframes.

Good, I think to myself. His absence from the CCTV at Benny's does, on the face of it, seem extremely suspicious.

But then another thought pops into my head, and I make a mental note that a large glass of wine on a Friday evening appears to do wonders for me. I've just had a eureka moment, and despite being warned off by Dan, Patrick *and* Alex, I'm simply going to *have* to follow this up. It suddenly seems so clear, so obvious, hidden in plain sight, as they say.

The *only* thing putting me off is that, if I'm right, then I'm on the verge of corroborating Mark's alibi and possibly clearing him for the murder of his mother.

Forty: Dan

It's just as well my visit to the pub ended earlier than I would have liked, as Mum has pulled out all the stops for a family dinner tonight, which is a welcome distraction after the rather unexpected drama earlier.

I feel my mobile vibrate in my pocket and expect to see Kat's name appear on the screen, as she presumably hopes to supplement my supper with some humble pie.

I see that it's Alex, and excuse myself from the table.

"My sources tell me there might be trouble in paradise already," she says, which throws me for a moment.

"Sorry?"

"I understand that some journalistic relations may be a little tense."

"You've spoken to Kat?"

"We could make a detective out of you," she teases, and then tells me how Kat told her things were 'complicated'.

"If, by complicated, you're asking if I got my head bitten off simply for asking her to be careful, then yes, they're 'complicated' all right."

Sensing, quite rightly, that she's hit something of a raw nerve, Alex updates me on the investigation, and forewarns me that a statement will be issued by the press office around midday tomorrow.

"You're not officially announcing Lisa's death as a murder yet, then?" I ask, when Alex pauses for breath.

"Until we get all the toxicological tests, we're keeping an open mind," she replies.

"It's very intriguing," I say, "not to mention a bit risky on your part, I'd imagine. Are Lisa's family happy with this?"

"We're still appealing for witnesses," says Alex, "which we would be doing whether or not we're calling this a murder. We just need a bit of time to sort a few things out without any increased media spotlight, which is why we're very grateful for your co-operation."

"Grateful enough to give me a bit of a steer?" I venture. "Off the record, of course. Kat said you'd mentioned something about some 'common factors' relating to the two deaths. Was Lisa tied up in her car? Is that the common factor? Or is it that Amanda also had a cocktail of drink and drugs, presumably forced into her?"

"You and Kat *have* been swapping notes, haven't you?" says Alex. Is it my imagination, or could there be a hint of jealousy in her voice. Ha, probably my imagination, feeding my male ego.

"Come on, Alex," I say, "there's obviously something you're not telling us."

"I can't," she says. "It's, er, *complicated*. Basically, the only reason we can say with some certainty that the same person is responsible for both deaths is because of certain details which have not been put into the public domain. If there was to be a third victim, and those circumstances emerge again without having been made public, it will give us a strong indication that it's the same killer."

"Do you think he *will* strike again?" I ask.

"When we found Amanda," she says, "taking into account all the circumstances, I was convinced that her death was a one-off. There were elements about it which made it appear very personal."

"And which presumably helped to point the finger firmly at Mark, particularly given his charming nature."

"But now, this second one; we're struggling to find a meaningful link between the two victims."

She pauses, and it sounds to me as if she has taken a slurp of something warm, comforting and alcoholic.

"Sorry," she said, realising that I probably figured out what she had just done.

"Don't apologise, I think you've probably earned it, after the week you've had."

"It's more like Dutch courage for what I've got to do once I've finished speaking to you," she says, "and no, I can't tell you what I'm doing to do. One thing that is bothering me though; did you fall out with Kat because of Mark?"

"What makes you say that?"

"Because I got the impression, from my chat with Kat earlier, that she is determined to prove Mark is the killer."

I tell Alex about my conversation with Kat and that ultimately it was my warnings to her to steer clear of Mark that prompted Kat to leave the pub.

"I've probably not helped matters," says Alex, who tells me she has undoubtedly added some fuel to the fire by telling Kat about Mark being absent from any town centre CCTV footage later in the evening.

"I'm on good terms with the editor of the Herald," I say. "Perhaps I'll give him a call. If Kat takes exception to you and me warning her off, perhaps she'll respect him."

"She did say I was the third person to warn her," says Alex. "If you were the second, perhaps the editor has already had a word?"

"She's still less likely to argue with him than she is with us, so I'll call him and say we're all a bit worried about her. She gets full marks for enthusiasm, but that isn't going to do her any good if Mark gets his hands on her and…." I tail off. I don't want to think it, let alone say it.

"I assume Pieter is now in the clear," I say, trying to push Mark to the back of my mind. "I guess there's now Ross, from the Herald, in the picture now, too. Kat told me Ross been sleeping with Amanda. I must admit, I didn't see that one coming."

"We'll be speaking to him," says Alex. "But I honestly don't think he could kill anyone. Just a gut-feeling, you know?"

"Yeah, I know," I say. "Just the same as my gut feeling tells me it isn't Mark. Tho I can't seem to convince Kat of that."

"I don't know what to think," says Alex. "We, er, we do know that Mark was in the woods this morning."

"Oh?" I can feel my heart start to pound again.

"Yes. He told my colleague, Tam."

"Another expert at social interaction," I say. "Those two are like twins separated at birth. So, Mark admitted being in the woods?"

"Goes running there every morning, apparently, including this morning, which means we have him at both crime scenes within a similar timeframe to our victims being attacked."

Never mind running, my mind is racing to Kat, hoping she hasn't gone off on another wild goose-chase in her blinkered quest to prove he is the killer.

Alex thanks me again for co-operating, and not rushing to the nationals with news of Lisa's murder.

"It does go against my instincts," he says, "and it certainly convinces me that you guys are holding out on me; you're clearly keeping a few things very close to your chest. But a second murder so soon will have all the nationals here, and I'll be sidelined. And I feel too involved to let go of it now."

"As soon as I can tell you more," says Alex, "I will, I promise. I do appreciate, as does Simon, that it has to be a two-way street."

"That's good to hear."

She pauses, then says, "Oh, here's a bit more information which might be of interest. Simon is going to speak to a criminal psychologist. You were asking if you thought he might strike again; we're trying to figure out why he targeted these two women, and if that shows some kind of pattern which may help us identify a potential next target."

"Interesting," I say. "Thanks. Maybe, once Simon is done with the psychologist, you can put me in touch, so I can do a piece, getting into the mind of a killer…"

"I'll see what I can do. Look, duty calls. Thanks again, Dan. And try not to worry too much about Kat. Hopefully, in the cold light of day, she won't do anything reckless."

"I hope not. And if anything exciting happens with whatever lead you're following up tonight…"

"If I can say anything about it, you'll be the first person I call."

"Not Kat?"

She laughs. "I'll call you first next time, OK?"

It doesn't take me long to write out a story for the nationals tomorrow, although I won't file it until the formal statement is issued by police, just in case something new comes to light. But as soon as that statement is issued, I will be able to tweak my story if required and then send it straight away.

I pick up Mum's copy of the Herald and thumb through it.

Old habits die hard, and I find myself naturally flipping through to the Births, Marriages and Deaths section, the inadvertent source of so many interesting snippets and leads over the years.

And this issue was no exception, for as I browse the columns of dense text, I spot something which seems to have slipped under the radar of everyone else and which, clearly, family members were hoping to keep quiet.

Amanda Shepton's funeral is taking place on Tuesday.

Forty One: Alex

With my calls to Kat and Dan made, I can't put off my next task any longer.

Following Tam's revelation about Warren James being a college governor, Simon instructed me to visit the Coroner's Officer, sooner rather than later.

Having remembered, from our time in the woods this morning, that he had taken the day off, I had called his office, before phoning Kat and Dan, and was told that Warren had only gone away for the day, to visit some relatives, but had been informed of Lisa's death and so was heading home tonight rather than staying away for the weekend, as he had apparently planned.

Which means, of course, that he is likely to be even less welcoming than he usually is.

It hadn't been said openly during our meeting earlier but if Tam's information proves correct, then suddenly Warren becomes a member of what, to the best of our knowledge right now, is a very small group – a group of people with a clear link to both Amanda and Lisa.

If *my* theory is correct, about the phrase 'wicked tongue' or 'vicious tongue' being the link, then that puts Warren into an even more exclusive little club, because I suspect Tam is right, and Warren will have seen both Sam Shepton's suicide note and Phillipa Player's complaint.

And *that* means, as uncomfortable and unbelievable as it sounds, that Warren suddenly becomes a 'person of interest'.

Tam had volunteered to visit Warren and threw a salvo of daggers my way when Simon ordered me to do it. Simon felt Tam and Warren were a little too friendly, a little too close, and that this visit may have to be a little more formal.

It was also a little disconcerting that Simon suggested, in a way that meant it was actually not an advisory suggestion but a demand, that I don't go to see Warren alone.

Warren lives in a large, detached, home on the lower slopes of Hillside, in one of the older parts of town.

Wildly-growing trees and thick, high, hedges surround the property and the house itself, set back from the road at the end of a short, private drive, almost looks like a film set for a low-budget horror movie; the sort of property some lost hikers would stumble upon during a midnight thunderstorm on a remote, windswept moor.

It looks dark, cold and foreboding.

There's a large black 4x4 on the drive and I pull up behind it.

DC Foreman and I get out of my car and stomp across the gravel drive to the heavy wooden front door, which has a large metal knocker on it and an extremely old-looking doorbell. If I had to describe the whole scene with one word, it would be 'creepy', which is the same word I would use to describe the occupant. Perhaps even 'menacing'.

I'm about to raise the large metal knocker when it pulls away from my grasp as the front door creaks slowly open, causing me to gasp.

"Acting DI Nicholas," says Warren, "I've been expecting you."

DC Foreman gives me a bemused look but I'm not entirely surprised. Tam! The disgruntled Detective Sergeant had clearly tipped his friend off that I was on my way.

The door opens a little wider. "Oh, and I see you're not alone," sneers Warren, knowingly. "Should I be concerned?"

"May we come in?" I ask, choosing to ignore his question.

"I suppose," he says opening the door wider still and stepping back, allowing us to enter the dark, dank hall, our footsteps echoing loudly on the bare flagstone floor.

He leads us through a side door into a study. He picks up a pile of letters from the top of an old-looking desk. "I've not been in long."

"We won't intrude on you any longer than we have to," I say.

"You probably know more than I do about Lisa Davidson's death," he says.

"We're following up leads on possible links between Lisa and Amanda Shepton," I explain.

"You mean other than them both having their tongues removed?" he replies dryly.

"Quite," I say. "We're trying to find people who had access to certain information which potentially links both women."

He raises an inquisitive eyebrow.

"We're keen to identify anyone who may have seen Sam Shepton's suicide note *and* Phillipa Player's letter of complaint to the college governors."

Warren freezes like one of those 'living statues', and a couple of letters slip from his fingers and fall back onto the table.

His eyes narrow. "Do I need a lawyer?" he says.

"Do you?" I counter. "What makes you say that?"

His cold eyes bore into me, then glances at DC Foreman, and then back to me. "You clearly know that *I* had access to both the documents you mentioned. *Acting* Detective Inspector, are you suggesting that I might be a suspect?"

"You've been around policing long enough," I reply. "You know we have to follow up every possible lead. Yes, I know you would have had access to Sam Shepton's suicide letter. This evening, we learned that you are a college governor, which we did not know before."

"And why would you?"

"Quite. What I came here to ask was, can you confirm that you did, indeed, see both documents, and can you tell us of anyone else who, to the best of your knowledge, may have had access to both of them? We're trying to compile lists and want to see if there are any common names."

"Well, there's *my* name, for starters, of course," he says.

"There is," I say, swallowing hard. This is becoming even more uncomfortable than I thought it would.

"If you want me to account for my whereabouts around the time of both deaths, I'm sure I can," he says. "I left town late last night, having booked today off, with the plan of spending a long weekend visiting friends and family, a good ninety-minute drive away, at least."

"Last night?" I say.

"Yes," he nods.

"I would need to consult my diary to see what I was doing last weekend, around the time of Amanda Shepton's death."

"Mr James, I'm not implying…" I start.

"Of course you are," he snaps. Then the stern expression on his craggy face suddenly softens just a little. "You're right, Detective Inspector, I have been around policing long enough, so it is perfectly logical that, in all the circumstances, you would want to speak to me, if you think that there is some kind of link between those two documents and the two deaths."

He smirks a little, and adds, "I'd be a little disappointed in you if you didn't. But if I need to formally say it, then no, I did not kill either of these two women. I had no reason to. I was many miles away when Lisa was killed. And I'm sure that if I consult my diary, I'll be able to tell you what I was doing when Amanda was killed. But yes, I confirm that I did, indeed, see both the documents you mentioned."

We will, of course, confirm that he did leave town last night but my instinct is telling me he is telling the truth, which would put him in the clear as far as killing Lisa is concerned.

"We were hoping you might be able to help us identify anyone else who may have had access to both documents," I say. "We haven't yet got a list of all the college governors."

Warren picks up the letters that had fallen onto the desk and flicks through them. "Let me think."

He pulls one of the letters to the top of the pile and regards it intently for a few moments. He tries to insert his little finger into the flap of the envelope but it appears to be firmly sealed.

He slowly lifts his head and fixes me with an unnerving look.

"Now that you come to mention it," he says, partially turning his back on me and reaches across the table towards a small container filled with pens, a plastic ruler and other items of stationery. When he turns round again, I see he is effortlessly slicing through the envelope with something in his hand. "There is someone that you should perhaps speak to," he says. "One of the other governors who sat on the panel which considered the complaint from Miss Player was Stuart Shepton."

Sam's brother! Someone who seems to have gone out of his way to evade us so far and who would certainly be aware of the full contents of his brother's suicide note.

"I think you'll find Stuart would have seen both documents you've referred so," says Warren. "There were other governors who saw the letter from Miss Player, of course, but I can't imagine how any of them would also have seen the late Mr Shepton's suicide letter."

He pulls the contents from the envelope, speed-reads them, tosses the paper onto the desktop and starts to open the next envelope.

"That's probably about as much help as I'm able to provide," he says. "If anything else occurs to me, naturally I will let you know."

I hear his words, yet it's as if I'm somewhere else. I'm aware of what he has just said, yet I am not really focusing on him. I am, instead, fixated on how he is now swiftly, cleanly, effortlessly and efficiently he is opening his letters.

"Miss Nicholas?" I kind of hear him say. "Detective?"

"Er, yes, yes," I mumble. "Stuart Shepton. He's not been too keen to speak to us so far, but I guess now I've got reasonable grounds to be a little more assertive. That's been very helpful, thank you."

"Are you alright?" he asks, more with a tone of veiled suspicion than any kind of genuine concern for my apparent vacant moment.

"Yes, I'm fine," I say, "thank you. It's been a very long day."

"Indeed it has," he says.

"You've been very helpful," I say, "thank you for your time."

"Of course," he says.

We step outside and only after the heavy door thuds shut behind us does DC Foreman turn to me. "What was all that about? Did you have a funny turn or something? It was quite stuffy in there."

"Sorry," I say, "I was just a bit distracted. I've just never seen someone open their post with a pair of surgical scissors before."

Forty Two: Kat

I drape my coat over the back of my chair and am about to sit at my desk when Patrick calls me into his office.

He tells me Ross won't be in at all this week; he has been granted 'compassionate' leave.

I'm not entirely surprised; I know he'll spend a few hours, at least, one day this week providing a formal statement to the police, not only in relation to his story about Lisa, but also his shocking relationship with Amanda, which I'm still struggling to comprehend.

I find it hard to recall the growing respect I had for Amanda. She seemed like such a successful, popular, happy person on the surface, who seemed to be doing many positive things.

Yet clearly there were some serious family issues, leading to her husband's suicide, her 'difficult' relationship with Mark, and her apparent, seemingly insatiable, penchant for younger men.

Patrick says he has reviewed the copy I filed over the weekend about Lisa's death; the police press office issued a fairly bland statement early on Saturday afternoon, and I've added a few extra details to it, but not anything that would betray the trust Alex has shown in me.

I'm bursting to tell Patrick what I discovered at the weekend but he knocks all the wind out of my sails when he tells me Dan called him yesterday, they met for a drink and talked about the two deaths and, apparently, about me!

This little revelation catches me totally off-guard and I forget how keen I was to talk to Patrick, to tell him what I'd learned by following my instincts. I wanted to show him what a good journalist I've been. But all I want to do now is let him say his piece and get out of his office as quickly as possible.

I only half-hear Patrick's words, because I'm feeling a mixture of emotions; I feel upset and extremely angry. In fact, right now, I'd go as far as to say I even feel a bit betrayed, by both Dan and Patrick.

Men! Pah.

I've been trying so hard to be professional and do the right thing; I've kept Dan at arm's length because I've been so worried that if we got together, no matter how discreet we tried to be, Patrick would find out and would suggest that, in our business, mixing business with pleasure was, if not forbidden, then certainly heavily frowned upon. Would I weaken, lower my defences, and disclose all my leads to Dan during some post-coital pillow talk?

That's why I've tried to resist Dan's interest in me and to resist my interest in him. This is my first proper job. I don't want anything to distract me from it, to compromise my career. It's the classic heart-versus-head moral dilemma. And at this early stage of my working life, I can't afford to let the heart win. Can I?

And what happens? My editor and my 'forbidden paramour' are meeting for drinks, discussing the story and talking about me!

Patrick should be talking to *me* about the story, not Dan!

"Kat? Kat!" Patrick raises his voice and shakes me from my thoughts. "Have you heard anything I just said?"

"Sorry," I mumble.

He sighs, but in a good way. And he smiles. "I know what you're thinking; *why* am I talking to Dan?"

My cheeks burn as they redden. Am I so transparent? So easy to read?

"It's all a means to an end. If you promise to listen, I'll give you the short version."

"Sorry," I mumble again.

"Warren called me last night and said the police are now turning their attention towards Stuart Shepton."

"Stuart?"

"Yes. Obviously he is linked to Amanda. But he's also a college governor, which loosely links him to Lisa. Since Dan met Stuart last week, I thought I'd see if I could prise a bit more information out of him, try to see if there's any merit in Stuart being a suspect."

"But what about Mark?" I hear the words come out of my mouth before I've even spoken them.

"There isn't much to link Mark to Lisa," Patrick says.

"You mean, apart from admitting to being in the woods around the time she died, and the fact that he has an extremely short fuse, hot temper and a tendency to spontaneous outbreaks of violence?"

"I think the links between Stuart and both victims *are* worth exploring. There's something else Warren told me, something I haven't told Dan." He hesitates, and for a moment I wonder if he is going to tell me, as well. After all, he and Dan seem so cosy right now, I'm surprised to hear Patrick has held something back.

The awkward silence seems to last forever. It probably wasn't even a full minute, but it felt a lot longer; Patrick seems to be reluctant to say much more, yet realises he has probably already said too much.

"As Coroner's officer, Warren saw Sam Shepton's suicide note," he says, speaking slowly as if very carefully contemplating every single word. "As a governor, he also saw the full allegations made against Lisa. There was something about the language used in both documents, coupled with - well, with circumstances surrounding the deaths which have not been disclosed - which suggests a clear link."

"Wait! Warren is a college governor? Wouldn't that make *Warren* just as viable a suspect as Stuart?" I ask; the words blurt out before I could stop them. Patrick looks horrified.

"What? Warren? No! He wouldn't, he…" Patrick pauses. "Well, technically, I suppose he did have access to both documents. And Alex did visit him on Friday night, but only to find out who else may have had access to both documents, which is when Stuart's name came up."

"Maybe Warren was diverting attention from himself," I suggest.

"Kat! Come on. I've known Warren a long time. He may not be the most, er, amiable chap, not necessarily what you'd call a people person, but I don't think he's so short of business that he needs to go and generate more of it for himself."

"I suppose," I say.

"I also learned from Dan that the SIO is consulting a criminal psychologist, to see if the language used in the letters, and the nature of the deaths, are linked."

"I wonder what it is about the deaths? What aren't we being told?" I say, thinking again about those common factors Alex alluded to.

"Nothing that we would publish," Patrick says sternly. "Believe me, Kat, you wouldn't want to know."

"Do *you* know?" I ask.

"I know enough," says Patrick. "I know enough to know when to stop asking questions. Warren has gone out on a limb telling me this much. But what it does mean is that I think we need to look a little closer at Stuart Shepton. And having spoken to Dan about it, while I didn't tell him everything I know, I'm sure the fact that we spoke about Stuart at all will raise Dan's suspicions."

Another thought suddenly occurs to me. "Ross," I whisper. "He has links to both women, too."

Patrick simply nods. "He does. But I…, well, I just can't believe it would be Ross."

"Nor can I," I say. "But then again, I can't believe he actually slept with Amanda, either. So, what about me?"

"Sorry?"

"You said that you and Dan also spoke about me."

"Ah," says Patrick, who rolls his eyes, almost as if he was hoping I had forgotten about that bit. "He told me you stormed out of the pub after he suggested you forget about Mark Shepton. He, well, he asked me to have another word with you. He's worried about you."

"Oh, for goodness sake!"

"I don't blame him, Kat. Mark is dangerous. He has a horrible temper. Look at poor Tony!"

"All the more reason to help get him locked up!" I say.

"Look. Dan and I had a chat…," he starts but pauses when he sees the look on my face. "OK, look, what *I* am trying to say is that it's Amanda Shepton's funeral tomorrow. I'm going to go, to represent the Herald. However she may have conducted herself in her private life, she did a lot of good work for a lot of organisations in the town, so I think it's appropriate to respect and recognise that. And that's why I will go, on behalf of the paper. And that's why I want you to keep well away from the crematorium."

"What?"

"I don't want you anywhere near the funeral."

"But…"

"Mark will be there, and I expect Stuart will be there, too. Which means you will be able to visit his office, without the risk of bumping into him, use your clear journalistic skills to talk to staff, see if you can find out anything of interest."

"But…"

"It's non-negotiable, Kat. Please. This isn't about protecting you. Well, it is. Of course it is. But it is more about the story. Our latest information suggests Stuart is now a person of interest, and I want you to follow that up, do some digging, see what you can find out while Stuart is occupied at the funeral."

I glare at him, but the look on his face tells me that his mind is made up. I turn, leave his little office and almost certainly slam the door a lot harder than I intended to. But seriously? When is he going to stop wrapping me in cotton wool? I'm so fed up with him and Dan both treating me like I'm some kind of fragile little girl.

I'd been so excited to share what I had learned at the weekend with my editor, to show him what a good journalist I am.

But now, there's only one person I think I can trust with what I've learned. If I tell Patrick, I'm not at all sure he won't tell Dan, and what I've discovered is the kind of the thing the tabloids would go crazy for, I'm sure.

No, there's only one person I can tell.

I tell Hannah I'm not lunching with her today because I have some errands to run. I leave the office and send a text to Alex; I've no doubt she's busy, but she'll want to hear what I've got to say. I tell her I need just five minutes of her time, because I've discovered something she will want to know.

Alex replies quickly, telling me she could use a change of scene and a short break. She suggests we meet in the same High Street coffee house that Dan and I went to last week.

When Alex joins me at my table, she can see I'm agitated.

"Everything OK?" she says.

"Just men," I mutter.

"You haven't made up with Dan yet then?"

"He seems to be more interested in climbing into bed with my boss than he is with me," I say, and immediately blush. It's not really the kind of language I use. Yet I feel increasingly comfortable with Alex.

"They did used to work together, so I guess they're just renewing their acquaintanceship," she offers.

"As well as conspiring to try to tell me how to do my job," I say.

Alex says, "I'll see Dan and your boss, and raise you a Tam Fawcett." She makes me smile. Then the smile fades. "I really don't have very long. What have you got?"

"I *know* where Mark Shepton was on Saturday night," I say, and the look on her face says I've suddenly captured her total undivided attention.

"What? Where? How?"

"My sister never needs too much persuasion to hit the town on a Saturday night," I say. "So, we went out, and I took the opportunity to do a little, er, investigative journalism because of what you told me about the town centre CCTV."

"And?"

"And I found out that the reason you didn't have any footage of Mark in Benny's last weekend is because he wasn't in Benny's. When my sister and I go out, and don't want to be pestered by horny guys on the pull, we, er, we go off the beaten track a bit."

"Meaning?"

"We went to Pride," I say. "And we got talking to a few people, and…"

"Pride?"

I nod, and I see her eyes widen.

"You're not suggesting…", she starts.

I nod again. "Yes. Our grunting, macho man Mark is not quite the alpha male he would have us believe. He's gay."

Alex opens her mouth, but can't find any words. And I can't help myself; I know that I'm now grinning like the proverbial Cheshire Cat. She's looking at me with the same mixture of shock, surprise and professional admiration that I was hoping to see on Patrick's face, had

I got the chance to tell him earlier, but his confession at talking to Dan about me made me uninclined to share.

"There's more; lots more," I say. "The rugby team, they all know. And while they don't necessarily understand it, Mark is one of their star players, so they've been protecting him and his 'reputation' as one of the lads. But here's the thing; once I got talking to the landlord, he wouldn't stop. Which is why yesterday afternoon, I visited the home of Mark's ex-boyfriend."

"You *have* been busy," says Alex, with what I can only describe as genuine tone of respect in her voice.

"Amanda didn't approve," I say. "She was fiercely homophobic. And, er, well, she seduced Mark's boyfriend, and as I understand it, basically told Mark that if his boyfriend could be 'turned', then so could he!"

"She slept with her son's lover?"

I nod. "Mark was, by all accounts, heartbroken. *This* is why he had such a problem with his mother. Then Sam Shepton killed himself, apparently because of Amanda, which only added insult to injury to Mark. His ex apparently approached him on Saturday night in Pride, to offer some support and perhaps try to persuade Mark to take him back, but Mark was, by all accounts, angrier than ever."

"It's no wonder he hates, er, hated, his mother," says Alex.

"I know," I say. "I almost feel sorry for him."

"Almost?"

I nod again. "I can't condone murder, no matter what the provocation."

"So you still think Mark killed Amanda?"

I nod. "When I first had the hunch about why you didn't have CCTV of Mark, I had mixed emotions, because I felt that if my hunch proved right, then actually I might end up corroborating his alibi, proving that he was in town like he said he was. He just wasn't at the same bar as the rest of the rugby team. But Allan - that's Mark's ex - said Mark went crazy when he approached him in the bar, and stormed out in a rage. I think Mark approaching him opened up all the raw wounds, and Mark then went to kill Amanda."

"I have to admit, there's a logic there," says Alex.

"I think Mark can't control his temper. Amanda's interference in his love life destroyed her relationship with her son. Then Sam Shepton kills himself. And then Mark is drowning his sorrows in town and is approached by Allan…I think it tipped him over the edge. She made it clear she was ashamed of his homosexuality and her attitude made him determined to keep it a secret, too, as much as he could. But ultimately he was just pushed too far."

I realise that Alex has been scribbling furiously in her notebook for the past few minutes.

After a short while, it dawns on her that I have stopped talking. She stops writing and lifts her head.

"Assuming you're right about all this," she says, "it certainly reinforces Mark's motive for killing Amanda. But what about Lisa?"

"I haven't had chance to look into it yet," I say. "I've been kinda busy. But my theory is that perhaps Lisa is homophobic, too. Mark was pushed over the edge by his mother, and maybe found out that Lisa was homophobic too, and couldn't help himself. It's like, once he was pushed over the edge, he hasn't been able to come back. Was there - was there anything in Sam Shepton's suicide note or Phillipa Player's allegations to suggest homophobia? Is this the 'common link' you mentioned before?"

"No," says Alex, "that's not it."

I can't hide my disappointment.

"Warren told Patrick that you're looking at Stuart Shepton because he had access to both documents…" I say. "If homophobia was evident, perhaps Stuart told Mark…"

"Both women were accused of having wicked or vicious tongues," says Alex, softly. "That's the common link. And the common circumstances surrounding their deaths are that both women had their tongues removed."

Forty Three: Dan

Every now and then it occurs to me that Patrick still thinks I'm that rookie reporter he employed at the Herald a good few years ago.

I think he sometimes forgets that I'm older and at least a little wiser now. I called him yesterday to arrange to meet for a drink for two reasons; I wanted to sound him out about this arrangement the Herald and myself made with the police concerning Lisa's death, and also to talk to him about Kat, because I'm concerned about her determination to pursue Mark. I asked Patrick if he would consider trying to keep Kat away from Amanda's funeral and he readily agreed.

But the conversation then turned into a journalistic interrogation, mostly about my meeting with Stuart Shepton, since I appear to have been the only person to have been able to speak to him recently.

Patrick confessed to being tipped off that police are interested in Stuart. Lisa's death had all but cleared Pieter, and I'm not at all convinced about Ross. And, despite Kat's own theories, I've just got a feeling that it isn't Mark.

But Stuart *did* have links to both women, being Amanda's brother-in-law and a college governor, which prompted Patrick to try to persuade me to recall as much as I could about my fairly brief visit to Stuart's office last week.

In all the circumstances, it wouldn't take Sherlock Holmes to deduce that the source of Patrick's tip-off was Warren James, but why would Warren want to be *quite* so helpful?

I know that he was fairly candid with Patrick; they'd known each other for years, but even so, Warren was generally distrusting of the media. The Herald just happened to be the lesser of all the evils.

Why would Warren provide a tip-off of information so potentially sensitive? I tapped out the college website address on my laptop and within a few moments found a list of the governors and my suspicions were confirmed; a few lines below Stuart Shepton's name was that of Warren James.

I remember how Stuart hadn't hesitated to point an accusing finger at Pieter, perhaps to deflect suspicion away from Mark. Was Warren using the same tactics? Was he suggesting that Stuart Shepton was a potential suspect in order to ensure no one looked at *him* too closely?

I feel like calling Alex, but she and Kat seem to be developing quite a decent rapport, and I don't want Alex tipping Kat off about anything I tell her.

And I honestly don't think I'll get much joy if I approach Paul in the press office, or Sergeant Davey. Which leaves me with one option; to turn into a hardball hack. If I can just push the right buttons, perhaps I can loosen the tongue of a disgruntled police officer.

I know enough about the way the internal phone numbers work at the local police station, from my Herald days, to enable me to avoid calling the switchboard and try a few direct phone numbers. After a few wrong numbers, I get through to the incident room.

"DC Foreman," says a voice.

"DS Fawcett, please," I say.

"Who's calling?"

"BBC News," I say, gambling that the officer won't want to risk being caught saying anything to a journalist. Sure enough, I hear him call across the office, and I can just make out a distance voice say "put it through to the guv's office. I'll take it in there."

A few seconds later, the gruff Scotsman speaks to me. "DS Fawcett. Who's this?"

"Dan Barton," I say.

"Barton? Since when did you work for the beeb?"

"I don't. But I thought you might not take the call otherwise."

"Aye, that's about right. So, what do you want?"

"I want to cut the bullshit," I say. "Look, Alex asked us to be wary of what we report about Lisa's death, and we agreed, right? But any kind of deal like this has to be a two-way street. Alex seems to be speaking to the Herald a lot more than she's talking to me. And that isn't fair."

"If you want to cut the bullshit," he says, "then I'll tell you this; Alex is out of her depth."

"That's what I thought," I say, my confidence growing because I can sense Tam is taking the bait. Now I need to try to press his buttons a little harder. "She's happy to speak to the Herald because she thinks she can wrap Kate around her little finger. She's worried about talking to me because I might ask some proper questions."

"Aw, and I thought you and Alex were tight," says Tam.

"Are you kidding me? Been there, tried that, too much hard work."

He laughs. Yes! I punch the air. I'm getting through. Hopefully.

"Besides, I'm more interested in Kat. Kate. That way, I can keep an eye on what the Herald is being told. You know, pillow talk and all that."

"You're a cold bastard, Barton," Tam says, and I can almost picture the smug smile on his face.

"The latest I've heard is that Warren James might be a suspect, which I find very hard to believe…"

"Warren?" says Tam, and I detect a mixture of both surprise and anger in his voice. "I told the guv he should have let me speak to Warren. That's Alex all over, barking up the wrong tree like she has been from day one."

"Oh?"

"Aye. I said right from the start I thought this had all the hallmarks of a serial killer. That's what I said. Did she listen? Did she want to use the benefit of all my experience? No. She was adamant Amanda's death was a one-off. A personal crime. I told her, it's a serial killer, lassie. But she wouldn't listen. And now we have a second murder, and she's trying to keep the press all quiet about it, because she knows she has screwed up, but doesn't want to admit she was wrong."

The bitterness in his voice is thick. I get the impression that he's been wanting to speak out for a while, but it's as if he didn't know who he could speak to. This could so easily have gone the other way, but it looks like my gamble paid off, which is a huge relief.

"So, what about Warren? *Is* he a suspect because he saw Sam Shepton's suicide note and Phillipa Player's letter?"

"You are well informed," says Tam, who then considers what I've told him, and says, "is this what Alex has told the Herald?"

"I guess so."

"Warren was spoken to, because he has seen both letters, aye. And I know she had to check his alibi for both deaths. Well, on Friday he wasn't even in town; he was visiting relatives. And it just so happens that on the night Amanda Shepton was killed, Warren was in the pub with me. But he *did* then tell us what we had not realised, which is that Stuart Shepton also had access to both documents."

"It's just as well I checked then," I say.

"Damn right," says Tam, who obviously feels quite happy at being able to apparently discredit something Alex may have been suggesting.

"I don't know how much longer I can keep silent, though," I say. "I mean, if Alex is talking to the Herald, it hardly provides me with much motivation to keep quiet, and go along with the ruse that Lisa's death may have been a suicide, does it?"

"See?" says Tam. "Another thing Nicholas has got wrong; the media strategy. No offence, Barton, but we shouldn't go around trying to make deals with journalists."

"None taken," I say. "But since we're talking so openly, and since Alex seems to be talking even more openly with the Herald, perhaps you can give me some idea about the common factor in those letters?"

"More than my job's worth," he says, as if to reinforce his previous point."

"Well, I guess I'll just have to speak to Simon, tell him what you've told me about Warren…"

"You really are a bastard, aren't you?" says Tam.

"I wouldn't want to give Alex any ammunition to use against you, but look at it from my side. I'm keeping my end of the bargain, and I'm getting nothing back."

"Alright, laddie," says Tam. "You can have this, and make of it what you will. Careless talk costs lives. Women are renowned for loving nothing more than a good chin-wag, a good gossip, to let their tongues run loose. And as Chaucer so eloquently put it, "A wicked tongue is worse than any fiend.""

"Eh?"

The line goes dead.

I'm not sure what has surprised me most; the fact that I managed to get Tam to speak to me at all, let alone provide Warren with an alibi (mind you, after seeing them together in the pub last week, I did think then that they appeared to be as thick as thieves), or the fact that he has just quoted Chaucer at me.

I'm trying to make sense of what I've just heard when the phone rings again.

"Is that Dan Barton, the journalist?" says a woman's voice. I don't recognise her, but there's a quiver in her voice which suggests she has either been crying, or is on the verge of crying.

"Yes," I say, "how can I help?"

"I want to meet you in person, tomorrow. I want to tell you who killed those two women."

Big news stories inevitably end up resulting in both the police and media outlets receiving a number of calls from people claiming to have information. Some people call the police because they think they have some genuine information, others seem to do it for kicks.

When it comes to the media, some people call us because, for one reason or another, they don't want to have direct contact with the police. Others call the media because they think we might pay them a handsome fee for a decent tip-off, regardless of whether or not it has any substance to it, and some are just eager to get their fifteen minutes of fame.

What has struck me immediately about this woman is not only the emotion in her voice, but the fact that she has suggested the same person has killed twice, which has certainly not been anywhere near the public domain yet. So either she is a complete crank who is clutching at straws and has made a lucky guess or assumption, or she has some kind of link to the investigation team - it does seem a little suspicious that her call has come just minutes after my fairly frank and open conversation with Tam; could this be a mind game on his part, getting a female colleague to call me with a tip off?

"Can you not tell me over the phone?" I ask.

"No," she says, and I can hear clear distress in her voice. "No, you never know who is listening. I need you come to my house."

"Listen, if you really know who the murderer is, why do you want to tell me? Shouldn't you be telling the police?"

Of course I want her to tell me, but at the same time I am trying to find out if she is genuine. Perhaps she won't approach the police because they know her, and she is a serial crank caller. They are out there.

"I can't tell the police," she says, her voice trembling. "If….if he thinks for one moment that I have spoken to the police, then he'll come for me. I'll be his next victim."

She certainly sounds sincere, and she certainly sounds very afraid.

"If you're so sure he'll come after you, why speak out at all?" I ask.

"Because I don't think he can stop himself, and it's only a matter of time before he kills someone else. When I heard about Mrs Shepton, I thought perhaps it was a one-off. But then I heard about that other woman, and I realised he's been pushed too far. You reporters are always quoting anonymous sources, so you can tell the police without my name being mentioned. Please, you've *got* to help. He *will* kill again."

She starts to sob, and I have to admit it, if she *is* a crank caller - and I've had my fair share over the years - then she's a damn good one. Right now, I'm inclined to believe she's quite sincere.

"Please," she says. "Three deaths are enough. He must be stopped."

"Wait, three? Did you say three? I'm only aware of two deaths."

"It's three," she says. "The first was a long time ago, and we thought it was over. But something has set him off again, and I'm afraid now that he can't stop himself."

My mind is racing. *Three* deaths? My nose for news is definitely twitching. I'm still not entirely sure if this woman is genuine or not, but as soon as she mentioned a third death, I think I decided right then that I would have to at least meet her once and follow this up. And then another thought occurs to me.

"Hang on," I say. "If I go the police with the killer's name, aren't I going to set *myself* up as his potential next victim?"

"No," she says, "because he only targets women with wicked tongues."

And that was the clincher.

Tam's choice of Chaucer quote included the term 'wicked tongue'. It felt like too much of a coincidence for this woman to use the same phrase, too. All of which means I am not going to be attending Amanda Shepton's funeral tomorrow, as I had planned.

Instead, every journalistic instinct I have tells me that I am going to discover the identity of the killer.

Forty Four: Alex

Simon isn't about this afternoon; he's been called to force HQ to give the Chief Constable a detailed briefing on our case, which means I've been able to shut myself away in the DCI's office to draw breath.

I suspect the Chief is uneasy about our tactics of not being entirely truthful about the second death. The golden rule is that we don't lie to the media; if you're caught out, it could undermine public confidence in policing. We police by consent in the UK, and it's vital that we do everything we can to keep the public on-side.

Right now, we can just about justify it by maintaining the 'open mind' approach, until the results of toxicological tests following the post-mortem, so we're not lying outright, but we are pushing the boundaries, and I suspect that this is making the Chief uncomfortable.

Uncomfortable is definitely something I am very used to, these days.

I felt uncomfortable over the weekend, as we issued that vague statement about Lisa's death. And of course, her death itself has left me feeling extremely uncomfortable. I was convinced that the nature of Amanda's murder seemed so personal that it had to be a one-off. But the fact Lisa also had her tongue cut out is simply too coincidental.

And in all the circumstances, I guess that the thing that's making me feel most uncomfortable of all is that it means Tam might be right; we're dealing with a serial killer.

It's useful that Kat and Dan are co-operating; this will help Simon, too. We haven't blatantly lied to the media; in fact, we are trying to do some damage limitation. We *all* agree that the worse case scenario, particularly when it comes to public confidence, will be to have hordes of headline-hungry hacks prowling around the town.

Tam makes me uncomfortable. I'm pissed off that he warned Warren that I was on my way to visit him on Friday. Simon chose me to make that visit, rather than Tam, for a reason; it's no secret that Tam and Warren are drinking buddies.

Tam would never have been able to approach Warren with anything like impartiality. Not that it was any easier for me.

Warren is renowned for being something of a prickly character at the best of times but could we really be considering him as a suspect? Could Warren be capable of committing two callous murders? Then again, what's that old cliché? It's always the person you least suspect?

I was definitely spooked when I saw the way he so deftly handled those surgical scissors when he opened his mail. That sent shivers down my spine.

Then, of course, there's the fact that Warren called the editor of the Herald in order to encourage them to focus their attention on Stuart Shepton. Was that an attempt to deflect the growing attention on him?

And where does Tam stand in all this? Warren and Tam are close. Does Tam know more than he's letting on? Could Tam be protecting his friend?

I did a little research into Warren over the weekend; it was no great hardship to access his personnel records; while he doesn't work for the police force directly, he has such close links that it was pretty easy to look into his background. A pretty flawless career history; one or two complaints about him appearing 'rude' and 'insensitive' at times; 'cold' seems to be the most commonly-used word.

As for anything personal, very little. Most notably, no indication of him ever being married. No suggestion - even anecdotally, now that I come to think of it - of him being involved in anything approaching a serious close relationship with anyone. No rumours of him having any kind of casual relationship, come to that.

Maybe he simply doesn't like women.

I shudder. Perhaps it goes further than that. Perhaps he has a *problem* with women. And that is now manifesting itself, turning him into a killer?

After my uncomfortable visit to his home on Friday, a place which most definitely lacks a woman's touch, I was seriously starting to think that we should be considering Warren to be a suspect. After all, we agreed the common factors; written references to wicked tongues, coupled with both victims having their tongues removed.

Warren would have seen Sam Shepton's suicide note and Phillipa Player's allegations against Lisa; it makes Warren a stronger suspect for both murders than Mark, who we can still only loosely link to Lisa.

And then came my meeting today with Kat, which has thrown up a whole new scenario, and one which I am increasingly inclined to lean towards.

Maybe this is not a case of Tam protecting Warren, or in some other way colluding with him.

Perhaps it's a case of Stuart Shepton colluding with his nephew.

Stuart had access to both documents. Stuart certainly had plenty of reason to despise Amanda. Perhaps he has a problem with women with 'wicked tongues', which is why Lisa also strayed into his sights.

Perhaps Stuart is the 'brains' of the operation, and his nephew is the brawn. It's no wonder Stuart has been avoiding all our attempts to contact him.

And I remember Dan telling me about his meeting with Stuart; Stuart said Mark had plenty of motive for killing his mother, which presumably alludes to Mark's sexuality, and Amanda's issues with it. But then Stuart was quick enough to point the finger of blame away from Mark, and onto Pieter.

My mind is whirling.

I've tried to get hold of Stuart Shepton over the weekend, but he has been in London; Amanda's daughter, Sarah, is flying in from Canada to attend the funeral and Stuart drove to pick her up from Heathrow Airport.

I've mentioned my suspicions to Simon, of course. He feels we should let the family have the funeral tomorrow, and then we can ramp-up our investigation. For now, the right thing to do is show due respect to the deceased.

In saying that, of course, it goes without saying that Simon expects us to have a presence at the funeral. It will be interesting to closely observe Sam and Mark. Also, it will be interesting to watch Warren and Tam; see if anyone acts suspiciously or says anything that may give us a better idea of who is responsible for killing Amanda and Lisa.

I'm sure Mark is not going to be happy about us being there.

He'll be even less happy if Dan and Kat turn up.

That's another thing that makes me feel uncomfortable; I know Dan and her editor have warned her to keep her distance, but something tells me Kat will be there, and that's all the more reason for us to have a presence there, because if Mark sees her, it's going to be like a red rag to a bull, I'm sure.

A shiver runs down my spine.

Stuart Shepton is the 'brains' of the operation, and Mark Shepton is the 'brawn'. The more I think about it, the more it makes sense.

And Kat's own detective work at the weekend, placing Mark at Pride but not for long enough to completely rule him out of Amanda's death, only adds more fuel to that particular theory.

The Shepton family has been well-respected in town for many years. Sam and Stuart as prominent businessmen, Amanda as the charitable-socialite, Mark as the star of the local rugby team.

Their collective reputation has already been tarnished by 'black widow' headlines; Mark's fiery temper and assault on the Herald photographer hasn't helped *his* reputation. If it turns out that Stuart and Mark are conspiring to commit multiple murders - partly in retaliation for Amanda's objection to Mark's homosexuality - then the Shepton's are likely to become this town's most infamous family; their reputation will be in tatters.

And yes, Mark's sexuality. Boy, I didn't see *that* one coming at all. But it almost makes sense. His overly-aggressive behaviour, his apparently blatant alpha-male tendencies - all a cover to disguise his true self; a disguise he felt compelled to wear, because of Amanda's attitude.

And does that mean we now have *another* suspect to throw into the mix? Allan, Mark's ex. He would certainly have the motive to kill Amanda. Is there a link between him and Lisa? Perhaps Allan is a former student. Maybe he has a weakness for the older woman, as well as for men. If Amanda could seduce him, perhaps Lisa did too? We're going to need to look into Allan now as well.

And then, of course, comes the biggest question of all, the question which, now that I come to think of it, makes me feel even more uncomfortable than accepting that Tam was probably right about Amanda's murder *not* being a one-off personal crime.

So, the biggest question of all; a question of when, rather than if, the killer will strike again.

My phone rings, distracting me from this stream of uncomfortable thoughts. My caller ID tells me that it's Dan.

"Hey," I say.

"Hi Alex," he says, and I detect a subdued excitement in his voice. He's trying to be cool, calm and collected, but he isn't. He's wired about something. "Are you going to Amanda Shepton's funeral tomorrow?"

"Yes," I say. "Why, are you asking for a lift? Some protection?"

"No," he says, "at least, not for me. I'm not going. I need you to do me a favour, please. Keep an eye on Kat."

"You think she'll turn up, after your and her boss have urged her not to?"

"What do *you* think?" he says.

I think about this for a moment, then sigh. "I think I'll be more surprised if she isn't there than if she is."

"Then please, promise me you'll keep an eye on her. If Mark sees her, I don't know what he'll do."

"What's so important that you're not going to be there to protect her yourself? Don't tell me you've been taken off the story?"

"Not at all," he says, and I sense a slight change in his tone, his obvious and genuine concern for Kat being overtaken by that excitement I detected when I first answered his call. "Far from it. Just promise me you'll keep an eye on Kat, keep her safe. And promise me you'll keep your phone switched on."

"My phone? Why?"

"Because if all goes as I expect it to, I'll be calling you tomorrow with the name of the killer."

Forty Five: Kat

The crematorium and cemetery sits on the outer edge of town at the top of a gentle rise, affording unspoiled views of the level rolling fields beyond and the majestic hills a few miles further away.

A sweeping road carves a picturesque path through lovingly manicured lawns towards the modern, wooden-fronted, chapel building.

To the right of the chapel is an enclosed garden of remembrance where people usually gather for a short while once the formal ceremony has finished. Further to the right is a large car park.

To the left of the chapel, the extensive, beautifully-landscaped grounds stretch away, filled with memorial stones, statues, benches and colourful floral arrangements.

Directly behind the chapel is a thick forest which contains a myriad of woodland walks where many trees have been planted as lasting tributes to lost loved ones.

I'm not surprised to see a large number of cars already here. Not many people know as much as I do about Amanda's lifestyle. The general feeling among the great and good of the town is that she was very much one of them, a kind-hearted servant to the community who supported many charities and other worthy organisations.

That, coupled with the sudden, premature, nature of her death meant there are plenty of people who want to pay their respects.

As I slowly reverse into a space towards the back of the car park, I spot Elizabeth Page, the Mayoress, walking towards the chapel and a cluster of many other members of the town council.

I wanted to get here early, hoping to hide in the background, observing, watching, but there are plenty of people here already.

There are several police cars parked up and as my gaze scans the mourners, I spot Alex Nicholas talking to Patrick. I momentarily freeze; I really hope I can stay out of Patrick's sight for as long as possible. He won't be at all happy that I am here.

Nor will Dan, no doubt. But I can't see his car anywhere, which surprises me. If he was here, I suspect he'd be following me around like a personal bodyguard, which I can live without, although I was sure he would be here. I'm curious.

I'm so lost in my thoughts, I've almost forgotten that I'm not alone. Allan is sitting patiently beside me, his eyes darting back and forth nervously between the chapel, a short walk ahead of us, and me, waiting for me to dictate our next move.

Alex and Patrick part company; I can't see where my editor has gone, but Alex is stepping away from the group, as if she is surveying the wider scene.

I get out of my car and immediately catch her eye. She nods just enough to acknowledge my presence, then casually walks towards me.

"Surprise?" I say, as soon as she is within earshot.

"Not really," she says. "I didn't think you'd stay away, although I wish you had."

"Have you seen Dan?" I ask. She doesn't reply. Her eyes are looking past me, as Allan gets out of the car. She then looks at me again, her eyes inviting an introduction. Is he the reason why you've seemingly gone cold on Dan? That's what her expression tells me she's thinking.

"This is Allan Jones," I say. "He's, er, he's Mark Shepton's former partner. He wanted to be here…"

Allan steps forward.

"Acting DI Nicholas," says Alex, formally. "Once this afternoon's out of the way, you and I are going to need to have a chat."

Allan looks a little sheepish and awkward, but nods. "Of course."

Alex turns to me again. "Does your editor know you're here?"

I shake my head.

"He told me to be on the lookout for you," she says. "I think he knows you're not going to be able to stay away."

"I couldn't," I say. "Truth is, I was getting on quite well with Amanda until, you know. And despite what I know about her now, I still want to pay my respects. And observe everyone else, of course."

"Well, just keep out of harm's way," says Alex. "And I'll do my best to try to ensure your editor is looking the other way."

"Thanks," I say. "So, have you seen or heard anything from Dan?"

She smiles. She obviously knows my interest in Dan, whether I am happy to admit it or not, goes beyond professional rivalry. "He's not coming," she says.

"Oh?"

"He called me late yesterday," she says, looking a little sheepish herself. "He asked me to keep an eye on you, too, because he couldn't be here himself. He said he had a hot new lead."

"About the murders?"

She nods. "Apparently. He hung up before I could get any more out of him. I tried to call him back, but he wouldn't answer. The only other thing he told me was to keep my phone on, because he hoped to call me with some significant information if things went the way he thought they would. I'm assuming he didn't say anything to you, then?"

"No," I say, and I'm unable to hide my disappointment. "Not a word."

"Alex!" A voice from the direction of the chapel calls out. Tam Fawcett is looking at us. He nods to his right and we turn our heads to see a large black hearse glide slowly along the road towards the chapel.

"I've got to go," says Alex. Her soft features suddenly turn stern. "Low profile, Kat, OK?"

I nod, and she turns and strides back towards the chapel.

Allan stands beside me. "Don't worry," he says. "If Mark spots us, he's far more likely to focus on me rather than you."

All I can offer is a feeble smile in response, because Allan's words offered cold comfort. Suddenly I'm wishing Dan *was* here, and starting to wonder whether I've made a mistake in coming.

I smile briefly; Dan often mentioned how he liked to see me in black, and here I am, black fitted trousers, my best black blouse, black jacket, and he's not here to see it.

What's he up to? Whatever this new lead is, he must truly think it is pretty hot for him to miss the funeral. While we're not obliged to share information with each other, we have had quite a few frank and open exchanges since Amanda's murder, so I thought he would have said something to me, even if to tease me about his new 'scoop'.

Who is he talking to? What has he got?

It's going to drive me mad, I know it is.

The hearse sweeps elegantly around the looping road which brings it in front of the chapel.

Behind it is another large ceremonial black car which comes to a smooth halt far enough behind the hearse to enable the coffin to be carefully removed in due course.

Mark Shepton steps out of this second car, turns, extends his hand inside and helps another passenger get out. "That's Sarah," says Allan, quietly. "Mark's sister. She flew in from Canada at the weekend."

Mark is wearing a black suit, white shirt and black tie. His stocky form doesn't look right in such formal attire. He looks like a petulant child who has been forced to get all dressed up for the very first time in order to attend the wedding of a distant relative he barely knows.

Sarah's wearing a simple, knee-length, expensive-looking black dress.

A third person gets out of the car, a short, slightly-built, older man. "That's Stuart Shepton," says Allan.

A tall figure steps towards the trio, hand extended in sympathy.

It's Warren James. For a fleeting moment, my mischievous inner voice says, 'Oh, if the devil could cast his net', but I shake my head.

Whatever else has been going on here, I shouldn't forget that this is about paying respects to Amanda. It's also about me remembering that, no matter what she might have done, surely no one deserves to die like she did?

Something Alex said at the coffee shop yesterday quickly returns to haunt me. "The common circumstances surrounding their deaths are that both women had their tongues removed."

I had been so shocked when Alex said this that I hadn't been able to ask her to explain more. Maybe, in truth, I didn't want to hear any more. I'm not surprised police had been so reluctant to provide us with any further details about the injuries Amanda and Lisa had suffered.

If Dan knew this, and told the tabloids, reporters from every national paper, broadcaster and agency in the country would be laying siege to the town.

Black widow has tongue ripped from her mouth after being tied to a chair in her own home? It's a tabloid journo's dream!

I think about Ross, my colleague. I can't for one second imagine he'd be capable of doing that to someone. From what I know of Pieter, I don't think he'd be able to, either.

But Mark? Well. He's got the strength to overpower anyone if he sets his mind to it. And he has that raging anger. Could he be capable of ripping his own mother's tongue out? Yes, I think he could.

I shudder at the thought of it and find myself subconsciously leaning into Allan, as if I need some reassurance. For all my own bravado, I suddenly feel like the vulnerable little girl that Dan and Patrick have been suggesting I might be over the past few days.

Warren steps aside as others step forward to offer their condolences to Amanda's family. But Sarah is the only one of the three who looks genuinely sad. Mark and Stuart have resigned looks on their faces, as if they feel compelled to go through the motions and keep up appearances, because it is what is expected of them.

Mark's head starts to turn towards our direction and I instinctively flinch and cower behind Allan. "It's OK," he says. "He hasn't seen us. He's talking to someone else."

I slowly lift my head an am relieved to see one of the coaches from the rugby club put an arm around Mark's shoulder, and guide him in the opposite direction.

Warren James is in deep, almost conspiratorial, conversation with Tam Fawcett. I'd love to be a fly on the nearest wall to those two.

I sigh; listen to myself. I'm becoming suspicious of anyone and everyone. I'm not sure I like it.

A large number of people start to drift into the chapel.

Allan and I look on, in silence, as we watch the pallbearers slowly lift the coffin from the hearse and carry it inside, with Mark, Stuart and Sarah walking solemnly in its wake.

"Looks like a large congregation," says Allan. "If only they knew the *real* Amanda. They wouldn't all look so sorry then, they'd be glad to see the back of her."

The venom in his voice surprises me momentarily.

But then, how much of his anger is directed to Amanda and how much towards himself? I didn't feel comfortable, when I met him on Sunday, going into detail about how Amanda seduced him and how much, if any, resistance he offered. Was the older women really able to get the better of him?

Perhaps there's as much guilt within Allan as anger.

Not everyone who had gathered outside the chapel went in.

Some now return to their cars and drive off, their 'token appearance' at the crematorium enough.

Allan and I stand in silence and, for a few minutes, it's blissfully peaceful. The only sounds are the gentle rustling of the trees in the forest directly behind the chapel building in the slight breeze, and the tweeting of birds.

I close my eyes and just for a few moments lose myself in the peaceful tranquility.

Hmm, I wonder if Dan has called Alex yet. What has he found out? With those thoughts, my brief respite is ended.

"They're coming out," says Allan.

I've obviously been daydreaming for longer than I thought. The doors at the side of the chapel have opened and Mark, Sarah and Stuart step from the chapel into the walled garden of remembrance.

"I'd like to get closer," says Allan. Without waiting for a response, he walks towards the stone garden wall. Through gaps in patterns in the stones on top of the wall, we can see into the garden.

Mark, Sarah and Stuart have their backs to us and stand shoulder to shoulder. Those who attended the service file past them in turn, offering condolences, handshakes, hugs and words of comfort.

Some drift out of the garden and to their cars. Others gather in little groups, presumably making small talk about what a lovely send off it was, how sad it all is and, in much lower voices, speculating about what had happened to Amanda and who was responsible.

Elizabeth Page steps out of the chapel with Patrick alongside her.

I note that Mark is shrugging his shoulders a lot when people approach him, almost as if he's saying 'whatever', or 'yeah, right' in response to whatever comfort they are trying to offer him.

"I need to speak to him," Allan says, and starts to walk towards the gap in the wall which opens onto the car park from the garden.

I tug at his sleeve. "What?" I hiss. "Do you really think that's a good idea?"

"Not really," he says, and I see tears welling up in his eyes. "But I have to."

Mark is standing close to the entrance to the garden. Allan approaches cautiously. "Mark," he says softly, without actually stepping into the garden.

Mark turns and his eyes widen. I can't tell if he's pleased to see Allan, shocked, or angry. He stares impassively at him.

Allan takes a small step towards Mark. "I wanted to be here," he says. "For you. I'm so…"

"What the fuck are you doing here?"

For a split second I conclude Mark is obviously angry to see Allan, after all. It takes me a split second longer to realise he's talking to me.

As Allan stepped closer to him, Mark was able to see over the shoulder of his ex, and saw me lurking behind him.

"You've got some fucking nerve, I'll give you that, showing your face here," Mark says, loud enough to capture the attention of everyone else in the garden.

Then he stares at Allan again and puts two and two together. "Did you come with *her*?"

Allan nods.

"You just can't fucking leave me alone, can you sweetheart?" he says. "Well, since you clearly know my secret, then you know you're not my type, don't you? Who the fuck do you think you are, bringing him here? What's this all about, eh?"

His anger is now split between myself and Allan.

"What's up? You two conspiring for the next front-page headline? 'Gay lovers reunited following the funeral of the disapproving black widow who split them up in the fucking first place.' Is that it?"

Everyone is now looking at us; in my peripheral vision, I see Patrick staring at me disapprovingly. Almost everyone else is motionless, shocked, wondering what exactly is going on.

Allan tries to placate him. "I want to be here, it's nothing to do with her."

"It's everything to do with her! Is this you way of getting back at me, because I walked out on you in Pride? What are you doing, selling your sob story to the fucking press, to get back at me?"

"No! I wouldn't do that, you *know* that."

"All I know is that *she* has been on my back from the start, invading my privacy, following me around like a lovesick bitch on heat."

I wince at his words, and feel my face redden. This is not what I wanted. There's a growing ferocity in Mark's voice. "Who the fuck do you think you are, sticking your nose into other people's private lives, into other people's grief? And for what? To sell a few extra fucking copies of that pathetic rag you write for?"

"No," I hear myself say, and I realise that I am fighting to hold back tears myself.

"You're fucking evil!" he cries. "Pure evil!"

"That's not you talking," says Allan. "That's your grief!"

"Grief?" bellows Mark. "I'm not fucking grieving! You, more than anyone, knows that! I'm glad my mother is dead. I'm glad we've just burned that witch. But you know what? My dad always said my mum had a wicked tongue, and fuck knows, she did. But that little cow over there, she has the wickedest tongue of them all. Only she doesn't speak her words out loud, she uses her poison pen to put everything into print for all to see! The pen is mightier than the sword, and it's fucking true." He turns and glares at me. "My mum's cruel words remained private, but what comes out of your wicked tongue is put into print for everyone to see. You do more damage than anyone! You have the most wicked tongue of all!"

Mark steps towards me and Allan intercepts him, blocking the entrance to the garden with his arm, which Mark pushes against.

"Calm down," says Allan, which is like a red rag to a bull.

"Who the fuck are you to tell me to calm down? You're not welcome here! I didn't ask you to come!"

With that, Mark smacks a clubbing fist into Allan's face and begins to push past him. "You want a piece of me, bitch? Well, here I come!"

Mark tries to barge past Allan, who was briefly stunned by the punch, and strides towards me with menacing purpose, while I stand motionless, petrified.

The pure, undiluted hatred in Mark's eyes is indescribable.

Allan lunges at Mark, wrapping his arms around his ankles in a textbook rugby tackle, bringing a struggling Mark crashing to the ground just a few feet away from me.

"Kat!" yells Allan. "For goodness sake, run! Run!"

I've never felt such fear and panic. What do I do? Where do I go? I'm like a rabbit in the headlights.

But then I see Mark kicking and struggling to release Allan's grip on him, and some sort of deep survival instinct kicks in.

I just start running, as fast as I possibly can.

"You can't run from me! I'm going to silence your wicked tongue!"

The nearest place that offers any possible refuge is the wooded area behind the chapel, so I sprint towards it.

My heart is pounding, my lungs feel as if they are going to burst.

I can hear many voices shouting, but the loudest belongs to Allan. "Mark! No! Come back!"

Shit! He's coming in here after me and who knows what he's going to do! I've never ever seen anyone look that angry before. If he catches me before anyone else catches him, what the hell is he going to do to me? Rip my tongue out?

I leave the forest path and crash into the thick undergrowth.

I hear voices calling my name. I'm sure one of them is Alex; maybe Tam, too. They're calling to me, they're calling to Mark.

I'm losing all sense of direction; I'm getting giddy and dizzy. My head is spinning.

"You can run but you can't hide, bitch!" yells Mark, and I hear the sound of someone charging through the forest like an enraged rhino, a wild, feral, beast. Or worse still, in this environment, a primitive predator, and I am his intended prey.

He sounds so close!

Tears start to cascade down my cheeks as I run, in absolute blind panic.

Mark cries out and I hear a large thud, as if he's run into something hard, or had the wind knocked out of him.

"Fuck off, Allan!" he yells.

I hear the sound of blows being exchanged, but I have no desire to stick around to see who is fighting with who; I am fighting for my life.

I plunge deeper into the forest, branches ripping across my face and body as I try to seek refuge among them.

My foot snags on something.

I turn, lose my balance, my left ankle twists inwards beneath me and I crash to the ground.

Everything goes black.

Forty Six: Dan

It takes me just over an hour to get to Margaret's house, in a small village pretty much miles from anywhere, and that was with me admittedly driving a lot faster at times than I should have done.

I've no idea how old she is, but my first impressions are that this weary-looking woman has the weight of the world on her shoulders, which is probably making her look even older than she actually is, though if I had to guess, I'd say she had to be in her late seventies.

She certainly doesn't look like the usual kind of crank caller type.

The house is clean and tidy. She appears as if she looks after herself, despite the signs of stress and worry written all over her face.

"Thank you for coming," she says, the quiver in her voice coming more from emotion than her age.

She shows me into her lounge and offers me a seat on the small, two-seat sofa while she settles into a chair closer to the fireplace.

As I watch her ease herself into the chair, I notice several small picture frames on the mantelpiece surrounding the fire. I notice them because they are all reversed, so I can't see the actual photographs. Is this something she usually does, or has she done it just because she knew I was coming?

I pull a small notepad from my jacket pocket, and a pen.

"I'm so grateful you're here," she says. "I'm so sorry for what has happened. I should have spoken out before, but I didn't want to believe it. I couldn't believe it. I thought it was all over. And now, well, like I told you on the phone, if I go to the police, and tell them his name, if he think's it was me who spoke to them, he'll accuse me of having a wicked tongue, and then he'll come for me!"

It's obvious that, whether she truly does know the identity of the killer or not, this woman is terrified.

"Why don't you start at the beginning?" I say. As much as I would love her to cut to the chase and just give me a name, but somehow I think this needs a slightly more sensitive approach.

"Decades ago," she says, her quivering voice almost a whisper. "My brother. My dear, beloved, brother, took his own life."

She pauses. Her eyes are glistening with tears.

"Take your time," I say. "Can I get you a drink or something?"

She shakes her head. "No. Let me tell you what I need to tell you. Then I'll make us a drink."

"OK," I say. "When you're ready."

"My brother. He took his own life. Whiskey and pills. He was found in the shed at the bottom of his garden by his young son, my nephew. He adored his father. He was heartbroken."

Her eyes momentarily flicker towards the reversed photo frames on the mantelpiece.

"Poor kid," I say. "Why did your brother do it?"

"His wife," she says, and the tone of her voice changes. The sadness now also has traces of bitter resentment. "He was what you might call a henpecked husband. She made his life a misery, constantly complaining, nagging, putting him down, moaning and groaning, morning, noon and night, non-stop. In the end, he just couldn't take it any more."

I start scribbling some notes.

"He wrote a several notes, one of which was to his son. But the boy's mother wouldn't let him see it. The boy kept a diary."

Margaret leans over and fumbles around by the side of the chair, before sitting up again with a battered book in her hand. There's a bookmark sticking out from the middle of it. She opens the book.

"This is what he wrote," she says, "when *my* mother, his nanna, showed him the note his father had written. He said, 'Daddy told me he loved me very much, and that he was so very sorry that he left me. He said Mummy had a wicked tongue. That was the words he used; wicked tongue. And he said he could not cope with her shouting at him anymore.' And that's how I know that he has started killing again."

Wicked tongue. Those words again.

"He wrote that diary entry after the inquest into my brother's death. That's when he found out that my brother had written him a note. His mother had kept it from him."

I continue to scribble some notes.

"A couple of weeks later, my mother telephoned the house and could tell that the boy was upset. It seems that his mother had now turned her wicked tongue on him. My mother went to the house and the two women argued. Janice dragged her son upstairs, while bellowing at my mum, saying such horrible things that it made my mum cry. And that was it. All the pent up emotion, grief and rage in her own son boiled up and exploded. My mother told me it was as if the boy had become possessed by a demon. He pushed his mother down the stairs with a strength nobody knew he had. He'd always been such a kind, gentle, good-natured, boy. He would cry if he stepped on an ant in the garden, and would have to hold a little funeral for it. But on this day, he was simply pushed too far. He ran down the stairs after his mother, and…and…"

Margaret pauses and turns her head away from me. When she turns back, I can see the glistening tracks of her tears down her wrinkled, sunken, cheeks.

"And what?" I say, softly.

"And even though she was already dead, he tore her tongue out of her mouth with his bare hands and tried to rip it into pieces, yelling 'Mummy won't be shouting at anybody, ever again'."

"Wow," I hear myself say.

"The authorities wanted to take the boy into care, but we couldn't have that. He was family. It wasn't his fault. It was hers, that wicked witch my brother had gone and gotten himself married to. My mother wanted to take him in, initially, but I said she was too old and had been through too much, so I took him in, and I raised him as my own."

"So, what you're telling me is that the killer is your son?" I ask.

"As good as. Biologically, no. But to all intents and purposes, yes, I raised him as my own, and was more of a mother to him than his biological mother ever was. Of course, we had years of social service visits, counselling, various psychiatrists and psychologists. No one could blame the boy for what he had done. It wasn't his fault."

A thought suddenly occurs to me. "And you say that this was *decades* ago?"

She nods, and I write two words in my notepad, and then put a heavy line right through them; Mark Shepton.

If the man who killed Amanda and Lisa really is the same person Margaret is now telling me about, then it can't possibly be Mark. It has to be someone older.

"So," I say. "He kills his mother. You raise him, and what then? Does he have a troubled life?"

She shakes her head and fresh tears start to flow.

"I - I thought I had raised him well," she sobs. "I even thought he was happy. He got a good education, he - he got himself a nice job, that he loved. We didn't speak about the past; it was like a long-forgotten, childhood nightmare. But now it has come back to haunt us. Now he has started killing again."

"But why?"

"Something one of the psychologists said, a long time ago. It was those words, 'wicked tongue'. Somehow, for some reason, they released all the anger and emotion he had bottled up over the death of his dear father, and all the anger that he had been suppressing, all the rage towards his mother, who he blamed, quite rightly, for his father's death. We asked, years later, after he had left home and seemed to be settled and content, if there was ever a chance that it could happen again. The psychologist said he would never be able to say for sure, of course. But there was an outside chance that if that poor boy ever came across that phrase 'wicked tongue' again in the right circumstances, then it could be like a trigger, or like a giant key, unlocking and releasing that terrible rage and hurt which he has managed to bury so deep inside for so very long."

I'm now scribbling furiously.

"I heard about that woman who was killed," Margaret continues. "And I heard about her husband, who had killed himself just a few weeks before. I was horrified! I couldn't believe it! I mean, what were the chances! Fate can be so very, very, cruel. What were the chances of something like that happening in the same place where my boy was now living, miles away from where he was brought up? What were the chances? It's so very, very, unfair."

She pauses and sobs quite openly for a few minutes.

"It's not his fault. He can't help it. I know that the woman's husband - what was his name? Shipton? Something like that? I know that he had used the phrase 'wicked tongue' in his suicide note. And that was enough to trigger my boy, to release all his inner demons after all these years. And....and, well, I know I should have spoken out then. But I couldn't. I knew they would lock him up, and it's not his fault. It's a terribly, terribly cruel twist of fate, and a million to once chance that something so similar would happen again, and that he would learn about it. If he had been living in London or someone else, he'd probably never ever have heard of Shipton or whatever his name was, and would still be happy and would never have killed again. What are the chances, eh? How cruel can life be?"

I shake my head. What answer, what comfort, could I possibly provide? My heart breaks for her. I feel a little sympathy towards her son, or adopted son, too.

But that doesn't change the fact that he is a killer.

Margaret isn't done yet. "I, well, I heard about the murder then, of Shipton's wife. And I thought, I hoped, that that was it. The circumstances had been so similar, it triggered him off, but it was done and, by all accounts, it sounds like that man's wife was just as nasty a piece of work as my brother's wife. So maybe, in a way, it was justice. But then I heard about another death, and that's when I realised the tragic truth. When I learned that both women had had their tongues removed and cut up, I knew that he isn't going to stop. He can't stop. He can't help himself. The inner demon has been awakened, and this time is not going to be buried again. He'll kill any woman who is accused of having a wicked or vicious tongue. And that's why I called you."

I lean forward and find myself resting a palm gently on one of her bony knees. "You've done the right thing, Margaret," I say. "Um, did you say their tongues were taken out and, er, cut up?"

She nods. "It's the whole 'wicked tongue' thing. It's his way of feeling that he has silenced their wicked tongues, by removing them."

No wonder the police kept that aspect of the murders quiet! Imagine the panic! Imagine the fear! Imagine the media headlines!

"Now do you understand why I couldn't tell the police myself?" says Margaret. "He'd accuse *me* of having a wicked tongue, and he wouldn't be able to help himself. He'd come and kill me, and take my tongue out."

If I can somehow persuade Alex or Tam to confirm, without any cryptic games, that Amanda and Lisa both had their tongues removed, then I think I'm pretty sure Margaret and I are, indeed, talking about the person who killed them, as well as killing his own mother so many years ago.

Tam had all but confirmed it during our recent chat. What was it he said? "Careless talk costs lives. Women are renowned for loving nothing more than a good chin-wag, a good gossip, to let their tongues run loose. And as Chaucer so eloquently put it, 'A wicked tongue is worse than any fiend'."

My instincts are telling me that I don't actually *need* confirmation. The man Margaret raised as a son, who killed his own mother at such a young age, is, indeed, the same man who killed Amanda and Lisa.

"If - if you'll excuse me for a moment, I need to use the bathroom," says Margaret. "I'll put the kettle on, too. Perhaps you'd like a cup of tea."

I help Margaret to her feet and watch her shuffle out of the lounge.

My mind is reeling.

I hear Margaret slowly climb the stairs and I hear the sound of the bolt on the back of the toilet door slide across.

Without hesitation, I walk over to the mantelpiece and pick up the nearest reversed picture frame.

I turn it around in my hand.

I actually hear myself gasp, as I take two involuntary steps backwards while the picture frame slips from my fingers and clatters to the floor, causing the glass to crack and splinter.

Staring at me through the shattered glass is a younger, smiling Margaret and, beside her, with his arm lovingly draped over her shoulder, is the younger, but unmistakable, face of Warren James.

Forty Seven: Alex

If I wasn't witnessing it for myself, then I simply wouldn't believe it.

The funeral has descended into absolute chaos.

Right now, Kat is being driven to hospital, after being found unconscious in the forest and Mark is on the run, after beating the living daylights out of his former partner, Allan, and, for an encore, doing pretty much the same to Tam.

Every able-bodied and, far more worryingly, less able-bodied man who was in the garden of remembrance when it all kicked off is, despite my pleas and protestations, in the forest looking for Mark.

Sergeant Davey was able to round up a number of officers very quickly after I called him, and DC Foreman brought everyone from the incident room here to help find and detain Mark.

From what I've seen so far, he is not going to come quietly.

I'm still in a state of shock.

Everything had been going as well as I could have hoped for.

I wasn't remotely surprised to see Kat turn up, although I was caught out by her accomplice. I'm not quite sure what she hoped to achieve, but after speaking to her, I was reassured that she intended to keep a low profile.

I was very aware of Tam and Warren James speaking conspiratorially in a little two-man huddle, throwing nasty little looks in my direction every now and then.

I had even managed to grab a quick word with Stuart Shepton, who agreed to come down to the station later in the week and make a formal statement.

It was all going so well.

I had not intended to sit inside the chapel for the actual ceremony, but after having my little word with Stuart, he invited me to stay and I felt it would have been rude, and disrespectful, to decline. Not that Amanda Shepton has done too much to command my respect, although it's undeniable that she did do a lot of good work in the town.

It was as I was leaving the chapel, near the back of the long line of people who were slowly processing past Amanda's family in the garden of remembrance, that I saw Allan near the other entrance to the garden, far too close to Mark for comfort.

And there, lurking a little way behind him, and looking more than a little uncomfortable, was Kat.

And then it was as if someone lit the blue touch paper, and stood well back, because all hell broke loose.

Allan approached Mark, and said something to him. Then Mark spotted Kat and, as I feared, wasn't exactly thrilled to see her. Mark lunged for her and Allan brought him down with the kind of tackle that would immediately earn him a place in Mark's rugby team.

Then Allan was screaming at Kat to run, Kat shot off like a rocket into the woods; thank goodness she was wearing trousers rather than those long skirts she seems to favour.

Mark broke free from Allan and set off after Kat, screaming like a man possessed. Tam and I forced our way through the onlookers to try and bring some sense of order to the situation, while at the same time calling for back up, but just about every man in the crowd set off after Mark.

Allan was in hot pursuit, but everyone else was chasing them, too, presumably all fearing what on earth he would do to Kat when - because it did seem as if it was more likely to be a case of when, rather than if - he caught her.

Allan, Stuart and Tam ran into the forest yelling Mark's name; Warren and Patrick, Kat's boss, ran into the woods yelling her name. It was carnage.

I feel my phone vibrate in my pocket. There's so much commotion going on around me that I'd never hear it actually ring.

Caller ID tells me that it's Dan. Christ, he certainly knows how to pick his moments. Well, he's going to have to wait. I've got far more pressing matters to deal with, other than whatever snippet of information he thinks he may have gleaned.

I cancel the call but before I have time to replace my phone in my pocket, it vibrates again. This time, it's a text message from Dan.

All it says is *Emergency. Pick up.*

My phone rings again.

"Dan, it's really not a got a good time," I say.

"Where's Kat?" he says. He sounds breathless and panicked. "She's not answering her phone."

"She's on her way to hospital," I say. I'm too emotionally exhausted by everything that's going on to mess around playing cryptic word games with anyone.

"What??? What's happened? Is she OK? What the hell…"

"She should be fine," I say. "Calm down. You sound like you're in a wind tunnel somewhere, and that you're about to go pop."

"I'm driving," he says. "And yes, I'm driving fast. What happened to Kat? Is she OK?"

"She should be," I say.

"Should be? What does that mean?"

"Like I said, she's being taken to hospital right now."

"What the hell happened?"

"Mark Shepton took exception to her being at the crematorium."

"The stupid, stupid, cow!" he says.

"But she wasn't alone," I say.

"Eh? Who was she with? Patrick?"

"No. She was with Allan. He and Mark were lovers until Amanda intervened."

"What???? Mark's gay? Allan…holy shit, I go away for a day and everything goes batshit crazy."

"Mark and Allan had words, then Mark saw Kat and turned his attention on her. He told her she had a tongue even more wicked than his own mother, or something like that."

"WHAT?" yells Dan. "Alex, say that again? Did Mark say Kat had a wicked tongue?"

"He screamed it at her."

"Who heard him?"

"Just about everyone; when Mark screams, he makes himself heard."

"FUCK!" yells Dan.

"What is it?" I ask. I expected Dan would be alarmed when he found out what happened here, but there seems to be a level of panic in his voice that tells me there's something far more serious going on.

"Alex! No bullshit, I just want a straight answer, OK?"

"OK," I say.

"Did Amanda Shepton and Lisa Davidson have their tongues removed?"

Who the HELL has he been talking to?

"ALEX! Tell me, yes or no, no bullshit. Did they? Am I right?"

Something in his voice tells me that he already knows the answer, so it would be pointless to lie to him.

"Yes," I say. "But what's that got to do with…"

"Did Mark get his hands on Kat? What happened?"

"No," I say. The desperate urgency in Dan's voice seems to compel me to simply answer pretty much anything he asks me, without wondering why.

"What happened?"

"Kat ran into the woods. Mark chased after her, and just about everybody else chased after them both."

"Everyone? Like who?"

"Allan, Tam, Stuart Shepton, Warren, Kat's editor, some local councillors. I tried to stop them but it was useless."

"Did Mark knock Kat out?"

"No, we don't think so. She was found unconscious in thick undergrowth with a bump on her head. To be honest, I think if Mark had found her, the mood he was in, she'd have more than one little lump on her head. I think she probably tripped and fell. We were going to call an ambulance but then someone apparently offered to drive her to the hospital, as it's just down the road and it would probably get her into the treatment area quicker than if we waited for the ambulance."

"Someone *apparently* offered to drive her? Who took her?" Dan asks.

"I don't know, I didn't see who found her or who drove her to hospital. I was busy tending to Tam's bruises, and talking on the radio to get some extra resources here to help hunt Mark down."

"Who took her?" he asks again, with even more desperation in his voice.

"I don't know," I repeat. "And frankly, I don't care, because I've got Mark running wild in the forest beating the living daylights out of anyone who gets near him, so as long as Kat is getting treatment, I don't really care who takes her to hospital. I've got other concerns."

"Well you should care," snaps Dan. "Because she could be in the hands of the killer right now."

"What? How? Who? Where have you been? Who have you been talking to?"

Dan tells me about his afternoon, his visit to Margaret, and how he turned around the picture frame to reveal a photo of Margaret with Warren James.

"Warren?" I gasp, and I frantically look around, twisting my head left and right. "He *was* here, and I know he ran into the woods, but I can't see him at the moment."

"Alex!" yells Dan. "Alex! ALEX! Listen! When Margaret came back into the room, she saw the picture frame on the floor so I asked her flat out, 'is Warren James your son?' and she said yes."

"Shit!" I say. "Tam! Foreman! Get on the radio. We need to find Warren James."

"Warren? What about Mark?" Tam says.

"Screw Mark. We need to find Warren. NOW!"

"ALEX!" screams Dan.

"What???"

"It's NOT Warren," he says.

"But you said…"

"Yes. Margaret is Warren's mother. Warren has been telling her everything, because he knows everything. But he is NOT the killer. All this time, he has been looking out for, and protecting his cousin."

"What?"

"Margaret considered him a son because she raised him as a son, but alongside her own son. Warren isn't the killer; his cousin is. They grew up together; 'thick as thieves' Margaret said. Warren has been watching over him for years."

Forty Eight: Kat

My eyelids feel too heavy to open; my head is pounding. My arms feel like lead weights. I feel dazed, confused.

It takes a considerable effort to open my eyes, but I do.

I'm home, I'm staring at the ceiling of my bedroom. Presumably from my bed. The heavily-lined curtains are drawn; the room is dark.

Thank goodness. What a bizarre dream.

Ow, my head is pounding. I'm groggy. I'm sore. *Was* it a dream? I'm confused. Something's wrong. I try to move. I can't. Am I paralysed? Have I been in an accident?

What's going on?

I open my eyes wider, which takes some effort.

I try to move my arms. I can't. What the hell?

I try to lift my head from the mattress but it hurts; my head aches. I manage to tilt my head backwards, and flick my eyes up as far as I can.

My hands are bound tightly together with a belt from my dressing gown, and are tied above my head to one of the thick wooden struts of the headboard.

I shake my head. Perhaps *this* is a dream.

Or a nightmare.

I try to move, but I can't.

I have a sudden, terrifying, thought, and throw my eyes downwards, over as much of my body as I can see. I appear to be fully clothed. That's some small comfort, at least.

Come on, Kat, I hear myself say. Wake up. Wake up!

I pull at my hands. My wrists are sore; the belt from my dressing gown digs into my skin. Why did I insist on buying such a solid headboard? The cheaper ones had struts that would probably snap like toothpicks if enough pressure was applied. But no, I had to go for the solid, strong one. I'm not going anywhere until whoever tied me here decides to let me go.

A wave of panic sweeps over me. Amanda Shepton was tied up. No! It can't be. NO!

A rush of images flood into my mind, as if I'm watching a film with my finger holding down the fast forward button on the remote.

I'm at the crematorium. I'm with Allan. Who's Allan? Oh. I remember. I see Alex. We talk. There's Elizabeth. Where's Dan? He isn't here. Shit, there's Patrick. I don't want him to see me. He told me not to come. There's Warren. He gives me the creeps. He's talking to Tam, and they look as thick as thieves. Is that Sergeant Davey? I'm not sure.

Shit! It's Mark. And he's seen me.

He's yelling at me. No, it's more than that. He's shrieking at me. Make him stop! It's not true! I'm not a nasty person. I'm not evil. I'm just doing my job.

He's after me. He wants to hurt me! I'm running. Fast. Heart pounding. I'm in the woods. My leg catches on something, I fall. Ow, my head. It goes dark.

There are voices.

"Is she breathing?"

"Yes."

"Did Mark hit her?"

"I don't think he found her. He was fighting with Allan."

"Who found her?"

"I did. I think she must have tripped over."

"She needs to go to hospital. Let's call an ambulance."

"I'll drive her. The hospital is five minutes away. By the time an ambulance gets her, I'll already have her in A&E."

"Are you sure?"

"Of course."

I must have passed out again, because I can't remember anything else.

Did I go to hospital? How long ago did all that happen? Did I go to hospital, get some treatment, and then come home? Maybe. Everything is still quite hazy.

Did the person who took me to hospital also bring me home?

Did that person also tie me to my bed? Why?

Someone's here! I'm not alone.

I hear the sound of somebody flushing the toilet, and then the sound of someone washing their hands.

"Hello?" I say. "Hello? Is someone there?"

Someone turns the tap off. There's absolute silence again.

My heart starts to race. What the *hell* is going on?

"Hello? HELLO????"

I hear a floorboard creak.

I try again to free my hands, but the dressing gown belt is tied far too tightly.

Another floorboard creaks, closer. I turn towards the bedroom door and see the figure of a man.

In the gloomy light, I can't see much detail. He appears to be wearing dark clothing. But then, if he was at the funeral with me, that's hardly surprising, pretty much everyone was wearing black. There's something odd about his face.

Then it dawns on me. I know that face. I recognise it.

It's one of mine.

He's wearing the latex old witch mask, with hair and headscarf, which I bought for a fancy dress party last Halloween!

"Hello," I say.

"Hello," he whispers. Why is he whispering? Does he have a speech impediment? Or is he simply trying to disguise his voice.

"Dan, is that you?"

"Would you be pleased if I said yes?"

"What? No, I'll be fucking furious because this isn't funny."

"I'm not Dan," he says.

I'm momentarily terrified that it's Mark; maybe he did catch me in the woods, after all, and knocked me out. Maybe he's finally going to make good on his many threats, and punish me for not leaving him alone.

But no. Mark is short and stocky. This man is taller, thinner. It's not Mark Shepton.

He steps into the room.

"Who are you?" I ask. "What do you want?"

"It doesn't matter who I am," he says.

He reaches behind him, presumably to a back pocket, and pulls out what looks like some kind of fabric wallet of some kind. He tugs at the Velcro fastening, and opens the wallet up.

The first thing I see is a pair of surgical scissors and another wave of panic sweeps over me. Who is this guy? What does he want?

A voice right at the back of my mind tries to tell me that it's should be absolutely obvious who this is; it's the killer. But I don't want to listen to that voice. I'm too scared that it might be right.

"What do you want?" I ask again.

"It's not about what I *want*," he says. "I don't *want* to do this. I have to. I need to."

"Do what?" I say, although I know I really don't want to hear the answer.

He pulls a pair of thin surgical gloves from the front pocket of his trousers, and pulls them onto his hands.

"I was there," he whispers. "I heard."

"Where? Heard what?"

"You have a wicked tongue," he says. "I heard. Everybody heard. You have a wicked, wicked tongue."

He picks up the wallet, which he had placed on the mattress beside me, and slowly removes the scissors.

"You have a wicked tongue, and wicked tongues *must* be silenced. They MUST!"

I hear another voice, but this one is inside my head. It's Alex. "Both women were accused of having wicked or vicious tongues," she says, softly. "That's the common link. And the common circumstances surrounding their deaths are that both women had their tongues removed."

I yank as hard as I can with my hands, but the strut on the headboard won't budge.

"No!" I say, as floods of tears start streaming from my eyes. "Please, no!"

"I *have* to."

"You don't!" I plead. "You don't have to do this at all. Why are you doing this? Why me? I've never hurt anyone!"

"You have a wicked tongue. The wickedest tongue of them all!" he whispers.

"I don't!" I plead but already I feel as if I've lost the will to fight. I can't see any way of getting out of this.

I think about my parents. I see my sister's face. Oh, Mel! I think about my cousins. I see Hannah's face. Ross, Tony, Mervyn, and Patrick, with a sad 'I told you so' expression on his face. I see Elizabeth Page, Warren James, I see Alex, Tam, Simon, Sergeant Davey. And I see Dan, with that - yes - that attractive smile.

"I *don't* have a wicked tongue," I protest. "Mark was lying. Mark is a nasty piece of work. You should hurt him, not me."

"It doesn't have to hurt," he says softly, which completely throws me off guard.

"What?"

"It doesn't have to hurt."

He steps out of the room and a few seconds later I hear the tap in the bathroom running again. He returns to the room with a glass of water in his hand, which he places on the bedside table.

He reaches into an inside pocket and produces two small bottles of pills.

"If you take these, you'll just gently drift off to sleep," he says. "It doesn't have to hurt."

"And then what?" I say.

"Sleeeeeep," he says. "You'll just drift off to sleep."

"And *then* what?"

"And then, nothing. You'll sleep forever."

He glances towards the scissors. "And then I'll do what I must."

"No!" I say.

"I have to."

"You don't!"

I start to sob. I can't help myself. And once I begin to cry, it's as if the floodgates have opened. Before I know it, I'm wailing, releasing more tears than I ever thought one person was capable of crying.

My whole body is shaking in fear.

"Please, I'll give you anything. I-I'll *do* anything. Please. Just tell me, and I'll do it. Anything!"

"I want you to be silent," he whispers.

"No! Please! Pleeeeeaase!"

He unscrews the cap from one of the bottles of pills.

"It won't hurt. It will be like falling asleep. Gentle, peaceful."

"FUCK YOU!" I scream. I bend one of my legs as hard as I can and then release it, thrusting my heel into his kneecap with as much force as I can manage. The sudden movement catches him by surprise, and before he can comprehend what has happened, I deliver a second kick with my heel.

I think it almost hurts me as much as it hurts him. Almost.

He cries out and stumbles backwards.

I start twisting and turning my body, thrashing wildly with my legs. Who knows, I might get lucky and kick him right in the face, perhaps make him fall over and bang his head.

Who am I kidding?

I'm not going to be able to keep this up for long. I know that. But I've got to try something. I can't just lie here and let him put me to sleep and then, what? Cut my tongue out with those scissors?

No, if he's going to kill me, then he's going to have to fucking well work for it.

I hear so many familiar voices in my head now, cheering me on, encouraging me, willing me to fight. So many voices.

The man seems to have recovered himself a bit.

He walks towards the bed again, but with a noticeable limp. I turn my body as much as I can and begin to kick wildly with my feet.

I close my eyes. I'm young. I'm in a swimming pool with Melissa. Our father is teasing us, threatening to duck our heads under the water. As he approaches us, we both cling to the side of the pool, and start thrashing at the water with our legs, kicking as hard and fast as we can, splashing daddy with water so that he can't get near us.

I catch the man on the knee once more with the heel of my right foot, using every ounce of strength I have.

He instinctively bends his body down in reaction and I swing my left foot over as hard as I can. It connects with the side of his face, forcing him head-first into the bedroom wall.

There's a kind of surreal crashing, splintering, sound, which doesn't seem quite right for the impact of his head against the plasterboard, but when he stands up again, I think I may have been mistaken and under-estimated my own strength, because there is now a deep indentation the same shape as his head, as the plasterboard gave way when he hit it.

He lunges for me again; I try to lash out with my feet but this time he anticipates it, grabs my legs and pins them down, as he climbs onto the bed and straddles me, forcing my breath out of my lungs.

I bend my legs and drive my knees into the small of his back as hard as I possibly can.

He leans forward. I shake my head violently from side to side as his hands slowly move towards my throat.

Oh no. Oh shit. Please. NO!

I hear voices again. My mum, crying. My dad, Mel. They're all crying.

His hands reach my throat, wrapping around my neck. He starts to squeeze. No!

I hear Alex.

I hear Dan. They're all calling my name.

"Kat!" says Dan. "KAT!"

Then another voice. It's Alex. But she isn't calling my name.

"Get away from her. Now!"

Shocked, the man releases his grip on my throat and turns.

I hear a funny buzzing, crackling noise which I can't quite place, and suddenly the man's entire body seems to go rigid and very upright. Then he shakes a little, as if he is having some kind of spasm or fit, and then he slips off me and onto the floor.

I look up to see Alex standing in the doorway, holding her Taser out in front of her.

From behind her, Dan pushes his way into the bedroom and drops down on top of the man, as if to make sure he is well and truly down.

Alex cuffs him while Dan comes over to me.

"Sorry," he says, "Alex and I have kind of demolished your front door. Er, are you alright?"

He glances at the wallet, sees the surgical scissors, and uses them to cut the dressing gown belt, releasing my hands, which I then wrap so tightly around his neck, he could be forgiven for thinking I'm about to strangle him.

"H - how did you find me?" I gasp.

"I found out who the killer was," says Dan. "And then worked out where he would most likely take you after he found you in the woods at the crematorium."

"But who…" I say, as I look over Dan's shoulder just as Alex removes the fancy dress mask to reveal the anguished, tormented face of my editor, Patrick.

Forty Nine: Dan

I'm sitting in our favourite coffee shop clutching a copy of today's special edition of the Herald, waiting for Kat.

I'm early, of course, but that's so that I could enjoy watching her make an entrance and walk the length of the shop to me.

We haven't actually seen each other face-to-face since the day Alex and I knocked the door of her flat down and rescued her. But we've spoken on the phone a lot, even started flirted again, and exchanged a lot of emails.

She had a couple of weeks off, to help recover, but has now returned to the office.

Today's Herald contains a pull out, an in-depth feature by myself and Kat, about the three murders committed by the former editor.

The pull-out is eight pages long; conclusive proof, I feel, that Kat and I *can* work together; no, better than that, we are good together.

As a journalist, I should be well aware of the power of words; but my appreciation of that power has moved to a whole new level now.

Wicked tongue. Two little words. But that's all it took to unlock and trigger that deep-rooted trauma within Patrick, which he and his loved ones had thought had been beaten and buried decades ago.

But no, it waited, a slumbering, dormant demon, imprisoned, waiting to be freed; wicked tongue; that was the secret password, the key, the magic words, the trigger needed to release that demon.

For the Herald's special feature, I interviewed the criminal psychologist Simon consulted after Lisa's was killed, when police were forced to accept that Amanda's death was not a personal 'one-off'.

Patrick had gone through years of therapy before moving to a new town, to start a new life. He got married. He got himself a good job; journalist, chief reporter, editor, of a respected local newspaper. He played golf at the local club and was a well-respected (despite his sometimes less than reputable profession) pillar of the community.

Two words. That's all it took to make him a multiple murderer.

The psychologist said Patrick had suffered an immense emotional trauma, after finding his father, reading his suicide note, and then unleashing his despair and rage by killing his mother.

But it appeared as if killing his mother seemed to satisfy this rage. Patrick was deemed emotionally capable of moving on.

Margaret not only agreed to raise her late brother's son but formally adopted him. So when I visited her home, it's no wonder I assumed the killer was Warren, after I saw that photograph.

While Warren was her biological son, Patrick's cousin, Margaret raised both boys as her own, and considered both her sons. The only reason for there being no photo of Patrick on her mantelpiece is that he hated having his picture taken which, once she mentioned it, I realised was true. When I was at the Herald, even at our Christmas parties, Patrick would always shy away from the cameras.

Now, poor Patrick is being detained indefinitely at a secure psychiatric hospital. He won't be held criminally responsible for the three murders. The psychologist told me that, in layman's terms, what happened to Patrick could be considered a kind of 'demonic possession'; a red mist descended and he simply couldn't help himself. He was most likely aware of what he was doing, but it would have been like an out of body experience; as if he was watching someone else.

The most tragic part of all this is that if Patrick had not found out that Sam Shepton used the phrase 'wicked tongue' in his suicide note, in circumstances so incredibly similar to the death of Patrick's own father, the chances are that his inner rage would never have been triggered. Ever.

Fate can be so cruel! I think there's better odds of me winning the lottery two weeks' running than there are of this heartbreaking coincidence happening. But it did happen. Against all the odds, it did.

And now my heart goes out to Warren.

He knew Patrick had suffered an emotionally traumatic experience, but had been spared the full details. The boys grew up together, living more as brothers than cousins.

They were so close that, when Patrick decided to move and start a new life in a new town, Warren said he would move to the same place.

When, as he so often did, Warren provided some 'off the record' help to Patrick, by showing him Sam Shepton's suicide note, the coroner's officer had absolutely no idea that the words 'wicked tongue' would prompt Patrick to kill Amanda.

Warren told Margaret about Amanda's death and she realised immediately what had happened, and who was responsible, and told Warren the full story. He was wracked with guilt, blaming himself. But he didn't, and couldn't, blame Patrick.

He convinced himself that the human race might even be better off without the likes of Amanda; it wasn't Patrick's fault; he couldn't help himself. So Warren became determined to do everything he could to protect Patrick.

Once triggered by such a staggering coincidence of circumstances so similar to the tragic death of his own father, it wouldn't take too much to make Patrick kill again and again. And he wouldn't need such similar provocation. When Ross showed him the paperwork regarding the college story and Patrick read Phillipa's accusations against Lisa, the trigger was pulled again. His killing would inevitably escalate and he would most likely end up targeting anyone perceived as a strong, outspoken woman, whether they were a 'bully' or not.

Warren now faces possible criminal charges, which is why we've had to be quite vague in that part of our article.

Kat and I will have to save the full details for the book.

For my part, I guess I'll always be in Warren's debt, as it turned out it was him who gave Margaret my name, which ultimately ended in me being able to save Kat.

Once Patrick was triggered, getting to Amanda was easy. They knew each other by sight, so it was simple enough for him to just knock on her door, presumably on the premise of writing a tribute to her husband in the paper.

But this is the bit that makes me feel particularly uneasy; Margaret and the psychologist were clear that, in their view, Patrick couldn't help himself. He was 'possessed'; it was as if he was two different people; the avuncular mentor Kat and I admired and respected, and the callous killer who appeared to be on the verge of a serial crimewave.

I was told Patrick was probably not even aware of what he was doing. But for me, Lisa's death contradicts that. While there had been no reason for Patrick to become a suspect, he had even ensured he had an alibi, playing golf.

The golf club had quite a casual approach to its most regular members, particularly in the very early mornings, outside peak hours. So Patrick killed Lisa, then went to the golf club, but rather than start on the first fairway, he started half-way round. And if anyone spotted him, as indeed Simon had done, they would simply assume he had been there from very early on, starting on the first hole, and was making his way around the course.

So perhaps Patrick was more aware of what he was doing than anyone thinks, having planned his alibi.

Or perhaps the demon had taken over, and the Patrick we knew was nothing more than a thin disguise.

There were so many similarities between Sam Shepton's death and that of his father that one can see why this might have triggered him. But once triggered, it would not take much to keep him killing, just something 'vaguely similar enough', hence him targeting Lisa and then going after Kat, after Mark's outburst at the funeral when he accused her of having the wickedest tongue of all.

Maybe there was enough of the old Patrick still there, though, which is why he chose to wear a mask while watching himself attack and, had it gone the way he wanted, kill, Kat.

I shudder at the thought of that.

Alex and I had arrived in the very nick of time.

The coffee shop door opens and there she is, wearing that long, smoky blue-grey skirt that suits her so well.

She's also carrying a copy of the Herald.

She buys a coffee from the counter near the front of the shop and then joins me at my table. And yes, I enjoyed watching her walk towards me every bit as much as I hoped I would.

"It's good to see you," I say.

"You, too," she smiles.

"You look great."

"Don't start," she says, but in that slightly flirty tone which tells me she has no objection.

"How are you?" I ask, and lower my voice. "Really."

"I'm good," she says, and then mimics me. "Really, I'm good."

"Good enough to let me take you out to dinner then? Or perhaps, in all the circumstances, you should take *me* out, for rescuing you…"

"My hero," she says, coyly, feigning the look of a swooning damsel in distress.

"You know, when I saw you in that room, your hands tied to your bed, dressed all in black, I was quite tempted to leave you there for a while, and enjoy the view…"

She blushes and playfully slaps my arm. "You wish."

She pauses, then adds, "I'm glad you didn't. Leave me there, I mean. Not like that."

"I know," I say. "I'm just so glad I got there when I did."

"Me, too. How…how did you know?"

"When I found out it was Patrick, I figured it was the only place he could take you. There would be other people in the Herald office, his wife would be at home, and you lived alone."

Kat reaches across the table and takes my hand. "Thanks."

I glance at the Herald's pull-out on the table. "See? We make a good team, you and I. We're good together."

She sighs. "It won't work," she says. "Whether I want it to or not."

"Do you?"

"What?"

"Want it to?"

"It doesn't matter. We'll always get funny looks. I mean, Patrick…" She pauses when she says his name, for obvious reasons. "He liked you, encouraged you, but the new editor, well, he or she might not share the same view. It will be too awkward."

"Ah, the old 'sleeping with the enemy' scenario," I say.

"Don't," she says, and she looks pained.

"Well, it just so happens that the new editor will whole-heartedly approve. I know, because I was offered the job yesterday, and accepted."

"You're kidding. You think sleeping with the boss is going to be any easier than sleeping with the enemy?"

"There's only one way to find out," I say, as I squeeze her hand affectionately and find myself smiling like the proverbial Cheshire Cat when she doesn't pull her hand away. I have a feeling that we're about to start writing a new story of our own.

Acknowledgements

After self-publishing a number of very silly books which I think are quite funny (some may argue otherwise), *Wicked Tongue* is my first attempt at something a little more serious, and I didn't do it entirely on my own.

First, I need to thank my wife, Debs, for never complaining when I shut myself away in the computer room for hours here or there, and during days off, and for putting up with me on the frequent occasions that I decided I hated the book, and for always supporting me in everything I do, or try to.

I would also like to thank author Vicki FitzGerald. I helped edit her book *Kill List*, which made me think about pursuing an idea I had for a crime thriller. I'd had the first three chapters of *Wicked Tongue* for years. I shared them with Vicki and she insisted that I write the whole thing. She gave me valuable constructive criticism during the writing process, and believed in this book on the frequent times that I didn't, and encouraged me to write it. She then persuaded me to be patient and allow her to proofread it before I pressed the 'publish' button, which I am very grateful for. I doubt I would have finished this book without her support.

I would also like to thank Ceri Doyle, for assisting me with some character insights, and Jeff Foreman (and, through him, Geoff Wessell) for clarifying some police procedural details.

And finally, thanks in advance to anyone who actually reads this, especially if you feel inclined to write a review, and even moreso if that review just happens to be a good one!